Picasso's Motorcycle

Marc Sercomb

Copyright © 2020 Marc Sercomb

All rights reserved. No part of this book may be reproduced or transmitted in any form or by any means, electronic or mechanical, including photocopying, recording or by any information storage and retrieval system without permission in writing from the publisher.

Blue Dog Press – Los Angeles, CA
ISBN: 978-0-578-68007-1
Library of Congress Control Number: 2020907164
Title: Picasso's Motorcycle
Author: Marc Sercomb
Digital distribution | 2020
Paperback | 2020

This is a work of fiction. The characters, names, incidents, places, and dialogue are products of the author's imagination, and are not to be construed as real.

Dedication

For my beautiful wife Robin, my inspiration, for believing in me and encouraging me every step of the way.

And for Chandler, my confidant and writing partner for ten amazing and fruitful years. I miss you, my dear friend…

Prologue

The legendary Benelli motorcycle racing dynasty began in 1911 when the recently-widowed Teresa Benelli sold off a parcel of family land and opened a modest machine shop and garage for her five sons to operate. The Benelli Garage of Pesaro, Italy, initially focused on the repair of bicycles, motorcycles, and automobiles, specializing in the machining of difficult to find, and often prohibitively expensive, factory replacement parts. During the Great War, the garage was kept busy machining replacement parts for war vehicles of the Italian military.

Upon the return of eldest sons Giuseppe and Giovanni from Switzerland, where they had studied engineering, the small shop began to branch out into the making of early motorcycle prototypes. In 1919, the Benelli brothers built their first motorcycle engine, a single-cylinder two-stroke 75 cc powerhouse, and attached it to the frame of an ordinary bicycle. Their first proper motorcycle, with a larger 98 cc engine, was built in 1920, and the Benelli legend began to take flight.

The youngest brother, Antonio "Tonino" Benelli, did not work in the shop with his older siblings – he had more heady ambitions. Tonino was set on becoming a motorcycle racing champion, and continuously nagged his brothers to design and build ever more powerful engines for their evolving motorcycles. They eventually presented young Tonino with a new 150 cc model, which he promptly rode to second place in his very first race. There were many races to follow, with Tonino "The Terror" honing his skills and quickly making a name for himself and the Benelli marque with his aggressive riding style and dashing matinee idol looks.

Soon, Tonino was winning more than losing, and Italian racing fans began to take note of the young upstart and his fast new machine. The increased publicity Tonino provided with each new win meant increased sales for the little company. The new income provided the brothers with the means to buy new machine tools to create a new four-stroke motorcycle – their most powerful and advanced machine yet. It had a 175 cc engine and a sleek roadster design, and featured a stack of intricately-designed gears and an innovative overhead camshaft.

It was an impressive, rugged machine, and turned heads all over the Italian racing circuit. Tonino rode it to victory in the Italian Championship in both 1927 and 1928. On the heels of these wins, the Benellis were able to put together a professional racing team, scoring several more big wins throughout 1929. Tonino won the Italian Championship again in 1930, cementing his legend and achieving his dream of becoming the top motorcycle racer in Italy.

Tonino entered race after race well into the 1930's, urging his brothers to build him ever faster machines to beat the stiff competition provided by the likes of Moto Guzzi and Ducati. Head engineer Giuseppe Benelli exceeded Tonino's expectations with a new double overhead camshaft 175 cc bike with a footshift and four-speed gearbox – a mechanical marvel and a match for anything the other manufacturers could throw at them.

Tonino then embarked upon a legendary trek across Europe, winning Grand Prize races in France, Belgium, Holland, and Switzerland. The Benellis now dominated the 175 cc class on the European circuit. Then, in 1932, tragedy struck when a bad crash during a race forced Tonino to abandon racing altogether. In 1937, the former champion, still a relatively young man, died in a rather ordinary road accident outside Pesaro.

Tonino's legend came to an end, but the Benellis soldiered on. In 1938, they abandoned the tried and true 175 cc platform and built a powerful new 250 cc bike that could easily achieve speeds over a hundred miles per hour. The new 250 routinely beat other bikes with bigger engines, catching the eye of English champion Ted Mellors. Mellors garaged his 350 cc Velocette and approached the Benellis about riding their 250 in the prestigious Isle of Man race in 1939. Mellors – and Benelli – easily won the day.

But as World War II loomed, the racing world saw many changes. Races became mini "proxy wars" between nations, and old fashioned ideals like sportsmanship and comradery were left by the wayside. Just as war was breaking out and Germany invaded France, the Benellis had designed and built their fastest racer yet – a four cylinder, 250 cc supercharged engine with twin overhead cams, capable of speeds of up to 146 miles per hour. But not wanting their masterpiece to fall into the wrong hands, the Benellis hid the bike in a barn in northern Italy for the duration of the war.

When the Germans came to shore up Mussolini's crumbling defenses, they took over the Benelli factory and trucked away all of the fine machine tools the brothers had accumulated over the past decade. Then when the Allies landed in Italy, the factory was completely destroyed in the fighting. When the war ended, the Benellis set about tracking down some of their precious tooling machines in Germany and Austria, and, at great cost, had them trucked back to Italy. They rebuilt the factory and within two years after the war, were building motorcycles again.

With a new racing team in place, champion rider Dario Ambrosini won a string of high-level races in 1948 and 1949 riding the supercharged Benelli 250. The world was slowly putting itself back together after the greatest upheaval in modern history, and Benelli was back in the game winning races and designing innovative motorcycles. And Tonino "The Terror," with his daring love of speed and his vision to take the Benelli marque to the top of the heap, lived on in the hearts and minds of racing fans all over the world.

Part One
The Bicycle Repairman

Chapter 1

By most accounts, the village of *Nulle* was perhaps the smallest and most inconsequential village in eastern France. Tucked cozily into a tiny, isolated valley, it was a sleepy, long-forgotten place that the entire world seemed to pass by without noticing. It was so small that most of the people in the surrounding villages had never heard of it. It was so small that it didn't even appear on most maps of the region. It was so small that the nearest railway station was seven kilometers away.

So it was all the more surprising when a preposterously young yet keenly tenacious priest from Strasbourg, with a ten year old blond orphan boy wearing a Tyrolean jacket and lederhosen in tow, stumbled into the remote location late one bitterly cold winter night in 1936.

Holding tightly to the orphan's hand with one of his own, and carrying a well-worn suitcase in the other, the priest walked down the main street of the village with stern determination, looking for the bicycle repairman's shop.

It proved not difficult to find. It was a drab, forlorn little shop with "Monsieur E. Renaud, Expert Bicycle Repair and Maintenance" painted in faint letters across the dusty front window.

"Monsieur Renaud!" the priest shouted, pounding on the shop door and trying to peer inside through the dark front window. "Monsieur Renaud! Open up, if you please!" The priest's spirits began to sink. "Oh, dear. It appears no one is home."

The priest put the suitcase down and continued pounding. "Monsieur Renaud! I really must speak with you! It's really rather <u>urgent</u>, I'm afraid!"

Finally, a light came on and a large, bear-like man with an aggressive mustache and wearing a soiled undershirt opened the door.

"What is it?" the man growled through his mustache.

"Monsieur Renaud?" the priest asked anxiously.

"It's very late," the older man grumbled, scratching the prodigious stubble on his greasy cheek. "Who are you?"

"I'm Father Gerard, from Strasbourg."

"_Father_?" The shop-keeper's mustache twitched in surprise. "Recruiting them rather young these days, aren't they?"

"Well, I took my vows only last fall..." the young priest stuttered, smelling the alcohol on the older man's breath and noticing the dark rings around his eyes.

"What do you want?" the shop-keeper demanded suspiciously.

"Well, I, I..."

"Where did you say you were from?"

"Strasbourg. It's...I mean, I'm afraid it's about your brother..."

"My _brother_?" The shop-keeper's eyes narrowed into almost imperceptible black slits.

"Yes, I'm afraid I have some rather bad news," the priest began haltingly. "Well, you see, there's no other way to say it, but...your brother and his wife have both died."

The priest looked up to examine the shop-keeper's face, but saw no reaction to the news. Finally, Renaud spoke.

"You have made a mistake, Father. I have no brother."

"You are Monsieur _Renaud_, are you not?" the priest blanched. "Monsieur Emile _Renaud_?"

"I told you, I have no brother," Renaud repeated impatiently. "Good night, Pere." The grubby shop-keeper started to close the door. Father Gerard stopped the door firmly with his foot.

"Well, I'm afraid it's a little more complicated than that," the priest explained. Renaud gave him a blank look.

"You see, this is _Daniel_," Father Gerard continued, pulling the boy in front of him and placing both hands on his shoulders.

"Who?"

"Daniel – your brother's son. Your _nephew_..."

Renaud stared coldly into Father Gerard's eyes. He didn't glance down at the boy at all.

"I don't know what you're talking about," Renaud repeated evenly. "I have no brother, so I cannot have a nephew. Now you are going to have to leave."

With great force, Renaud managed to push the priest's foot out of the way and slam the door shut.

"Don't be absurd, Monsieur Renaud," Father Gerard shouted through the glass window in the door. "I *know* you had a brother, and I *know* Daniel is your nephew!"

Saying nothing, Renaud drew the blinds over the window and turned out the light, returning the shop to darkness.

"But Monsieur – this is highly <u>irresponsible</u>!" The priest called through the closed door. "For the boy's sake, please reconsider!"

"Go away, or I will call the gendarme!" Renaud shouted back. "And take the boy with you!"

He stamped away from the door and started to climb the stairs to his flat above the shop. Then he stopped, thought for a moment, listened intently, walked stealthily back to the door, and peered through the blinds to see if they were still there.

The Priest and the boy were now sitting on the curb directly across the street from the shop, the suitcase between them.

"*Mon Dieu!*" Emile sighed, closing the blind. He lit a cigarette and paced the room, deep in thought. He kept pacing and thinking furiously until the cigarette had burned down to a nub.

"They must be gone by now," he muttered, dropping the butt on the floor and walking quickly to the door to peer through the blinds again.

They were still sitting on the curb as before, but now it had begun to rain lightly. Exasperated, Emile growled like an animal and shouted through the door, "I'm a very stubborn man, Pere!"

"I am also!" he heard the priest shout from across the street.

All this shouting isn't good, Emile thought to himself, rubbing his brow. *The neighbors will be getting involved soon...*

He walked to a table and poured himself a glass of wine. He drank the wine in three gulps, his mind racing for a way out of this trap.

Five minutes passed. He poured another glass of wine and drank it slower this time. Another five minutes passed, and then another.

"Surely he has come to his senses by *now*," Emile said to himself out loud, and peered through the blinds again.

"Still *<u>there</u>*!" he sighed, opening the door quickly. "Look – I'm calling the gendarme now!"

"You won't," the priest predicted confidently. It was raining heavier now. The boy was huddled against Father Gerard's side, the priest trying to shelter him with part of his frock.

"You are crazy, *Pere!*" Emile couldn't help shouting. "Take the boy and find shelter, before you both catch your death!"

"Not until you admit he's your nephew!" the priest said defiantly.

Emile bit his mustache, unable to force himself to say it. Finally, he broke. "All right, he is my nephew! But why have you brought him all the way <u>here</u>?"

"Well, Monsieur, you see, there is…no one <u>else</u>…"

"What the hell do you expect me to do with a <u>kid</u>?"

"You're his <u>uncle</u>…I merely presumed…"

"You presumed too much, *Pere!*"

"You won't take him, then?"

"Take him back to Strasbourg," Emile said flatly. "Take him to his <u>*mother's*</u> family."

"As you wish, Monsieur." Father Gerard stood up, picked up the suitcase, took the boy by the hand, and began to lead him away. Then he stopped and turned back to Emile. "I brought him here first because I didn't think you would want your nephew – your own brother's son – to be raised in the German-speaking part of Alsace. By <u>*Germans*</u>. But, as you wish, Monsieur…"

Emile growled, lowered his head, and rubbed the back of his neck roughly. "<u>Wait</u>," he barked.

Father Gerard stopped in his tracks. "*Monsieur?*"

Emile sighed deeply. "My younger brother was an irresponsible, selfish dreamer. <u>I</u> was the responsible one. <u>I</u> was the one who always had to follow him around and clean up his messes, fix his *mistakes*. When he married that German trollop, that was the last straw. I told him I was through taking care of him. I swore I wouldn't fix any more of his mistakes, <u>ever</u>. I haven't spoken to him since that day."

Emile and Father Gerard stood staring at each other for a full minute. The rain had let up slightly. Finally the priest broke the silence.

"What are your intentions now, Monsieur?"

Emile, his back against the wall, growled loudly and spit on the ground. "Put his case inside. Then get the hell out of here…"

When the priest had gone, Emile took the boy upstairs to the flat above the shop. He led him to a small back room where there was a bed, a chair, and an ancient wardrobe with off-kilter doors. He set the suitcase down and said, "This is where you will sleep."

"Now then, let's have a look at you." Emile turned on a single overhead light bulb. Daniel was small, blond, wet, and shivering like a rat. Emile regarded the boy with something like disgust, sighing ruefully and shaking his head in disapproval.

"Not much to look at," he grunted, handing the boy a moth-eaten blanket. "Here, put this around your shoulders before you catch a cold. You won't be of much use to me with pneumonia."

Daniel put the blanket around his shoulders and sat on the bed. "Merci," he said between chattering teeth.

"Oh, so he _does_ speak French, after all!" Emile observed sardonically. "I suppose you speak German, as well, eh?"

The boy nodded, warming up slightly inside the cocoon of the blanket.

"Well, there'll be no German spoken here!" Emile growled angrily. "We will speak French only in this house, understand?"

Daniel nodded.

Emile glared down at him through the dim amber light from the overhead bulb, but somehow still managing to not make direct eye contact with the boy. "The toilet is down the hall. If you have to use it during the night, don't wake me. I rise early, and so will you. After breakfast – and this is not the _Hotel Continental_, mind you – we will put in a full day's work in the shop."

Emile spoke to him gruffly, distantly – more like a master addressing a new apprentice than an uncle to a nephew.

"If you have any dry clothes in that suitcase, you'd better put them on." Then he turned off the light and closed the door roughly, leaving young Daniel in the dark.

Outside the door, Emile paused a moment to listen. He heard gentle sobs coming from inside the room, but the slightly pained, stony expression stayed fixed to his face as he walked down the dark hall to his own bedroom.

***

Daniel awoke early the next morning to the smell of sausages and coffee, and the faint smell of burned leather. Where he had left his lederhosen draped over the bedpost the night before, there was now a very proper-looking pair of French boy's short pants. He put them on and went down to the kitchen.

His uncle sat at the table drinking a cup of coffee, intently studying a newspaper. A plate of bread and butter and sausages, as well as a mug of coffee, sat waiting for him.

"Sit down," Emile grunted impatiently. "Eat."

The boy complied.

"Where is my lederhosen?" he asked.

"I burned them. In the back yard. You're a Frenchman now, and you'll dress as one."

"Papa thought they looked smart."

"Your Papa was a twit. A confused twit. Marrying that woman only made matters worse."

Daniel picked up the mug of coffee and sniffed it hesitantly.

"I don't like coffee."

"You'll be working a full day, as I do. You'll start with a cup of strong coffee, as I do." It wasn't a suggestion.

Daniel took a sip from the mug, and grimaced. "What about school?"

"School!" his uncle sniffed. "What good is *school*? It's nothing but a waste of time!" And that was that.

Daniel took a large bite of bread and butter. "Have you any jam?"

"Does this place look like a *Bistro* to you?" Emile grumbled without looking up from is newspaper.

"Mama always had jam."

Emile made a face behind the newspaper, but did not answer the boy.

Daniel ate in silence a moment. Then, "Don't you want to know…how it happened?"

"It doesn't matter to me," his uncle said coldly. "Your father and I haven't spoken for many years, ever since he married that kraut. I got fed up chasing him around and fixing his stupid mistakes. But, just like him, now he's left me with one more. So, we will simply put on a brave face and make the best of it."

After breakfast, Emile took Daniel downstairs to show him around.

"This is my bicycle shop," Emile declared proudly. The place was a mess, with bicycle frames and tires hanging from the low ceiling and dusty parts strewn everywhere. "I fix bicycles here. Do you know how to ride one?"

"Yes, Papa taught me."

"Good. You can deliver them back to their owners once they're repaired. But you will polish them up nice and shiny first. Your duties will also include sweeping the floors, washing the windows, fetching my lunches from the café, and anything else that needs doing around here. Understand?"

Daniel nodded.

"Good. And listen, you sound like a moron when you talk, so you'd better just keep your mouth shut around the customers. I don't want to lose any business because of you. Your insipid Alsace accent grates on the nerves, like fingernails on a chalkboard." Emile handed him a rag and a bottle of polish. "Start with that blue one there. It goes straight back to Officer Le Pen, the gendarme, as soon as it's spotless. Now get to work!"

Daniel started polishing the gendarme's bicycle while Emile opened up the shop. The first customer of the day was Jacques, the village butcher.

"I've been waiting outside since seven," he complained, wheeling his bicycle through the shop door. "You're opening later and later each day, Emile."

"Nonsense," the bicycle repairman growled. "What do you want?"

"The chain is slipping again," Jacques declared accusatorially.

"The chain is fine," Emile insisted.

"It's _stretching_ again, I tell you!" the butcher argued. Daniel stole a quick glance at the man. Jacques was almost as big as Emile, but had slicked back hair and a pencil thin mustache, like a Hollywood movie star. He had on his trademark blood-stained butcher's apron and a pencil pinched over his right ear.

"It's your imagination," Emile laughed.

"Look at the _slack_ in it!" Jacques shouted. "It nearly fell off on the way over here."

"All right, settle down. Let me take a look at it." Emile bent down to examine the chain. "Ah, you are right, Jacques. You need a new chain."

"Who said anything about a <u>new</u> chain?" the butcher protested. "Can't you just fix this one again?"

"You can only fix an old chain so many times," Emile patiently explained. "At some point, you will still need a new chain."

"You're always trying to sell me parts I don't need," Jacques insisted. "This chain is fine."

"But you just said it was slipping."

"It is," the butcher explained, "but the <u>chain</u> itself is fine."

Emile lit a cigarette and scratched his head. "I don't follow you."

"Look, let me explain it to you, Emile: There is nothing wrong with this chain, so I don't need a new one. Just fix *this* one…"

"But what will I be fixing if there's nothing wrong with this chain?" Emile asked.

The butcher was getting red in the face now. "I don't know – *you're* the bicycle repairman, just fix it so it doesn't slip anymore – like you did *before*…"

Emile sighed and rubbed the back of his neck, looking down at the chain thoughtfully. "All right, I'll take a look at it and see what I can do. But you'll have to leave it here for a few days."

"A few *days*?" Jacques protested, now turning bright crimson. "I can't do that! How will I make my deliveries?"

"You can always make your deliveries with a slipping chain, then…"

"No, no – I'll leave it. Just try to fix it quickly."

"I'll see what I can do," Emile repeated, finishing off his cigarette and grounding the butt into the floor with his shoe.

Daniel, fascinated with the butcher's bloody apron, had been sneaking glances at him since his arrival.

"Who's boy is that?"

"*Him*?" Emile cocked his head without looking at Daniel. "My imbecile brother, he married a German. The sorry result of this tragic union stands before you. Then my brother dies, and some priest from Strasbourg drops him off in the middle of the night." Emile shook his head in disgust. "Look at him: blond and fair, just like his kraut mother!"

"What are you going to do with him?"

Emile thought a moment, then scratched a dark, stubbly cheek. "Raise him, I suppose…"

The butcher broke out in laughter. "*<u>You</u>*?"

"Why not?" Emile looked indignant. "You think I don't know how to raise a boy?"

"Why don't you just send him back? Or to the orphanage in St. Claire?"

"I thought about it," Emile admitted. "Of course, that would be the easy thing to do. But I've decided to take the challenge."

"What challenge?"

Emile took his time lighting another cigarette, slowly formulating his thoughts with each smooth movement and gesture. "The poor boy is half German. But he's also half French. Perhaps there is still a chance for him, there's still hope he can be…I don't know…*rehabilitated*."

"*Rehabilitated*?" the butcher asked.

"That's right. You see, he's only ten years old. Perhaps it's not too late to, to… *purge* the German-ness out of him."

"That's an interesting challenge, Emile."

"Besides, I can put him to work around here," Emile added.

"How's that going?"

"He's useless, just like his no-good father!" Emile growled, as if Daniel weren't even there. "But we'll change *that*, I can tell you!"

A few minutes after the butcher left the shop, Claude the postman entered with his bicycle. A slender man of average height, Claude was well-groomed and his postman uniform was always neatly pressed.

"The front tire is a little soft," the postman declared. "I fear I've picked up a tack on Rue St. Denis."

"Let me have a look at it then," Emile said.

Claude glanced around the shop as if looking for something. "Who's the boy?" he asked, without surprise.

"My German nephew," Emile grunted derisively.

"I know," the postman nodded ruefully. "I met Jacques on the way back to his shop."

Emile bent down to examine the tire.

"Jacques says the boy is from Dusseldorf, and speaks only German," Claude reported, eyeing Daniel suspiciously. "He says both his parents are krauts and the boy doesn't speak a word of French."

"Since when do you listen to *anything* Jacques has to say?" Emile asked, spinning the bicycle's front wheel and lighting another cigarette. "It's not as bad as that. The boy speaks a little French."

"Jacques says that you actually intend to raise the boy," the postman declared. "That you intend to make a proper Frenchman out of him. Is this true?"

Emile carefully felt around the circumference of the tire, looking for the tack – squeezing here, pinching there. "Being somewhat of a Frenchman myself, I think the boy will be in good hands."

"Yes, I'm sure of that, Emile," Claude conceded as Emile continued to work on the tire. "But have you thought of the consequences? This is a very small village – have you given any thought to what everyone will be thinking and saying about this…this…*situation*?"

Emile stood up and wiped his hands with a rag. He still had the cigarette dangling from the corner of his mouth. "The tack did not penetrate the tube. I removed the tack and plugged the hole in the tire. Good as new."

"Oh, *merci beaucoup*, Emile," the postman sputtered. "But, what do you intend to do about all the, you know…"

"Gossip?"

"*Exactly.*"

"Leave the boy to me," Emile winked and patted the ruffled postman's shoulder. "No charge for the tire. Now, be on your way…"

Emile knew the word would spread quickly. Jacques the butcher would have a half dozen customers before noon, and each of those would talk to three or more villagers before the day was out. Not to mention the postman, who was sure to spread the gossip to the rest of the village on his rounds.

So he was not surprised by the stares and hushed whispers that greeted them when he and Daniel entered the café at lunch time.

"This is where you will fetch my lunches each day," Emile instructed him sternly. Daniel looked around the crowded café with trepidation: silent, stone-faced shop-keepers and assorted local characters all crammed in around tiny round tables, smoking, drinking *pernod*, and eating hearty plates of potatoes, bread, beef and vegetables.

"Bonjour, Monsieur Renaud!" a young woman behind the counter exclaimed cheerfully.

"Bonjour, Mademoiselle Prenet," Emile replied, lifting his cap slightly. "This is the boy. He will be fetching my lunches from now on."

"Does he have a name?" Mademoiselle Prenet asked.

"*Oui*," Emile answered curtly.

"Well, what is it?" the cheerful young woman persisted.

The boy answered for himself. "*Je m'appelle* Daniel."

"Well, *bonjour* Daniel," she smiled, reaching over the counter to shake his hand. "It's very nice to meet you."

"It's very nice to meet *you*," the boy replied in stilted French.

"He's from Alsace," Emile explained.

"You make it sound like an apology," the girl said, still smiling at Daniel. "I think his accent is charming."

"Eh," Emile muttered, shaking his head in disagreement.

Mademoiselle Prenet handed Daniel a wicker basket with the lunch tied up in a big red checkered napkin.

Emile looked at the basket. "You included more than usual. What's the extra for?"

"Well, the boy has to have something, no?"

Emile merely grunted in reply. "Don't forget the beer."

"I haven't forgotten," the girl said cheerfully, handing Emile two dark bottles.

"You see, <u>two</u> bottles of beer," Emile instructed Daniel. "And make sure <u>both</u> bottles are filled to the top, or you will be making a second trip back here to top them off. Understand?"

Daniel nodded. Emile paid Mademoiselle Prenet and looked around the still silent café. "What are you all looking at? Have you never seen a German boy before?"

The crowd just continued gaping.

"Yes, everyone take a good look. Here is the German boy they sent me to raise. He speaks more German than French! My crazy brother, who did *this,* was a radical. A liberal. And his German wife – <u>his</u> mother – was a well-known libertine. Well, that's the worst of it. Now you know everything, and you can all get on with your lives, eh?"

Nobody said a word.

"Why so quiet? Come on, what are you all thinking? 'Ah, well, he is young…perhaps it is not too late to undo the damage, eh?'"

Tears started streaming down Daniel's cheeks. Emile reached down and brushed them away with the back of his hand. "Don't weep. You are a Frenchman now! Germans weep, not Frenchmen!"

Emile turned back to the crowd. "You see? I am not surprised. My brother was the same way when <u>he</u> was a boy." He turned back to his nephew. "Back to the shop now, and don't drop the lunch! Germans weep like schoolgirls, not Frenchmen!"

They left the café and started walking back to the bicycle shop. Daniel was clutching the lunch basket, still sobbing quietly. Emile stopped him, knelt down before him, and brushed the tears away with the back of his hand again.

"I said stop crying. Listen to me. This is not Strasbourg, this is a small country village. You've got to be tough, or you won't survive. They don't look like much – just simple country peasants, right? But they can be brutal, let me tell you. Like animals. You've got to understand that, or you'll never make it here. Now stop crying like a mama's boy and act like a Frenchman!"

Daniel did his best to control the sobs.

"There. We'll go back and have our lunch," Emile said. "Then you'll sweep the floors and tidy up the shop for the afternoon."

After lunch, Emile finished his second bottle of beer and pulled his cap down over his eyes to take a nap in a chair while Daniel swept the floors and tidied up – trying his best not to wake his snoring uncle. Then Emile woke up with a snort, lit a cigarette, and tinkered with a sprocket and some gears at his workbench for most of the afternoon.

There were no more customers after lunch. It was like the whole village just closed up and went to sleep. Emile didn't speak to the boy – didn't acknowledge his presence in any way – just smoked and puttered around the shop until the shadows began to grow long in the streets outside. Finally, he put his tools down, hung the "Closed" sign in the window, and locked the shop door. Then, without a word to the boy, he trudged upstairs and began fixing supper.

They ate their supper that night without a word passing between them. Emile seemed more sullen than usual. After they were finished eating, Emile slowly poured himself another big glass of wine and finally spoke to the boy for the first time since lunch.

"You'd better go on to bed now." It wasn't a suggestion, it was a demand. Daniel obeyed. He slipped out of his chair and padded quietly to his little bedroom. He felt like telling Emile that he wasn't tired yet, but he knew from the look on his uncle's face that it would have been a grave mistake.

He undressed and got into his squeaky bed, pulling the covers up under his chin. It would be a cold night, and the warmth of the bed felt good, but he still had a hard time falling asleep. Through the closed door, he could hear his uncle pacing heavily in the small kitchen. The floors creaked as the agitated, anxious pacing went on and on, for hours.

Finally, Daniel drifted off to sleep. He was awakened sometime later by the sensation of someone hovering over his bed.

"Get dressed and come into the kitchen," Emile ordered, then turned and walked out of the room. Daniel got dressed and went out to the kitchen. It felt like the middle of the night, but Emile had not slept at all.

They sat down at the table across from each other. There were several empty wine bottles and glasses on the table between them. "I…I need to tell you something…I need to explain something to you."

"Yes, uncle?"

Emile sighed, anxiously rubbing the back of his neck. "Today, after lunch, I had decided to send you back to Father Gerard…back to Strasbourg. Let your German relatives have you. It just didn't seem to be working out…"

Daniel listened, staying quiet.

"But, tonight…I changed my mind," Emile continued. "I don't believe in God the way the Church does…the way the priests describe Him. But I believe in some kind of higher power, which we can call, say, 'providence.' Do you understand?"

Daniel nodded.

"I am not going to send you back to Strasbourg. Now I know that Father Gerard bringing you here was not a mistake. It was providence, it was *meant to be*. The good news is, even though you are my imbecile brother's son, you are still half French. So, I am going to *save* you, boy. I am going to wash the German out of you like a filthy stain! That's right, I am going to make you into a proper

Frenchman! That is my *mission*. That's why you were brought here!"

The boy just stared at his uncle blankly.

"Ah, you have no idea what I'm talking about, do you?" Emile sighed. "But you will – you will understand, in time. And you will thank me, Daniel. Mark my words: you will come to thank me."

It was no drunken tirade, or momentary whim. It would not be put aside or forgotten in the soberness of the morning light. From that moment on, Emile truly and honestly embarked on a campaign to "purify" Daniel by introducing him to proper French culture, cuisine, and values, and Daniel had no say in the matter. His "lessons" would consist of long sermons and diatribes on what was wrong with German culture and cuisine.

He started first thing in the morning, at breakfast. "We've already talked about the language question. There is no question: French only, no German from now on." Emile displayed a new-found spark – he was absolutely energized by his mission. "As for food, I don't know what kind of German *merde* you are used to eating, but there will be no *schnitzel* here, young man. German food is not worth eating, and tastes like shoe leather, even when one is starving to death. And their wines – their wines are thin and yellow and taste like cat-piss! No, what you need is good French country cooking, the kind of simple peasant food you can grow strong on!"

Emile slid a plate in front of Daniel. The boy sniffed it unappetizingly. "What is it?"

"Quail eggs cooked in garlic. Rabbit filets with rosemary. The kind of good, solid French cooking that's going to turn you into a man!"

Daniel picked up a piece of cheese and sniffed it. "Uncle, this smells terrible!"

"Our local variety, made from raw goat's milk! It'll make you strong, like me. You'll get used to it!"

The gastronomical lessons continued that night at supper. After a hard day polishing bicycles and tidying up in the shop, Daniel stared down into a plate of unrecognizable mush.

"Uncle, what is this?"

"*What is this?*" Emile repeated is disbelief, somewhat offended. "This, I'll have you know, is none other than *pork rilletes*. A staple of French cuisine, both in the country <u>and</u> in the city. Look, you smear a little on a piece of toast, and voila – *heaven!*"

"And this?" Daniel poked a sticky glob of meat with his fork.

"That? That is *cervelle de veau.*"

"What's that?"

"Calf's brains."

Daniel made a face. "And these black slices? Mushrooms?"

"*Mushrooms!*" Emile looked offended again. "Those are truffles, you dense oaf! Sauteed to perfection in butter and garlic."

"What are truffles?"

"Ah, well…a type of *fungus.*"

Daniel stared at the plate in confusion. His uncle looked angry. "You are not going to eat it? Calf's brains, truffles…they pay a *fortune* for a meal like this in Paris!"

"May I just have some bread and butter, uncle?"

Emile did his best to cover his disappointment and disdain. "This was my mistake," he sniffed petulantly, snatching the plate away and tossing it into the kitchen sink. "Obviously, too much too soon for your delicate German sensibilities. I should have known. I'll take it a little slower from now on, so as not to overwhelm you…"

Chapter 2

One afternoon, a few days after Daniel's arrival, Father Pascal, the village parish priest, paid a visit to the little bicycle shop. He was accompanied by Officer Le Pen, the village gendarme.
Emile wasn't at all surprised to see the pair.

"*Bonjour*, Emile," the priest greeted the shop-keeper in a formal tone. He was a gray-haired man in his late sixties, with a large, round, unusually young-looking face and large, plump lips. Father Pascal considered himself the indispensable moral authority of the village, and he'd brought the village legal authority, Officer Le Pen, along as back-up.

"What can I do for you fellows?" Emile asked warily.

The priest did all of the talking. "We came to have a look at the boy."

Daniel was in the back of the shop, polishing the baker's bicycle. Emile waved him forward.

"Have a good look," the shop-keeper said compliantly.

Both the priest and the gendarme examined Daniel with a disquieting, unblinking thoroughness. Finally, Father Pascal blinked. The gendarme, who suffered from a condition in which his eyes produced an over-abundance of tears and therefore rendered blinking unnecessary, did not.

The priest's verdict was inscrutably pithy. "Curious...extremely *curious*..." Then he seemed to be at a loss for words.

The gendarme whispered something in the priest's ear, who nodded approvingly.

"What are the boy's religious inclinations?" Father Pascal demanded.

"I don't know," Emile confessed. "Nor do I care."

Father Pascal bent down to address Daniel himself. "What are your views on God, my son?"

"Mama said God always watches over us."

"Indeed. Was your mother an adherent of the Holy Church of Rome?"

"I don't know," Daniel answered honestly. "We lived in Strasbourg."

The priest and the gendarme looked at each other. Father Pascal looked at a loss again, so Le Pen obligingly whispered in his ear again.

"Well, the boy's spiritual state is, of course, of great concern to us…" Father Pascal observed.

"To us?" Emile asked.

"What I mean is, to the village as a whole," the priest quickly clarified. "You have taken on a great responsibility, Emile. I would expect to see the boy attend mass on a regular basis, starting this Sunday morning."

Emile thought a moment, scratching his stubbly cheek. "I'll let the boy decide for himself when he comes of age."

The priest looked horrified. "Monsieur Renaud, I am well aware of your views on the Church, and that you have not attended Mass in over ten years –"

"Fourteen, to be exact, *Pere*," Emile corrected him.

"Be that as it may," Father Pascal continued. "But I would fully expect you to see to the boy's proper religious instruction."

"As I said, I leave that up to him," Emile repeated. "Is there anything else?"

The priest was unable to answer, until Le Pen whispered into his ear.

"Yes, there is one more matter we came to discuss," Father Pascal declared. "Have you enrolled the boy in school yet?"

"No."

"Well, why not?"

"It's a waste of time," Emile said without hesitation. "I can teach the boy everything he needs to know – how to work, how to earn a living –"

"But surely you agree that the boy needs a proper education!"

"From that imbecile teacher Monsieur Closson? No, he will be much better off in *my* hands."

The visitors looked at each other again and this time, instead of whispering in his ear, the unblinking gendarme merely cocked his head earnestly in Emile's direction.

"The boy is going to have to be enrolled in school, Emile," Father Pascal said firmly. "It's a legal matter, isn't that right, Le Pen?"

The gendarme nodded judiciously.

"But I need him to help out around here," Emile argued.

"The village ordnance states that every child of school age <u>must</u> attend school – no exceptions," Father Pascal insisted.

"No exceptions, eh?" Emile asked.

"I'm afraid not."

Emile turned to Daniel. "Do you want to go to school?"

"*Oui.*"

"Then I suppose the boy will go to school."

"Splendid," the victorious vicar beamed. "I will pick him up early in the morning and take him to school myself. *D'accord?*"

"*D'accord.*"

After Father Pascal and Officer Le Pen had left, Emile turned to Daniel and tried to salvage his lost pride. "Ah, well, perhaps it is not so bad, eh? It will help you with your French, and perhaps to fit in a little better around here. But don't get too comfortable, mind you. You'll still put in a full afternoon around here after school each day."

The priest was good to his word. He arrived bright and early the next morning to walk Daniel to the small schoolhouse on the edge of the village, and to see to it the boy was properly enrolled. On the way, Father Pascal explained the school situation in Nulle.

"There are actually <u>two</u> schools in our village – one for boys, and one for girls," the priest – who, despite his age, was a very fast walker – informed Daniel. Daniel struggled to keep up. "So you will be attending an all-boys school. The girls' school is at the other end of the village, and it's run by nuns. This has proven a very satisfactory arrangement, as it keeps the boys apart from the girls and everyone is better able to focus on their academics and stay out of trouble. The headmaster, Monsieur Delfont, is in charge of both schools, but his office is at the boys' school, so you'll be seeing quite a bit of him."

The boys' schoolhouse was a large gray building with a red slate roof at the end of a narrow lane lined with cypress trees.

When they arrived at Monsieur Delfont's office, the headmaster was waiting for them. To Daniel, at least, it appeared to be a typical headmaster's office, except for the great number of photographs and

diagrams of insects that lined the walls. Every possible square inch
of wall-space, it seemed, was covered with pictures of every type of
insect imaginable: beetles, ants, weevils, locusts, roaches, wasps,
grasshoppers, and centipedes, to name just a few.

"This is the boy I told you about," Father Pascal said to Monsieur
Delfont, seemingly unaware of the bizarre army of insects crawling
up and down the walls. The headmaster was neatly dressed in a dark
suit and tie. He had an unfortunate, irregularly shaped mustache that
crawled across his upper lip like a deformed gray caterpillar, and
over-sized spectacles that made him appear comically bug-eyed.

"I feel that it is my solemn duty to warn you, Daniel," the
headmaster began in a dry voice, "that the standards of admission to
our school are quite rigorous. Quite rigorous, indeed."

"*Oui, Monsieur*," Daniel replied.

"You see, at this school we have one purpose, and one purpose
only," Monsieur Delfont continued with as serious a tone as he could
muster. "Would you like to know what it is, Daniel?"

"*Oui, Monsieur*."

"To take young boys, and mold them into *men*."

"*Oui, Monsieur*."

"Discipline. Honor. Patriotism."

"*Oui, Monsieur*."

"These are the characteristics that will see you through life,
Daniel."

"*Oui, Monsieur*."

"Are you ready to be <u>shaped</u>, Daniel?"

"*Oui, Monsieur*."

"Are you ready to be <u>molded</u>, Daniel?"

"*Oui, Monsieur*."

"I detect a slight accent," the headmaster said to Father Pascal.

"He's from Alsace," the priest explained.

"Alsace, you say?" the headmaster asked, ripping the glasses off
his face and squinting hard at Daniel for several seconds. "How old
are you?"

"Ten, Monsieur."

"Ah, yes," Monsieur Delfont said, replacing his glasses. "Now, to
the academics. How are your numbers?"

"*Bien*, Monsieur."

"And your letters?"

"*Bien*, Monsieur."

"Can you recite Voltaire? Rimbaud?"

"A little, Monsieur."

"Do you know most of the words to *La Marseillaise*?"

"I think so, Monsieur."

The headmaster stood up stiffly and extended his hand over the desk. "Congratulations, Daniel. You have just passed the enrollment interview. I officially welcome you to our school!" Daniel shook the headmaster's hand.

Father Pascal looked very pleased. "Then, gentlemen, I will leave you to it!" He shook hands with Monsieur Delfont and patted Daniel on the head. "Well done, my son. Congratulations, and good luck in your studies!"

When the priest had gone, the headmaster gave Daniel a serious look. "And now, I will take you to meet your new teacher, Monsieur Closson." He led Daniel out of his office and down a short hall to the classroom.

"By the way, I am preparing a fascinating series of lectures on the insect kingdom," Monsieur Delfont confided proudly. "From time to time, I may be popping into your classroom to deliver them. A lesson here, a lesson there – you know, to give Monsieur Closson a little break."

"I will be looking forward to it, Monsieur," Daniel smiled.

"Discipline. Order. Structure. Obedience. There is much we can learn from the insect kingdom, Daniel."

"*Oui, Monsieur.*"

They reached the classroom door. "Are you ready?" the headmaster asked.

"*Oui, Monsieur.*"

"I think you are going to like Monsieur Closson a great deal," the headmaster predicted, opening the classroom door and ushering the boy inside. Butterflies in his stomach, Daniel stood dead still and took in the scene. The room was musty and well-worn. The overhead lighting was old and inadequate, but a row of large windows along the back wall bathed the room in plenty of golden sunlight. Rows of battered old desks were arranged neatly, facing the teacher's desk in the front, which sat on a slightly raised platform. Sagging shelves contained dozens of dusty old books, and curled, yellowed posters of human anatomy, medieval knights, and prints of impressionist paintings lined the walls.

Daniel loved it.

Then he saw the fattest man he'd ever seen in his life, lodged behind the teacher's desk, reading aloud from a book of poetry. Monsieur Closson stopped reading and lowered the book when he saw Daniel and the headmaster enter.

"Forgive the interruption, Monsieur Closson," the headmaster said deferentially. "This is the new boy I told you about. His name is Daniel. Say *bonjour* to your new teacher, Daniel."

"*Bonjour*, Monsieur Closson," Daniel said in a timid voice.

Monsieur Closson's voice boomed out in reply. "*Bonjour*, Daniel. Welcome to our classroom." The corpulent teacher was dressed in a somewhat tattered tweed jacket and coffee-stained tie, and a burgundy cape flung rakishly over his left shoulder provided a calculated amount of dramatic flair. His tousled hair was unkempt and kept falling into his eyes, giving him the look of an overweight English sheepdog and making it necessary for him to brush it back nonchalantly with a stubby hand every now and then. He was neither young nor old, and he was the first person that Daniel had met in the village of Nulle that didn't seem to really belong there.

"Well, I can see that you're in the middle of a lesson," the headmaster observed, "So I will take my leave, and bid you a well-disciplined, productive day." He bowed his head slightly in Monsieur Closson's direction and left the room quickly, leaving Daniel standing self-consciously by himself. He glanced around the room, finally noticing the rows of boys in their neat blue uniforms and suddenly realizing in horror that _he_ was not wearing a uniform.

"The order of seating is determined by the grades you earn," Monsieur Closson explained, brushing his bangs out of his eyes. "Those who earn the highest grades sit in front. Those who earn the lowest grades, in back. Since you are new and have no grades yet, Daniel, you will sit in the back for now. Don't worry, if you are bright, you will be able to make your way to the preferential seating in the front in no time. It's just my little incentive system to keep everyone sharp and on their toes."

One of the taller boys in front, a handsome, self-possessed lad wearing a neat blue tie, stood up to address the teacher. "Um,

Monsieur? There is an empty seat next to me. May we please allow Daniel to sit there?"

"That's very kind of you, Remy," Monsieur Closson said. "But what about my *system*?"

"And a grand system it is, Monsieur, to be sure," Remy said cheerfully. "But if he sits here, next to me, I can help him with the class routines and procedures. I mean, him being new and all…"

"Very persuasive, Remy," the teacher conceded. "Your sound reasoning and good judgment have won me over. Daniel may sit next to you – but just until he learns the ropes around here, so to speak."

"Very good, Monsieur," Remy said, and sat back down. Daniel walked to the empty seat next to Remy and sat down.

"Remy, why don't you get Daniel's books and materials together for him," Monsieur Closson suggested. "And anything else you can think of that will help him get up to speed. I'll leave him in your capable hands."

"Splendid idea, Monsieur," Remy replied, then flashed his most charmingly comforting smile at Daniel. "Don't worry, I'll help you, Daniel," he said to his new classmate. "I know how nervous you must feel on your first day. I'll show you around, and introduce you to all the fellows at recess."

"*Merci*,' Daniel said shyly.

As the day went on, Daniel's butterflies seemed to flutter away and he began to relax. He was relieved and grateful to find that his first day in the new school was so painless, so, so…*enjoyable*. It was all he had dreamed of. After a rocky start in his new life in Nulle, maybe things were beginning to look up for him, after all.

Daniel kept up with the day's demands while absorbing everything going on around him like a sponge. Very quickly, the dynamics of the class began to emerge. He could tell, by the deferential treatment of the other boys, that Remy was not only the smartest boy in class, but something of a class leader, as well. Remy seemed charming, kind, and helpful – both to Monsieur Closson and Daniel – and Daniel was a bit overwhelmed at having such a noble and intelligent friend on the very first day.

At recess, Remy fulfilled his promise to introduce Daniel to the other boys. There was Charles, and Rene, and Bernard, and Francois, and Nicolas, and Edgar, and Andre, and – well, too many names to even remember right now. Each one seemed as friendly as Remy, as well as curious to know more about him.

"I think your accent's right smart," Edgar told him. "Where are you from, anyway?"

Now the center of attention, Daniel carefully explained where he had come from and how he had arrived in Nulle. The group of boys listened, thoroughly enraptured by the tale. When he'd finished, Francois called out, "Here, Remy – don't forget to tell him about the Sport Club."

"Sport Club?" Daniel asked.

"That's right," Remy explained. "We've got a Sport Club after school. And we want you to join."

"Yes, I'd like that very much," Daniel responded.

"Splendid. We meet behind the schoolhouse right after school."

After recess, the boys piled back inside the schoolhouse for math lessons. Monsieur Closson picked up a piece of chalk and began the lesson, but what he wrote on the chalkboard looked nothing like any math Daniel had ever seen before. A few minutes in, he was completely lost – and starting to panic. What if Monsieur Closson suddenly turned around and called on *him* for an answer? He quickly scribbled "Completely lost...Help!" on a scrap of paper and quietly handed it to Remy.

Remy read the note and smiled. "Don't worry," he leaned over and whispered. "Math's not his strong suit. None of us can follow him. Just pretend it makes sense, and you'll be all right. And don't worry about the old man – he's an easy grader...if he likes you, you're aces."

Monsieur Closson stopped writing on the chalkboard and turned around. "What was that, Remy?"

"Um, nothing, Monsieur Closson," Remy flashed his charming, toothy grin. "I was just explaining your advanced technique to Daniel. Carry on, you're doing a splendid job!"

"Oh, thank you, Remy," the teacher said absent-mindedly, brushing the hair out of his eyes. "That's very kind of you...now, where was I...Oh yes..."

Admittedly, Daniel's attention began to wander as the afternoon wore on. Monsieur Closson's pedagogical efforts aside, Daniel could not help but find himself daydreaming about going home after school and telling his uncle about all the wonderful things that had happened, and all the wonderful new friends he'd made on his first day of school. Surely, even his grouchy uncle would be happy and proud to hear that things had gone so well.

As Monsieur Closson was wrapping the day up and assigning homework, Remy leaned over to remind Daniel: "Don't forget the Sport Club. Behind the schoolhouse right after school."

"I've been looking forward to it all day," Daniel replied.

When the dismissal bell rang, all the boys quickly emptied out of the classroom and gathered behind the schoolhouse. There was an overgrown sports field with a deep mud hole right in the middle of it.

Daniel could barely contain his excitement. "What's the sport?"

All the boys laughed.

"What's going on?" Daniel asked, sensing a seismic shift in the mood. Something had changed since leaving the classroom.

"Don't you get it?" Remy sneered. "<u>You</u> are. <u>You're</u> the sport!" Then he pushed Daniel down into the mud hole. All the boys stood around him, laughing, jeering, and pointing at him.

"Come on, guys – let's go," Remy said, walking away. "And he actually thought we would be friends with a dirty *kraut*…" Remy and the other boys left, congratulating each other on the success of their elaborate joke.

Daniel lay there in the mud, immobilized and stunned. *What had just happened?* Then the enormity of it crept over him slowly, like a strange, sickening shadow. It had all been a ruse – the smiles, the friendliness, the promises to include him in their games – it had all been carefully planned to set him up for *this*.

Daniel slowly crawled out of the hole. He was covered with thick, gooey mud. He felt numb, extinct. Like he no longer existed. He couldn't even cry.

All he could do was slowly leave the schoolhouse and head in the direction of home. Before he got back to the shop, he stopped at the fountain in the village square and tried to clean himself up the best he could. He knew there would be work waiting for him when he got back to the bicycle shop, no matter how humiliated and rejected he now felt.

When Daniel arrived at school the following morning, things appeared to be absolutely normal. There was no mention of the previous afternoon's events behind the schoolhouse. Remy and the other boys acted as if nothing had even happened.

This, of course, created a great deal of apprehension in Daniel. As the day continued to progress in as normal a fashion as could be expected, he couldn't help being overtaken by a dark sense of impending doom. *When would the other shoe fall?*

Then it struck him: it was all an act. Remy and the boys were staging a *performance* – the perfect young men, gentlemen and scholars, one and all – solely for the benefit of Monsieur Closson, who was surely keenly unaware of what had transpired behind the schoolhouse the day before.

Daniel sat stiffly and uneasily beside Remy, as Remy continued to show the kindness and helpfulness of the day before – again, for the benefit of Monsieur Closson, who needed to believe that the new student was being treated with the utmost respect and courtesy. *No,* thought Daniel, *if the hazing is to continue, it will not be carried out in the classroom in full view of Monsieur Closson, but after school when the teacher would not be able to witness it.*

As the day wore on, it became apparent to Daniel that Monsieur Closson only knew one lesson, which he repeated, in one form or another, at various intervals throughout the day. The heart of the lesson was always his intense love and devotion to the life and poems of Arthur Rimbaud. The lesson would usually begin with a dry lecture on the poet's life ("The great poet was born in the provincial town of Charleville, the second child of Frederic Rimbaud and Marie Catherine Vitalie Cuif, and was raised a devout Catholic by his mother…") and inevitably wind up with an impassioned recitation of one of his poems. Monsieur Closson would become so overcome with the weightiness and profundity of the material that the recitation would often end in uncontrollable weeping and protracted periods of anguished silence while the overwhelmed teacher attempted to recover his faculties. To anyone's knowledge, Monsieur Closson had never been able to make it through one of Rimbaud's masterpieces without experiencing this debilitating emotional reaction.

The rest of his curriculum consisted chiefly of teaching the boys how to box by the Marquess of Queensberry rules, as well as the fine art of embalming (he had worked briefly as a mortician before entering the education profession.) But mostly he slept. He was always falling asleep in class, and the boys had a game of piling their coats and other items on top of him as he slept so that he would inevitably awake with a start to find a mound of objects covering him.

Apparently, the headmaster, Monsieur Delfont, was of the mind that Monsieur Closson needed all the sleep he could get. Just before recess, Monsieur Delfont entered the classroom to impart some valuable information to the students, only to find Monsieur Closson tilted back in his chair, snoring away. Without missing a beat, the headmaster cheerfully ordered, "Boys, be quiet. You'll wake Monsieur Closson." Monsieur Delfont then proceeded to divulge the vital information he had come to impart: "I'm very pleased to announce that tomorrow I will be delivering my first lecture on the insect kingdom. Everyone be sure and be here tomorrow, you won't want to miss it!" Then he left the room without Monsieur Closson so much as stirring.

After recess, Monsieur Closson felt sufficiently refreshed to administer an impromptu lesson on political science. He sat hunched behind his desk and cleared his immense thoat – his signal that he was ready to begin a lecture.

"Boys, do not read communist literature, or other writings by social reprobates such as Marx or Engles," he admonished seriously.

"Why not, Monsieur?" Remy asked innocently.

"Well, literature such as this does not contain proper French virtues," the teacher ad-libbed, brushing the bangs out of his eyes.

"Like what, Monsieur?" Remy asked with seemingly great interest.

"Well…virtues such as…as…" Monsieur Closson was clearly flustered. "I…I seem to have lost my train of thought…"

He sprang up suddenly from behind his desk, "Boys, get the boxing gloves. We're going outside for some fresh air!"

***

As the day wore on, Daniel watched the classroom clock with much trepidation. *What was going to happen after dismissal today?*

When the dismissal bell rang, he lagged behind the other boys, with the pretext of getting his desk in order and his books ready to carry home for homework. When all the boys had left, Daniel waited an extra five minutes, for good measure.

Monsieur Closson, working at his desk, looked up suddenly and brushed the hair out of his eyes. "Daniel. What are you still doing here?"

Daniel considered telling him about the mud hole, but thought better of it. *Perhaps it was just a first-day hazing ritual, after all. No need stirring things up unnecessarily by informing on the lads...*

"I...I'm just getting my things ready, Monsieur..."

"Well, see you tomorrow, bright and early," the teacher said, then stopped. "Say, how do you like our school so far? Getting along all right, are you?"

Daniel nodded. "I like it well enough, Monsieur."

"Fine. You let Remy know if you need anything," Monsieur Closson said off-handedly, returning to his work. "He's the one to go to when you need anything around here..."

"*Oui*, Monsieur..." Daniel picked up his things and left the classroom. He exited the schoolhouse and began walking down the cypress-lined path to the village, listening to the crunching sound of the gravel beneath his feet. Then he heard it: "Look, it's the kraut who likes to wallow in the mud like a pig!" It was Remy's voice.

Daniel stopped and froze. He closed his eyes, paralyzed, unable to run or even move. He heard the crunching of many feet on the gravel, and forced himself to open his eyes. There were all the boys, now surrounding him. They had come out from behind the lush, green cypresses lining the pathway like indifferent, unhelpful guardian giants. And there was Remy, standing right in front of him, holding something dark brown in his hand.

"He likes the mud so much, maybe he likes to *eat* it, too!" Remy continued, extending his hand. Daniel could now see what he was holding: mud. In his own mind, he saw himself running away swiftly, like a gazelle. But he knew in reality, his feet were planted as firmly as the roots of those cypress trees.

He didn't know what to do.

Then there were two boys, one on either side of him, pulling him to the ground on his back, and holding him down. Remy was over him with the mud. "Staying behind in the classroom isn't going to save you. You can't stay behind all night. Now, eat it, kraut!"

Remy smeared the mud against Daniel's lips. Daniel fought to keep his mouth shut tight.

"Oh, a fighter, eh?" Remy chuckled. "Bernard, force his mouth open!"

Daniel felt fingers between his lips, then inside his mouth. He bit down hard, like an animal.

"Owwww!" Bernard screamed, pulling his hand away.

"He bites like a pig, too!" Remy laughed. "You've almost got to admire his spunk! Francois, a stick!"

Daniel felt a stick being inserted into his mouth, and his jaws being pried apart. It was too great a force to withstand. He felt his mouth opening, and the slimy mud being systematically forced into it. He choked, gagged, and sputtered. He felt like he was suffocating.

"All right, enough, lads," he heard Remy order. "I think he's had his fill – for now."

Daniel lay there, in utter defeat.

"And now, as if on cue, the water-works!" he heard Remy say triumphantly. It was impossible not to cry. All the boys jeered and laughed derisively. "Stupid *kraut*!" "Dirty *kraut*!"

"Come on lads," Remy called. "A good afternoon's work. Let's get home now to our suppers!"

Relieved, Daniel stayed prone until he was sure they had gone. Then he sat up, looked around warily, and began removing the rest of the mud from his mouth.

That night, Daniel had no appetite for supper. Lying in his bed, he seriously considered telling his uncle that he'd given up on school, that Emile was right – he should just stay home and labor at the shop each day. Maybe someday, become a bicycle repairman, like his uncle.

Then something else rose up in him. This was his village now, his school – his *life*. Suddenly, the thought of letting Remy and the other boys cheat him out of what was rightfully his was unthinkable. No, he would go back in the morning, and the next day, and the next. How long could they keep this up, after all? He decided to let his determination guide him, perhaps win them over, win their respect, through sheer determination and courage.

Suddenly, he felt brave. He felt a courage that he didn't know he had. Then he fell into a deep, peaceful sleep until morning.

Remy looked surprised when Daniel entered the classroom the next morning and took his usual seat in front. "Back for more, eh?" the bully smiled. "That's fine. We've got <u>plenty</u> more…"

Monsieur Closson looked up from his desk and saw Daniel. "How is everything going, Daniel?"

Daniel hesitated, fighting the urge to tell him.

"Daniel is doing splendid, Monsieur," Remy flashed his toothy grin at the teacher. "He's really catching on. Quick study. He's going to be fine, Monsieur. Just fine."

"Glad to hear it," Monsieur Closson said, suddenly distracted by some horseplay in the back of the room. "Now everyone, take out your penmanship books and get ready for today's practice…"

Once again, the day went by without incident – until dismissal time. This time, Daniel didn't lag behind after the bell. He left with the rest of the boys, so as not to arouse Monsieur Closson's suspicions. Halfway down the path, just out of eyesight of the schoolhouse, they began to surround him like a pack of wolves.

Looking ominously at Daniel, Remy pulled a rag out of his pocket and waved it in the air. "Hey, kraut! I hear you like to shine bicycles in your uncle's shop. Here, shine my shoes!" Daniel looked down at Remy's shoes. They were covered in thick mud.

"No," Daniel said quietly.

"What's that?"

"I won't shine your shoes."

"Ho-ho, what's this? What's *this*?" Remy taunted heartily. "The kraut's suddenly grown a backbone? <u>Boys</u>." Francois and Edgar came alongside Daniel and held his arms. Remy walked up and stood in front of him, making a fist. When he saw no change in Daniel's demeanor, he drew back and punched him hard in the eye.

"Go ahead." Remy flung the rag in Daniel's face disdainfully. "Make them nice and shiny, or it's back in the mud where you belong!" Francois and Edgar let him go, and Daniel picked up the rag, bent down, and started cleaning Remy's shoes, fighting back the tears.

And so it went, day after day.

Daniel fantasized about telling Monsieur Closson, but he knew that would only make it worse. Then, one day, Monsieur Closson announced the boxing championship, and Daniel saw a faint ray of hope…

Emile had been noticing the black eyes when Daniel came home from school, but said nothing. Daniel would come into the shop each afternoon after school, put his apron on, and start polishing bicycles or sweeping the floors without saying a word about it.

One day, Mademoiselle Prenet came to the shop with a chocolate éclair for Daniel. She saw his eye and gasped.

"What happened?"

"He's trying to make friends at school," Emile explained.

"Are you going to do anything about it?"

"He's got to work it out on his own," Emile shrugged.

Mademoiselle Prenet shook her head disapprovingly. She gently pulled Daniel's head back and examined the black eye. "I know just the thing for that," she said decisively, handing him the éclair. "Here, you eat this. I'll be right back."

Daniel put the broom down and bit into the delicious confection. He felt better instantly. Mademoiselle Prenet was back in no time with a raw steak.

"Here. Hold this on your eye," she ordered. "Believe me – this will do the trick!"

That evening after supper, Emile noticed Daniel reading a book.

"What's that? *Boxing for Gentlemen*?" Emile asked. "Where did you get that?"

"From school," Daniel answered evasively.

"You can't learn to fight from reading a book!" Emile growled, snatching it out of his hands and tossing it away. "Come with me."

Emile took him into the tiny yard behind the shop.

"Now, put your hands up, like this," Emile demonstrated. Daniel put his hands up.

"No, no – like *this*." Emile pulled Daniel's hands up higher. "You've got to protect your head <u>and</u> your body, at the same time. Now, before your opponent makes a move, you kick him between the legs, <u>hard</u>. I guarantee you, the fight will be over before it even begins."

"No kicking," Daniel said. "Monsieur Closson insists on gentlemen's boxing. Marquess of Queensberry rules."

"Ah, that's not *fighting.*" Emile sniffed, spitting on the ground.

"It must be Queensberry rules," Daniel insisted. "Monsieur Closson announced a boxing tournament tomorrow. I don't want to be disqualified."

"All right, no kicking," his uncle relented. "Put your hands up again. Keep your head down. Just remember, when your opponent tries to hit you, push his hand aside like <u>this</u>." Emile demonstrated.

"Now <u>*you*</u> try it," Emile said, reaching out and slapping him across the face.

Daniel was surprised. "Why did you do that?"

"You were supposed to brush my hand aside, like I showed you. Now try again!"

Daniel raised his hands, and Emile reached out and slapped him again. "Why aren't you brushing me aside?"

"I'm trying. You're too quick."

"The other boy isn't going to be slow," Emile pointed out. "Now, try again!"

Daniel tried to push his hand away, but got a slap instead. His cheek was beginning to turn red.

"Again. Come on, brush it aside!" He slapped Daniel again. "You're fighting like a girl! Come <u>on,</u> Little Bo Peep! Fight! *Fight*!" Daniel flailed, but could not deflect Emile's repeated slaps. Finally, Daniel dropped his hands in frustration, tears streaming down his face.

"You're all <u>crazy</u>!" Daniel exploded. "Everyone in this village is <u>crazy</u>!"

"Ah, *there* it is!" Emile broke into a huge grin. "There <u>is</u> a little French in you, after all!"

"What are you talking about?" Daniel asked, sniffling and wiping away tears.

"<u>*Anger*</u>!" his uncle replied triumphantly. "You've got to *use* the anger! Now, let's try again. Use it!"

Emile reached out to slap Daniel again, but this time he brushed him aside.

"Again!" Emile cried, with the same result. "You see, you <u>*can*</u> do it! Now, when you brush my hand aside, my whole body is exposed. That's when you go in for the <u>*kill*</u>. Get it?"

Daniel nodded, grinning.

"All right, now <u>*show*</u> me."

Chapter 3

The next morning, Monsieur Closson assembled everyone in the schoolhouse's rundown gymnasium for the annual boxing tournament. A padded section of the floor had been cordoned off with ropes to represent a make-shift boxing ring, which the rotund teacher stood in the center of in order to address his students.

"Boys, this will be a gentlemen's tournament, adhering strictly to the Queensberry Rules of Boxing," he enthusiastically announced. He then proceeded to enumerate the said rules with an almost parliamentarian sense of decorum.

"Rule number one: to be a fair stand-up boxing match in a twenty-four foot ring, or as near that size as practicable. Rule number two: no wrestling, kicking, or hugging allowed. Rule number three: the rounds to be of three minutes' duration, and one minute's time between rounds…"

He went on to recite all twelve rules by heart, having memorized them sometime in his youth.

"This will be a single elimination tournament, meaning the loser of each match is immediately eliminated from the competition," Monsieur Closson explained. "Each winner will then play another winner, and so on, until the final match. The winner of that match will be champion. Only the twelve oldest boys will be competing."

Daniel crossed his fingers to make the list.

"And the twelve oldest are: Remy, Edgar, Francois, Bernard, Charles, Rene, Jean, Nicolas, Andre, Patrick, Henri, and Frederic."

Daniel's heart sank.

"Um, excuse me, Monsieur," Remy raised his hand.

"What is it, Remy?"

"Jean is absent today," Remy informed him.

Monsieur Closson did a quick head-count. "Ah, you are correct. *Merci*, Remy. In that case, the next oldest boy is…Daniel."

Daniel's spirits soared.

"Remember boys, it's not about who wins and who loses," Monsieur Closson sagely cautioned them. "It's about the traits you display here in the ring today. Courage. Decency. Fortitude. Perseverance. Sportsmanship. Fairness. These are the trademarks of a winner."

"Here, here!" Remy cheered. "Well-said, Monsieur!"

Monsieur Closson then led the boys in singing a ragged but heartfelt rendition of *La Marseillaise*, and with that, the tournament began.

The first round of six matches took most of the morning, one match at a time. These matches took the most time due to their sheer number and the freshness and exuberance of the boys.

Daniel was paired with Nicolas in this round. They were fourth up. Slipping on his gloves, Daniel went over and over his uncle's instructions from the night before: *head down, hands up, brush attacks aside, look for openings*...The other boys stood confidently around Nicolas, wishing him luck. "You've got this," Edgar assured him. "*Oui*, I say the kraut goes down in the first round," Frederic agreed. Nicolas looked cocky.

The two fighters climbed into the ring, met in the center, and tapped gloves. Then they retreated to their corners and waited for the bell.

Daniel's heart was beating out of his chest. Then the bell rang, and he had to will his legs, which felt like numb stumps, to carry him to center ring.

Nicolas was already there, dancing around Daniel, sizing him up and planning his first move. Though of a slender build, Nicolas was slightly taller than Daniel, meaning Daniel would be punching up.

A tentative jab from Nicolas grazed Daniel's chin, reminding him to tuck his head in and raise his hands higher to protect his face. Another jab got through and landed on his chest. It didn't hurt; his opponent was merely probing his defenses, looking for weaknesses.

Then another jab landed on the left side of his torso, and this one *did* hurt. It got Daniel's attention, woke him up. He was able to brush away a fourth attack, then dodge a fifth. Nicolas was feeling more at ease, getting more aggressive, but also breathing more heavily at the same time.

Then the bell rang, ending the first round. Each boxer returned to his corner – Nicolas to congratulations from his friends, Daniel to a lonely corner and moral support from not a single soul.

During the minute's rest, Daniel tried to take stock of his performance so far. Nicolas had landed four blows so far, while he hadn't even attempted a jab. He knew that would have to change, or he'd have no chance of winning the match. In that case, he'd be eliminated from the tournament.

The second round bell rang, and Daniel emerged from his corner determined to seize the initiative and show more aggression. He tried a tentative jab to Nicolas' face, but his nimble opponent drew back without contact.

"Oh-ho, what's this?" Nicolas asked, surprised. "Now we've got a match, eh?"

Daniel answered with another, more confident attack, landing a blow to Nicolas' right side. Nicolas winced; it hurt him, but he tried not to let it show.

Of course, the crowd cheered wildly – all for Nicolas. "Go, Nicolas!" "You've got him now, Nicolas!"

Now Nicolas went on the offensive, with a flurry of blows that Daniel, using his uncles coaching from the night before, was able to turn away with his upraised arms. This resulted in no new points for Nicolas, just greater fatigue for his efforts.

The bell rang, ending the second round. Daniel was tired, but Nicolas looked more tired.

In the third round, Daniel continued his strategy of trying to outlast his opponent and win through attrition. Nicolas continued to try to pummel him, using up much of his strength, with very few blows making it through Daniel's defensive posture. In the meantime, Daniel was matching Nicolas blow for blow, until it was impossible to tell who was ahead in points.

The rest of the match progressed in this manner, Daniel buying time, trying to keep just outside Nicolas' reach, eventually looking more like a stalemate than a decisive victory for either boy. For the sake of time, Monsieur Closson had limited each match to six rounds. As the bell rang after round six, the boys, neither one having landed a decisive knockout, disengaged and made their way to their corners to await the results.

It took some time for Monsieur Closson to count the tally marks on the rolling chalkboard he'd been using to keep score. The room was absolutely silent during the process. Finally, he put down the piece of chalk and walked to the ring.

"Gentlemen, we have a winner for this match," he announced as the crowd waited breathlessly. "It's Daniel, with fourteen points, to Nicolas' twelve points…"

The boys were stunned. "Are you sure, Monsieur?" Remy asked incredulously.

"Quite certain," the teacher answered, brushing the bangs out of his eyes. He reached over the ropes and jerked Daniel's gloved hand up into the air. "Congratulations, Daniel! You will be moving on to the next round!"

Many of the boys still couldn't believe it. *How could this be?* A few of them tried to comfort Nicolas, who didn't look like he was taking it well at all. "It's all right, Nicolas. He just got lucky, that's all…"

Between rounds, Daniel had time to rest and think. He knew he had done well putting his uncle's coaching to work, at least in a defensive sense. But he was still missing something. What was it – the missing element that would provide the *aggression* he was lacking?

Ah, the anger! Without that, he knew was trying to fight with his head, like an automaton, instead of with his heart. He remembered his uncle's words: *Use it. Use the anger!*

In the second round, Daniel was paired with Bernard, the boy whose fingers he'd bitten that day after school when they'd forced him to eat mud. He knew from the look Bernard gave him that it was going to be personal. *Bien*, thought Daniel. *I remember that day, too. I can use that anger…*

From the opening bell, Daniel knew this match was going to be different. Bernard came right out of his corner and immediately began stalking Daniel, to great cheers from the crowd. No tentative dancing and probing, like Nicolas – Bernard was clearly coming after Daniel. He immediately attacked Daniel with a right-left-right combo that forced Daniel to fall back and tuck his arms in close to his sides in a purely defensive posture. Then Bernard went for Daniel's head – right, left, right – causing him to tuck his head and crouch down lower as he took several more steps back. He was almost on the ropes, very close to disaster, when he began to have a peculiar taste in his mouth.

What was it? Musty, gritty, salty – like soil. Mud! The memories started flooding in on him – being held to the ground, jaws pried open, that horrible muck being forced into his mouth. The laughter, the jeers, the humiliation, the tears – everything crashed in on him at once. Then he began to feel it – the *anger*.

Bernard was pummeling him. He was against the ropes, and Bernard was preparing to finish him off. But he was still standing.

"I can still taste it," he said to Bernard through the flurry of blows.

"What?" Bernard asked.

"I can still taste it!" he said, louder.

"Taste what?"

"The mud!"

Bernard stopped a moment, confused. "*Mud?*"

Then Daniel saw it: Bernard had left an opening, left his torso exposed. Before Bernard could cover himself, he hit him hard in the left side, just below the ribs. Bernard staggered back in surprise, Daniel took two steps forward and was off the ropes. The crowd had gotten quiet, not sure what was transpiring. Daniel, sufficiently roused, went on the offensive.

"I can still taste it!" he told Bernard, advancing on him and hitting him again in the same spot under his ribs. Bernard went down on one knee, the wind knocked out of him. The rest of the boys were absolutely silent now, except for one. "Get up, Bernie!" someone pleaded in a quivering voice. Daniel knew not to hit a man when he was down, even on one knee, and waited for Monsieur Closson to start the countdown. Instead, the bell rang ending round one.

Bernard was saved. He stood up shakily and walked to his corner, not quite sure what had just happened. Daniel returned to his corner and waited for round two, determined to keep his anger stoked until the bell rang.

When round two began, Bernard had roused himself from his stupor, but his legs still looked a little shaky. Daniel, on the other hand, seized the momentum and pounced on Bernard like a leopard. He tried to break through and land another punch in Bernard's soft spot, his side, but Bernard was able to keep his flanks well protected by his arms. Daniel tried for his head, but Bernard was able to keep his blows from landing there, as well. Stymied, Daniel started looking for another opening, and Bernard provided one.

Bernard made a sudden, impulsive jab at Daniel's head, but Daniel deflected it with an outward movement like Emile had taught him. Then he took advantage of the opening Bernard had left and landed a crushing blow to his right side. Bernard hadn't seen it coming. He staggered back, sucking air and trying desperately to stay on his feet.

Then it was like something took Daniel over. A Zen-like serenity descended on him like a soothing ocean mist. His movements became fluid, graceful, *precise*. He had no fear, no apprehension, no uncertainty. It was just like he somehow knew – innately, instinctively – what to do. His feet, arms and hands moved in beautiful harmony as he approached Bernard, feinting here, jabbing there, waiting for an opening to present itself. He *was* a boxer.

Bernard attempted another desperate jab at his head. Again, Daniel deflected it with ease and delivered another crushing right hook to Bernard's side. Bernard went down on one knee again, trying to get his wind back, but unable to get back on his feet. Instead, he pitched back on his rump, his arms dangling uselessly at his sides. Monsieur Closson started the count.

Bernard merely shook his head, knowing he was finished.

All the boys were rendered speechless by what they had just witnessed. Two of them came and helped Bernard out of the ring, while Monsieur Closson finished the count and declared Daniel the winner of his second match.

"Winner, in the second round," the teacher said, holding Daniel's hand in the air. "This was some incredibly accomplished boxing, young man. Incredibly accomplished, indeed!"

There were only three competitors left in the third round: Remy, Francois, and Daniel. Monsieur Closson had them draw straws. Daniel drew the short straw, meaning Remy and Francois would fight first, and Daniel would take on the winner.

Daniel carefully studied the match between Remy and Francois. It was obvious from the start that Francois was quite outmatched; Remy's technique and execution was impressive for a boy his age. Where many of the other boys had been flailing and thrashing their way through their matches, Remy executed legitimate boxing moves with precision, fluidity, and timing. Consequently, he was able to dispatch his opponent in the middle of the third round.

That left Remy and Daniel for the final bout.

Monsieur Closson, no doubt feeling that some sort of heartfelt oration was in order, solemnly addressed his students. "All of you, to a man, have acquitted yourselves like champions, like chivalrous knights of old," he sermonized, brushing the bangs out of his eyes. "I am proud of all of you. You stand as shining examples to your school, your village, and, yes, to all of France. And now, we have reached the end, the final match of our tournament. I am certain both combatants will acquit themselves with the utmost honor and chivalry. And, no matter the outcome, I'm certain we can all be proud to call ourselves Frenchmen. *Vive la France!"*

And with that, Remy and Daniel met center ring and tapped gloves. Remy had an ironic grin on his face. "Who could have predicted this, eh?" he asked out loud. "Well, good luck."

Daniel merely nodded, and the two boys retreated to their corners. Daniel had no strategy in mind. Watching Remy fight Francois, he had seen no apparent flaws, no weaknesses to exploit – except, perhaps, over-confidence. When the bell rang, Remy shot out of his corner like a rabbit and took up position in the center of the ring. It appeared to Daniel that he was trying to dominate the space, to claim it for his own, to make Daniel feel like the interloper.

Daniel hesitated.

"Come on," Remy taunted. "Are we going to fight, or not?"

Daniel came out to meet him, his guard up. Remy immediately executed two quick right jabs and a beautiful left hook. The hook caught Daniel in the side of the head, causing him to stumble slightly and shake his head several times to set his vision straight. Daniel reflexively stepped back, and Remy went on the attack again: a rapid-fire series of jabs and crosses that kept Daniel on the defensive. This elicited boisterous cheers from the crowd and calls for Remy to "finish him off for good."

Remy followed him around the ring, throwing punches when he could, keeping Daniel in a crouch with his head down low, for the rest of the round. When the bell rang, Daniel retreated to his corner. He knew it wasn't going his way, but he didn't know what to do, how to turn it around. As things stood, it seemed hopeless.

Then the second round bell rang, and there was Remy, center ring, taunting Daniel with his crooked, charming grin. Daniel forced himself out into the ring, resigned to accept whatever punishment Remy was willing to dish out. Remy came in close and said, "Krauts don't know how to fight," careful that Monsieur Closson wouldn't be able to hear. Then, apparently unwilling to chase Daniel around the ring for another round and wanting to end things quickly, he shot his foot out and tripped Daniel while he was attempting to back away. Daniel fell backwards and went down hard.

Monsieur Closson *did* see this, however, and stopped the fight.

"It was an accident, Monsieur," Remy insisted innocently.

"Nevertheless, I'm going to have to deduct one point from your score," Monsieur Closson informed Remy.

Remy wasn't happy. "*Oui*, Monsieur," he said sullenly.

Daniel got to his feet. "Are you able to continue, Daniel?" the teacher asked.

"*Oui*," Daniel answered, feeling his anger rise.

Monsieur Closson rang the bell to continue the round. Remy was hyper-aggressive, all over Daniel once again. But this time he met with resistance. Daniel stood his ground, successfully deflecting Remy's blows and even landing a right-cross on Remy's chin. This was the first glove Daniel had laid on him, and although it didn't hurt much, Remy tried not to show his surprise.

He retaliated with a flurry of jabs and crosses that Daniel was able to deflect or dodge without much trouble. But landing another blow on Remy was proving difficult after his initial success – Remy was much more cautious now. Nevertheless, Daniel knew he needed to touch him again, and waited patiently for the opportunity to present itself.

It did a moment later, when one of Remy's usually machine-like right crosses went wide and exposed his right side for a split second. Daniel immediately took advantage and landed a crushing blow to Remy's ribs. Stunned, Remy staggered back and tried to regain his breath. Daniel stepped forward, keeping his guard up but going on the offensive with several well-placed blows.

"Don't let him win!" someone called from outside the ring, but Remy's form was disintegrating as quickly as his confidence. Then the bell rang, and the fighters retired to their corners. Remy looked sweaty and out of breath, but far from defeated. Daniel was tired but elated at his own recent headway. For the first time, no one was sure just how this was going to end.

The third round started, and Remy came out trying to regain his poise and confidence. He landed a couple of decent blows on Daniel's body, but Daniel was doing a good job keeping himself protected and deflecting most of Remy's efforts. Daniel kept his head tucked in and gloves in front of his face, waiting for his next opportunity to strike. It came in the middle of the round, when Remy launched another wide cross and left his ribs exposed again. Daniel was ready, hitting him hard again in the same spot as before. Remy staggered back, pain and disbelief written across his face. Then, the tears started filling his eyes and flowing down his cheeks – whether from pain or frustration, Daniel could not tell.

Recovering quickly, Remy wiped the tears away with his gloves before any of the other boys could see. *Tears!* Even if the others didn't see him crying, Daniel had, and it gave him a wonderful sense of satisfaction.

Remy regrouped in the fourth round, connecting with a right hook to Daniel's jaw that sent him reeling, but he stayed on his feet. Then Remy came in heavy with a left-right-left combination that dropped Daniel to one knee. Remy stood over him, waiting to see if he would get up or not. Daniel wavered, tired and out of breath, but determined not to give up. He rose cautiously and raised his gloves to continue.

"Why don't you just stay <u>down</u>?" Remy asked.

Daniel shook his head. "No."

The rest of the round saw Remy on the offense, moving Daniel around the ring, and Daniel counter-punching but unable to land a decisive blow.

At the beginning of the fifth round, Daniel felt himself fading. Two more rounds of combat seemed unthinkable, if not impossible. Remy emerged from his corner and went on the offensive, swinging away with several quick jabs and a right cross that caught Daniel square in the eye. Remy also slipped a sneaky below-the-belt punch to Daniel's groin that even Monsieur Closson didn't see.

The pain shot through Daniel's body, turning his legs to gelatin. There was no way he could stay on his feet. He went down, and Monsieur Closson began the count as Remy danced around Daniel in victory. The boys went wild cheering for Remy. As Monsieur Closson finished the count and gently lifted Daniel to his feet, the boys pulled Remy from the ring, lifted him onto their shoulders, and carried him around the gymnasium like a conquering hero.

"Are you all right, Daniel?" Monsieur Closson asked. Daniel nodded bravely through the still-burning pain, fighting back tears and determined not to let it show. He almost told Monsieur Closson about the below-the-belt punch, but thought better of it. If they bullied him this badly as it was, what would they do to a snitch?

The boys were still carrying Remy around the gymnasium, singing an old French battle song in victory.

"You did very well today, Daniel," Monsieur Closson said kindly. "You can hold your head high. Now go home and rest."

***

Miraculously, the bullying ended after the boxing tournament. Daniel returned to school the next morning, sporting the black eye from one of Remy's last punches, fully expecting the bullying to continue, if not get worse. So he was not surprised when, upon leaving the schoolhouse at the end of the day, Remy and the boys surrounded him on the gravel path as they had done so many times before.

"Don't worry, we're done with the bullying," Remy assured him with his sly grin. Daniel was pleased to see that Remy's nose was slightly swollen from one of his own punches the day before. Remy noticed him staring at it. "I guess we've both got our battle scars, eh? That was a good one, by the way…"

Daniel remained silent, not sure where this was going.

"The boys and I have got something to tell you," Remy continued. "We, um, we think you showed a lot of honor and courage yesterday. No kidding. That was pluck, way beyond anybody's expectations. You impressed us. Nicely done, Daniel."

"*Merci*," Daniel said, still unsure.

"And that's not all. You didn't snitch on me cheating. That was real stand-up of you. In fact, you never snitched on us, whatever we did to you. That shows character. That shows loyalty. So, the boys and I got to thinking, and, to get right down to it, we all took a vote and we're going to let you join our gang."

Daniel had a skeptical look on his face.

"Relax, Daniel. This is on the up-and-up. We're inviting you to join our gang. No more hazing, no more bullying. From now on, you'll be one of us. What do you say?" Remy extended a hand. Daniel made no move to take it. "Come on, no tricks. I promise…"

"All right, then," Daniel said, shaking his hand.

"Splendid!" Remy beamed. "Of course, there's a probation period."

"A probation period?" Daniel asked.

"*Oui*, everyone has to go through it," Remy explained. "It's nothing, really. You just have to fulfill some initiations to earn all the rights and privileges of full membership…"

"Initiations? Like what?"

"Oh, just little things – pranks, really – you know, just to prove your loyalty beyond a shadow of a doubt. And after the initiations, you just need to remain willing to do whatever we ask you to do, when called upon. Then, after you've proven yourself, you're off probation – you're one of us! *D'accord?*"

"*D'accord*," Daniel agreed.

"Splendid! Now, the first initiation won't be too difficult, I promise. I'll tell you what it is first thing in the morning. Welcome to the gang, Daniel!" All the boys gathered around and patted him on the back, chumming it up with smiles and words of welcome. Although confused, Daniel felt a twinge of relief and began to see a faint ray of hope that life in his new village may actually improve.

The next morning, as soon as the boys had taken their seats at their desks, Remy revealed the first initiation. "Monsieur Closson keeps a small bottle of brandy in his bottom desk drawer," Remy whispered into Daniel's ear. "This afternoon, when he falls asleep, we want you to get it."

"But how?" Daniel asked.

"Easy," Remy assured him. "He's a very heavy sleeper…"

"I don't know, Remy…"

"Come on, you want to be part of the gang, don't you?"

Daniel thought about it a moment. "All right. I'll do it."

That afternoon after lunch, Remy watched Monsieur Closson like a hawk. As predicted, it didn't take long for the corpulent teacher to start to nod off.

"There he goes," Remy nudged Daniel. "He's <u>under</u>. It's all yours."

"Are you sure?" Daniel asked nervously.

"Positive," Remy assured him. "He'll be out for at least twenty minutes. Now go on, you're wasting time…"

Daniel got out of his chair and took his shoes off. He walked stealthily towards the teacher's desk, stopping to make sure Monsieur Closson didn't awaken whenever he stepped on a squeaky floor plank. Finally, he made it to the desk and stopped.

"Go *on*!" Remy hissed from his desk. The whole class was silent, watching Daniel's every move. He carefully got down on all fours and crawled around to the back of the desk. Monsieur Closson snored loudly, but stayed asleep. Daniel reached a hand up and slowly pulled the bottom drawer open. He peaked over the side of the drawer, and reached in to grab the bottle.

Just then, Monsieur Delfont, the headmaster, burst into the classroom in an unusually animated state. Startled, Daniel dropped to the floor and tried to stay hidden behind the desk. Monsieur Closson snored loudly again.

Monsieur Delfont stopped abruptly just inside the door. "Ah, I see Monsieur Closson is resting," he said to the class. "No need to wake him. I just came in to tell you that tomorrow I will be delivering my second lecture on the Insect Kingdom."

Nobody stirred. Everybody was holding their breath. Daniel lay on the floor as still as a corpse, praying the headmaster wouldn't see him.

"This one will be on the <u>ants</u>," Monsieur Delfont elaborated. "The ants, as you may know, have developed an extremely sophisticated society. I think you're going to be fascinated by the complexity of their social order…"

It was like a classroom of statues. Oblivious, Monsieur Closson snored again.

"Well, I'll let you carry on with your work," the headmaster said cheerfully. "See you boys tomorrow!" He left the room and closed the door. Everyone breathed again. Daniel reached into the drawer and grabbed the bottle by feel. When he had it, he carefully closed the drawer and slinked across the floor back to his desk. Sitting upright in his chair again, he quickly passed the bottle to Remy who shoved it down his trousers just as Monsieur Closson snorted awake.

"Well, I seem to have nodded off for a second there," Monsieur Closson admitted as he came back to consciousness. "It's rather warm in here, isn't it?"

After school, the boys shared the brandy back behind the schoolhouse, passing it around like seasoned drinkers. Remy made the first toast: "Here's to Daniel, who proved himself a fine fellow today!" Daniel couldn't help but feel a pang of pride – as well as relief for not getting caught – at finally being accepted by the group.

The next morning, Remy had the next initiation ready. He presented Daniel with a small gift box and instructed him to open it. Daniel did so, and nearly jumped out of his skin. Inside was the fattest cockroach he'd ever seen.

"Wh-what do you want me to do with *this*?" he asked, his skin crawling.

"You're going to put it in Monsieur Delfont's jacket before he comes to give his insect lecture today," Remy smiled.

"H-how do you expect me to do that?"

"Don't worry, we wouldn't send you into battle without doing our homework first," Remy assured him. "Before his lectures, Monsieur Delfont always washes up in his office bathroom. While he's in there, you'll sneak into his office and plant the cockroach in his jacket pocket."

"But what if he catches me?"

"He won't, because you're too sneaky," Remy argued. "You <u>do</u> want to get off probation, don't you?"

Daniel agreed to do it. Just before it was time for the lecture, he asked permission to leave the classroom to use the toilet. Then he snuck into the headmaster's office and sheepishly looked around. As Remy had said, Monsieur Delfont was in the adjoining bathroom with the door closed. He could hear the sounds of running water and Monsieur Delfont humming through the door.

The headmaster's jacket was hanging over the back of a chair. Daniel quietly walked over to it and pulled the small box from his trouser pocket. With an involuntary shiver, he opened the box and dumped the cockroach into the jacket's breast pocket. He heard the running water stop and a rustling of towels in the bathroom. Quickly stuffing the empty box back into his trouser pocket, he scurried out of the office and closed the door behind him.

Back in the classroom, Remy seemed anxious. "How'd it go?"

"You'll see," Daniel smiled. A few moments later, Monsieur Delfont entered the classroom, freshly washed and neatly coiffed, wearing the jacket. He stepped to the front of the classroom and took his place behind the lectern, smiling in anticipation.

"*Bonjour*, boys!" he beamed.

"*Bonjour*, Monsieur Delfont," the class replied in unison.

"Well, as promised, today's lecture will be on the ants," the headmaster began. Every eye in the room was trained expectantly on his jacket. "Industry. Community. Loyalty. Make no mistake: the ants can teach us much about ourselves and our human aspirations…"

Two long feelers suddenly appeared, sticking up out of the headmaster's breast pocket.

"Ants are eusocial insects of the family Formicidae and, along with wasps and bees, belong to the order Hymenoptera. As we all know, ants live in communities called *colonies*, consisting of anything from a few dozen individuals to millions of citizens…"

The feelers twitched, and a cockroach head appeared.

"Larger colonies consist mostly of sterile, wingless females, or *workers*, and fertile males called *drones*," Monsieur Delfont continued, oblivious to the hideous creature beginning to emerge from his breast pocket. "Of course, all colonies have one or more fertile females, or *queens*. There are also *soldiers* who protect the queen and the colony from hostile foreign invaders."

The giant cockroach crawled completely out of the pocket and rested on the headmaster's lapel, like a broach. Francois emitted a stifled snicker, but Remy flashed him a grimace and he quieted down.

"What strikes one most about these enterprising creatures, is the way they seem to work together, all doing their distinct jobs, for the good of the queen and their colony. The support, protection, and nurture of the colony is of paramount importance to every ant. In fact, one often becomes emotionally overwhelmed when one contemplates the degree of loyalty these creatures – " and there was a slight catch in the headmaster's throat here – "display for their queen." He pulled out his handkerchief and delicately blew his nose.

The cockroach slowly climbed up the lapel, and disappeared down Monsieur Delfont's shirt collar. It was all the boys could do to keep from exploding in laughter.

"When one contemplates the proto-typical ant colony, with its division of labor, communication between individuals, and uncanny ability to solve complex problems, one can only marvel at the parallels with the sophisticated societies and advanced development of modern human beings..." The headmaster's shoulder twitched involuntarily. "Where did this ability come from? From whence came this sophisticated intelligence?" His left arm now convulsed reflexively.

Unable to control himself any longer, Francois burst out laughing, then covered his mouth with his hand. Daniel, eyes glued to the twitching headmaster, was determined to hold it together.

"How, for instance, are they able to communicate with each other, you may ask?" Monsieur Delfont was now showing unmistakable signs of distraction. He gripped the lectern tightly with both hands in an attempt to minimize the twitching. "Well, experts believe they use their feelers, or *antennae*, to transmit signals to one another through touch..." His left arm twitched again, and the cockroach emerged from his shirtsleeve, sat on the back of his hand a moment, then crawled to the middle of the lectern and seemed to look out at the audience. The temporarily relieved headmaster somehow remained unaware of its presence.

Several boys began to crack up. Monsieur Delfont gave them a stern look, then stoically continued. "It is also believed that these sensitive antennae can detect chemicals, air currents, and slight vibrations in the ground and air..." The cockroach jumped onto the headmaster's *other* hand, then scurried up his right shirtsleeve. The creature must have run up the length of his arm, for that unfortunate appendage suddenly rippled and twitched in a most curious, wave-like manner. "My apologies, boys, but there seems to be something inside my *shirt*..." he said, following his discovery with a twitchy, jerky little jig. Then his arms flailed in the air as he tried in vain to reach around to his back.

Now the whole room erupted in unbridled laughter. Monsieur Delfont's head turned and bobbed comically in unison with his shoulders as he shivered in disgust; the wild, involuntary physical contortions made him appear to suffer from some type of nervous disorder.

"I'm afraid we're going to have to finish our lecture another time..." He headed quickly for the classroom door, already tearing his jacket and shirt from his ravaged body. When he was gone, Monsieur Closson pounded his desk with a book for order.

"Now, I know one or more of you had something to do with this," he finally said, when all the laughter had ceased. "I am asking the guilty party to do the honorable thing and step forward, or I shall be forced to punish the whole class." Monsieur Closson looked around the room, examining each face. Poker faces from everyone, especially Remy and Daniel. "No? Then no recess for two weeks, for everyone!"

To all the boys, Daniel included, two weeks without recess was well worth the spectacle they had just witnessed. "Besides, the Old Man will forget all about it in a few days," Remy told Daniel after school. And he was right: they only had to forfeit three days of recess before Monsieur Closson commuted the sentence and things returned to normal.

Remy proved uniquely gifted when it came to inventing pranks. "Come on," he told the boys one day. They all followed him to the butcher's shop, just in time for the butcher to take off on his bicycle with a package of meat.

They followed Jacques to a small cottage just outside the village, hiding in the bushes as he got off his bicycle and took the package inside. "To everyone else, he sends his delivery boy," Remy explained knowingly. "But to the widow Deschard, he delivers the sausage <u>himself.</u>" Then they listened beneath her open bedroom window and heard passionate sighs, giggles, and the squeaking of mattress springs.

A gleam in his eye, Remy led them around to the butcher's bicycle. "Watch this," he grinned, letting the air out of Jacques' tires. Then they hid in the bushes again until he came out, tucking his shirt-tail into his pants and flattening down his hair. When he saw his deflated tires, he swore loudly and pushed his flat bike all the way to Emile's repair shop in the village. "Monsieur Renaud!" he shouted. He only used the proper title when he was especially upset. "My tires are flat. These are defective tires you sold me. I demand new tires at once!"

"There is nothing wrong with these tires," Emile retorted. "Perhaps you have been riding through a briar patch, or perhaps you need to lose a few pounds, eh?"

"This is not a joke! I want new tires!"

Emile shook his head. "There is nothing wrong with these tires." He pumped them up, putting his ear close to the tread for hisses. "You see? They are holding air now."

"Every time I go up Prassis Lane, they go flat!"

"Ah. And who lives up Prassis Lane?" Emile smirked.

The butcher turned red, blustered something about his delivery boy being sick, and declared, as if to save face: "I am telling you: there is something wrong with these tires!" The boys watched, laughing, as he grabbed his bike and sped away in a huff.

Every time the butcher made one of his deliveries, the boys followed him to the widow's house. Again, listening underneath the bedroom window and giggling to themselves. "Boy, the widow Deschard sure orders a lot of sausage!" Edgar observed wryly.

This time, Remy gave Daniel the honor of letting the air out of the tires. "If you do this, consider yourself off probation," he promised Daniel. "You'll be one of us." Daniel went to the bicycle and started deflating the tires while the others hid in the bushes.

Just then, Jacques came out of the cottage unexpectedly and caught Daniel in the act. "Aha! So you're the one who's been doing this, eh?" Before Daniel could run, the butcher grabbed him by the ear and wouldn't let go. "We're going straight to your uncle!" Jacques pulled him by the ear (while riding the bike) all the way back to Emile's shop. Daniel had to run the whole way to keep up.

"Now I know who has been letting the air out of my tires!" the butcher raged when they'd reached Emile's shop. "I saw other boys running away. Who are they?" he demanded, twisting Daniel's ear. "I want names!" Daniel said nothing. "Oh, not talking, eh?" the butcher said, and boxed Daniel's other ear.

"Enough, Jacques," Emile said calmly but firmly.

Jacques boxed Daniel's ear again. The boy looked right in his uncle's eyes, but did not cry. Jacques reached back to box him again, but Emile grabbed his wrist with his strong hand and staid the blow. "I said, _enough_, Jacques!"

Jacques released the boy. "Well, I want my tires inflated immediately. And...and I want a new wicker basket on the front." Emile nodded in agreement. "All right, Jacques." Emile looked at Daniel, nodding slightly, acknowledging his lack of tears, and something unspoken passed between them. He knew then that his uncle was not going to punish him for the prank.

Later, after the butcher left, the boys sheepishly gathered at the shop to see Daniel. "How's your ear?" Remy asked.

"It'll be fine," Daniel said.

"You didn't rat us out," Remy said in awe. "You are now my brother."

As winter faded into spring, life for Daniel began to settle into a pleasant routine. There was school, working in the bicycle shop afternoons, and exploring the countryside around the village on weekends. The boys fished and loafed and played "knights," strapping pillows to their torsos and beating each other with stick "swords." Mademoiselle Prenet dropped by the shop several times a week bearing chocolate eclairs, cream puffs, or tarts for Daniel.

"I just want to make sure the boy isn't wasting away," she explained, shooting a reproving, sidelong glance in Emile's direction.

Even Emile's lessons on "French-ness" became less didactic and more integrated into the fabric of their lifestyle. In the meantime, Daniel and Remy became fast friends. As Daniel got to know him better, he began to see the true dimensions of Remy's complex personality emerge. Remy was alternately kind, unctuous, charming, manipulative, loyal, vain, generous, and even cruel – in short, whatever he needed to be at any given time to get what he wanted. But he was also brilliant, Daniel soon discovered. He was the type of boy who could master pretty much anything he set his mind to: chess, electronics, languages, intricate cons, and harmless pranks. Everything in Remy's world had the potential to be mastered and leveraged to his advantage, and as long as one was aware of that, one could get along with him just fine.

As time passed, Emile began to soften somewhat, and even put Daniel to better use in the shop. He began to teach Daniel how to fix flats, change tires, and do other common repairs on the bicycles. As part of his training as a proper Frenchman, Emile, who was a good cook himself, began to teach Daniel how to prepare proper French dishes. Since a vital part of cooking is procuring the materials, Emile set about to teach Daniel the proper techniques of hunting and fishing. This required weekend camp-outs in the woods, which Daniel began to look forward to with great relish.

Emile taught him how to load a shotgun and dress a wild hare. He taught him how to build a fire on the forest floor and cook the hare in a stew with garlic, cloves, and wild onions. He taught Daniel the patience required of a hunter. "If you want to eat, you sit quietly and still. You don't <u>hunt</u> them. You sit and wait for <u>them</u> to come to <u>you</u>." The logic of this didn't seem completely correct to Daniel at first, but he slowly began to understand what his uncle was talking about.

On clear crisp spring mornings Emile would close the shop and take Daniel down to the stream for fishing lessons. He was quick to point out that they were not "sluffing off" work, but engaging in important instruction in skills which every proper Frenchman was expected to exercise when confronted with a body of water. The first time, Daniel approached the stream and trudged noisily into the water. Emile snatched him by the shirt-collar and yanked him violently back onto the bank.

"*Lourdad!* What are you *doing*?" Emile shook the boy savagely. Apparently, the patience Emile exhibited while crouched in the forest waiting for his prey did not translate directly to delivering a fishing lesson to an energetic and over-eager boy. "You announce yourself like a column of clumsy German tanks! Do you <u>want</u> the fish to hear you coming?" Emile demanded, again shaking the boy for emphasis. Calming down somewhat, Emile released the boy and sat down on a large rock. "Come here," he said, patting the rock beside him. Daniel complied. "They must not know you are here. You must *sneak* *up* on them, without a sound, until they are completely relaxed and certain there is not a loud, clumsy oaf of a German boy within a kilometer of them. You see?" Daniel nodded. "Good. Now let's try it again. And remember: *they must not know you are here*!"

Daniel, staying on the bank this time, took his rod and tried to cast the hook into the stream. Of course, the line became hopelessly tangled. Emile growled, but patiently untangled the line. "Look. You've got to cast it with a smooth motion, like this..." He demonstrated for Daniel, then had the boy try again, with better results. "That will do for now," his uncle muttered grudgingly.

After a few minutes, Daniel asked, "When will the fish bite?"

"When he feels like it," Emile said flatly. "If you're not willing to wait, you shouldn't be a fisherman."

"How will I know when it happens?"

"Ah, now you're asking some good questions," his uncle said, more engaged now. "You see, it's not as straightforward as one thinks..." Emile went on to explain that when the trout bite, there isn't a tug on the line as one would think. Instead, a bubble will rise to the surface.

"When you see the bubble, you tug *upward*, not to the side," Emile explained. "Then, when you're sure you've hooked him, you pull the fish along the water, not hoist him into the air."

"Uncle, there's a bubble!" Daniel called excitedly.

"Shhhh! You'll scare him away!" his uncle cautioned. "Now, tug upward!"

Daniel did so, and started reeling him in.

"No no no no! You are jerking the line too much! Reel it smoothly, like this, see?" It was a nice twelve inch trout. That afternoon, Emile showed him how to prepare fresh stream trout with a sauce of wild almonds and lemon.

"I am pleased," Emile told him after the meal, though without much affection. "You are learning fast." His belly full, Emile felt chatty. "Your father, of course, was no outdoorsman. He had no interest in any of this, and would not be able to teach you what I am teaching you. I suppose he reckoned he would take his meals in the café every evening, while he persued his writing, and not have to bother with all of this. A typical artist – head in the books, no sense of the outdoors or the practicality of finding your own food. Listen to me, Daniel. A Frenchman must know how to take care of himself, how to live off the land..."

"Perhaps he knew how to do things, from reading books..." Daniel suggested.

"Books? Pshaw! How do you learn these things from _books_? No, your father was weak and useless."

"But he was your brother," Daniel pointed out. "Was there never a time you loved my father?"

"I...I...ENOUGH! Men don't speak of such things! You're just a boy...you don't know what you're talking about..." and Emile ended the discussion by rising, stomping away from the camp fire, and relieving himself against a tree.

When Emile came back and sat down again, he was calmer. "It was an accident," Daniel finally said.

"What are you talking about?"

"How they died. They were run down by a car while crossing the street. It was just an accident." Emile said nothing. He just sighed, scratched a stubbly cheek, and picked a stick up off the ground.

"Uncle, why do you hate the Germans so?"

"Why? I fought them in the war," Emile answered, digging at the campfire with the stick. "I saw things…they, they did despicable things, Daniel…"

"Just the Germans? Didn't your side – *our* side – do terrible things, as well?"

"Yes, yes I suppose in war, there are no innocent men," Emile admitted. "I saw things I cannot tell you about. You're too young to know such things. But I cannot erase them from my memory. I suppose I never will. Life in the trenches was…I can't explain it, there are no words for such things. Sometimes, the supply lorries just didn't make it to the front for weeks at a time. We were so hungry, we did things…we ate things…that civilized people shouldn't talk about." He shuddered, then smiled suddenly as a long-forgotten memory resurfaced. "One time, a starving dog chased a starving rat into our trench. Ten starving soldiers, they didn't stand a chance. We ate the rat as an appetizer, and the dog as the main course!" Emile laughed heartily at the memory. Daniel laughed, too. Here they were, sitting beside a stream with full bellies, on a beautiful spring afternoon. On days like this, life didn't seem so bad.

Snooping around in an old building behind the shop one day, Daniel found an interesting shape with a cover over it. Curious, he pulled the dusty cover off and saw that it was an old motorcycle. Thinking nothing of it, he sat on it and pretended to ride it. Every day for weeks he went back to play on the motorcycle, imagining himself winning a number of great races. But he never mentioned it to Emile, for fear of getting in trouble for playing on it.

Chapter 4

Three years passed, Daniel grew, life in the village continued quietly. There was talk of war with Germany but it seemed far away. Daniel continued to go to school, work in the bicycle shop, and hunt and fish with his uncle. Emile slowly softened towards Daniel, and now treated him like a son. He was clearly proud of Daniel, but still didn't show much open affection to the boy.

Daniel had grown quite fond of his uncle, as well. Still, he kept two secrets from him. First, every night in bed before he fell asleep, he carried on imaginary conversations, in German, with his mother. Second, he had been playing on the motorcycle in the shed for three years. He couldn't help it, even though he knew his uncle would not be pleased. For some reason, it was as if he were being *drawn* to that old motorcycle.

Then one day, Emile pulled the motorcycle out of the shed and wheeled it into the shop. "Here Daniel, I want to show you something." Daniel thought he was going to be punished for playing on it behind Emile's back.

"It's all right. You can touch it…" Emile told him. Daniel slowly reached out and touched the handlebars. "Don't be so timid, Daniel. I know you've been playing on it for years."

"How…how did you know?"

"I noticed the dust on the seat was imprinted with the pattern from your trousers," Emile shrugged.

"And…and you don't mind?"

Emile shrugged again. "Boys and motorcycles…what's to mind?"

Emile then told Daniel that this was no ordinary motorcycle. "This motorcycle belonged to Pablo Picasso." Then he told Daniel a long, beautiful story: "While on a trip to Italy in 1928, the famous artist and his mistress witnessed an Italian championship motorcycle race. Picasso's mistress couldn't stop talking about the excitement of the race and the courage and derring of the riders themselves. She was so effusive about the event that the artist began to grow jealous that she was not paying enough attention to *him*. He saw the way she looked at the handsome young winner of the race, and he didn't like it. So he went up to the winner and insisted that he celebrate his victory by allowing Picasso, and his mistress, to take him out for a night of eating and drinking in Rome.

"Well, who would deny the request of such a famous man as Pablo Picasso? And so the three of them went out drinking that evening and hit it off so well that the party lasted until dawn. Picasso, of course, noticed through his smile that his mistress didn't take her eyes off the dashing Italian racer all evening. Indeed, the feeling must have been mutual because the Italian also found it difficult to peel his eyes off of the attractive young lady. Finally, Picasso could take it no more and very bluntly (albeit playfully) offered to render a sketch of the lovely woman on the spot and present it to their new Italian friend as a keepsake so he would never forget this evening and the exquisite beauty of the young lady.

"Sketch paper and a pencil were provided by a waiter, and Picasso set about sketching his lovely mistress by candlelight. In almost no time at all, he presented the stunned Italian motorcycle rider—whose name was Tonino—with a sketch of such profound beauty that he was immediately enraptured and rendered completely speechless. Indeed, many intrigued tablemates and by-standers were heard to suggest that the girl in the sketch was *even more *beautiful than the actual flesh-and-blood woman sitting at the table with the Italian motorcycle racer and the esteemed Spanish artist. It was unanimously concluded by everyone crowded around the table that the artist had not only brought to bear every ounce of his prodigious artistic ability on the evening's impromptu project, but that he had accomplished a remarkable feat and created nothing less than a masterpiece that would surely find a place in his already prestigious artistic canon. In truth, the artist's formidable creative inspiration had come from equal parts artistic skill and sheer, green-eyed jealousy. Then the scheming Picasso played his Ace card: since the sketch had exceeded everyone's modest expectations, and since the Italian was clearly mesmerized by its seductive beauty, perhaps Tonino would be willing to engage in a bit of a trade. Say, the motorcycle he had just ridden to victory a few hours earlier? Tonino heard the artist's proposal well enough, but remained speechless. "How about it, Tonino? One work of art for another?"

"Picasso then signed and dated the sketch, and that was the final straw. Unable to surrender the lovely and hypnotizing sketch before him, Tonino nodded in agreement and consented to the trade. When the deal was done, Picasso asked the stunned Italian, in front of the entire crowd, if he had any regrets. After all, this was the fastest motorcycle in all of Italy, or perhaps all of Europe. The racer just gulped down a glass of wine, smiled broadly, and answered, 'I'll just have my brothers build a <u>faster</u> one!'

"And so it was that Pablo Picasso, the greatest artist in the world, simultaneously took command of his storied jealousy, created a new off-the-cuff masterpiece in a smoky little bar in Rome, and broke the Italian motorcycle champion's spell over his beautiful mistress in one eventful evening following the 1928 Italian Championship motorcycle race.

"Picasso – and the mistress – rode this motorcycle all the way back to Paris," Emile said triumphantly.

Daniel was absolutely transfixed. He had no idea his gruff uncle could be such a captivating storyteller. "That story is wonderful, Uncle. But it can't be true!"

"Of course it's true! What do you know?"

"What happened to the beautiful sketch of the mistress?"

"Nobody knows," Emile replied. "Perhaps the motorcycle racer still has it, but keeps it to himself and lets no one else see it. Or, perhaps he burned it when he realized he would never know the love of the beautiful mistress."

"But, how did *you* get the motorcycle?"

"One day ten years ago, I was on my way to Paris in a borrowed lorry to pick up some bicycle parts, when I came across a very well-dressed man whose car had broken down on the side of the road." Emile went on to relate how he stopped to assist the well-dressed man, and after an hour of work under the bonnet, he was able to get the car started. The man insisted on paying him, but he refused. He finally agreed to follow the man to his home in Paris, where the man bestowed the motorcycle upon him as a reward.

That's when the well-dressed man told Emile the story: He was an art broker who knew Pablo Picasso well. He said the artist had lost interest in the motorcycle after his mistress broke up with him and took up with a sea captain in Marseille. Picasso gave the art broker the motorcycle to cover a debt he owed him. The broker did not ride motorcycles and had no use for it. So Emile threw it in the back of the lorry and brought it back to the village.

"Did you ride it?" Daniel asked.

"A few times. But not in many, many years. It's been sitting in the back gathering cobwebs since then. I thought we might, you know, see if we could get it running again…"

"Really?" Daniel asked.

Emile and Daniel worked on the motorcycle together, cleaning it up, repairing it, and finally getting it running. In the process, and to Emile's surprise and delight, Daniel showed a great aptitude for mechanics. Before long, Daniel was zooming along the country roads around the village, wearing an old aviator's cap and goggles that Emile had laying around the shop. At night, he would lie in bed and tell his mother how happy he was and how good life had become for him, and that she shouldn't worry about him at all. Then he would say a prayer for her, and fall asleep and dream of becoming a championship motorcycle racer.

One day, a handsome man in his early thirties wearing a cap and goggles pushed his disabled motorcycle into the village. The first person he met was Claude the postman, who, quickly noticing the motorcycle had a flat tire, promptly directed him to the bicycle repair shop. Emile was out of the shop at the time, but Daniel took a look at the tire and told the man it would be repaired in half an hour. "You can wait in the café down the street, if you wish," Daniel told him.

"Wonderful," replied the man, who was breathing heavily due to his recent exertions. "I had to push it the last four kilometers, and I'm quite thirsty."

Daniel quickly identified the problem: a nail had pierced the tire's tread all the way through. Within half an hour, he had the tire patched and inflated, ready for the road. When the man returned from the café, refreshed and relaxed by a couple of afternoon *aperitifs*, he was pleased to see his motorcycle ready and waiting for him.

"Splendid!" he exclaimed happily.

"I checked the oil level and adjusted a brake cable that was a tiny bit loose," Daniel informed him.

"And polished it as well, I see," the man said in a pleased tone.

"That's all part of the service," Daniel explained. "No extra charge."

"No extra charge!" the man repeated in astonishment. "I can tell you, young man, that I am well-pleased with your service. Well-pleased indeed."

"*Oui*, Monsieur."

"I shall remember this place, in case I am ever in this area again."

"*Merci, Monsieur*."

"This is a bicycle shop," the man observed. "Where did you learn to take care of motorcycles?"

"My uncle taught me."

"Do you ride yourself?"

"*Oui*, Monsieur," Daniel said, leading him to the back of the shop where his motorcycle sat. The man was impressed.

"If I'm not mistaken, that is an Italian racing cycle," the man predicted, studying the vehicle carefully. "Custom built, probably late 1920's?"

"That is correct, Monsieur."

"How did you come by it?"

Daniel shortened Emile's amazing story considerably. "It was given to my uncle by a man in Paris as payment for repairs on his auto."

"Indeed, indeed..." the man was lost in thought. "I should say, your uncle came out on the right end of the deal, don't you think?"

"*Oui*, Monsieur."

"Well, if you ride as well as you repair them, then you must be quite good," the man smiled.

"I don't know about that, Monsieur. But I would like to be a championship motorcycle racer someday."

The man's handsome eyebrows arched. "Would you? Very interesting. Good luck with your ambition, then!"

"*Merci*, Monsieur."

"Well, let's settle up, and I'll be on my way," the man said, handing Daniel money.

"This is far too much for the flat tire, sir," Daniel told him.

"No, no. I want you to keep the rest as a tip," the man insisted. "For the excellent service, and the splendid conversation."

"*Merci*, Monsieur."

"And please take this," the man added, pulling a business card from his breast pocket and handing it to Daniel. "If you ever find yourself in need of a job, I could use a good mechanic." Then he bid *adieu* and took off on his motorcycle. Daniel looked at the card. It read : "MONSIEUR SIMON LE GRUN, ESQUIRE, DISTINGUISHED AND ESTEEMED MOTORCYCLE AND AUTOMOBILE SPEED CHAMPION, 17 RUE DE LA PAIX, NEUFCHATEAU, FRANCE."

Daniel had to read it twice in order to comprehend what was written on the card. It was unthinkable to him – actually meeting a real motorcycle racing champion here in *Nulle* was something he'd never dared to contemplate before. He carefully slid the card into his pocket, already composing the words he would use when he got a chance to tell Remy and the boys about meeting the dashing Monsiuer Simon Le Grun, Esquire, Distinguished and Esteemed Motorcycle and Automobile Speed Champion!

***

Meanwhile, there was a lot of talk in the village of escalating tensions with Germany, and possibly even war looming. Even in the bicycle shop, it was all the customers could talk about. Emile was certain the Germans were going to cause more trouble. "There will be another war with them, mark my words," he told Jacques one day.

"Oh, it's just the Paris newspapers stirring things up, worrying people in order to sell more papers," the butcher poo-pooed.

"No, there's going to be war," Emile insisted. "The Germans are a destructive, war-like people."

Every week there was a new headline: "Hitler invades Sudetenland." "German soldiers march into Austria." "Germany over-runs Czechoslovakia." Cinema newsreels showed phalanxes of goose-stepping Nazis marching through cosmopolitan European capitals such as Vienna and Prague. The radio breathlessly reported Hitler's latest threats against Poland and Benito Mussolini's vows to annex Albania. It seemed that fascism was an unstoppable wave moving across Europe, threatening even the great empires of Britain and France.

The villagers breathed a brief sigh of relief when Monsieur Chamberlain, the British Prime Minister, returned from meeting

Hitler in Munich and declared "Peace for Our Time." There was a small celebration in the village square, with people waving newspapers and breaking open bottles of wine. But Emile would have none of it. "That man doesn't know who he's dealing with," he shook his head in disgust. "What a fool!"

It was a tense summer, with people sticking close to their radios and hoarding the Paris newspapers, scanning them for every tidbit of news they could find. Then, in the fall, the headline everyone was dreading appeared like a thunderbolt: "Germany Invades Poland!" It was a bombshell. Everyone knew what it meant. The Allies had been duped; there would be no peace. Sure enough, two days later, Britain and France declared war on Germany. Everyone was gathered around the café radio when they heard the news.

"Well, if there's to be war, it will be a quick one, anyway," Jacques predicted. "The Germans are no match for the French Army."

"That's right," Pierre chimed in. "Czechoslovakia and Poland are one thing, but he'd never invade a country as powerful as France."

"I wouldn't be so sure," Emile cautioned.

The boys were all gathered outside. "Did you hear that?" Remy asked. "The radio said we're going to war with Germany! I hope it's not over too soon – I want a chance to get in on the action!"

"Me, too!" Francois echoed. "I hope the grown-ups save some Germans for us!"

Remy turned to Daniel. "It's a good thing you're French now – at least you'll be fighting for the right side!"

That night at supper, Emile was especially quiet and somber.

"Remy said it's not fair that the grown-ups get to fight in the war, and we don't," Daniel finally said. "Remy said the war will be over before we get a chance to share in the glory."

"What does Remy know?" His uncle asked distractedly, slurping his soup. "War is not a game, Daniel. There's nothing glorious about it."

"Do you think it will last long enough for me to fight in it?"

Emile put his spoon down and wiped his mustache on his sleeve. "I hope not. You don't know what you're talking about. If you knew what it was really like, you wouldn't wish for it. I pray you never have to experience it."

That Sunday, Father Pascal announced from the pulpit that a group of nuns from the Paris diocese would be arriving in the village to conduct a blood drive. "War is coming, my children. It is every villager's patriotic duty to give blood for the French cause. Some brave men will soon be giving their blood in battle." The announcement caused quite a stir in the little village. The shopkeepers and leading businessmen all met in the little café that afternoon after church to discuss the situation.

"Why are they coming to Nulle?" Pierre, the baker, asked harshly. "We're just a tiny village. There are so many other places for them to go…"

"They will be going to every village," Jacques predicted. "The government and the Church want this war. They're going to suck the blood from every village in France."

"Wait a minute, Jacques," Claude the postman said hotly. "It's every Frenchman's patriotic duty to give blood."

"Let's tell Father Pascal to tell them not to come," Monsieur Beauvais, the grocer, suggested.

"He can't stop them," Jacques protested. "He's just a little country priest. They'll go right over his head!"

"I'm not letting them stick a needle in me!" Jean Philippe, the cheese shop owner, vowed.

"You can't go against the Church, you fools!" Le Pen, the gendarme, chimed in.

"That's right, never question the Church!" Emile interjected sarcastically. "You can see where that's gotten us…"

"Jean Philippe is right – they can't force us to cooperate," Pierre insisted. "It's called a *donation*. Donations are given by free will!"

"Don't be so sure," Emile said pessimistically.

"Officer Le Pen is right," De Leon, the cobbler, offered. "We cannot go against the wishes of the Church!"

"What are you talking about?" Jacques challenged. "You're an atheist!"

"I am not an atheist," De Leon corrected. "I am a *nihilist*."

"It's only a little blood, for Heaven's sake!" Claude pointed out. "Our bodies will just make more!"

By the end of the impromptu meeting, the consensus was overwhelmingly skeptical. Remy, Daniel, and the boys were outside the café hanging on every word. "Well, what do you think, guys?" Remy asked his gang.

"I'm not keen on it," Francois volunteered.

"Me neither," Edgar agreed.

"What do we get out of it?" Andre asked.

"Exactly!" Remy said. "Good point, Andre. We've got to look out for ourselves, you know."

"But what about for the good of France?" Daniel asked.

Bernard looked at Daniel. "Oh, you don't have to worry. They don't want *German* blood."

After the meeting in the café, Le Pen went straight to the village church to give Father Pascal the news. "They don't like it. Four to one against it. Very negative. Very skeptical. Many of them say they're not going to donate at all." This was not good news for the Father, who had specifically written to the Paris diocese touting Nulle's unusual level of patriotism and requesting to be one of the first villages in France to bleed itself dry for the French cause. His reputation and credibility with his superiors was now on the line.

The priest sighed deeply and buried his head in his hands. "Oh, Lord, why have you given me such a stiff-necked and obstinate people to shepherd?"

Even with the near-unanimous unpopularity of the blood drive, it was still something of an event in a very sleepy little village in which events were often in short supply. So, out of sheer curiosity, Daniel, Remy, and the boys, along with half of the adult population of the village, turned out for the nuns' arrival at the church.

Father Pascal had been in the sanctuary all night on his knees, praying for a turnaround in the hearts and minds of his flock regarding the blood drive. Perhaps the Good Lord had indeed heard his prayers, because the moment the male population of the village got a look at Sister Beatrice, all resistance instantly evaporated. It was a miracle!

Sister Beatrice's youth and beauty was otherworldly. Her large round eyes were the color of dark Belgian chocolate and her skin shone like Chinese porcelain. Her movements were as fluid and graceful as a swan. She radiated innocence and piety. She was the Church's secret weapon for turning around unsuccessful blood drives.

Word soon spread throughout the village. More villagers – especially men – showed up and eagerly qued up to donate their precious bodily fluids. Men and boys jostled one another to be first in the beatific nun's glowing presence. The line was soon so long and boisterous that Officer Le Pen had to be called in to restore order. "Everyone remain calm!" the gendarme shouted, waving his arms in the air. "Everyone is going to have a chance to donate! Remain calm!"

Father Pascal was positively beaming. "I am happy to see French patriotism so alive and well in our wonderful village!"

The four nuns from Paris pumped blood out of villagers all day long.

"We have never seen such generosity," a shocked but pleased nun told Father Pascal. "Some of these brave men have such a love of France that they've returned several times to give more." As she spoke, several perturbed wives marched up and yanked their sheepish husbands out of the line and frog-marched them home by the collars.

The boys went back again and again in hopes of being touched by the angelic nun, until they were so weak they were passing out in line. Daniel went back a third time, but instead of Sister Beatrice, he was man-handled by an ugly old nun, whose face is the last thing he saw before passing out.

At five o'clock, there was still a long line of men waiting patiently to give more blood. Most of them were second or third timers, who had been home to change clothes and hats in an attempt to disguise themselves. "Most of you have given enough for one day," the head nun said. "Come back again tomorrow, when you have more strength."

"I am so proud of all of you," the priest beamed from the pulpit the following Sunday. "The blood drive has been so successful, the sisters have decided to stay another week and keep collecting blood. This must be the most patriotic village in France!"

Noticing who was the most popular blood drawer, the nuns placed Sister Beatrice front and center, along with the more attractive nuns.

Daniel, who, like all the boys, was absolutely smitten with Sister Beatrice, told his uncle that he wanted to marry a nun.

"Idiot. You cannot marry a nun."

"Why not?"

"Because they are already married. To Christ."

"Why does Christ need so many wives?"

Clearly having no answer, Emile closed his eyes, trying to summon patience. "Go ask the priest," he sighed.

Daniel went banging on the parish door. The priest answered, saw the boy, nodded silently, and bid him follow. He took Daniel to his study, where all the other village boys were already sitting. Daniel sat down among them.

"I take it this has something to do with Sister Beatrice?" Father Pascal asked Daniel.

"Well, actually, I have a question," Daniel responded. "Why does Christ need so many wives?"

"Our Savior had no wives."

"But the <u>nuns</u>."

"Ah, I see." The priest explained that those who are baptized in Christ are <u>all</u> married to Christ, in a figurative sense. "It's a metaphor. We – Christ's whole church – are all his bride."

Remy piped up. "How do we become a priest?"

"Well, we'd better slow down a bit," cautioned the priest. "Perhaps we should start on a lower rung of the ladder. I could always use some new altar boys."

So that's how Remy's gang all became altar boys. This position, however, sadly offered them no special access to Sister Beatrice. At the end of the second week, the nuns packed up their equipment and prepared to head for the next village. Everyone turned out to see them off.

"They drained every drop of blood they could squeeze out of us," Jacques complained, rubbing his sore arm. "I feel like I've got nothing left…"

"I didn't see anyone with a gun to your head," Emile growled in response.

The boys looked depressed as the nuns drove off in their car. "I'm going to run away," Francois vowed, forlornly watching the car disappear down the road. "I will go to Paris and find her. Then we'll be happy for the rest of our lives."

"Didn't you hear what Father Pascal said?" Remy snapped at him. "She's already married – to Christ."

"Then I will kill myself," he said dramatically, as only a Frenchman can.

The departure of the nuns might have meant a severe decline in interest in being altar boys, if Father Pascal had not firmly held them to their deal. So the boys decided, as usual, to make the best of it.

Knowing that the priest measured the communion wine with a ruler each week, they quickly developed the habit of nipping at it and carefully re-filling the cask with water. It soon became so watered-down that even the parishioners began to notice and comment on it. Finally, Father Pascal confronted them.

"Has anyone been tampering with the communion wine, boys?" he asked sternly. Each boy instantly made their most earnest angel face – large, round eyes, innocent pouting lips: *Communion wine...what communion wine?*

"No? Well, let me just remind you, this is no ordinary wine. This wine represents the blood of our Savior. Drinking it for any purpose other than worship is a grave sin!"

The boys nodded innocently, but found it impossible to change their habit, sin or no sin.

Finally one day it was so weak that the boys knew they had to do something. "It's too watered- down," Daniel said. "He'll taste the difference."

"I know what to do," Remy said, running home and returning with a bottle of cognac under his robe. "This will put the kick back into it," he said, pouring it liberally into the wine cask.

After the service that day, Father Pascal called the boys into his study. The wine cask was on his desk, and his eyes were a little red. He'd been tasting the wine, an empty glass sat on his desk.

"I have never seen such fervor for communion among the congregation before," the priest admitted, a little puzzled. "Several of the older men tried to return for a second round, and not a few of the older ladies as well." The boys were as silent as statues. Father Pascal poured more wine into the glass and sipped it absent-mindedly. "In fact, his Honor the Lord Mayor told me that if one pass at communion makes you holy, two passes should really do the trick. Then he set the example himself by stepping forward to lead the congregation in a second round. Highly unorthodox, mind you, but how does one argue with his Honor the Lord Mayor?" The priest shook his head, sat the glass back down, and dismissed the boys. They were off the hook!

Communion, it seemed, would never be the same.

The following week during Mass, Remy surreptitiously disabled the church organ just as the organist was about to play Fugue in C Minor. When the organist started playing, what came out instead was "Take Me Out to the Ball Game," thanks to an old phonograph player Remy had hidden beneath the altar. But communion was such a hit, no one seemed to notice except the church organist.

Remy's well of pranks and hoaxes seemed truly bottomless, and he spent most of his time defending his title as "King of the Pranksters." His uncle, for instance, had learned Japanese while in the merchant marine. He'd been teaching Remy the language for some time, and Remy had been passing it along to the other boys. At first, the boys merely used the language to fool around and amuse themselves. But Remy being Remy, soon he was using the talent to embark upon an ambitious series of pranks in the village.

Being something of an electronics whiz, Remy had been working part-time in the cinema. There, he had figured out how the projector worked, how to splice and edit film when it broke, and all sorts of technical tricks and gimmicks having to do with film and sound. "I'm going to be a famous director in Paris when I grow up," he used to tell everybody, and everybody believed him. Putting Remy in charge of the projection booth was a little like letting a child with a sweet tooth run wild in a candy shop. He soon became technically adept at adding his own homemade special effects to movies and quirky, nutty sound effects to the soundtracks. He and the boys were always doing fun things, like showing the movies sped-up, slowed down, or even backwards, just for kicks – usually late at night when the audience was too drunk to notice or care.

So, when a long-sought-after print of "Gone with the Wind" arrived, Remy knew exactly what to do.

"Film has two parts, a visual part and a recorded soundtrack so you can hear the music and what the actors are saying," Remy explained to the boys, sounding something like a professor. "The soundtrack is synchronized to the pictures, so the movement of their mouths matches the dialogue." A couple of the boys were completely lost. "Don't you see? We can change the soundtrack, but the pictures stay the same! We can make the actors say *anything* we want them to say!"

"Why would we want to do that?" Bernard asked, with a puzzled look on his face.

"Look, in Paris, they overdubbed 'Gone with the Wind' in French," Remy patiently explained. "Everyone's expecting to hear Clark Gable speaking in French. Well, we can make him speak in any language we want him to! Get it?"

Remy was able to cobble together the equipment needed to edit the soundtrack: a microphone, an old tape recorder, and an editing machine. The boys worked in the projection room all night over-dubbing Clark Gable's lines in Japanese. What words Remy didn't know, he just used oriental-sounding gibberish.

The next night was opening night for the film. The village had been waiting for this film for some time, and the cinema was packed. People were even standing outside, hoping to hear a snippet of the movie here and there. When the lights went down, everyone applauded excitedly and settled down to watch the movie. All of the music and the other actors' dialogue were normal, but whenever Rhett Butler opened his mouth to speak, it came out in Japanese. At first, people were simply puzzled. But as the movie went on, and Rhett continued to speak nothing but Japanese, people began to get surly.

Jacques stood up in the stream of light from the projector and shouted "What is this?"

Claude the postman's wife popped up. "I don't understand a thing that's happening!"

Claude joined her. "I'm very disappointed in this film!"

Pierre the baker stood up next. "It's not the film. It's those bastards in Paris, playing a trick on us country *paysans*!"

De Leon the cobbler joined them. "This is an outrage! I demand my money back!"

Monsieur Passy, the cinema proprietor, appeared in front of the screen to try to calm everyone down. "I am so sorry, I don't know what has happened…"

"This was supposed to be a masterpiece, and now it's ruined!" someone called from the audience. "A whole evening, wasted!" shouted someone else. "This cinema never gets anything right!" another shouted. People began to leave, kicking the seats and mumbling in disgust.

"I'm afraid there has been some kind of mistake," Monsieur Passy fretted. There was a huge close-up of Rhett Butler embracing Scarlet O'Hara romantically and wooing her in Japanese behind him as he spoke. "I will get to the bottom of it, I promise. I'll have another print sent here in no time…"

"Of course, they're going to drop everything in Paris and rush another print to *Nulle!*" someone, who sounded a bit like Emile after two glasses of wine, shouted back at him.

In the projection room, Remy, Daniel and the boys were rolling on the floor, tears of laughter running down their cheeks.

A few days after the cinema disaster, the village received some news that made everyone forget about "Gone with the Wind." Due to the overwhelming generosity of the villagers during the recent blood drive, an official from Paris and the head of the French Red Cross would be coming to Nulle to present His Honor the Lord Mayor with a special award. As the news spread through the village, people were overcome with pride and began making preparations for the important visit. The honored guests would be welcomed with pomp and circumstance, the award accepted by His Honor the Lord Mayor himself, and then the whole village would sit down to a wonderful feast and revelry that would extend well into the night.

Preparations began immediately. Shopkeepers painted their store fronts in bright colors and washed their windows until they gleamed like Austrian crystal. Window boxes all along the main street were filled with colorful flowers, and banners and French flags were festooned all over the buildings, trees, and store fronts of the tiny village. A dais was erected in the town square where speeches would be given and awards accepted. Old-timers remarked that the village hadn't looked this festive since the end of the Great War.

A day before the great event, Officer Le Pen paid a visit to Remy's house and asked to speak with the boy. "Monsieur Passy tells us that you are quite handy with electronic equipment," the gendarme informed him. "His Honor the Lord Mayor would like you to rig up some sort of contraption to make his voice louder for his special acceptance speech tomorrow. Would you be able to oblige?"

Of course, Remy was not about to let an opportunity like this go to waste. "I think I'll be able to throw something together…"

"Fine," the gendarme smiled. "We knew we could count on you, young man!"

The next morning, Remy borrowed a large speaker and a microphone from the cinema. He and the boys set up the microphone on a stand on the dais, and rigged the speaker up on a pedestal off to the side, facing where the crowd would be. Officer Le Pen and His Honor the Lord Mayor inspected the equipment as the boys worked. His Honor the Lord Mayor was a short, round, balding man with an old-fashioned shiny black waxed handlebar mustache, carefully curled into a double-o shape at each end.

"And you're sure this will make my voice loud enough for everyone to hear?" he asked Remy. "We're going to have quite a large crowd, you know."

"Oh, I guarantee they'll hear you, Monsieur," Remy flashed his winning, crooked grin. "All you've got to do is speak clearly into this microphone, and let me do the rest."

"Splendid," the Lord Mayor beamed, admiring the microphone and speaker setup. "Simply splendid. Carry on, lads…"

As the time of arrival of the dignitaries from Paris approached, everyone began to gather in the town square. The shopkeepers and business leaders and their families were all dolled up in their Sunday best clothes, the men shaved, hair neatly oiled, and mustaches duly waxed. The women and girls paraded around the square in their pretty dresses, ribbons and bows. Father Pascal, Officer Le Pen, Monsieur Delfont, and His Honor the Lord Mayor all stood in front of the dais, waiting for the honored guests to arrive.

Suddenly, Pierre, who had been posted on the edge of town as a watch, came riding his bicycle into the square shouting "They're here! They're here!" All the gentlemen in front of the dais smoothed down their hair and adjusted their hats, coats and ties one more time. As a large black car pulled into the square, a motly band of villagers who fancied themselves musicians began playing a lurching *La Marseillaise* on an assortment of horns, violins, and squeeze boxes. The car stopped near the dais, and two well-dressed men from the city stepped out and looked around. The musicians played on, even though the French national anthem was completely unrecognizable to the visitors from Paris.

His Honor the Lord Mayor stepped over to the men and presented himself. "Gentlemen, it is truly an honor!" he gushed. "Welcome to our humble village!"

The man in the gray suit extended his hand first. "Marcel Poussaint-Levy, Assistant Director to the Minister of the Department of Rural Purview and Provincial Administrative Oversight," he said, without a touch of irony. The Lord Mayor shook his hand like it was Charles de Gaulle.

The man in the black suit extended his hand next. "Rodney Fouche de Roche de Chenaille, Departmental Administrative Assistant to the Vice Under-Secretary of the President of the French Red Cross." The Lord Mayor grabbed his hand and shook it for far too long, refusing to let go.

The man in the gray suit squinted and looked around the village. "Are you sure this is the right place?"

"Oh, this is the right place, your honor," the Lord Mayor assured him. "The Village of *Nulle*, the nuns from Paris, the most blood..." The man in the black suit had to pry the Lord Mayor's fingers off of his hand to get him to stop shaking and let go.

"I see," said the man in the gray suit, unenthusiastically. "Charming. Um, if I may, what exactly does *Nulle* mean?"

"Nothing," the Lord Mayor answered. The dignitaries from Paris appeared confused.

"I say, do you mean that the word actually has no meaning, or that the meaning of the word is literally 'nothing?'" the man in the gray suit asked.

"I'm afraid you've lost me," the Lord Mayor confessed.

"What my colleague is trying to determine, if I may interject, is that he's wondering if the name of your quite charming little village has a meaning or not, and, if so, is the meaning literally 'nothing?'" the man in the black suit tried to clarify.

The Lord Mayor blinked at him uncomprehendingly.

The man in the grey suit turned to his fellow dignitary. "Let's give him the award now."

The Lord Mayor, Officer Le Pen, Monsieur Delfont, and Father Pascal all gathered once again in front of the dais. The dignitaries from Paris retrieved a plaque from the car and joined them. The musicians were still playing something that had a remote connection to music, and the Lord Mayor waved at them frantically to stop.

The man in the gray suit did the honors. "On behalf of the Government of France and the French Red Cross, we would like to honor the village of Nulle for its patriotism and generosity in not hesitating to rise to the occasion when desperately needed by your country. In these troubled and unsure times, it is your gallantry and selflessness that shines so bright a light on the path ahead that has been darkened by the ominous clouds of war. Please accept this plaque in the spirit of gratitude and service in which it is given." He handed the plaque to the Lord Mayor, who cradled it in his arms like an infant. Claude the postman snapped pictures of the Lord Mayor and the dignitaries with an ancient camera.

"Thank you, thank you," the Lord Mayor repeated over and over, as people cheered. "You can search France over, and not find a more patriotic village than this, I assure you." Now in pure politician mode, the Lord Mayor gingerly handed the plaque off to Father Pascal and climbed up onto the dais to give the acceptance speech he had labored night and day on since first hearing of the award. He reached into his jacket, pulled out a thick stack of crumpled paper, and carefully unfolded them. The he wiped his brow, cleared his throat, and launched into the speech of his lifetime.

Halfway through the opening line, he knew something wasn't right. He was reading the words on the pages, but something *else* was coming out of the speaker that Remy had set up. Some confusing, clanging clutter of a language – incomprehensible gibberish. *<u>Japanese!</u>*

Nobody had noticed that the microphone on the dais was a dummy. It wasn't even plugged in. Behind the stage, down a narrow alley space between two buildings, Remy had the real microphone, the one plugged into the speaker next to the stage. It worked perfectly: to the audience, it looked and sounded exactly like the Lord Mayor was giving his speech in Japanese.

The Lord Mayor saw the looks on the faces in the crowd. He saw the two dignitaries squinting and shaking their heads in confusion. He saw Officer Le Pen signaling for him to stop by making a cutting motion across his throat. But he panicked. He panicked, and he kept reading from the pages. He kept reading from the pages, not knowing what else to do, not even being able to think. Just reading the elegant words he had crafted so carefully, the lovely words that nobody was hearing.

When he had finished his speech, he stopped talking, neatly folded up the pages, and put them back inside his coat. Then he mopped his brow.

The crowd was silent. Officer Le Pen led the Lord Mayor gently from the stage. The dignitaries from Paris got back into their car without a word, and drove away.

There was an investigation. Officer Le Pen interrogated Remy and the boys that evening at police headquarters. "I know you had something to do with this," he told them soberly. "Now, out with it. How did you do it?"

"Do what?" Remy asked.

"You know – you were in charge of the equipment," Officer Le Pen stammered. "Come on – what happened?"

"That was the same speaker that caused all the trouble in the cinema," Remy pointed out. "It's obviously a faulty speaker. There it is."

"A faulty speaker?" the gendarme asked incredulously. "Since when do speakers translate French into Japanese on their own?"

"It could have faulty wiring," Remy calmly bluffed. "It could have picked up radio transmissions from a Japanese submarine."

"We're nowhere near the Pacific Ocean!" Le Pen argued.

"Well, the Japs and the krauts are in kahoots, are they not?" Remy asked reasonably. "They could actually have submarines off the French coast, for all we know…"

Le Pen took a deep breath, calming himself down. "Look, the Lord Mayor had a nervous breakdown. He's resting at home tonight…"

"Well, that explains everything then, doesn't it?"

Le Pen stared hard at Remy. "I <u>know</u> you had something to do with this. But I can't prove it. You're free to go – but watch yourself! All of you – watch yourselves!"

Chapter 5

The next morning at school, Monsieur Delfont and Father Pascal came to class to make an important announcement. "Boys, I have exciting news," the headmaster declared. "This year, due to popular demand, we will be having a spring social ball. This special ball is intended for all school-aged children – boys <u>and</u> girls – and will be held in our own school gymnasium. Monsieur Closson will be supervising you in the cleaning up and decorating of the gymnasium before the event. Of course, the ball will have to follow all moral precepts, and all participants must conduct themselves with the utmost morality and chivalry at all times. Father Pascal is now going to say a few words about that."

Father Pascal stepped forward and cleared his throat. "Boys, in the past the Church has frowned upon dancing as a sinful, immoral activity best left to the unsaved heathen. But now it is 1939, and the Church recognizes the need to change with the times, so I whole-heartedly endorse this social ball. However, it is important to remember to always conduct yourselves as gentlemen when in the presence of young ladies. Our separation of boys and girls in the academic arena, I believe, has been a smashing success. Keeping boys and girls away from each other at all times keeps *everyone* out of trouble. But at this ball, you will be mixing with the fairer sex, and I don't want anything untoward to happen. No monkey business. No hanky panky. No shenanigans. Do I make myself clear?"

"*Oui, Pere,*" came the corporal reply.

"No touchy-feely nonsense," the priest continued. "No fooling around. No slap-and-tickle."

"*Oui, Pere.*"

"No going off in a dark corner and 'necking.' We all know what *that* leads to…"

"*Oui, Pere.*"

"If we aren't careful – if we aren't on our _guard_ – something might happen. The rhythm of the music. The closeness of the forbidden fruit. The stuffiness of the warm gymnasium. The heat starts rising…" Father Pascal took out a handkerchief and mopped his brow. "Before you know it, passions you are not aware of at your tender young age start emerging. Urges you've never felt before begin to take over –"

"I believe the boys understand completely, Father," Monsieur Delfont quickly cut him off. "_Merci beaucoup_ for coming in and talking to us. It's been most enlightening…"

"Of course, of course – my pleasure, Headmaster," the priest said, recovering his composure.

After school, it was all the boys could talk about. A social ball, with music, refreshments, and _girls_. They all wanted to go.

"But I don't know how to dance," Daniel admitted.

"None of us do," Edgar said. "How can we learn in a week?"

"Let's ask our mothers and sisters to teach us," Andre suggested. Everyone gagged and wretched out loud. "No, I suppose that won't do."

"I can teach you," Remy declared. "But I'm not dancing with you lot. Men don't dance with other men."

"What if one of us dresses up as a girl?" Bernard suggested. "Would you dance with him then?"

Remy considered this. "I believe that would be an acceptable accommodation, under the circumstances. Who's it going to be, then?" No one volunteered. "We'll draw lots," Remy decided. They found some sticks on the ground, and Remy prepared them. "Short lot has to be the girl."

Charles drew the short lot. "Wait. I don't want to go through with it."

"Sorry, mate," Remy said firmly. "Can't back out now. I'm afraid I'm going to have to hold you to it." Everyone nodded in agreement, relieved it wasn't going to be them. "Here's the plan: everyone go home and pinch all the gear you can from your mothers and sisters – raid the clothesline, rifle through the bureau drawers, that kind of stuff – and meet me at the old barn on the edge of town in an hour. Got it?" They all nodded. "And you'd better show up, Charles!"

An hour later, they all regrouped at the barn. "All right, let's see what we've got," Remy said. Daniel had a woman's slip. "Where'd you get that?" Remy asked, holding it up.

"From Madame Deshcard's clothesline," Daniel answered proudly.

"Well done," Remy said. "Francois?"

"My sister's dress."

"Jean?"

"My auntie's wig."

"Bernard?"

"Some of my mother's make up."

"Henri?"

Henri handed Remy a plus-size brassiere. "It's my grandmother's."

Remy looked at the brassiere, then at Charles, and shook his head. "Won't be needing that." Remy surveyed the pile of articles and concluded they had more than enough to work with. "Let's get to work, then."

When they were through, the transformation was stunning.

"Charles – you're *beautiful*!" Francois exclaimed. It was no exaggeration – Charles was an absolute doll.

"I never would have guessed!" Edgar said in amazement.

"Kiss me, *mon cherie*," Bernard joked, reaching for Charles.

"Cut it out – it's not funny," Charles protested, slapping Bernard across the face.

"Oh, I love it when you play rough!" Bernard said, rubbing his cheek.

"All right, lads, everyone knock it off," Remy ordered. Never one to let a useful accident go to waste, he began concocting a new scheme on the spot. Ever since hearing about the ball, Remy had been perversely trying to think up a way to subvert it. Now he'd found it. "This is it, lads. This is the *one*," he said, his mind whirling.

"What are you talking about?" Daniel asked.

"The Big One," Remy repeated. "The hoax of all hoaxes – on the *girls*." The whole plan came to Remy in one glorious flash: "Charlotte," Charles' cousin from Paris, is in town for the week and will attend the social ball."

"I didn't know Charles had a cousin in Paris," Henri said.

"He doesn't, you oaf," Remy explained. "*Charles* is 'Charlotte.' We'll invent a whole glamorous backstory for her. Some kind of mysterious past that will drive everyone crazy. The girls will go *mad* when they find out how bad they've been had!" Remy crowed, bursting with zeal.

"It'll never work," Jean scoffed.

"Of course it will – *Look* at him!" Remy countered.

"But how can he be Charles and Charlotte at the same time?" Daniel asked.

"He doesn't have to be," Remy argued. "On the evening of the ball, we'll tell Monsieur Delfont that Charles is home with a fever. It's brilliant!" Remy was clearly letting himself get carried away with the plot. The others weren't so sure – but they knew that once Remy got going on a scam, it was no use trying to stop him. "Now all we've got to do is convince Monsieur Delfont to add a dance contest at the end of the ball."

"A dance contest?" Daniel asked. "Why?"

"For the *climax*," Remy said, a bit exasperated. "All right, look. Every hoax has to have a climactic moment. It's neither here nor there if 'Charlotte' just shows up and dances with a few blokes. She's got to win the dance contest! She's got to be the center of attention – all eyes have to be on her – for the big reveal to have the ultimate impact. Don't you see?"

The other boys reckoned they had to defer to Remy's expertise in this field, being mere apprentices themselves at the art of deception. So they decided to stop questioning the plan and take Remy's assurances at face value. If he said it would succeed, then it more than likely had a good chance of doing just that.

It proved less than difficult to convince Monsieur Delfont to incorporate a dance contest into the ball. Remy knew the best chance was to make him believe it was actually <u>his</u> idea.

"I know that after so much planning and preparation, we all want to see a successful Spring Social Ball," Remy told the headmaster in his office. "But, I have to tell you, I'm very concerned about participation – especially on the part of the boys."

"Participation?" Monsieur Delfont asked, looking alarmed.

"That's right. The lads are hesitant about the whole thing because they just don't feel confident in their dancing skills. If there was just some way to *motivate* them…"

"Motivate them?"

"Exactly! You know, they're a very competitive lot."

"Competitive?"

"That's right, if there was some sort of, I don't know, award involved, it just might be the thing to light a fire under the lads…"

"Hmmm," Monsieur Delfont rubbed his chin. "Competitive. Award."

"You know, like maybe a dance contest…"

"A dance contest?"

"Brilliant idea, Monsieur!" Remy exclaimed. "I knew *you* would be the one to come up with just the right solution…"

The boys spent the week cleaning the old gymnasium and decorating it with streamers, banners, and bunting in the blue, white, and red colors of the French flag. Given the new war reality, the unofficial 'theme' had to be patriotic. After school, the boys adjourned to the abandoned barn, where Remy and Charles practiced their dance moves and taught the other boys enough to get them by. Remy proved a knowledgeable teacher, but the hapless Charles proved to have two left feet when it came to dancing.

"To learn to dance, you've got to know your left from your right," Remy said in frustration. "It's like trying to teach a cow!"

"Well, you don't have to dress this way and pretend to be a girl," Charles shot back, visibly upset. "You don't have to dance in these bloody heels. It's got me all turned around!" He was close to tears.

"There, there, it's all right," Remy said, softer now, as if addressing a distraught young lady. "You'll catch on. Let's just try it again. Count out loud with me: one-two-three-four, one-two-three-four…"

They carried on, and Charles slowly began to catch on. Everyone noticed a change in Charles when he was dressed as 'Charlotte.' He was more sensitive and emotional. His feelings were so easily hurt. Little things that would never have bothered Charles – a snag in a fingernail, a run in a stocking – became major issues for 'Charlotte.' As a result, the gang eased up on him and started treating him more gingerly.

By the afternoon of the ball, Remy knew they were never going to be the Fred Astaire and Ginger Rogers of *Nulle*. But when Charles donned his disguise and became 'Charlotte,' he was sure they were going to be able to pull the masquerade off. "As long as you remember to let me lead," Remy reminded Charles sternly.

But suddenly there was another crisis. Someone – Andre or Bernard, perhaps – made an off-hand comment about the shape of 'Charlotte's' *derriere*. At first, 'Charlotte' became quiet and sullen, but then could hold it in no longer. "I *hate* this bloody dress!" Charlotte exploded. "It makes my ass look like a sack of potatoes!" Then the tears came.

"Oh, it's not that bad, love," Remy said immediately, trying to contain the damage.

"Yes it is, it's *terrible*," Charlotte sobbed. "I'm not wearing this potato sack to the ball!"

Thinking fast, Remy said, "All right, everyone back to your homes and bring in every dress you can scrounge. Come on, off with you!"

While they were gone, Remy did his best to console 'Charlotte,' who finally stopped sobbing and agreed to try on some different dresses. Within half an hour, the boys were back with a variety of dresses. Remy carefully laid them out for 'Charlotte' to inspect.

"Now, which one do you like?" he asked. 'Charlotte' studied each dress carefully, as if shopping in a Paris boutique.

"This one." It was a nice yellow chiffon mid-length number with a big white bow in front and puffy, ruffled shoulders.

"Nice choice," Remy enthused. "Try it on."

'Charlotte' started to slip out of the 'potato sack' dress, then stopped. "Do you mind?"

"Of course not – turn your backs, fellows!" Remy ordered. Everyone turned their backs, while 'Charlotte' changed into the new dress.

"How does it look?" 'Charlotte' hesitantly asked.

"Wonderful!" Remy said.

'Charlotte' wasn't convinced. "Does it make my ass look too big?"

"Not at all," Remy assured. "Very flattering. Right, boys?"

Everyone nodded in affirmation, holding their breath for the final decision.

"Well, all right then," 'Charlotte' finally said. "I suppose it will have to do…"

The plan was simple: everyone would show up at the ball on time, except for 'Charlotte,' who would arrive fashionably late. This would create the desired buzz, as 'Charlotte' became the center of attention and all the girls would wonder who this lovely new creature was. At this point, Remy's plan would go into full gear.

Everything went according to plan. Father Pascal, Monsieur Delfont, and the nuns from the girls' school were the chaperones. The boys and girls stood on opposite sides of the gymnasium, separated by the dancefloor in the center. When the music started, the girls looked shyly across at the boys and giggled. The boys made no move to cross the no-man's-land and ask the girls to dance. They remained separated in this manner, like combatants unwilling to engage the enemy, through three songs.

Along one wall stood a table supporting an ancient phonograph machine and a stack of records which were nearly as old. Remy looked through the records with discouragement. They were all old French records – slow music, anguished, romantic ballads – not at all the type of records to dance to.

"This won't do at all," he said. As Remy kept watch on the chaperones, Daniel and the other boys deftly switched the records on the table for a stack of American jazz and big band records that Remy's uncle had procured while in the merchant marine. "That ought to liven things up a bit," Remy smiled. Then it was time for 'Charlotte's' entrance. Only she didn't arrive. They waited several more minutes, through more music without dancing. Anticipating another snag, Remy was about to go looking for her when…there she was, standing just inside the entrance, looking as demure and lovely as a spring flower.

The reaction of the girls was immediate and profound. Shy, gay smiles evaporated. Giggling stopped. Stunned faces with wide eyes turned to one another in a flurry of urgent, alarmed whispering. Others stood staring at 'Charlotte,' mouths wide open, in shock and disbelief. It was just the kind of impact Remy had been hoping for.

Remy went into action, directing the boys to start spreading the rumors they'd been preparing all week: 'Charlotte's' parents were very well-connected in society. Her father was the ambassador to Lichtenstein and her mother was a distant cousin to the wife of the King of Denmark. She lived in a chateau in Paris. She'd been in the movies. She spent summers in Milan. She knew Gertrude Stein and corresponded with the son of the King of Morocco on a regular basis.

The rumors were elaborate and impressive, yet somehow believable. In no time, the girls were in a tizzy of gossip, whispering, and dizzying recrimination – something like a hornet's nest that's been stirred to a frenzy with a stick. Most of all, they couldn't seem to tear their eyes away from her. And nobody seemed to notice that Charles was nowhere to be seen.

The boys buzzed around 'Charlotte' like bees, each seeking the first dance. One of the nuns changed a record, and instead of Edith Piaf, loud American jazz blared from the old phonograph. Father Pascal shot a sharp glance at the nun from across the room, but all she could do was shrug her shoulders. The disappointed priest, a scowl of scorn written across his face, directed several nuns to look for the approved French records, but, of course, they were nowhere to be found.

Remy and 'Charlotte' were the first to dance. The girls just watched in silence, their mouths agape, as the pair smoothly executed all the dance moves they'd been practicing all week. 'Charlotte' was doing an admirable job, although more than a few times she could be heard counting the dance steps out loud. For the next song, 'Charlotte' changed partners, and, on cue, the other boys approached the girls and asked them to dance. The ice had been broken, and, not about to be one-upped by the interloper from Paris, the girls danced with a vengeance.

When it became apparent the slow music would not be recovered, Father Pascal surrendered to the new reality with a sense of grudging resignation. In order to prevent further catastrophe, however, he went around measuring the distance between boys and girls with a ruler. Those who were less than twenty centimeters apart received a sharp rebuke and a gentle nudge of separation. He also directed the nuns to check the closets and hallways every ten minutes for hugging, fondling, necking, or other unseemly activities.

Before long, 'Charlotte' had danced with all the boys at least once. Between songs, they hovered around her offering small-talk and glasses of punch, laughing at her jokes and hanging on her every word. The girls were furious.

Before the dance contest, Father Pascal instructed Monsieur Delfont to call for a cessation in the dancing for "passions to subside." Andre, who wanted to dance with her again but had been denied the opportunity, was inconsolable. "I'm in love with 'Charlotte!'" he moaned in agony. "But 'Charlotte' is *Charles*," Daniel reminded him. "I _know_..." Andre said, slumping in anguish as only a Frenchman can.

Monsieur Closson and Mademoiselle Prenet, who had a layperson's knowledge of ballet, would judge the contest part of the evening. Father Pascal urged them to award points for "decency and honor" as well as execution and precision. Then a big band swing song by Tommy Dorsey filled the gymnasium, and the contest began in earnest. The dance floor was crowded with couples, but of course all eyes were on the team of Remy and 'Charlotte.'

They did a fast jitterbug, a dance Remy had memorized from seeing too many American movies in the cinema. When Remy executed a smooth around the waist twirl with 'Charlotte,' the look of disapproval on Father Pascal's face was plain to see. When 'Charlotte' leap-frogged over Remy, Father Pascal had his eyes closed and looked like he was praying. When Remy spun 'Charlotte' in front of him and slid her between his legs, it looked like Father Pascal was about to faint. When Remy grabbed his partner by the waist and attempted a 'dive-bomber' lift, Father Pascal ripped the needle off the record and the music came to an abrupt stop.

"That will be quite enough!" he bellowed, mopping his brow with a handkerchief. "Let's give out the awards now." Monsieur Closson and Mademoiselle Prenet conferred as everyone gathered around to hear the results. When they finished, they handed a piece of paper to His Honor the Lord Mayor, who was charged with awarding the trophy.

"It is my great honor to award this trophy to the winning team," the Lord Mayor said in his best politician's voice. "All of you acquitted yourselves admirably. However, one couple must be chosen the winner, and that couple is..." He pushed his glasses up his nose and squinted at the paper. "...Remy and 'Charlotte.'"

There was wild applause and cheers from the boys, and quiet, polite applause from the girls. "Well, I don't think a girl from Paris should be allowed to enter *our* contest," one girl was heard to complain. She just happened to be the Lord Mayor's daughter. Several others quietly agreed. Ignoring the less than gracious remarks, Remy and 'Charlotte' stepped forward to receive the trophy from the Lord Mayor who, as always, was pleased to be doing his civic duty and representing the village in such a distinguished manner.

"Congratulations," the Lord Mayor beamed, handing the trophy to Remy. "You are a remarkably talented young couple!" The Lord Mayor's daughter could no longer hold her tongue.

"Papa, I'm afraid there's been an egregious miscarriage of justice committed here," she exclaimed, causing everyone to turn and look in her direction.

"What – what's that, my dear?" the Lord Mayor spluttered.

"A fraud. A flouting of convention. A complete and utter disregard for civilized rules."

"What are you talking about, my dear?" the Lord Mayor asked, trying to hold his public smile.

The Lord Mayor's daughter, whose name was Penelope, pointed at 'Charlotte.' "She's a fraud!" Surprised, Remy looked at the Lord Mayor, then at Penelope. *How did she know?*

"A…fraud?" the Lord Mayor asked unsurely.

"Yes. She's not even from our village," the girl continued. "She's from Paris! And that's against the rules!" Remy breathed a sigh of relief.

"Is that so?" the Lord Mayor asked Monsieur Delfont.

"Well, there's no rule about being from our village, that I know of…" the headmaster announced weakly.

Remy and Daniel exchanged a glance. They both nodded: it was time for the big reveal.

"Actually, Your Honor, 'Charlotte' is indeed a resident of our village," Remy explained.

"What are you talking about?" Penelope shouted. "You said she was from Paris!"

"'Charlotte' is from Paris," Remy continued. "But *Charles* – "and at this he ripped the wig off Charles' head – "is from Nulle!" There was a gasp from the crowd. The nuns crossed themselves. Father Pascal rolled his eyes Heavenward and kissed his crucifix. Penelope shrieked. His Honor the Lord Mayor fainted dead away. The girls gaped in horror. Charles held the trophy high in triumph. The boys hoisted Remy and Charles unto their shoulders and marched around the gymnasium in a triumphant procession.

Of course, when the dust settled, the trophy was stripped from Remy and Charles. Remy, however, remained unrepentant, regally declaring to everyone present, "I'm <u>not</u> sorry. It was the grandest hoax of all!"

The punishment was decided upon quickly. For their part in the fraud, and for making the Lord Mayor faint, Remy and the boys would have to paint His Honor's house and walk his dogs for a month. He had about a dozen poodles of all shapes and colors, and a large *maison* high on a hill on the outskirts of the village. The boys were put to work painting the house the following day. The Lord Mayor wanted his house painted blue to "cheer the place up." So the boys worked hard and finished the job in about a week, without incident – except for spilling a bucket of blue paint over one of the Lord Mayor's poodles. The Lord Mayor was pleased with his house, and gave the boys some cold lemonade when they were finished.

But…there were several buckets of paint left over. "What are we going to do with all this paint?" Henri asked. Of course, Remy had a solution. He looked at the one blue poodle and shook his head. "That just won't do. They've got to match." So they each grabbed a paint brush and painted the rest of His Honor's dogs blue, then took them for a walk through the village to get a reaction. Children laughed and pointed, adults gaped, Officer Le Pen shook his head and sighed, "His Honor is not going to like *this*…"

But they still had paint left over. "Come on, grab the paint," Remy ordered. "I've got another idea…"

They took the paint to a farm outside the village and painted all the farmer's sheep blue. Then they made posters and put them up all over the village. Village kids came swarming out to the farm, where Remy and the boys charged them two sous each to look at the blue sheep. Kids were lined up all the way down the road, so they sold them the Lord Mayor's lemonade while they were waiting.

When the farmer saw his sheep had been painted blue, he trudged into the village to find Officer Le Pen. Officer Le Pen accompanied the farmer to his farm to see the blue sheep for himself.

"Well, what are you going to do about it?" the farmer demanded.

The gendarme thumbed through his well-worn book of municipal codes. "Well, I see no law against painting sheep blue…"

"Destruction of property!" the farmer suggested, red-faced.

Le Pen looked at the sheep grazing peacefully in the field. "They do not look destroyed to me."

"So, you're just going to do nothing?"

"Not exactly," the gendarme corrected. "I am going to the café for an *aperitif*, and if anything else strikes me, I'll let you know."

But the farmer was having none of it. He marched back into the village and lodged a formal complaint with the Lord Mayor himself. "It's your fault for painting your house blue!" he accused.

The Lord Mayor directed Officer Le Pen to take the boys out to the farm and have them wash all the paint off the farmer's sheep. Then they came back in the middle of the night and stole the farmer's cow. Using a bucket of oats, they led the cow all the way up to the top of the church bell tower and left her there. "It's well-known that cows will walk up stairs," Remy explained. "But they're always afraid to come down..."

At sun-up the next morning, Officer Le Pen was awakened by pounding on his door. It was Pierre, the baker. "What are you doing sleeping?" the baker demanded.

Officer Le Pen was confused. "It's early..."

"There's mooing coming from the church bell tower," Pierre told him.

"What?"

"There's mooing coming from the church bell tower," the baker repeated. The gendarme got dressed, still wondering what the deranged baker could be talking about. When they got to the church, a crowd had gathered below the bell tower. The baker was right – there was mooing coming from the top of the tower.

"As everyone knows, cows will walk up stairs, but they're always afraid to come down," Emile observed sagely.

"I didn't know that," Officer Le Pen admitted, looking up at the tower. A long discussion ensued about the best way to get the cow down, with everyone throwing ideas out.

"Let's send Jacques up there to butcher it," Pierre suggested. "Then we can carry it down in pieces."

"Let's fool the cow by making her come down the stairs backwards," Claude, the postman, offered.

"Lower her down from the window with ropes," Monsieur Beauvais, the grocer, said confidently, folding his arms across his chest.

After much serious deliberation and discussion, they sent Pierre on his bicycle to fetch the firetruck in the next village. An hour later, an ancient firetruck rattled up to the church. Pierre was standing on the running boards with several firemen, his bicycle strapped to the hood of the truck. The fire chief hopped out of the cab and shouted "Where's the fire?"

"There's no fire," Officer Le Pen calmly informed him.

"Pierre said there was an emergency."

"*Oui*, there is."

"Well, what is it?"

"There is a cow in the bell tower."

"What?"

"There is a cow in the bell tower."

"What do you want <u>us</u> to do?"

"Get it down."

The chief reached up under his helmet and scratched his head a long time. "We'll see what we can do," he finally said.

The firemen climbed up the tower with heavy coils of rope over their shoulders. They tied a rope around the cow's neck, and two firemen pulled while three firemen pushed the cow from behind. The cow would not budge.

After an hour, the firemen gave up and climbed back onto their truck.

"You're leaving?" Le Pen asked in astonishment.

"That is one stubborn cow," the chief told him, sliding into the cab of the truck.

"But what should we do?" Le Pen asked woefully.

"You'd better milk her," the chief called out the window as the truck drove away.

Next, Pierre was sent on his bicycle to another village to retrieve a farm veterinarian. When the veterinarian arrived, Le Pen took him to the top of the tower. The veterinarian looked at the cow and asked "What exactly is the problem?"

"The cow will not walk down the steps," Le Pen explained.

"Ah, yes…" the vet said knowingly, not venturing to ask how she got up there in the first place. "Did you try using psychology?"

"*Non.*"

"Ah, but you see, you must use *psychology*" the vet nodded confidently.

"Psychology?"

"That's right. Any animal will understand psychology. Leave it to me."

The vet went right to work. After three hours of using "psychology" on the cow, the frustrated vet emerged from the tower with a grimace on his face.

"It didn't work?" Le Pen asked.

The vet pointed dramatically up at the tower. "That is an *abnormal* cow!" Then he went back to his village.

The next morning was a Sunday, and the cow still had not been removed from the bell tower. Father Pascal had no choice but to go ahead with Mass as scheduled, though it was punctuated with loud calls from the cow. It was the day of Daniel's confirmation, but Father Pascal began the service with a hymn and a sermon on the Ten Commandments. Jacques and his wife, as well as the widow Deschard, were in attendance.

"I am the Lord thy God, ye shall have no other gods before me," the priest began solemnly. He was going through the commandments in order, and as he got closer to number six, Jacques kept sliding down lower and lower in his pew. The cow mooed after each commandment, as if on cue. After reading number five, Father Pascal cleared his throat portentiously and intoned, "Thou shalt not commit adultery." Then he paused and looked at Jacques a long time. Jacques was sitting so low in his pew, his head was barely visible.

Jacques glanced nervously at the widow Deschard. The widow Deschard glanced nervously at Jacques' wife. Father Pascal glanced at the widow Deschard. Jacques' wife glanced at Father Pascal. Father Pascal glanced at Jacques. Jacques' wife glanced at the widow Deschard. Jacques glanced at his wife. The cow mooed.

Jacques' wife glared at Jacques. "*Her*?"

Jacques covered his face in shame with an open hymn book. His wife grabbed the hymn book and hit him over the head with it. Then she sprang up and chased the widow Deschard around the church, trying to hit *her* over the head with the hymn book.

"Madame, may I remind you: the sacred hymns are not to be used as an instrument of violence!" Father Pascal called out.

Without missing a beat, Remy shot to his feet. "The Word of God is as sharp as a two-edged sword!" he called out, causing Father

Pascal to bury his face in his hands. The widow Deschard ran from the sanctuary with Jacques' wife and the hymnal in hot pursuit. Officer Le Pen ran out after them, trying to catch up to Jacques' wife. Jacques stayed down low in the pew, still as a statue. Father Pascal regained his composure and motioned Daniel to the altar. Daniel approached the priest in his clean white altar boy smock. He was nervous, but somehow comforted that Emile was there, making a rare appearance at Mass, just to see him be confirmed.

Daniel knelt at the altar and Father Pascal anointed him with oil, making the sign of the cross on his forehead. "Be sealed with the gift of the Holy Spirit," the priest said.

"Amen," Daniel answered. The cow mooed.

"Peace be with you, my son," the priest said, shaking his head. "That is, if you still want to be a member of this church…"

Two days later, Jacques was dead. He had eaten a bad mushroom placed into his soufflé by his wife. "It was an accident," she sobbed to Officer Le Pen. "I got confused." Officer Le Pen, finding no physical evidence of a crime (Jacques had eaten the entire soufflé), closed the case and allowed her to go free.

The whole village turned out for Jacques' funeral. It was more out of curiosity, for he was not a well-liked man. His wife, the widow Deschard, and several widows from neighboring villages knelt at the altar and wept before his open casket. The undertaker had done a wonderful job on him; his hair was slicked back and his mustache neatly waxed, just like when he was alive.

"His skin looks better than ever," Claude remarked quietly to his wife, who nodded in agreement.

"He looks so life-like," De Leon, the cobbler, said to his wife after peering into the casket. "Like he could just stand up and walk right out of here."

Father Pascal took his place behind the pulpit. "In sad times like these, it is customary to remember the good that the departed has done. But in the case of Jacques, nothing comes to mind. There are many words that describe Jacques, but I'm afraid 'good' is not one of them. He was selfish, vain, egotistical, vulgar, mean, rude, petulant, nasty, immoral, unfaithful, dishonest, and many, many other things. I liked Jacques. But he cheated old women in his shop and berated customers. And I'm sure he would be in hell this very moment if not for the lavish saving grace of our Lord Jesus Christ. Now let us pray.”

Everyone bowed their head. The cow, still stuck in the tower, mooed loudly.

“Our Father, who art in Heaven,” began Father Pascal, “forgive our brother and his many sins, unholy deeds, and shortcomings as a man. May his life of decadence, depravity, and unbridled greed stand as a tarnished testament to how great and powerful your loving mercy truly is. Amen.” Everyone raised their heads to find Jacques’ casket empty.

“Where _is_ he?” his wife shrieked.

“He’s been stolen!” someone called out.

“He’s been resurrected!” someone else shouted.

“No,” Father Pascal shook his head emphatically. “The Lord would never resurrect Jacques without running it by me.”

They broke into groups and searched the whole village. Two hours later, they all regrouped in the town square. “He’s nowhere to be found,” Officer Le Pen reported to Father Pascal.

“Has anyone tried the café?” Emile asked.

“What would a dead man be doing in the café?” Monsieur Beauvais asked.

They headed for the café like a mob. Bursting in, they found Jacques sitting at a center table enthusiastically eating a four-course meal.

“Jacques – what are you _doing_?” Father Pascal demanded.

Jacques looked up at him as if he were simply enjoying a typical supper. “I’m hungry. I haven’t eaten for three days…”

With a little digging by Officer Le Pen, it was discovered that the mushroom ingested by Jacques when he ate the soufflé was not, in fact, fatal. In actuality, it was a type of mushroom which merely caused severe paralysis and physiological conditions _resembling_ death, which typically last three days. Instead of relief over her husband’s remarkably sudden recovery from death, however, his wife found herself preoccupied with questions as to the identities of the several widows from surrounding villages who had somehow found their way to _his_ funeral.

***

The cow in the tower would not stop mooing. They carried hay and water up to it every day and lowered buckets of its waste out the window on ropes, but still it would not stop mooing. Over the course of three days, its mooing grew more and more anxious, more and more plaintive, until finally His Honor the Lord Mayor called a village meeting. Everybody met in the church.

"I've tried everything," the Lord Mayor opined. Officer Le Pen nodded his head in solidarity behind him. "I've even called Paris asking for help, but they said it was a local problem. Does anyone have a suggestion?"

No one stirred. Finally, Daniel stood up. "Maybe she's lonely."

The Lord Mayor looked confused. "Did you say 'lonely?'"

"Yes. Maybe she's lonely, and wants to see another cow."

"See another cow?" the Lord Mayor was taken aback. "Well, we're certainly not going to take another cow up there..." Behind him, Officer Le Pen made a face and shook his head dramatically.

"That's not what I'm suggesting," Daniel clarified. He went into Father Pascal's study and took down a wall mirror. The Lord Mayor, Officer Le Pen, and all the villagers followed him outside and stood beneath the bell tower. "Wait here," he told them, then motioned for Remy to follow him up to the top of the tower. Holding the mirror up to show the cow her own reflection, Daniel led her down the steps while Remy made mooing sounds behind him. It worked brilliantly.

When Daniel and Remy emerged from the bottom of the bell tower with the cow, the whole village erupted in surprised applause. "How did you do it?" The Lord Mayor asked in astonishment.

"Simple," Daniel explained. "She thought her own reflection was another cow. She was so lonely up there, she forgot all about being afraid of going down the steps."

His Honor the Lord Mayor and the entire village was so impressed and grateful that they held a special ceremony that evening, during which the French national anthem was played, speeches were made, and commendations and Medals of Honor were awarded to the two boys.

The festivities were somewhat quenched, however, when Claude the postman came riding up on his bicycle with urgent news. "The Germans have just invaded Holland and Belgium! It's on the radio now! They're headed for France!"

Chapter 6

The news was true, and it wasn't good. Everyone crowded around the old radio in the café, straining to hear the frantic broadcasts of the BBC and French National Radio. After months of inactivity, the Germans were on the march, smashing through Holland and Belgium and swarming over the French border in droves. Daily life in *Nulle* almost ceased, as the war was all anybody could think or talk about. Day after day, the same news came through the radio speaker: on the frontier, the vaunted French Army collapsing in confusion beneath the successive waves of *Stuka* dive-bombers that preceded the endless columns of *panzer* tanks. In the cities, panic took hold.

A large-scale evacuation of Paris sent waves of terrified refugees into the surrounding countryside, seeking shelter and safety from the advancing German Army. The British rushed reinforcements across the Channel, but it was too late; the French Army, smashed beyond recognition, had ceased to exist as a cohesive fighting force, and soon the Nazis were goose-stepping through the *Arc de Triomphe* in Paris.

The weary villagers listened as the BBC reported that the Germans had trapped 300,000 British troops on the beaches of Dunkirk, and threatened to annihilate them if they did not surrender. They listened as thousands of small fishing boats crossed the channel to rescue the soldiers and ferry them safely back to England. They listened as Paris, Lyon, and Tours all fell to the German forces, and as General Charles De Gaulle encouraged the tattered remnants of the French Army to fight on at all costs. They listened to other government officials who argued for a ceasefire and armistice with the Germans before more Frenchmen died.

Then they listened as Marshall Petain took to the airwaves to throw in the towel. He told the French people in a calm, dignified voice that resisting the Germans was futile, and would only lead to the complete destruction of France. In order to save the country, he said, France should surrender immediately and submit itself to German occupation. He ended the broadcast by declaring an immediate ceasefire, and encouraged all Frenchmen to stop fighting and cooperate fully with their new German overlords. "There has been enough bloodshed," he said emotionlessly. "We must now face reality."

"Traitor!" Pierre hissed at the radio. "How can he call himself a Frenchman?"

"What do you want him to do?" Jacques asked. "There's no more army. There's no more air force. He had to do this to save the rest of the navy, before the Germans sank it."

"What good does it do to have a navy, if the Germans are in charge of it?" Monsieur Beauvais argued.

"Marshall Petain knows what he's doing," Officer Le Pen assured everyone. "He's going to move the government to Vichy. We will still have a government, still have a France."

"Still have a *France*?" Emile spat. "They will call it a 'government,' they will call it 'France,' but it will be the Nazis who are pulling the strings!"

And so it went, not only in *Nulle*, but all over France. It seemed no one could agree; to half the country, surrender was the only option. To the other half, fighting on to the end was the noble thing to do.

To the boys, there was only one clear path. "I'm going to Paris and join the resistance," Remy declared. "Then, after we've licked the Nazis, I'm going to become a famous director and live in a lavish apartment over-looking the Champs-Elysees and wear dark glasses and date beautiful Italian movie stars…"

"*Oui*, I'm joining the resistance, too," Daniel chimed in. "Then, when Hitler's dead, I'm going to become a famous motorcycle racer and win races all over the world and live in America and drink chocolate sodas and watch the Yankees and marry Betty Grable and Jean Harlow…"

But, of course, it was all talk. Remy and Daniel did not join the resistance. Nobody from *Nulle* joined the resistance, despite all the bravado and tough talk. In fact, nobody in *Nulle* even <u>saw</u> a Nazi until a single officer riding in a motorcycle sidecar came putting into the village one day and asked to see His Honor the Lord Mayor. Officer Le Pen officiously led him into the Lord Mayor's office, where His Honor stood stiffly at attention behind his desk, not knowing whether to bow, salute, or extend a hand to the German.

The German officer was tall, strait, and blond. He wore an impeccable gray uniform, and never smiled. "You have no doubt received the orders of cooperation from Paris, and I expect nothing short of full compliance with that directive," he said icily, in heavily-accented French.

"*Oui*, Your Emissary," the Lord Mayor coughed hoarsely.

"You are responsible for making sure that your village adheres strictly to the new regulations, especially the rationing of premium goods," the officer continued. "You will also inform your farmers and shopkeepers that from now on two-thirds of their produce and goods will be forfeited to the German Army for the war effort. They may keep or sell the remaining one third. These regulations will be followed exactly to the letter, under penalty of death."

"I understand…"

"Lastly, have your gendarme confiscate all firearms and stockpile them in a safe place. I will send a truck to collect them in one week."

"It will be done…"

"You will report the names of any resistance fighters, partisans, or villagers who express anti-German sentiments directly to me from now on. There is a new order in France, Monsieur Mayor, and make no mistake, it is here to stay." And with that, the officer clicked his heels and left the Lord Mayor's office.

Life under the occupation was not much different than before the war, except for the curfew and the rationing. Even then, life was better in the countryside and small villages than in the cities. There was more food in the countryside, while rumors of disease and mass starvation in Paris and Marseilles abounded. Furthermore, there was more freedom and less scrutiny from the Germans, especially in a village the size of *Nulle*, where nobody felt like the Germans were looking over their shoulder or breathing down their neck. In fact, German soldiers were rarely seen in or around *Nulle*, and life under the occupation soon settled into a rather predictable routine.

Once a week, an army truck would drive into the village, and two soldiers would load the confiscated produce and goods into the back and then leave. They never checked shops, houses, or farms for any contraband or held-back wares. As far as the Germans were concerned, *Nulle* was on the honor system – at least so far. There was nothing about the tiny hamlet to arouse suspicion, anyway. Once in a while, a German patrol would stumble upon the village and spend a few leisurely hours drinking, smoking, talking, and laughing in the café before happily climbing into their vehicles and driving off again, with little concern or regard for the villagers themselves. In fact, they acted almost as if they were tourists on vacation, taking pictures of the scenery and chatting up the shopkeepers with small talk in stilted French.

Even the curfews were of little worry. Daniel and Emile were still able to hunt and fish in order to supplement the rationing, as long as they did it early enough in the morning to make discovery by a German patrol unlikely. While armed resistance was out of the question, the type of "passive" resistance most villagers in *Nulle* practiced brought at least a small amount of satisfaction. Emile refused to surrender his shotgun, which he kept hidden in a chest in the cellar in the event of a surprise raid. Most farmers and shopkeepers kept more than one third of their produce and wares, and the Germans never even suspected or knew. Sometimes city folks came to buy meat, chicken, eggs, or milk from the farmers at black market prices.

They also listened to radio broadcasts that were strictly *verboten*. General De Gaulle made weekly broadcasts to the French people from London on the BBC urging resistance and offering hope, a refreshing break from the diet of German propaganda found on Radio Paris and Radio Vichy.

But perhaps the greatest act of passive resistance occurred when "The Adventures of Robin Hood" arrived at the tiny village cinema. Showing an American movie, which somehow had slipped through the German censors in Paris, was resistance enough in itself, but the villagers who packed the stuffy cinema that summer evening expecting to see Errol Flynn swashbuckling his way through Sherwood Forest were going to get more than they bargained for.

Before showing the main feature, Remy and Daniel swapped the official Nazi propaganda newsreel with their own "mock" newsreel. It started with the usual newsreel bombast, but when the narrator began speaking it quickly became clear something was not right. "Adolf Hitler has revealed a lifelong dream to become a ballet dancer, debuting in the Berlin Ballet performance of *Swan Lake*," the narrator intoned, over footage of a male ballet dancer doing all kinds of acrobatic dance moves. The audience gasped in surprise.

The narrator continued: "Not to be outdone by his partner in crime, Benito Mussolini brought his lifelong ambition to become an opera singer to life in his debut of Puccini's *La Boheme*," over footage of a big-breasted, fat female opera singer wearing a Viking helmet. The audience roared with laughter.

"Meanwhile, the German people continue to loyally follow their Fuhrer anywhere," (footage of lemmings running off a cliff). "The German infantry surges across the frontier…" (babies crawling in a nursery, old men with canes racing each other). The audience went wild.

"The German Navy takes to the seas…" (women in old-fashioned bathing suits running into the water at the beach, a man in a rowboat with a gushing leak shooting up in the air like a geyser). "And the Nazi panzer divisions continue to plow through all resistance…" (Keystone cop cars in a chase scene, weaving, turning upside down, crashing into each other, wheels coming off and flying in all directions). More laughter, jeering from the audience.

"And the brave Luftwaffe dominates the skies over France…" (old biplanes trying to take off and crashing, wings falling off, bursting into flames on the runway, falling out of the sky in a trail of smoke). The whole audience was standing up now, laughing and cheering wildly.

"And the victorious *Fuhrer* visits Paris, where he wines and dines in style…" (Charlie Chaplin eating his own shoe with a knife and fork). "And stepping triumphantly into the annals of history…" (Chaplin in his tramp get-up, stumbling away from the camera as the shot fades out into a tight circle in the center of the screen).

It was bedlam inside the cinema. Delirious with joy, people were laughing, hugging, and kissing each other on the cheek. Young couples were passionately making out. Father Pascal, leaning against Jacques, wiped tears of laughter from his eyes. And for just a brief moment, they had forgotten the ugliness of war and the indignity of occupation.

Remy and Daniel watched the scene unfold below them from the projection booth. They had stayed up all night splicing together footage from old movies and doing the voice-over narration themselves. They were tired, but filled with a sense of exhilaration and pride. All the work was worth it. It was their gift to the village.

It was their love letter to *Nulle*.

***

From time to time, as Daniel lay in his bed at night having an imaginary conversation with his mother, he would pull out the card the young motorcycle champion had given him and run his fingers over the exquisite words printed on it, almost like he was reading some kind of wonderful braille: "MONSIEUR SIMON LE GRUN, ESQUIRE, DISTINGUISHED AND ESTEEMED MOTORCYCLE AND AUTOMOBILE SPEED CHAMPION." A feeling of exhilaration came over him whenever he looked at the card, and thoughts would begin to formulate in his mind of someday leaving *Nulle* to achieve his dream. How would he ever become a motorcycle racing champion here in *Nulle* – a tiny, inconsequential nook lost in the French countryside?

At times, he felt he could wait no longer. He felt like a candle that was slowly burning down, wasted here in the village. If he didn't act soon, there would be nothing left with which to reach his goal. One day, he summoned up the courage to approach his uncle with his intentions.

Emile brushed the idea aside like an irritating mosquito. "Out of the question. Leave the village? Are you crazy?"

"It won't be forever," Daniel argued. "I've just got to find Monsieur Le Grun. He said he would hire me on as a mechanic. I could watch from the sidelines and learn the racing game from a champion!"

"Listen to him!" Emile said to nobody. "The racing game! It's not a 'game,' Daniel. It's very dangerous."

"I'm ready to accept the challenges."

"You're fourteen."

"Almost fifteen."

"The dreams of a young boy," Emile said dismissively. "Wait until you're old enough."

"You can't keep me here," Daniel said defiantly.

"Oh, listen to him!" Emile said derisively. "That's right. You could run away. But you won't. You don't have it in you."

Daniel knew it was true. He probably wouldn't be able to do it without his uncle's blessing.

"I need you here, around the shop," Emile said, softening. "I'm not getting any younger, you know." And that was that.

That night, Emile stayed up all night pacing the kitchen floor. He did this whenever he was facing a dilemma or wrestling with a tough decision. Daniel listened as his uncle paced, smoked, and drank wine into the middle of the night. He finally dozed off, but was awakened in the wee hours of the morning by Emile standing over his bed. His eyes were bloodshot and he looked weary.

"This motorcycle champion, he is a nice man?" Emile finally asked.

"Very nice."

"Let me see his card."

Daniel handed it to him. Emile read it several times, deep in thought.

"If you can find him…and he agrees to hire you…I suppose it would make an acceptable apprenticeship for you…"

Daniel was overjoyed. "Thank you, Uncle!"

"But if it doesn't work out, you will come back here."

Daniel left later that morning. He took whatever he could strap to the back of his motorcycle: a small bundle of clothes, a sack of cheese sandwiches, a small *Michelin* road atlas, a compass, and a hunting knife. Before he left, Emile handed him some money. "Here, take this," he said, betraying no emotion. "Be careful. And remember to keep in touch."

"Thank you, Uncle."

 "I suppose it's natural for a boy to want to make his own way in the world," Emile said, then turned away. "Now go…"

It was a two-day ride to *Neufchateau*. Daniel stopped at the end of the first day and camped in a grove of eucalyptus trees off the road. It had been a pleasant ride on winding country roads, and Daniel was tired and ready to sleep after his cheese sandwich supper. He slept well in the warm late summer air, and woke with the rising sun to continue his journey. On the second day, he encountered more traffic on the roads: old lorries, cars, farmers on their tractors, and a few people on bicycles. Outside *Bourg-Saint-Marie*, there was a German roadblock. A lorry loaded down with farm produce was pulled off the road, and several German soldiers were searching it. Two other soldiers motioned for Daniel to stop on the road.

"Papers," one of them said, looking over the motorcycle. Daniel took his identification papers out and handed them to the soldier. "Destination?"

"*Neufchateau*," Daniel answered.

"The purpose of your journey?"

"I'm taking an apprenticeship there."

"What kind of apprenticeship?"

"As a mechanic with a racing champion."

"Racing champion?"

"*Oui*. Motorcycles." Daniel revved the throttle of his motorcycle for emphasis.

The soldier smiled. "How old are you?"

"Fourteen. Almost fifteen."

The soldier kept smiling. "Almost fifteen." He looked at the motorcycle again. "How did a fourteen year old come by an old racing bike like this?"

"My uncle gave it to me."

"Is he a motorcycle racing champion, too?" The soldier asked.

"No. He's a bicycle repairman in *Nulle*."

The soldier nodded. "Do you know how to maintain this thing?"

"*Oui*. He taught me everything."

"I like motorcycles. I have a BMW waiting for me when I get home. Have a pleasant journey." He waved Daniel through, and before he knew it he was on his way.

Neufchateau was a much larger village than *Nulle*. After stopping several times to ask directions, he finally found Number 17 Rue de Paix, the address on Monsieur Le Grun's card. Expecting to pull up a long gravel driveway to an expansive country estate, Daniel was surprised to find a rather modest cottage with ivy growing up the walls and colorful flowers in the window boxes. He parked the motorcycle in front, and let himself in through the garden gate. After knocking on the door several times, it finally opened to reveal a pretty woman in her thirties. She was very pleasant, but had a sad look on her face.

"*Bonjour*. I'm looking for Monsieur Le Grun," Daniel said.

"He's not here," the woman answered. Daniel heard a baby crying inside the cottage.

"He came to my village once," Daniel said. "I fixed a flat tire on his motorcycle. He gave me his card." He handed the card to her. She read it and handed it back without saying anything. There were tears in her eyes. "He told me to find him if I ever needed a job. I'm a motorcycle racer – I mean, mechanic."

"He's not here," she said again, wiping tears from her eyes. The baby cried again. "They took him away two weeks ago. To Germany. Forced labor."

"Why?" Daniel asked in shock.

"They're taking all the men who aren't in the army. They said they're short of workers in Germany. They said he'd be back after the war."

"Why didn't they stop them – Marshal Petain, our government –"

"It was our own government," she said bitterly. "They're the ones who took him. They – *Frenchmen* – rounded up their own countrymen and shipped them off to Germany. Petain – the police, everyone – they're all collaborating with the enemy now. I just don't know what's happened to the world…"

"I'm sorry," Daniel said quietly.

"You look like you've had a long journey," she said kindly. "I can offer you a cup of tea and bread. I'm afraid that's all I have to eat."

She let him in and led him to the small, homey kitchen. She put a kettle on the stove and went into another room. A moment later, she was back with a baby, which she placed in a high chair and gave a small piece of bread and jam. When the kettle whistled, she poured two cups of tea and put a small plate of bread, butter, and jam on the table in front of Daniel.

"I'm afraid the tea is weak," she apologized. "I must reuse the bags for several days, to stretch it. The rationing has hit us very hard."

"That's all right," Daniel said, gratefully sipping the hot tea. He took a piece of thick bread and jam and took a large bite out of it.

"You look hungry," she said.

"I am. I ate my last cheese sandwich this morning for breakfast."

"How far have you come?"

"From *Nulle*. You've never heard of it. It's a tiny place two days' ride from here."

"Did you encounter any Germans on your way?"

"Just once, but they let me through their checkpoint. The motorcycle captures their attention, and they become less suspicious and let their guard down a bit."

"I'm sorry you travelled so far for nothing," she said. "The least I can do is put you up for the night. We have a spare room. I'll make up a nice, comfortable bed for you."

"Thank you," Daniel said, taking another bite of bread. "I'll be on my way in the morning."

The woman got up to prepare his room, then stopped suddenly. "Forgive me, I haven't introduced myself. I don't know where my head is lately…My name is Anne-Marie."

"I'm Daniel."

"It's very nice to meet you, Daniel. You must very tired. I'll go make up your bed now."

It was a comfortable, soft bed with a cushy, over-stuffed feather pillow. Daniel sank down into it and was asleep in seconds. He awoke early the next morning to sunshine streaming in through the window. It took him a few moments to remember where he was.

Anne-Marie and the baby were in the kitchen. The baby was in the high chair, drinking milk from a bottle.

"He's gotten used to the powdered milk," she told Daniel as he sat at the kitchen table. "We haven't had real milk in a long time. The German soldiers take it all."

For breakfast, there was more tea with bread and jam. Anne-Marie sat down opposite Daniel as he ate. "Where will you go now?"

"Back to my village, I guess."

As Daniel was leaving the cottage, Anne-Marie gave him a small knapsack. "The neighbor had some ham. I made some sandwiches for your journey. There's also a few biscuits in there."

"Oh, I couldn't –"

"Please. I want you to take it," she insisted. "I wish my husband could have met you. He would have enjoyed working with such a nice young man."

"Thank you," Daniel said, taking the knapsack. "Good luck."

"*Bon voyage*," she said, and kissed him on the cheek.

As he secured the knapsack and got on his motorcycle, he decided to take a different way home. It would take a little longer, but he wouldn't have to explain to the soldiers at the checkpoint why he was coming back through so soon. As he rode through the village it was busy with pedestrians on their way to work, and a few German soldiers strolling on the sidewalks or lounging in the cafes over coffee. Then he passed some shops – the butcher, the baker, the cheese shop – and noticed long lines already forming outside. He knew that these people would spend hours on the sidewalk waiting for half a loaf of bread or a small piece of beef or pork – that is, if the shop didn't run out before they got to the front of the line.

In the hottest part of the day, he stopped in *Saint-Julien* for a cool drink of water in the village square. He checked his fuel tank and noticed it was low, but found a petrol station on his way out of the village. A large bellied attendant with a thick gray beard and a soiled racing cap pumped the fuel while Daniel counted out the money Emile had given him.

"You here for the big race?" the attendant asked.

"Big race?" Daniel's ears pricked up.

"*Oui*. Motorcycle race. Right here in *Saint-Julien* tomorrow. I hadn't seen you around here before, so I just figured you were here for the race."

"Perhaps I am," Daniel answered, his head spinning. He paid the attendant for the petrol. "You know, I forgot the chap's name – about the race, I mean."

The attendant smiled knowingly. "Go see Monsieur Albert. He's in a field about a kilometer down this road. That's where they're doing the qualifying."

Daniel found the field, and pulled his motorcycle into it. Several men were there, working on their bikes, smoking, drinking beer, and chatting. Daniel asked one of them about Monsieur Albert, and was pointed in the direction of a squat, powerfully built man with a mustache that looked like gray steel wool and biceps the size of wine casks. It was only as Daniel got closer to him that he realized just how short Monsieur Albert really was; Daniel literally towered over the diminutive man.

"I would like to enter the race, Monsieur," Daniel announced.

"Do I know you?" Monsieur Albert squinted at him with an air of suspicion.

"*Non*, Monsieur."

"You're very polite, I'll give you that." The small man's voice was exceedingly raspy, like sandpaper. "What's your name?"

"Daniel Renaud."

"How come I haven't heard of you before?"

"I can't say, Monsieur."

"How old are you?" Monsieur Albert barked, looking up at Daniel.

"Sixteen," Daniel lied.

"More like fifteen, I'd say," Monsieur Albert huffed, lighting a cigarette and holding it palm-up, like an aristocrat. "Have you raced before?"

"*Oui*, Monsieur…"

"Likely not, so I won't ask you which races," Monsieur Albert grimaced. "I don't usually take novices, but if you qualify, and you've got the racing fee, I think we can come to some sort of agreement."

"*Merci*, Monsieur."

The racing impresario pointed to some pylons laid out in the form of a course. "You qualify over there. Go around four times as fast as you can. And don't knock any pylons over."

Fighting the fluttering of the butterflies in his stomach, Daniel climbed on his bike and started around the course. He went around once at an easy clip, then picked up speed on each consecutive lap until he felt he was moving at quite a fast speed. He pulled up to Monsieur Albert feeling confident about his performance.

"Nice cornering," Monsieur Albert barked. "You controlled that antique well, but you need to work on your speed. But I see you can ride, so if you've got the racing fee, I'll let you race tomorrow."

Daniel could barely contain his excitement. This was a long-time dream coming true. He counted out Emile's money again, and was relieved he had just enough to pay the racing fee.

"Where are you staying?" Monsieur Albert asked, pocketing the money. Daniel didn't answer. He knew he couldn't afford a hotel room. "Well, some of the boys camp out in this field overnight. If you don't mind sleeping on the ground, you're welcome to stay here." He took a piece of paper out of his pocket, unfolded it, and handed it to Daniel. "This is a map of the race. Since you don't know the roads around here, you'll have to memorize this by tomorrow. Race starts at 8 o'clock sharp, so have your bike ready."

"*Merci*, Monsieur."

Daniel didn't at all mind sleeping on the ground – he'd sleep on a bed of nails to get a chance at competing in a real motorcycle race. As the sun went down, some of the other racers built a campfire and passed around bottles of beer and cognac, laughing and telling stories until late in the night. Daniel couldn't help but think they were all hardened, veteran racers, maybe even champions themselves. He built a small fire for himself, and sat next to it eating one of the sandwiches Anne-Marie had given him when he left *Neufchateau* that morning. That seemed like ages ago now, after his good fortune and the exhilarating events of the day.

One of the racers noticed him sitting alone and brought over a bottle of beer. "Now you have something good to wash that sandwich down with," the man said. "I haven't seen you before. Where are you from?"

"A small village called *Nulle*," Daniel answered.

"Never heard of it."

"No one has."

"First race?"

"*Oui*."

"Well, get some rest tonight. You're going to need it."

"*Merci*."

The man started to walk away, then stopped and turned back. "Listen, it gets a little rough out there," he said. "Don't take it personally. That's just the game. Be careful." Then he returned to his mates at the other campfire. Daniel went to sleep with a smile on his face, no place in the world he'd rather be than in that little field outside *Saint-Julien*.

At sun-up the next morning, the field quickly filled up with motorcycles and riders coming in from the hotel in the village. Riders revved their engines and checked their brakes, clutches, tires, and chains, making last minute adjustments in preparation for the race. In the growing sunlight, Daniel studied the map and quickly committed it to memory. It looked like a fifteen or twenty kilometer course, snaking its way through the countryside past villages, farms, and lakes. The racers would end up back in *Saint-Julien*, in this very field, when the race was over.

At 7:30, dark clouds gathered overhead and it began to rain heavily. Daniel felt crushed, until he learned that the race was not going to be cancelled because of the rain. "We race in rain, sleet, and snow," the man who gave him the beer the night before told him. Daniel's spirits soared at the prospect: nothing, it seemed, was going to get between him and his first race.

At 7:50, Monsieur Albert called the racers to line up in their starting positions. It was still raining, but no one cared. The adrenalin was already flowing through Daniel's body, so strong that he was barely able to stay in his position until the starter gun fired. At 7:55, everyone fired up their bikes and warmed them up for the race. Daniel looked around him and counted about two dozen racers; then one of the bikes stalled and the rider couldn't get it started again. Cursing and kicking, he pushed his bike off the road and started frantically working on the engine with a wrench.

At 8:00, Monsieur Albert fired the starter gun and the mass of bikes took off in a high-pitched cacophony of revving engines, squealing tires, and backfiring exhaust pipes. Daniel got chills; to him, there was nothing like that sound, and the excitement of rushing forward headlong into the wet countryside. But nothing could have prepared him for what was to follow.

The rain had turned the dirt road into a churning river of thick, oozing mud. Right off the starting line, three motorcycles lost traction and slid off the road into a ditch. They were out of the race. The riders in front lurched forward with spinning tires, creating a thick wall of mud, gravel, and smoke through which Daniel and the riders in back had to pass. Daniel's goggles were immediately rendered useless by a thick coating of mud. He had to continually reach up and wipe them with his gloves in order to see where he was going. At this point, the flying mud was so thick that he couldn't see the road at all – it was all he could do to follow the back fender of the bike in front of him.

Daniel felt his bike bounce violently over washboard-like ruts in the road and his back-end fishtail through the slimy mud. He just held onto the handlebars as tight as he could, trying to keep his legs wrapped around the bike and keep the bike upright and going in a forward direction.

He looked up briefly and saw that the rain had stopped. The dark clouds were parting and the sun was peeking through. He'd made it through the violent, uncontrolled initial rush of the start, and was still on the road. Then he noticed the pack had gotten away from him, and twisted the throttle for more speed. At almost full throttle, he suddenly realized it was going to be extremely hard to catch up to the leaders, who remained at least twenty meters ahead of him for most of the race.

The road was a little straighter now, but still treacherous with mud. He swerved suddenly to miss a rider whose bike had gotten stuck up to forks and couldn't get it free. Another one out. Approaching a narrow curve, two riders came up from behind and sandwiched him between them. Every time he sped up, they did the same, keeping right alongside him. He knew the curve was too narrow for three bikes, and realized they were trying to force him to pull behind them in order to make it around. But he wouldn't budge, so one of them fell behind while the other one tried to run him completely off the road. He backed off the throttle just in time to avoid complete catastrophe; they both shot ahead of him and went around the curve first.

Daniel sped up on the outside coming out of the curve, and caught up to them. They tried to box him in and block him again, but he squeezed through to the front. One of them came up and tried to run him off the road again, but lost control himself and crashed into a tree off to the right. The other one came up fast and rammed him from behind. Then he came alongside Daniel and kicked out at him, trying to topple him over. Daniel decided to become more aggressive, turned sharply into him, and forced him off the road. The rider flew off his bike just before it flipped headlong over a rock wall and crashed on the other side.

Welcome to the world of motorcycle road racing, Daniel thought to himself, adrenalin coursing through his body. Focused now on catching up to the pack, Daniel accelerated on a straightaway and could just make out their dust cloud about fifty meters ahead. They'd ridden out of the rain and the road was much drier and more solid now, so he made good time. Coming up behind the nearest bike ahead, he started to pass when the other rider's front wheel snapped off and flew right at him. Ducking reflexively, he was just able to avoid being decapitated as the rider and his bike went tumbling end over end off the road. The field of competition was being narrowed quite rapidly at this point, Daniel noted.

Up ahead, two more bikes crashed into each other, forming a spinning, twisted mass of steel and rubber that Daniel was just able to swerve around. The carnage was striking; mangled bikes and injured riders littered the roadside as Daniel whizzed past and continued to gain ground over the next two kilometers.

Then the road got twisty. Daniel saw a rider ahead take a curve too fast and go down on his side, causing a spectacular five-motorcycle pile-up. Realizing that this was what happened when too many motorcycles rode too close together too fast, Daniel decided to keep as much distance between himself and the others as he could. He counted about a dozen riders left in the race, most of them still ahead of him. *Pace yourself,* he thought. *Wait for your opportunity...*

Then another rider got his wheels stuck in a rut and couldn't get them out. Instead of slowing down, he sped up, hit a bump, flew over his handlebars, and was run over by his own motorcycle. Daniel swiftly bypassed him and gained on the pack even more. It soon became apparent, however, that the remaining pack represented the cream of the riders. These seasoned riders would not be making mistakes. They weren't giving up a meter, and they weren't going to give him any opportunities to overtake them. From this point on, he was going to have to draw upon everything he knew about himself and his motorcycle to have a winning chance.

Then he thought he saw an opening, and moved in to fill it. At the last second, the rider in front of him veered to block him. He had to brake hard and almost lost control on the gravelly dirt. Then he tried to pass them on the right and was similarly blocked. They were an impenetrable wall, and he began racking his brain to find a way over, under, or around them before the race was over. Then an opportunity appeared out of nowhere.

A road crew working up ahead had blocked the way and set up detour signs. The detour took the riders off the road and through a large meadow. Daniel turned off the road and followed the pack. Riding through the bumpy field, he looked to his right and saw an angry bull running alongside him for several meters. Finally, the bull turned away and started charging a nearby rider, who fell off his bike and had to climb a tree to escape a certain goring.

The detour soon took them back onto another smaller road, where they were immediately slowed down by a farmer on a tractor. All the riders whizzed past the tractor but one, who wasn't able to squeeze through and ended up going off the road and into a pond. The next obstacle occurred when they came upon another farmer herding his sheep across the road. Pandemonium ensued, as frightened, bleating sheep bolted in every direction and cursing riders tried to guide their bikes through the noise and confusion. At one point, the road forked and the path of the detour became indiscernible, with most riders opting for the road to the right. Daniel made a quick decision and took the road to the left, hoping for the best.

A rider came up beside him and shouted "You're going the wrong way! Turn around! Turn around!" Before Daniel could respond, a low tree branch swiped the rider right off his bike, which rode on in a straight line for a while before smashing into a tree.

Daniel realized he was on the right track when he looked back and saw the riders who had taken the other road had turned around and were now coming up behind him very fast. He tried to keep in front of them, but their newer, more powerful bikes easily overtook him. They tried to slam into him and force him into the trees as they passed in a swarm, but he was somehow able to keep his wheels on the road. Then Daniel realized a village was coming up fast. Before he knew it, he was roaring down the main street, which was lined with waving, cheering adults and children. He felt a sudden swell of pride – they were cheering for *him*! They thought he was a famous motorcycle champion! It was quite a rush for a fourteen-year- old with a dream.

He looked to the right and noticed two riders had stopped at a café. Their bikes were parked in front of the establishment, and they were drinking beers and chatting up some German soldiers at the next table! Daniel had no time for such nonsense – he'd entered this race to *win*. Leaving the village, he saw another rider on the side of the road trying to fix a flat tire. The rest of them were thirty or forty meters ahead of him.

Daniel knew it was the final stretch, and they were nearing Saint-Julien again. This was his last chance to overtake the pack, and he opened the throttle all the way to get every last ounce of power he could out of his bike. That closed the gap to twenty meters. Then ten. He was right behind them now. This was it – he knew he had to force his way through somehow. He had to start getting aggressive, or he was going to lose.

He inserted his bike into a narrow crack between the two in front of him. He could tell by the looks on their faces that they didn't like him being so close. One of them tried to ram him, but he dodged it and then slammed into the other rider. That bike's front tire blew, and he careened off the road and broke through a wooden fence. Without missing a beat, Daniel slammed into the other one hard, sending him flying off the road and into a nice, soft haystack. The explosion of hay upon impact was something of a comical sight.

Out of respect or fear, the other riders made way for him and Daniel now found himself one of the pack. But he was at the back, far from the leaders up front. By now, the church spire of Saint-Julien was visible in the distance. The end of the race was coming up fast. Several bikes in the lead suddenly broke away and surged far ahead. Determined not to lose them, Daniel made his way to the front of the pack and attempted to catch them.

These were the best riders, on newer bikes with powerful engines. Daniel knew this, and gave it everything his old bike had. Unfortunately, it just wasn't enough. He wasn't able to close the gap between them, and he rode through Saint-Julien and passed the finish line in sixth place. He pulled into the little field and saw that a crowd had gathered – but not for him. They were standing around the winner, slapping him on the back and breaking open bottles of beer and wine.

Daniel parked his bike and got off. His legs felt like rubber. His arms ached, and his hands were numb. He had used muscles he didn't even know he had. He was covered in dried mud from head to toe. The last two hours had been hell, and his body felt like it. And he'd loved every second of it. He'd never experienced anything like it. This was the day he discovered what he wanted to do with the rest of his life.

Monsieur Albert came up to him and shook his hand. "To be honest, I never expected to see you again. But you finished. You _finished_. That's quite an accomplishment – especially on this old relic."

"_Merci_," Daniel managed to croak out, the inside of his throat caked with mud and dirt.

"The next race is in _Val-de-Meuse_ in two weeks," Monsieur Albert said. "I'd love to see what you can do with a little experience under your belt."

This was it for Daniel. He was in. He wanted to enter every race he could find. Then he remembered: that would take money. The money Emile gave him was almost gone. He would need to find a job.

"I don't have enough money to pay the racing fee," Daniel told him.

Monsieur Albert pulled a newspaper from under his arm and opened it to an advertisement. He handed it to Daniel. "The circus is hiring, since the army took all the young men. You might find work there."

Part Two
Emily's Errands

Chapter 7

Daniel found the ragged little *Cirque d'Europa* pitched forlornly in a field outside St.-Julien. He parked his motorcycle and saw two men working on the engine of a large truck. Pulling the folded-up newspaper ad from his pocket, he approached them and announced, "Bonjour, Messieurs. I'm looking for work. Who do I talk to?" One of the men regarded him with vague interest, then spat on the ground and called out "Boris!" before returning to work on the engine.

A barrel chested-man of average height wearing a grubby sleeveless undershirt with holes in it approached him. "What do you want?" he squinted at Daniel.

"I'm here to apply for the job," Daniel informed him, holding the ad out. The man took the ad, read it over quickly, and returned it to Daniel.

"We don't need a kid. Go home, Sonny..." the crew boss said dismissively, lighting a cigarette and screwing it expertly into the crook of his mouth, where it remained for the rest of the conversation.

"But, I'm a hard worker," Daniel said, folding the ad and putting it back into his pocket.

"You're a pipsqueak," Boris barked. "We need strong men for this kind of work, not pipsqueaks." Daniel couldn't help but notice the tattoos that covered the man's big arms. On his left bicep was a tattoo of Lana Turner, and on his right was a surprisingly life-like portrait of Dorothy Lamour.

"Please, I need the work," Daniel pleaded.

"Come back in a couple of years, kid." Boris said with finality, then turned and walked away. Despondent, Daniel turned to the two men working on the truck. They didn't seem to be making much headway getting the engine started.

"Mind if I have a go?" Daniel asked.

"Sure, kid. Let's see what you can do…" The men stepped aside and broke open warm bottles of beer while Daniel got down to work. Daniel worked on it for half an hour, while the men sat in the shade, smoking and drinking beer.

"How's it going, kid?" the taller one, Val, asked.

"Almost done," Daniel answered. "Your carburetor was clogged, so I cleaned it out and adjusted the fuel intake. Then I noticed the spark plugs were fouled, so I cleaned them and re-set the gap. But now you've got a bad spark plug cable. Do you happen to have a length of cable about this long?" Daniel held his hands about twenty centimeters apart. The men found a cable and Daniel quickly changed it out. "There. That should do it. Try starting it up."

The shorter man, Denis, got behind the wheel and turned the key. The engine started right up. "Thanks, kid," Val said, handing Daniel a warm bottle of beer. "How'd you do that?"

"My uncle taught me," Daniel said, turning around and walking back to his motorcycle. Boris reappeared and asked how they got the truck running.

"The kid fixed it," Denis said in amazement.

"The _kid_?" Boris rubbed his chin, thinking. "Well, don't just stand there – go hire him!"

Val and Denis welcomed the overjoyed Daniel to the crew and informed him that his duties would include driving a truck, feeding and taking care of the animals, mucking their stalls, pitching tents, and anything else that needed to be done.

Cirque d'Europa was owned and operated by the Baron Almasy de Siklos, a Hungarian aristocrat of dubious reputation who lost his family's fortune in the casinos of Monte Carlo and, finding himself penniless, promptly married the daughter of legendary Austrian circus impresario Julius Gleich in a disastrously unsuccessful bid to restore his position in European society. The marriage didn't end well, with his father-in-law arranging a hasty annulment and signing the small, debt-ridden *Cirque d' Europa* over to Siklos in exchange for promises that the destitute Baron would never try to contact or see his daughter ever again.

In reality, it was Monsieur Victor, the ringmaster, who ran the show. A life-long veteran of the European circus, Monsieur Victor was about 4 ½ feet tall, with a dark black bottle-brush mustache and think caterpillar eyebrows. His costume was a dented bowler hat and an ancient, threadbare tuxedo jacket stretched over his large, round belly. He always had a limp cigarette drooping from the corner of his mouth, uneven grey teeth, and smoke curling up into his squinty eyes.

The "star" performer of the circus was Ballantine the Conjuror, an escape artist who attempted Houdini-type escapes from locked trunks submerged in tanks of water, and the like. Ballantine considered himself the "star" of the circus, and did indeed receive top billing, but in reality he was a washed-up former star who could no longer find work in any of the larger circuses. Nonetheless, he still walked around with a jacket draped over his shoulders like an artist, a black fedora cocked low over one eye, a pair of pince-nez glasses on the end of his nose, and an ivory cigarette holder (a gift from Harry Houdini himself, he maintains) pressed between his lips, for good effect.

More often than not, the aging, although still dashing-looking Ballantine was unable to escape on his own, and, desperately running out of breath, had to be rescued by the clown with an axe. Noticing that these dramatic rescues seemed to satisfy and thrill the audience just as much as the rare escapes did, the ringmaster decided to make them part of the act, narrating the dangers dramatically and whipping the crowd into a frenzy as the axe-wielding clown brought the rescue to its exciting climax.

"He couldn't fight his way out of a cracker-box," another performer once complained to Monsieur Victor. "Why don't you just fire him and hire someone else?"

"No-no," the ringmaster shook his head emphatically. "He's too good-looking to fire. The crowds <u>love</u> him."

Another performer, Madame Durand, induced an alligator named Horatio to yawn by reading him Proust while tickling his nose with a feather and feeding him Spanish almonds. According to Madame Durand, the Proust was just for show. The real key to the act was the Spanish almonds, which included an ingredient that reduced the flow of oxygen to the reptile's brain and therefore rendered him sleepy. At any rate, when he yawned she stuck her head inside his mouth, which never failed to elicit a gasp of alarm from the audience. Although Madame Durand had become very quick at extricating her head when Horatio suddenly felt like closing his mouth, it should be noted, somewhat gruesomely, that Madame Durand was, in fact, missing a large part of her left ear.

The high-wire act was a blind Jewish performer named Monsieur Nikolai, who, wearing dark glasses to underscore his visual disability, rescued several kittens stranded in baskets along the high wire, by collecting them all in a wheelbarrow which he pushed from one end to the other. This act, of course, was extremely popular with children. Monsieur Nikolai's other act was riding a bicycle along the tightrope while playing *La Marseillaise* on the violin, followed by a Capuchin monkey dressed in a miniature Napoleon Bonaparte uniform and hat, riding a tiny bicycle and playing a toy drum hanging from a rope around his neck. During down-time, this monkey, who had become addicted to cigarettes, infuriated the circus crew by crawling into the cabs of their trucks and pilfering their smoking material while they were working. He also liked to sit around with the men and smoke and spit and scratch himself and play cards at night. He often won.

The circus also owned an elephant named Socrates who did tricks like standing on a pedestal, rolling a barrel with a clown in it around the arena, and spraying water out of his trunk at a clown orchestra whenever they hit a sour note while performing popular selections from French composers.

The equestrian trick rider, Fernando the Magnificent, stood on the backs of two side-by-side trotting horses and did things like jump through hoops while drinking a cup of tea (without spilling a drop), juggling burning flares, playing a trombone, cooking an omelette, painting a landscape, or shaving with a straight razor.

The Strong Man was an intimidating giant named Lars Johannsen, known to the circus-going public as the "Helsinki Hercules." In reality, Lars was Swedish, not Finnish, but Monsieur Victor couldn't think of a good name to go with "Stockholm." His act consisted of lifting four clowns sitting side by side on a railroad tie, and then using the apparatus to fend off a pride of snarling tigers and save another clown dressed up as a damsel in distress.

Tivo, the head clown, was an alcoholic who suffered from depression and acute Tourette's syndrome, and the ringmaster was continually trying to keep him away from drink. Whenever Monsieur Victor's efforts failed (which was sadly too often), Tivo would get hammered and attempt suicide in various exotic ways.

There was a one-armed lion tamer named Monsieur Laurent, and a narcoleptic lion named Hector who sometimes felt the need to lie down and take a nap in the middle of the show. Ulysses the bear, wearing a tall wizard's hat, walked on a giant ball for up to five minutes at a time without falling off. A family of tightrope-walking geese kept the kids in stitches while clowns with long poles tried in vain to knock them off.

Of course, one of the highlights of the show was Madame Olga and Her Magnificent Trained Seals. In one of their most popular acts, the seals dressed in tuxedos and played instruments like an orchestra, with Madame Olga somberly conducting them. In another, the seals, in costume, re-enacted famous paintings by Degas and Delacourt, historical battle scenes such as Waterloo, or pivotal scenes from Shakespeare's "Hamlet" and "Macbeth." The crowd, especially the young ones, were never disappointed when Madame Olga and her talented seals hit the ring.

The trapeze act was called "Constantine and Emily," and it was well-known that the two partners were also lovers. Emily was petite and beautiful, and never failed to get the crowd's pulse going as she performed death-defying aerial feats while a pack of hungry tigers prowled in the ring below. Constantine did not get drafted into the French Army because he was born in Switzerland, a neutral country. Although he sympathized with the French, he used his Swiss citizenship as a cover – first with the French, and then with the Germans.

As it turned out, the circus had few difficulties operating during the early days of the occupation. The Germans liked circuses, and on most nights the audience was dotted with a few dozen grey uniforms. The German area commander, Colonel Fischer, was a huge fan, and even signed travel permits and authorized extra petrol rations for the circus trucks. Colonel Fischer's attitude seemed to be that if the population were allowed some kind of innocent diversion, such as a circus, they would be more likely to cooperate with the German occupiers. "Circuses are not political or subversive. Let them have their circuses!" he happily declared to his staff.

In fact, once the upheaval of the invasion and the exodus of refugees died down, people began to realize that the Germans weren't coming to rape, pillage, and destroy, as first thought. As long as the French authorities kept order, the Germans proved to be very hands-off – no atrocities, no suppression, no trying to change the French way of life. "As long as you can guarantee the safety and security of our troops, your citizens will be able to go about their daily lives with little disruption from us," Colonel Fischer assured the Lord Mayor of St.-Julien.

The worst thing to contend with was the rationing of food. Rumors were starting to circulate of mass starvation in Paris and the other cities, and even here in the countryside people were starting to feel the pinch. Each person was allotted 350 grams of bread per day, 50 grams of cheese, 60 grams of lentils, and, upon availability, 300 grams of meat per week. But meat was seldom available except for those willing to pay high prices in the black market. Most of the meat, eggs, and butter were going to feed the Germans.

Daniel proved quite handy, supplementing this meager diet by fishing for trout in the local streams very early in the morning, to avoid being charged with poaching. He brought home baskets of fresh trout, and sometimes even a rabbit or two, to cook up for himself and his circus co-workers. This led to Daniel's quick acceptance into the circus community. And Constantine, the trapeze artist, turned out to be very well-connected with the black market, supplying chocolate, whiskey, cognac, eggs, sausages, and Italian and American cigarettes to the circus workers. All of this made life in the circus, at least, more bearable than in the general population, and, despite the hard work, Daniel thrived. He was completely enraptured by circus life and all of his interesting new friends. Motorcycle racing aside, he was sure he had found what he wanted to do – at least for now.

As he settled into circus life, he realized he had to write to his uncle and let him know he was all right. First, he wrote a letter saying he had procured the apprenticeship with Monsieur Le Grun, but had second thoughts about lying to Emile and didn't mail it. He wrote another letter, explaining the truth, trying to convince his uncle that things had turned out even better than the apprenticeship would have been. This way, he reasoned, he could earn his own money to pay the racing fees and jump-start his own racing career without having to endure a long apprenticeship with no pay.

In the meantime, Daniel enjoyed his labors, driving, keeping the trucks running properly, and making friends with the animals as he fed them and cleaned out their cages. The seals were a delight, always clowning around with him, stealing the hat off his head and nuzzling into his pockets with their wet noses. Horatio the alligator liked to sleep all day in his dark cage, but perked up a bit when Daniel entered to feed him and rub him behind the ears. The tightrope-walking geese always squawked loudly and chased him around their cage when he came to clean it. Socrates the elephant never failed to squirt him with water from his trunk, as if he thought Daniel needed a bit of cooling off. Even Hector, the narcoleptic lion, was less grumpy when he saw Daniel approaching his cage with his huge raw steak.

One night after the show, the crew were unwinding around a campfire, smoking, drinking beer, and playing cards. It was a lovely night, and the stars were shining brightly in the black sky. Daniel felt very happy, living this charmed life, with so many new friends, accepted and liked by everyone. *How idyllic*, he thought to himself, feeling the warm glow of the fire and watching Monsieur Nikolai's monkey, Napoleon, carefully consider his hand of cards. He had them fanned out in front of him, just like he'd seen the men do, and was extremely careful not to let any of them show.

Lars, the strong man, was there too, thinking he had a good hand but trying not to let it show on his face. Val and Denis folded their hands, shaking their heads in disgust. The monkey kept his cards close to his chest. Lars peered around the circle, trying to decide whether to hold or fold, as the others had done.

"Come on, what are you going to do?" Val demanded impatiently.

"I'm staying in," Lars finally declared, laying his cards down face up. "A straight."

The monkey laid his cards down. "Look at that! A full house!" Denis exclaimed.

"He cheated again!" Lars thundered, reaching out to grab the hapless monkey. Quick as lightning, Napoleon grabbed the money in the pot and darted just out of the strong man's reach. Lars flailed around, trying to grab the dancing primate, but Napoleon absconded with the poker money <u>and</u> Lars' pack of cigarettes.

"I'm going to crush that damned monkey!" The Helsinki Hercules raged, while the others laughed. "I'm going to skin him alive and feed him to the tigers!"

"Calm down," Val advised, handing him a bottle of cognac. "Take a drink of this, and you'll forget all about the monkey."

"The Great Helsinki Hercules – undone by a monkey!" Denis teased, then stopped abruptly when Lars shot him a dirty look. "All right, my friend, it's only a joke. You're just upset you can't go back to Sweden, then everyone will know you're not really from Helsinki."

"Of course, you could go back to Helsinki, but you'll have the same trouble there," Val said, referring to the recent Soviet invasion and occupation of Finland.

"You might as well stay here, my friend," Denis suggested. "The Germans are much nicer than the Russians."

Daniel knew what was coming next: a heated argument about the Germans and the occupation. He knew the crew was split on the occupation, which invariably led to a lively discussion of current events. He wasn't disappointed.

"Petain has everything under control," Denis assured everyone. "The Nazis will be back in Germany in no time."

"Petain has to ask permission from the Germans before taking a piss in the morning!" Val said, trying to get a rise out of Denis.

"And where is De Gaulle, the savior of France?" Denis sniffed, spitting on the ground. "Leading the Resistance from the safety of his flat in London! While Petain is here, in France, standing between his people and the Germans!"

"The Germans pull Petain's strings, and he dances," Val scoffed, working invisible puppet strings. "De Gaulle is the one who will stand up to them!"

"*When*? There are no Germans in England. He should have stayed here if he wants to fight them. At least Petain didn't run away and leave his people on their own!"

Val stood up suddenly. "Take it back!"

"De Gaulle is nothing but a coward!"

"I said take it back!"

Denis stood up and faced him. "Make me!"

The two men grabbed each other and started wrestling each other to the ground. In a moment, they were down in the dirt, ineffectually kicking and hitting at one another, with no one actually getting hurt. Lars picked them both up off the ground and separated them, holding one in each hand.

"Boys, stop this now," he said, shaking them like rag dolls. "You don't want to fight."

"He insulted De Gaulle!" Val shouted, dangling from the Helsinki Hercules' arm like a fish. "He's not a patriot!"

"Not a patriot?" Denis protested. "I love France! Vive La France!"

"Vive La France!" Val shouted, even louder.

"All right, then. You both love France," Lars said, putting them down. "There's an end to it."

"Very well, but I'm not shaking his hand!" Denis vowed.

"And I'm not shaking _his_ hand!" Val declared, pointing an accusatory finger at Denis. They both dusted themselves off and sat down again around the fire.

Feeling the need to change the subject, Daniel blurted out the first thing that came into his head. "Why does Boris have Lana Turner _and_ Dorothy Lamour tattooed on his arms?"

"He can't decide which one he likes better," Val said, and they all laughed. The ice was broken.

"Some nights he likes the blonde, and some nights he's in the mood for a brunette," Denis added mirthfully.

"_Oui_, he's a real ladies' man, in his grubby undershirt and five o'clock shadow," Val continued. "You know, he's also got a tattoo of a belly dancer on his back."

"Really?" Daniel asked.

"Truly. Ask him to show you sometime."

It sounded like a set-up. Daniel gave him a skeptical look.

"No, truly. When he's had a few drinks, he takes off his shirt and flexes his shoulder blades. It makes it look like she's dancing."

"I don't believe you."

"We will get him drunk sometime, and show you," Denis pledged.

As the contented men sat around the fire smoking cigarettes and drinking more cognac, the conversation turned to Daniel. The men, who liked Daniel immensely and considered him one of them, wanted to know more about him.

"Why the circus, Daniel?" Val inquired. "What are you running away from?"

"I'm not running away," Daniel replied, surprised.

"Everyone who joins the circus is running away from something."

Daniel told them about his dream of becoming a motorcycle racer, and how he needed money to enter the races.

"So, you race that old rustbucket?" Denis asked. Daniel felt offended. "Ever win a race?"

"Not yet," Daniel answered. "But I'm not giving up until I do."

It was time to turn in, so Lars went back to his trailer and the crew retired to the cramped tent they shared. Daniel fell fast asleep and didn't wake up until early in the morning, when he heard the sound of hammering outside. He got dressed and went outside to see what the commotion was about. A few meters from the tent, Val and Denis were building what looked like a curved wall out of scrap lumber that had been discarded in a nearby farmer's field.

"What is this?" Daniel asked, still sleepy.

"A motordrome," Val answered cheerfully. "Or, we could call it The Wall of Death, like they do in America."

"What is it for?"

"For your motorcycle," Val answered, and went back to work. "Are you going to help, or not?"

As they worked, Daniel could see the motordrome taking shape. It began to look like a very large wooden bowl with sloping sides, and a hinged door which opened and closed flush with the planks. About noon, it was finished.

"A little rough, but it'll do," Val said, examining their work and nodding in approval. "Go get your motorcycle."

"You want me to ride inside that thing?" Daniel asked incredulously.

"Why not? It's all the rage in America."

"I'll kill myself!"

"You want to be a motorcycle racer, don't you?" Val asked rhetorically. "Well, you'll earn more money as a *performer* in this circus, instead of on the crew. Now go get your cycle…"

Daniel did so.

"Now, you just start riding around the bottom," Val explained. "As you gain speed, you'll climb up the side."

"It's not possible," Daniel objected. "It's too steep."

"I've seen it done in newsreels," Val explained. "Centrifical force keeps you up – as long as you keep moving, that is."

Daniel shrugged his shoulders, fired up his cycle, and lowered his goggles over his eyes.

"Just keep going, around and around," Val instructed.

Daniel rode his bike into the drome, Val closing and latching the curved door behind him. It took Daniel the whole afternoon to get the feel of it. Before long, he was strangely comfortable riding nearly vertically in such a tight circle. Climbing the wall was easy, but coming back down proved more difficult. He had to de-accelerate at a very slow rate in order to stay on the sloping track, until he was finally back on solid ground.

He pulled his cycle out of the drome and shut it off. He climbed off on somewhat shaky legs and tried to look straight at Val, but there seemed to be two of him. "I'm dizzy," Daniel groaned.

"It's all right, you'll get used to it," Val assured him. Daniel suddenly pitched to his knees and vomited on the grass. "Feel better now?" Val asked.

"A little."

"Good. Wait right here."

"Where are you going?"

"To get Monsieur Victor."

Daniel sat down on the grass and waited. As he waited, his skepticism about the motordrome faded into excitement. He realized he had actually enjoyed the sensation – it was a strangely weightless feeling, something like flying. Soon, Val was back with Monsieur Victor, the diminutive ringmaster. Denis, Lars, Monsieur Nikolai, and a few other performers were there as well.

"Well, show them, Daniel!" Val exclaimed.

Daniel fired up his cycle and did a hundred or so laps in the motordrome. When he was finished, the crowd had a stunned look on their faces.

"What *is* this?" Monsieur Victor wanted to know.

"Your next attraction," Val informed him.

"But what is it?" the ringmaster asked again, puzzled.

"It's 'The Wall of Death,'" Val replied enthusiastically. "It's defying gravity, defying *death* itself."

"But, will people want to see this?" Monsieur Victor asked.

Val, Denis and Lars went to round up more performers and crew members. When they had a good-sized crowd gathered, Daniel executed his third ride around the inside of the drome. It was his best ride so far – he was really getting the hang of it now. When he was finished, the crowd applauded loudly, gathering around him and his motorcycle as if he were a celebrity.

Monsieur Victor had a big smile on his face. "We will add it to the show tomorrow!"

And so, Daniel joined the ranks of the circus performers – with a catch. Monsieur Victor insisted on him continuing his duties on the crew as well as performing in the motordrome, with only a ten-percent raise in salary for his trouble. "We will see how this goes before I commit to any further changes in your status," he sternly told Daniel. Daniel, for his part, accepted the deal with innocent enthusiasm; after all, he was going to be a true *performer* now, well-paid or not.

The next morning, Daniel helped Val, Denis, and the rest of the crew construct a platform next to the motordrome so the spectators would have a better view of Daniel as he rode. A sign was made announcing "The Terrible Wall of Death" in chilling red letters, under which appeared the words "See our own daredevil rider defy gravity and laugh in the very face of Death," with a caricature of a disappointed Grim Reaper holding a drooping, bloodstained scythe. Daniel's name was nowhere to be seen, but he didn't care at all. All that mattered was that he was going to ride his motorcycle before a crowd of awestruck onlookers. He was in show business!

Daniel was the first performer of the day. The plan was to warm up the crowd with his motordrome antics, then usher them into the Big Top tent for the main attraction – the tightrope, trapeze and animal acts. The first day, everything worked according to plan: the drome was an exciting introduction to the festivities, slowly building to the more daring and lavish established acts inside the big tent.

The second day, the crowd for the motordrome was too big to fit on the platform – they piled onto it and hung off the edges like ants, little children hoisted up onto their fathers' shoulders in order to get a glimpse of the rider. The crowd was so large and boisterous that Daniel, becoming more comfortable with each lap, began trying out little tricks while he rode. First, he tried standing up as he went around and around. The crowd cheered. Then, he lifted one foot and put it on the seat. The crowd roared. Finally, he raised his left hand and waved at the spectators as he flew by. The crowd went wild.

He was a hit.

After his performance, the crowd funneled into the Big Top absolutely buzzing with energy and excitement, eager to see more thrills during the main event. Monsieur Victor had a huge smile pasted across his face. "More tricks, young man – more tricks! That's the ticket!" Daniel obliged by standing upright with both feet on the motorcycle seat during his next performance. The audiences were eating it up.

The next day, Daniel's name was added to the sign, and, due to his newfound popularity with the audiences, his duties as a crew member were drastically curtailed. In addition, the camp seamstress made a dashing, colorful new costume for him. And, oh yes, Monsieur Victor raised his salary another ten-percent.

***

"The Wall of Death" being a great success, Daniel began to reap the benefits of being one of the circus's most talked about new performers. He was now welcome to socialize with the higher-end acts, to rub elbows with some of the "stars" of the show. Madame Durand had him for tea. Fernando the Magnificent sought him out to "talk motorcycles," but didn't know much about them so they ended up talking about horses, of which Ferdinand indeed knew a great deal. Madame Olga invited him into her trailer for a cigar and a shot of vodka, and asked him if he thought it would be possible, indeed advisable, for him to teach one of her star seals how to ride a motorcycle. Daniel answered that while he thought it would be a challenge, it could possibly turn out to be a worthwhile endeavor and would certainly like to give it a go. Monsieur Nikolai, the blind tightrope walker, Monsieur Laurent, the one-armed lion tamer, and the trapeze artists Constantine and Emily always gave him a broad smile and exchanged pleasantries with him whenever they passed.

The only performer who continued to snub him was Ballantine the Conjuror, who would walk right by him wrapped in his cape and low-slung fedora without in the slightest way acknowledging his presence.

Of all the performers, it was Emily the trapeze artist who caught Daniel's eye the most. She was older than him, but delicate and childlike – she had to be in order to perform some of the amazing aerial feats that she accomplished with a graceful, swan-like ease on a daily basis. A former ballet dancer and artist's model, Emily carried herself with an enigmatic elegance and dignity, never

123

seeming to have to force the innate charm which radiated from her to whoever she came in contact with. But Daniel knew she was Constantine's girl. Constantine was a tall, athletic young man with blond hair and sea-green eyes, and he was an unmistakable leader among the little troupe of circus performers. Whenever Constantine talked to Daniel, however, he seemed genuinely interested in the boy – especially the motorcycle and Daniel's intuitive skill in operating it. Daniel felt both Constantine and Emily reaching out to him, and over time, the three became fast friends.

So it didn't come as much of a surprise when Constantine came to him one day and asked him for a favor. "Would you take Emily on a picnic?"

"A picnic?"

"*Oui*. You see, she simply adores picnics. I'm far too busy refining the act, and to be honest, I'm not much for picnics myself. The fact is, she's going to go on her own, and I'd like to have somebody responsible there to keep her company and look after her. It needs to be somebody I can trust with her, and I'm afraid you're it, *mon ami*."

"But, I've never really been on a proper picnic, you know, with a *girl*..."

"There's nothing to it," Constantine assured him. "You just sit under a tree and eat. That's all. And talk. And oh, by the way, she'll probably want to picnic two or three times a week. Whenever it strikes her fancy. You know women, right? I really would appreciate it if you would, you know, take good care of her for me."

Daniel, of course, readily agreed, little knowing how greatly his life was about to change.

Chapter 8

The next day, Daniel and Emily struck out for a mid-day picnic in the countryside outside the village. He tied the picnic basket to the back of his motorcycle and instructed Emily how to sit as a passenger on the seat behind him – she'd never been on a motorcycle before, and she was a little apprehensive.

"Just keep your feet up on the pegs, and let me do the rest," he told her, and then they were off. Daniel had never felt the touch of a woman like this – outside of his mother – and the sensation of having her arms wrapped around his torso as they rode sent a kind of novel – if entirely innocent – thrill through his young body.

When they were in the countryside, Emily seemed to be quite particular about the exact spot for the picnic. Daniel stopped twice at spots he thought would have been ideal for a picnic – beside a babbling brook, in a wildflower-covered meadow – but Emily vetoed both places.

Finally, they reached a grassy, gently sloping hillside off the road, and he felt her arms suddenly squeeze him tight. "This is it!" she said. Relieved, Daniel pulled the cycle off the road and parked it in the shade underneath a spreading oak tree. She spread a blanket on the ground while Daniel untied the basket.

"Yes, this is a lovely spot," she said, gathering her skirt and sitting on the blanket. "When Constantine told me you would be coming with me, I was so pleased. He doesn't fancy picnics much, and I so dislike picnicking on my own."

"It isn't safe, a girl picnicking alone," Daniel ventured, not exactly sure what to say. "You know, with the Germans and all…"

"Oh, the Germans haven't bothered me," she smiled. "Leave them alone, they leave us alone. Are you hungry?"

"Yes, I could eat something."

Emily reached into the basket and pulled out cheese, bread, plump sausages, and a bottle of wine. "Bon appetite," she smiled. Hearing the whine of a truck engine, Daniel looked down at the road and saw a German Army truck grind slowly by. It continued down the road a bit, and then turned into an arched gateway and drove up a long gravel driveway. Emily didn't seem to notice the truck as she passed him a piece of bread with cheese on it and poured two glasses of wine.

"Well, how do you like the circus?" she asked him pleasantly, biting into a baguette hungrily.

"I love it," Daniel admitted. "I've never seen anything like it."

"From a small town, are you?"

"Very small. Virtually unknown, in fact."

"So, how is it a nice young boy like you ended up in the circus?"

Daniel blushed. "I left home for an apprenticeship with a professional motorcycle racer in Neufchateau, but that fell through. So I joined the circus to earn enough money to pay the racing fees. You see, I want to be a professional motorcycle racer, as well, just like Monsieur Le Grun."

"Monsieur Le Grun?"

"Yes, he came to my village with a flat tire, then he gave me his card. But then he was sent to Germany as a worker, but it wasn't the Germans who sent him, it was our own government. Madame Le Grun, who has a small baby, said the government is collaborating with the enemy."

"I see," Emily said. "How sad."

Another German truck passed by on the road, and turned into the same driveway. Daniel absent-mindedly watched it travel up the driveway and saw that it was full of soldiers. Then he noticed, at the very end of the long gravel driveway, the trucks were pulling up in front of a large estate.

"And your parents? They're all right with you being away from home, travelling all over the country with a circus?"

"My parents died in an accident. They were hit by a car while crossing a street in Strasbourg. I was raised by my uncle in *Nulle*. He's a bicycle repairman. He gave me the motorcycle."

"Where did he get it?"

Daniel told her the story Emile had told him, word for word. He had committed it to his memory long ago. Emily listened, enraptured. When he was finished, she said "That's the saddest story I've ever heard!"

"Sad?"

"*Oui*, the Italian motorcycle champion doesn't get the beautiful girl, just her portrait. And he loses his wonderful motorcycle. And the artist eventually loses the beautiful girl, and gives the wonderful motorcycle away because it reminds him of her. Nobody keeps what they love. Sad."

"I suppose it is," Daniel admitted.

"It's also a beautiful story. But is it really true?"

"I've thought about that a lot over the years," Daniel replied pensively. "I've decided it doesn't matter if it's true or not. It just *is*."

They had finished eating, and Emily poured two more glasses of wine. They were quiet a while, and then she said, "My parents died, too."

She told Daniel that her parents had been extremely wealthy from the Persian rug import business, and when they died she was sent to live with distant relatives who took all her inheritance money and sent her to live in a convent. They were not especially religious people; they just didn't want her around. As a consequence, she was abandoned and raised entirely by nuns. Fortunately, she was loved and treated very well, and still considered the nuns her only real family. When she left the convent, her relatives told her they wanted nothing to do with her. They had squandered all of her inheritance money, so, penniless and alone, she ended up in Paris, where she worked as an actress and an artist's model.

She barely scraped by until a very rich but disturbed young man whose name she swore to never utter again saw her in a tawdry stage production supposedly based on a non-existent Victor Hugo novel. The very rich young man soon became violently obsessed with her, forcing her to cut her hair and dye it a different color and dress in particular clothing until he got her just the way he wanted her. She felt like a lifeless doll, like her own personality had been completely wiped away, but he worshipped her and gave her anything she wanted as long as she looked the way he wanted her to look.

Finally, he insisted she become a world famous ballerina, and paid for her tuition at a prestigious ballet school in Paris. She told him she didn't want to be a ballerina, but he insisted. She was actually quite an accomplished dancer, and her instructors had high hopes of her someday becoming a prima ballerina. But miserable and feeling suffocated, she couldn't bear it any longer and plotted her escape for weeks. After painstakingly inventing thirty-three different escape plans, she threw them all away and finally worked up the nerve to quietly slip away one night after a grueling twelve-hour ballet class.

She went straight to a hotel and cut her hair and dyed it a different color. She put on completely different clothes and wore dark glasses, like Mata Hari. She spent hours fiddling with her disguise until she was absolutely sure there was no way the very rich young man would recognize her. Then she boarded a train leaving Paris from Gare du Sud and met Constantine, who was also running away. In his case, it was from his domineering Swiss father, who insisted he become a taxidermist and take over the family business or he would be disavowed and cut out of the father's will. For years, Constantine had acquiesced to his father's desire, but just couldn't go through with it due to an aversion – a fear, even – of working with dead animals. It had been since childhood, when his father refused to let him have a household pet, instead forcing the young boy to grow up in a dark, spooky house full of taxidermied raccoons, lemurs, and Madagascar brown-throated sloths.

She asked him where he was going. He said he didn't know. She said *she* didn't know, either. He said, "We should start a trapeze act and join the circus." Neither one had trapeze experience, but she agreed because the man she was running from had a deep-seated fear of circuses and would never think to look for her there.

"So we went to Casablanca and worked up an act," she said, sipping wine. "And we've been together ever since. By the way, how many soldiers do you reckon fit in a truck like that?"

"What?" Daniel said, still reeling from her life's story.

"The German trucks. How many soldiers do you think they hold?"

Daniel's attention was directed to another German truck turning into the large estate's arched gateway. "Oh, I don't know…maybe twenty…"

"I'd say thirty," Emily said flatly, not taking her eyes off the truck.

"What do you suppose that place is?" Daniel asked.

"Oh, I'd say it was a German Army post of some sort," Emily answered, watching the truck travel up the long gravel driveway. "But who can be certain?"

"Well, there sure are a lot of Germans going in there," Daniel observed.

"Indeed," Emily said distractedly, sipping more wine. Daniel could almost see her mentally doing the math: *three trucks, at thirty soldiers per truck...*

"We've got to go now," she said abruptly. "Come on, finish your wine. I've got an errand to run on the way back..."

They packed up the picnic things and headed back to where the circus was camped. Emily was very quiet the whole way. "Go into this village up ahead," she ordered him curtly as they approached a small collection of shops and cottages. "Stop in front of the blue house with white gables. Wait for me outside. I'll only be a few moments. If anyone asks any questions, just tell them we stopped for some eggs."

"*Eggs?*"

"Please just do what I say..." she said, hopping off the bike and disappearing into the blue house with white gables. She was inside for several minutes. Through the front window, Daniel thought he saw a man push the curtain aside with his hand and take a good look at him. Then the man was gone, and Emily emerged from the house and hopped on the back of the motorcycle. "Let's go home," she said, a little more relaxed now.

When they got back to the circus, there was a great commotion at the tigers' cage. Everyone was crowded around the cage, a buzz of nervous talk and anxiety. Daniel and Emily got off the cycle and pushed their way to the front, where Monsieur Victor and Constantine were standing. Tivo the clown, clutching a bottle in one hand and Napoleon the monkey in the other, sat precariously atop the wall, his legs dangling over the edge of the open-topped cage. Below him, two anxious tigers paced back and forth on the cage floor.

"Tivo's latest suicide attempt," Constantine explained calmly, but Monsieur Victor looked worried and upset.

"I can't afford to lose another clown!" he moaned, shaking his head in anguish.

"He's traumatizing my cats!" Monsieur Pettibone, the animal wrangler, shouted. "What are you going to do about it?"

"Everyone just stay calm," the ringmaster advised, although he himself looked like he was about to panic. "Tivo, please…the audience will be coming soon!"

"They all laugh at me, every night," Tivo shouted drunkenly, almost losing his balance. "Especially the children!"

"You're a clown!" someone shouted up at him. "What do you expect?"

"I want to be respected! I want to be taken seriously!" Tivo lamented.

Constantine turned to Daniel. "He's a clown with a complex about being laughed at, poor soul…"

"Tivo, please come down so we can discuss this rationally!" the ringmaster pleaded.

"No, this is it. I'm going to do it this time. And I'm taking the monkey with me!"

"Not Napoleon!" Monsieur Nikolai, the blind tightrope walker, cried. "He's half of my act!"

"If anything happens to that monkey, I'll kill you again!" the Helsinki Hercules threatened.

Constantine was holding a piece of paper. "He left this suicide note: *'Hitler has been spreading nasty rumors about me again. I saw him and Groucho Marx giggling at me from the stands last night. Mussolini is in on the conspiracy, too. He sent me a dozen red roses with a card that read "Last week in Buenos Aries was very special for me." I can't take the ridicule anymore. This is definitely it. I'm not kidding. I know you don't believe me, but I'm* really *serious this time. Give my underwear to Boris. Goodbye.'*"

"Don't do this, Tivo!" Monsieur Victor entreated. "You've got too much to live for! You spread so much joy! And, it's almost show time!"

"Goodbye, all!" Tivo cried. "You should have appreciated me more!" Then, still clutching Monsieur Nikolai's monkey, he launched himself over the edge and down into the tiger cage. The crowd gasped in horror.

"Somebody <u>do</u> something!" Madame Durand shouted in alarm.

With a roar, the surprised tigers pounced on the inebriated clown at once. Napoleon worked himself free from the melee and clambered back up the side of the cage to safety. Tivo screamed and flailed beneath the powerful cats, but his cries soon turned to uncontrollable laughter. Instead of tearing him apart, the cats were standing on his chest and licking his face affectionately!

"Ow! That tickles!" Tivo called out, trying to fight them off. "Come on! Get off me!"

"Pussycats!" Lars laughed, shaking his head. Napoleon leapt into his arms and gave him a big kiss on the mouth, then jumped out of reach before Lars could grab him. "Disgusting creature!" Lars grimaced, wiping his mouth with the back of his hand.

Monsieur Pettibone distracted his cats with a feather on a string attached to the end of a stick, while Val and Denis quickly dragged the depressed clown from the cage. Monsieur Victor forced Tivo to drink a pot of strong black coffee, and, to everyone's amazement, he gave one of his best performances ever.

***

On their next picnic, Emily chose an idyllic spot in a shady grove of sycamore trees near the village railway station. They ate and talked and drank wine, but Daniel sensed something was off. Emily seemed unusually distracted. She kept looking at the railway station expectantly, as if waiting for something to happen. When a train finally chugged into the station, she sat up rigidly and watched the passengers disembark one by one, until the train cars were empty. Then the train pulled out of the station, and she relaxed.

About forty-five minutes later, they heard the whistle of another train approaching, and Emily stiffened again. As the train pulled into the station, they could tell it was different: this engine was adorned with bright red and black swastika flags. There were three passenger cars filled to the brim with gray-uniformed soldiers – no civilian passengers at all.

"Looks like a Nazi troop train," Emily said to herself, but loud enough for Daniel to hear.

Two German soldiers and an officer disembarked and began a thorough inspection of the station, while the others stayed on the train. Then the officer looked around and spotted them sitting in the grove of trees. He motioned for the two soldiers to approach them, and Emily went white as a ghost. "No, no…" she gasped. "Quick, kiss me!"

"What!?" Daniel gulped.

131

The soldiers approached. "Kiss me, now!" She grabbed Daniel and threw his arms around her. Then she leaned into him, closed her eyes, and put her lips against his.

Daniel didn't struggle.

Lips still locked, she opened one eye and glanced in the direction of the soldiers. "They're still coming," she whispered. "Kiss me, and don't stop!" Hearing the urgency in her voice, Daniel complied with the request. He kept his lips glued to hers and didn't flinch, wondering *How am I supposed to breathe?*

The two soldiers stopped a few meters away, close enough to see what was going on. They kept kissing with their eyes closed, pretending to be caught up in the moment, oblivious to the soldiers' presence. A minute ticked by. *How long are they going to stand there?* thought Emily. Then one soldier broke into a huge grin and nudged the other one with his elbow. They said something to each other in German and laughed.

And then they walked away! Back to the station, where the officer was waiting. Out of the corner of his eye, Daniel could see the soldiers explaining something to the officer, who laughed and shook his head. *Ah, young love…*

Emily finally broke the kiss. "Tres bien," she said, relieved. "Very good." Daniel looked stunned. "Now, I want you to do exactly as I say. I'm going to lay back on the blanket, and I want you to put your hand on my thigh, like this. Then I want you to stroke my hair with your other hand, and look at me like you're mad in love and you're reciting poetry to me. Do you think you can do that?"

"Oui," Daniel croaked. He put his hand tentatively on her thigh.

"No, no. Higher, like this –" she reached down and guided his hand in place. "We're in love, now make it look *good*!"

Daniel stroked her hair and tried to look like Valentino from the movies.

"Softer – I'm a woman, not a goat!"

"Sorry, I've never done this before." Daniel lightened his touch.

"That's better. Are they still watching?"

Daniel glanced over at the station. "Oui. They're looking over here from time to time."

"That's what I thought. Are the other soldiers disembarking yet?"

"*Oui.*"

"Bien. Now listen very carefully. I want you to count how many soldiers get off that train, and I need an exact count, so be careful. And don't let them see you counting."

"Why?"

"Don't ask questions, Daniel. Just do as I say…"

Daniel counted – ten, twenty, thirty, forty, fifty… "Sixty soldiers," he said, after the last one got off.

"Are you sure?"

"Oui, I'm sure."

A car arrived at the station and the officer got in. They could hear him barking some orders in German, and then the car drove off. The soldiers formed into columns and left the station, marching into the village. When the soldiers were gone, the train pulled away and blew its whistle. The station was quiet again.

Emily sat up and smoothed her hair, blouse and skirt. "Well done," she said, as if nothing had happened. "Was that really your first kiss?"

"Oui." Daniel blushed.

"Well, I hope it'll be a memorable one. Now let's go, I've got another errand to run."

They packed up the picnic gear and rode the motorcycle into the village – back to the blue house with the white gables. "Wait here," Emily ordered, and got off the cycle. She walked to the door and knocked three times. The bearded man he saw in the window the last time answered and let her in. He looked up and down the street carefully, then closed the door without acknowledging Daniel.

Daniel didn't quite know what he was involved in, but he was beginning to realize it must be something serious.

***

The following week, the circus packed everything up and moved to another village – but the "picnics" continued as before. And Daniel soon discovered that the picnics would always be followed by one of Emily's "errands." She seemed to have a curious amount of things to drop off and pick up from various shops and houses – and she was always secretive about it.

"Is it circus business, then? These errands?" he finally asked her.

"Better not to ask so many questions, my little man," she teased.

"I'm not little," he bristled. "I'm fifteen."

"I'm sorry, Daniel. I didn't mean to…"

"Who are the men – you know, the men in the houses?"

She puts her fingers to his lips. "SShhhh. You really shouldn't ask such things…" Then she kissed him with a long, moist, warm kiss, as if attempting to erase the question from his mind.

Truth be told, perhaps he really didn't want to know the truth. If she had suddenly stopped taking him on her "picnics" and "errands," he would have been crushed. To be honest, he looked forward to every moment spent with her. He knew he was falling in love.

One day she insisted on picnicking near a particular farmhouse a few kilometers outside the village. "Why here?" he asked. He was asserting himself more now, asking more questions, pushing back a little.

"I just like this spot," was all she said, and smiled that smile. While they were eating, a German patrol stopped near the farmhouse for lunch. Emily looked concerned. "I've got to get in that house. Chase me around this tree."

By now, Daniel no longer expected things to make sense, so he got up and chased her around the tree. After a couple of times around, she twisted her ankle and fell to the ground in pain. Horrified, Daniel knelt beside her. "Oh, Emily – I'm so sorry…"

"it's all right, Daniel. I'm fine. This is how we're going to get past that patrol and into that house."

Daniel looked puzzled.

"Just pick me up and carry me to the house…trust me…"

Daniel did as he was told. They walked right by the Germans, who didn't bat an eye. At the farmhouse door, the farmer answered. He recognized Emily, but hesitated, glancing nervously at the soldiers nearby.

"My girlfriend twisted her ankle," Daniel told the farmer.

The farmer looked at Daniel, then at Emily, then at the soldiers. "Bring her inside. I'll fix her up." Daniel carried Emily inside the house. The soldiers didn't even bat an eye.

"Put her on the kitchen table," the farmer said, rummaging through a cabinet for a roll of bandages. He brought it to the table and asked, "Which ankle?"

"The left," Emily answered. The farmer began slowly wrapping her left ankle. "We are expecting German reinforcements," Emily said quietly.

"*Oui*," the farmer said, continuing to wrap her ankle carefully. "A German officer came yesterday to buy my cows. I told him it was impossible, they are promised to the butcher in town. He told me I would have to sell them to the German Army instead. So I told him I could sell them two cows, but the rest must go to the butcher as promised. He turned and talked to his assistant. I heard them say in German, 'Two cows are not enough. We need enough beef to feed 200 men.' Then he turned back to me and said he'd meet the butcher's price, but he must have <u>all</u> the cows. So I could take his money, or he would take my cows anyway. I took his money."

"Thank you for the bandages," she said.

"I hope you feel better soon," the farmer said, doffing his cap.

Her ankle wrapped, Daniel carried her out of the house and past the German soldiers outside. He deposited her on the back of his motorcycle, and they rode back to the village. She took the bandage off her ankle when they were out of sight of the Germans. "Stop at the house with a green shade drawn in the upper window," she told him. She was inside the house for fifteen or twenty minutes, while Daniel waited on his motorcycle outside. While he waited, his mind began to piece things together. When she came out, Daniel confronted her.

"This is about the Resistance, isn't it? Well, isn't it?"

"Daniel, the less you know…the safer you are…"

"But I'm here with you," he argued. "If they capture *you*, they capture *me*…they don't care what I know or don't know…"

"We just didn't want to involve you in the details. This way, if we are captured, we can tell the Germans that you didn't know what we were up to."

"You're using me. Tell me what this is about!"

"All right. You're right. You're taking the risk, you deserve to know."

She told him they are gathering information and passing it on to the Resistance leaders. "'*Picnics*' is code for gathering intelligence, and '*errands*' is code for dropping off the intelligence to the Resistance. We just watch, count, and pass on the numbers. They decide what it means, and what to do. All we do is watch, and count…"

Of course, it all made perfect sense. A circus was the perfect cover for the Resistance. They were able to obtain travel permits sanctioned by the Germans so they could move from town to town, observing German troop numbers in various regions. The Germans loved circuses, so many times a town's entire German garrison would turn out for the show. All they had to do was count the grey uniforms in each evening's performance to estimate garrison strength.

"And the picnics, the conversations—the *kisses*," he said bitterly. "They're not real, just a 'cover.'"

"No, Daniel, I look forward to our 'errands,'" she insisted. "And not to watch trains and count Germans. Even with the world falling apart around us, we have managed to escape a little, no? I mean, from time to time, forget about all this madness…"

He didn't say anything. She moved closer and kissed him softly on the lips. "Don't be cross, *mon chere*," she cooed into his ear. "Please don't be cross with me…"

Daniel softened, too. Yet there remained the nagging doubt, in the back of his mind, that the sentimentality wasn't real and he was merely being used by the Resistance.

The next day, a German train blew up nearby. "Was that us?" Daniel asked Emily.

"That was us."

Mixed feelings for Daniel: pride and exultation for having a hand in getting a blow in for France, and the sobering reality that people died as a result of his actions. Working for the Resistance was important, and yes, *exciting*, but the risk of being captured by the Germans should have frightened Daniel. Only it didn't. Daniel was willing to take the risk to continue to spend time with Emily. He felt like a man riding with her on the back of his motorcycle. He enjoyed the picnics in the country, their long talks – and the tender kisses, which she seemed to dispense on an as-needed basis.

"Someday," he told her, "I would like us to go on a <u>real</u> picnic – no spying, no errands – just the two of us, with no war, or cares, or troubles…"

"Don't be silly," she stopped his musings with a finger to his lips. "You know I'm with Constantine."

"*I* could make you happy," Daniel responded defensively.

"You *do* make me happy!" she smiled.

"I mean like Constantine does."

"You're too young to understand," she said dismissively, not realizing what a fiery dart it was to his heart.

And so, Emily's errands continued. Wherever the circus went, there were Germans to count and troop trains to spy on. One day, while Daniel was mucking the animal's stalls, Val and Denis approached him. He could tell they had bad news, by the look on their faces. They had both received orders from the local police to report for a work detail bound for Germany.

"They can't do that!" Daniel exclaimed, then remembered the fate of Monsieur Le Grun.

"They say the Germans need more workers, to replace the men in the army," Denis said. "It's not a request, it's an *order*…"

"it's not right!" Daniel insisted. "You don't have to go!"

"Don't worry, my friend," Val said. "I am not going to Germany. I'm going to the mountains and join the armed resistance."

"You're crazy!" Denis declared. "Going to live in the mountains, where it's wet and cold! Marshall Petain says the conditions for workers in Germany are excellent! Nice living quarters, plenty of food – French workers are given special privileges, health care, everything you could want!"

"Marshall Petain says, Marshall Petain says!" Val mocked him. "It's all a lie! He's in with the Nazis, I tell you! I'm not going."

"If you don't go, that means somebody else will have to go in your place," Denis argued. "Perhaps somebody older, or weaker…"

"I don't care. We should <u>all</u> refuse to go."

"Well, I'm going," Denis vowed. "There's no future in France. They say the conditions are better than here. They say there's more food in Germany. They say the war will be over in a few months, and we'll all be coming home anyway."

"They say a lot of things," Val scoffed. "The workers who have gone to Germany will never come back. But you go, my friend, and I hope you are right – for your sake."

A going-away celebration was hastily arranged for that evening. Val and Denis were well-liked by the performers, and many toasts and good wishes were made in their honor. To mark the occasion, Boris even got drunk, stripped to the waist, and made the belly dancer on his back do an exotic dance. The troupe was well-entertained, and Val and Denis both left early the next morning, leaving the cramped crew tent almost entirely to Daniel.

After Val and Denis left, there was more bad news. Monsieur Victor called a special meeting in the mess tent to announce that, due to increased Resistance activity in the area, the amiable Colonel Fischer had been relieved of his command and sent to the Eastern front. His replacement was Feldcommandant Horst Dokken, a man with a reputation for iron-fisted rule.

"The Germans are really starting to crack down," Monsieur Victor warned. "The new commander has lowered the curfew to 6 p.m., doubled German patrols, and restricted all travel in the area. He's also revoked our special travel and petrol permits."

"For how long?" Boris asked.

"Indefinitely."

"But we can't stay open if we can't travel!" Madame Durand pointed out. "What will we do?"

"I don't know," the ringmaster admitted sullenly.

Everyone felt the same dreadful feeling in the pit of their stomach. Everyone knew what this meant for the circus, for their livelihood. Up until then, the Resistance hadn't really been effective yet, and the Germans were still acting like they were in France on vacation. Now that the Resistance was getting its legs, things were rapidly changing for the worst.

A few of the performers cursed the Resistance for causing trouble with the Germans and disrupting their lives.

"The Germans left us alone before," Ballantine the Conjuror complained to no one in particular. "Now the Resistance has stirred everything up, and everyone's in danger!"

"They're only protecting France, you old gas bag!" Madame Olga bellowed at him. "What are the Germans doing here, anyway?"

"Let them go back to their own country!" Monsieur Laurent, the one-armed lion tamer, shouted heatedly.

"Be careful what you say, the Gestapo has eyes *everywhere!*" Monsieur Nikolai, the blind tight rope walker, warned.

"Let them arrest me!" Monsieur Laurent said defiantly. "What can they do to me – cut off my *other* arm?"

Evidence of the German crackdown was immediate. Rumors circulated of a large Gestapo presence in the area, with officers nosing around the villages and rounding up Jews to be exported to Germany. In light of these events, Constantine, who had connections to the Resistance, told Emily and Daniel that their intelligence-seeking excursions would be drastically curtailed until things settled down.

"It's just too dangerous right now," he explained. "Better to lay low for the moment and see what happens."

Proactively, Constantine worked with Rene, the local Resistance leader, to create forged papers for the circus employees who the Gestapo would most likely arrest as "enemies." These were people who were not of French origin, or from countries Germany was at war with.

"Will this make us safer?" one of the clowns, who was from Russia, asked.

"It will help," Constantine replied honestly. "But there's no guarantee the Gestapo won't find out who you really are."

"What about me and my wife?" Monsieur Nikolai, who was a Jew, asked hopefully.

"I am sorry," Constantine told him. "I can get papers to say you are an Italian instead of a Russian. But I can't get papers that say you are not a Jew. It's not possible. The Gestapo will find out, one way or another."

"This isn't right," Emily protested. "We've got to do something for them. We're all family. We've got to take care of each other."

"I'll talk to Rene and see what we can come up with," Constantine promised. "But for now, there's really nothing we can do for them. They're *Jews*..."

Two days later, things got even more complicated. Monsieur Nikolai and his wife Rebecca, who was the company seamstress and costume maker, came to Constantine and Emily's trailer with a strange man, woman, and two children.

"This is Rebecca's brother and his family," the blind tightrope walker said sheepishly.

"More *Jews*?" Constantine hissed. "What are you thinking? Why did you bring them *here*?"

"I didn't," Nikolai clarified. "They just showed up. They have nowhere else to go."

Constantine regarded the ragged family, then shook his head. "We can't take them. It's too risky."

Emily intervened. "Constantine! We can't let the Germans take them!"

"We have troubles of our own," Constantine argued. "What do *we* do with them?"

Daniel had a solution. "Val and Denis are gone. The man can take their place on the crew, and the woman can help Rebecca with the costumes. If we blend them into our circus community, perhaps they won't stand out as much and the Germans won't notice them."

"Oh, the Gestapo is smarter than that," Constantine asserted. "They can sniff out Jews anywhere."

"We've got to give it a try," Emily said, taking the children – a boy and a girl – under each arm. Constantine knew her mind wasn't going to be changed.

"All right," he relented with a sigh. "I'll talk to Rene about what we can do for them."

And so it was settled: *Cirque d'Europa* had officially become a haven for refugee Jews.

Within two days, Rene had a solution: an RAF plane would be landing in a field outside the village of *Val-de-Meuse* in three days, to deliver weapons and ammunition to the Resistance. The plane would be able to take Nikolai and Rebecca, plus Rebecca's brother's family, back to England and safety.

"All we've got to do is get them to that field at the right time," Constantine said. They knew that would be difficult, given the new travel restrictions implemented by Feldcommander Dokken. Constantine and Emily called Nikolai, Rebecca, and Daniel to their trailer to work on a plan.

In three hours, they had one. Constantine, Emily, and Daniel would drive Nikolai, Rebecca, and her brother's family to the rendezvous with the plane in one of the circus trucks. The Jews would ride in the back of the covered truck, where it was dark. Hector, the narcoleptic lion, would be in the back with them. Naturally, he would sleep for most of the journey and be little danger to the children, who would be tucked up next to the cab and covered with blankets. If they were stopped by Germans, they would say that it was an emergency – that the lion was very sick and they had to get it to an animal hospital in Reims before it died. If the Germans looked in the back, the Jews would pose as veterinarians attending to the sick lion. If they insisted on searching the back of the truck, the "veterinarians" would tell them that trying to wake a sick lion would be very dangerous.

"Will it work?" Constantine asked skeptically.

"It's got to," Daniel replied. "It's our only chance."

"We've got to try," Emily agreed.

Constantine arranged with Rene for some fake documents for the Jews. Rene wasn't happy about the short notice, but said he would do his best. Daniel and Emily then embarked on one last errand, to pick up the forged papers from Rene's house in the village. They brought a picnic basket along with them, in case they were stopped by the Germans – then they would go into their old "two lovers on a picnic" routine.

When they got to the house with the green shade, Emily said, "You're in this deep now. Come inside and meet Rene."

They looked up and down the street for Germans. Then they approached the door and knocked three times, knowing they were being watched from a window. The door opened and they were pulled inside quickly. It was dark inside, and it took a few minutes for Daniel's eyes to adjust. A bearded man with a pistol greeted them – it wasn't Rene. The man tucked the pistol into his waistband and smiled at Emily. "Who's this?" he grunted.

"This is Daniel."

"Ah, the motorcycle rider," the man nodded. Daniel looked around the parlor. There was another man asleep on the sofa with his cap pulled over his eyes, snoring. A rifle was leaned up against the end of the sofa, near his head.

"Are the papers ready?" Emily asked.

The man nodded, and took a large bite out of an apple he was holding in his hand. "Follow me."

He led them into the kitchen, where Rene was sitting at a table eating a meal of potatoes and sausages. He looked up at Emily, then Daniel, but didn't say anything. He slid a box of chocolates across the table toward them.

"The papers are in a false bottom, under the chocolates," he said. "I stayed up all night working on them. It was a rush-job, so I can't guarantee anything. They might be good enough to fool a lazy corporal, but probably not an alert officer – unless you can distract him enough."

"We'll have a lion with us."

"That should do it."

Emily picked up the box of chocolates. "Thank you for everything."

"Good luck, you'll need it," Rene said, going back to his meal.

They left the house and started for the motorcycle parked in front. Just then, a German soldier was walking down the street. He stopped and looked suspiciously at the chocolates in Emily's hand. One glance from Emily, and Daniel knew to go into the "act."

"Oh, *mon cher*, thank you for the chocolates! They're my favorites!" she gushed, grabbing him and kissing him passionately. She kissed him until the soldier, satisfied, smiled knowingly and continued on his way. Then she stopped as quickly as she had started, and put the chocolates in the picnic basket, Daniel watching her and wishing it all wasn't just an "act."

Chapter 9

The next morning, they loaded the truck for the trip to *Val-de-Meuse*. At first, Monsieur Laurent was reluctant to loan them the use of Hector, but Daniel promised to take good care of him.

"I know he likes you," Monsieur Laurent said, handing him over to Daniel. "And it's all for a good cause."

Daniel, who had been watching Monsieur Laurent's lion-taming act for months, knew how to get Hector to jump into the back of the truck. The sometimes-grumpy old lion complied with Daniel's request just like they were old friends. When the Jewish family saw him, however, the children didn't want to get into the truck with him.

"He's really harmless," Daniel assured them. "He looks fierce in the ring, but that's all a show." He let them pet him and feed him raw chunks of steak until their fears evaporated. After playing with him for a while, the children were charmed with their new friend.

"He's really a lazy kitty," Daniel said, as he and Constantine helped the Jewish family climb into the back of the truck with Hector. "When we get on the road, he'll fall fast asleep for most of the trip."

With everyone loaded up and the truck's tank full of petrol, the little group warily set out for *Val-de-Meuse*. As predicted, Hector's narcolepsy kicked in and he was out for most of the trip. They attempted to stay on back roads as much as possible, in order to avoid Germans and remain inconspicuous. For the first few hours, traffic was light and the roads were clear. Just when it looked as if everything was working out in their favor, the road was blocked and they were forced to take a detour onto a busier thoroughfare.

"It'll be fine," Constantine assured Emily and Daniel from behind the wheel. "If we get stopped, just remember what we rehearsed…"

Soon, there was a problem. Up ahead, a lorry piled high with bales of hay had collided head-on with a sedan, leaving the smaller vehicle a crumpled, twisted piece of steel. The gendarmes were there, as well as a dozen or so onlookers. A farmer had attached what was left of the sedan to the back of his tractor and was attempting to haul it off the road. The damaged lorry blocked one whole lane, and traffic was squeezing through a small gap as directed by one of the gendarmes. Just as they approached the scene, the gendarme directed them to stop and allow the farmer on the tractor finish pulling the wreck off the road.

Sitting there and waiting, they began to attract the attention of some of the bystanders. Then a gendarme noticed them and walked up to the cab.

"Where are you coming from?" he asked.

"*Rougement,*" Constantine replied coolly.

"And the purpose of your journey?"

"We are transporting a sick circus animal to an animal hospital in Reims," Constantine answered, following the script to the letter.

"The circus?" the gendarme asked with interest. "I love the circus. Perhaps I've seen you – which circus is it?"

"*Cirque d'Europa,*" Constantine answered.

"No, I've never heard of you. Are you a small circus?"

The gendarme was asking a lot of questions, and questions made him nervous. It was impossible to tell whether the gendarme was suspicious, or just making small talk.

"Rather small," Constantine admitted.

"That's why I've never heard of you," the gendarme nodded. "You <u>are</u> aware of the new travel restrictions, aren't you?"

"Of course. This is an emergency."

"Well, it looks like you picked a bad day for an emergency."

The tractor had successfully removed the wreck, and the road was now clear.

"May we pass now?" Constantine inquired, trying not to sound impatient.

The gendarme looked into the cab and inspected Emily and Daniel. "And you two also work for the circus?"

They nodded. "*Oui*, officer."

Satisfied, the gendarme nodded and stepped away from the cab. "You may pass."

Relieved, Constantine slowly began to pull away.

"Wait!" the gendarme shouted. "Stop!"

Constantine almost panicked and kept going. Emily said, "You'd better stop…" He looked at her: her face was intense but calm. He followed her advice.

"I just wanted to tell you: you'd better get off this main road as soon as you can," the gendarme said. "Emergency or not, the Germans may not like you breaking their travel restrictions…"

"Thank you," Constantine gasped.

"Have a pleasant journey," the gendarme said, walking away.

They all started breathing again. "He's right, we've got to find a way off this road," Constantine said, putting the truck into gear and pulling away from the scene. A few kilometers ahead, he found a smaller road to take. "There will be more villages to go through, but less traffic than the main road," he told the others, visibly relieved. An hour and a half later, they found themselves entering a sleepy little village. In the center of the village, two German soldiers had the road blocked. The sidewalks were empty, the shops closed up and shades drawn.

"Oh, this doesn't look good…" Constantine murmured, stopping the truck.

One of the Germans approached the cab. "You can't pass this way," he said excitedly, in stilted French. "There's a partisan with a rifle in an upstairs window, shooting at everything he can see."

Just then, several rifle shots were fired from an upstairs window in a building on the left. Several German soldiers returned fire from shop windows across the street. On closer inspection, the village was crawling with Germans. They were running from door to door, taking shelter and then coming out to fire at the sniper whenever they could.

"We're in the middle of a battle," Daniel said breathlessly.

The German at their window ducked reflexively as several more shots rang out. "He's a crazy old guy," the soldier told them. "Wearing his uniform from the Great War, and firing an antique rifle from 1918." Several more shots rang out, and he ducked again. Daniel saw a German get hit and fall in the middle of the street, while other Germans fired a fresh volley at the partisan. Then he saw an armored German halftrack vehicle pull into the street in front of the partisan's building. It had a fifty caliber machine gun mounted on it, and a soldier began firing non-stop into the partisan's window. Then it stopped, and everything got quiet.

Two Germans came out from hiding and threw hand grenades into the partisan's shattered window. There was a great explosion, and smoke billowed out into the street. Six Germans ran across the street and busted the sniper's door down. More soldiers came over, and they all started going up the stairway to the top floor.

Flames now shot out of the sniper's window, but he wasn't going down yet. More shots rained down on the remaining Germans below. The armored car returned more ear-splitting machine gun fire. The Germans threw more hand grenades into the building. The soldier by their window crouched down again. "You'd better get out of here!" he shouted over the gunfire. "Take a different route!"

Constantine threw the truck into reverse and backed away. Then he turned around and drove back down the road until he found another way around the village. Within an hour, they were hopelessly lost. Constantine saw an on-coming truck and waved it down. It was a farmer with a dozen sheep in the back.

"We're lost," Constantine admitted. "We're trying to get to *Val-de-Meuse*."

"You're going the wrong way," the farmer said matter-of-factly.

"Which way is it?"

"Turn around and go back the opposite way about six kilometers," the farmer said. "When you get to the village of *Lille*, turn left. Stay on that road and it will take you close enough to *Val-de-Meuse* to find it without too much trouble."

"Merci." Constantine turned the truck around and headed in the opposite direction. The old-timer was right: after driving seven kilometers, they found themselves in Lille. Feeling much more confident, they turned left and ran right into a German roadblock. There was nothing to do but stop again.

A soldier came up to the cab. "What is your destination?" he demanded gruffly.

"Reims," Constantine lied, sticking to the script.

"*Reims*? Isn't that the other way? You're nowhere near there, I'm afraid…"

"We're unfamiliar with the area," Constantine said, not lying at all this time.

"Well, this road is closed," the soldier informed them. "Partisans blew up the bridge last night. They got one of our trucks with four soldiers in it. The bridge will have to be rebuilt. That will take months."

Constantine's head swirled. *What do we do now?*

"Your papers, please," the German said. Constantine handed him his documents. The soldier scanned them quickly and handed them back. "What is your business in Reims?" the soldier asked.

"We're from a circus. We've got a sick animal in the back. We need to get it to the animal clinic in Reims."

"Aren't you aware of the new travel restrictions?" the German asked harshly.

"It's an emergency," Constantine said. "We don't have time to apply for a travel permit. If we don't get it to the clinic, it will die."

"I need to check the back."

"Daniel, why don't you help me," Constantine suggested.

They got out of the truck and the German followed them to the back. Constantine opened the tailgate and the German peered inside. It was a real mess back there. Thankfully, Hector was predictably asleep, but he'd apparently gotten car-sick from all of the jostling on the back roads, and there was lion vomit everywhere.

The soldier looked at the scene in disgust. "Who are these people?"

"Our circus veterinarians."

"I need to see their papers."

Constantine collected everyone's false documents and handed them to the German, who unfolded them and painstakingly examined each one. Daniel caught a sideways glance, and thought they actually looked pretty authentic.

"There's something wrong with these papers," the German finally said. Everybody froze.

Constantine turned ghost white. "Wh–what's the problem?"

"There's something funny about the dates," the soldier said, looking closer at the forgeries. "And these signatures aren't right..." Daniel remembered what Rene had said: *Don't let them look to closely at these...*

"I've never seen stamps like these..." the soldier said, puzzled.

"They, they got those documents at the Swiss border," Constantine bluffed. "These veterinarians are from Switzerland..." It was all he could think of.

The soldier shook his head. "That shouldn't matter. I'm going to have to call these in…"

It was all Constantine could do not to shout out "NO!" He gulped and tried to breathe normally, instead. The soldier took the papers to a guardhouse and picked up a radio. Emily crawled out of the cab and joined them at the back of the truck.

"What's going on?" she asked, concerned.

"It's not good…" Constantine said. "He's calling their papers in."

"What do we do?" she whispered.

"I'm, I'm thinking we get in the truck and drive off. You know, take our chances…"

"They'll *shoot* us!" she whispered. A different soldier came over and looked inside the truck.

"What circus are you from?" he asked Emily, smiling. He was friendlier than the other one.

"*Cirque d'Europa*," she answered.

"Never heard of it." His French was slightly better than the other soldier's.

"Few have," she said. He smiled at her. Then he looked in the back of the truck.

"And these are the veterinarians. I come from a family of vets."

Constantine, Emily and Daniel looked at each other – *Uh-oh…*

"That's right, my mother and father were both vets," he continued in a friendly tone. "I grew up in a pet clinic, you might say. Even studied to become a vet for a while, until the Army got me…"

Daniel had a sinking feeling in his stomach. The Jews were frozen. They looked petrified.

"You there," the friendly German said to Nikolai. "Tell me what's going on with your patient."

Nikolai's wife pinched him on the elbow to let him know the question was directed at him. He cleared his throat awkwardly, trying to think of something to say, pretending not to be blind. "Well, he's very sick," he finally managed to choke out.

"I can see that," the soldier said, looking at the pools of vomit. "Perhaps he's just a little car sick."

"No, no – it's worse than that," Nikolai replied, trying to look in the direction of the German's voice.

"Well, tell me doctor, in your expert opinion, what do you think is wrong with him?"

"An ulcer," Nikolai replied. It was the only thing he could think of.

"A lion with an ulcer?" the soldier asked, surprised. "I don't think I've ever heard that."

"Circus life can be very stressful."

"I imagine so, especially for the animals."

"He also suffers from…acute performance anxiety," Nikolai added, and instantly wondered if he should have.

"Performance anxiety?" the soldier repeated. "I've never heard of that before, either. What are the symptoms?"

Nikolai thought quickly. "Paralysis. Difficulty breathing. Loss of appetite. Irritability. Impotence. High blood pressure. And, vomiting."

"Interesting," the soldier observed. "And you, doctor – do you concur with your colleague's diagnosis?" He was speaking to Nikolai's brother in law, whose name was Aaron.

"Yes," Aaron said, wide-eyed. Then, feeling the need to add something, he said "And colitis."

"Colitis?" the soldier asked. "My, this _is_ a very sick kitty, indeed. And tell me, just how would you go about treating such an illness?"

"Vitamins," Aaron blurted out.

"Vitamins?" the soldier repeated incredulously.

"And a change in diet," Nikolai intervened, hoping to save things. "Exercise. And rest – lots and lots of rest…"

"That's a very unusual treatment."

"We're from Switzerland," Nikolai explained, before realizing how little sense it made.

The friendly soldier's smile evaporated and his eyes narrowed into slits. "Hey, you're not really veterinarians, are you?"

Nobody spoke. "What did you do, steal this lion? That's it, isn't it?"

Just then, the first German put the radio down and called excitedly to his partner in German. There was a frenzied back-and-forth exchange in their language, most of which Daniel caught. The friendly soldier looked very excited.

"I think we're all right," Daniel whispered to Constantine and Emily. "They said the partisans who blew up the bridge are surrounded in a barn nearby, and they've been called in as reinforcements."

The first German seemed to have forgotten all about them. He was ordering the other soldiers to bring their rifles and get into the car. *"Schnell! Schnell!"* he was shouting.

"The Germans are leaving," Emily said.

"But they've still got our papers," Constantine reminded her.

Thinking quickly, Emily reached out and grabbed the friendly soldier's arm as he was leaving. "You're right, we stole the lion. We're an animal rights group, and we couldn't stand to see him suffer any longer in that cruel circus. Being an animal lover yourself, I'm sure you can understand!"

"Yes, yes…you're free to go on your way," he said hurriedly. "I've got to go!"

"But they've got our papers…we need them back!" Emily told him, squeezing his arm.

"All right, wait here." The soldier went over and got the papers away from his distracted partner. "They're all right, I'll explain later," he told him. Then he brought them back and handed them to Emily.

"Thank you!" she shouted over the commotion.

"Don't mention it!" he shouted, climbing into the car as it raced away. "Keep saving the animals!"

Minutes later, they were back in *Lille*, asking for new directions to *Val-de-Meuse*. They found they were actually closer than they thought. In another two hours, they had reached their destination and found the farm where the RAF plane was scheduled to land. The farmer, Gaspere, who was sympathetic to the Resistance, had been expecting their arrival. They would all be staying in his house until the plane arrived the following night.

Gaspere cut quite an imposing figure. Nearly six feet tall and powerfully-built, he had a shock of white hair that stood nearly straight up on his head, and a soft white beard. His eyes bulged when Daniel woke Hector up and prompted him to jump out of the back of the truck. Feeling somewhat better now that the car sickness had worn off, Hector stretched his front legs and looked around the farm contentedly.

"He's our cover," Daniel explained. "He did a magnificent job, even though all he did was sleep all day."

Gaspere was apprehensive. "He's not going to eat all my sheep, is he?"

"No," Daniel assured him. "He's a circus cat who likes his meat brought to *him*."

Daniel walked Hector around the farm a bit, then stashed him in one of the empty stalls in Gaspere's barn. He fed him some meat, said goodnight, and went into the farmhouse. Gaspere's wife had prepared a supper of onion and potato soup and bread for everyone, and it smelled wonderful. During supper, Gaspere smoked his pipe while he ate and regaled them with war stories.

"My hair wasn't always like this," he explained, happy to have a table full of guests to talk to. "It used to be as black as tar, until I was caught in a German gas attack in the war – the Great One – December 17, 1917. Mustard gas – that's what made my hair this way. Didn't blind me or damage my lungs, just turned my hair as white as snow and made it stand up on end like this. The doctors couldn't figure it out. They didn't know what to do with me. So they sent me back to the front and the mustard gas never bothered me again after that. And it's been standing up on my head like this ever since. Feel it." He bowed his head slightly and let Daniel touch it. "Stiff as a horse's mane. I can't even get it to lie down with a handful of axle grease."

Exhausted from the exertions of their journey, the weary travelers wanted nothing more than to sleep after the hearty supper. They all found various places to lay down in the modest farmhouse, and were soon slumbering peacefully.

The next day, everyone stayed inside the farmhouse all day in case a German patrol passed by the farm. They ate, slept, and rested, waiting for night to fall. After dark, Gaspere took a flashlight and led them to the plane's landing sight.

"This is the place," he told them, stopping in a wide, open field. "This is where it lands."

"When will it land?" Constantine asked.

"There is no telling," Gaspere replied. "It could be any time before sunrise." He untied a piece of cloth and handed each person a chunk of dark chocolate. "Here, eat this. It will keep you from catching cold."

Everyone sat down on the grass and ate their chocolate. Then he reached into his pocket and pulled out a flask of cognac. He took a slug and passed it around. "Drink this, it'll keep you warm." Next, he pulled out a knife and began whittling a piece of wood.

"I see you looking at my knife," he said to Daniel. "You like it? I got it off a dead German at Verdun. That's right, a colonel. We were in the trenches, we had nothing to eat, nothing to drink, no latrines – we just did it right there in the trenches, then sloshed around in it to the top of our boots. We lived like animals. The rats wouldn't even stay in the trenches with us. Friends would turn against friends. Steal your food, your socks, your cigarettes, photographs of your family or your girl back home and use them to wipe their asses with. We'd lost our humanity, we weren't human anymore. We weren't even animals. We were like senseless microbes, just breathing and thrashing and trying to survive.

"Then one night, I couldn't take it anymore. I just decided to do something, anything, except stay in that wretched trench until I died. So I took my rifle and snuck out of my trench and looked around. I'd been in that trench for six months. When we went in, the countryside was lush and green and there were cows and sheep and trees and rivers and…now, the landscape was unrecognizable. There were no more animals, no more trees, no more grass. Even the rivers were gone. The *rivers*. What could make *rivers* disappear? France was gone. It looked like the surface of the moon, or Mars. Craters everywhere. And the craters were filled with skeletons and rotting corpses. Somehow, I had been transported to Hell. I wasn't prepared for it. I screamed in horror – screamed for what felt like hours. Then something happened to my mind. It kind of snapped. And all I wanted to do was murder. Murder filled my mind. Murder filled my heart. Murder, murder, murder. Blackness and murder. There was no more goodness, no more God – no more *Me*. All I could think of was murder.

"Since I no longer existed, I vowed to murder the first living thing I came across. I started for the German side and crossed the No Man's Land. The barbed wire tore my flesh but I didn't care because I couldn't feel it. I didn't feel it because I had no more nerve endings, no more senses left in my body. I was a worn-down, senseless nub of scar tissue. I couldn't hear the shells exploding around me, the bullets whizzing past me. All I could do was propel my body forward to satiate my lust for murder. Germans started coming out of their trenches to confront me, but I shot them, one by one, with my rifle. When I ran out of bullets I stabbed and slashed them with my bayonet. But still they kept coming, they wouldn't stop. I killed them all.

"Finally, I reached their trench. I'd killed all of the Germans, except for one: their colonel. He stood there, astonished, with his handlebar mustache and his Kaiser helmet with the spike on the top. His eyes were large, he was looking at me as if I were an apparition. He started firing his luger pistol at me, but his hand was shaking so badly that every bullet missed. Then he was out of bullets. I came at him with my bayonet, and he took out his knife and started slashing wildly at me with it. He cut me many times, but I wouldn't stop. He was able to knock the bayonet out of my hands, but I pushed him backwards and he fell on his back. Then I straddled him. I took the knife away from him and wrapped my hands around his throat and started squeezing with all of my strength. Squeezing the life out of him, slowly. As slowly as I could, because I did not want him to die quickly like the others, I wanted him to suffer the longest, suffer for *everyone*. I wanted him to suffer for what we became, for turning France into a wasteland, for going down below and hauling Hell itself up to Earth's surface. He was going to pay for it all.

"Then, as if he read my mind, as if he knew my very intention, I saw his mouth moving. I couldn't hear what he was saying because my hands were still wrapped tightly around his throat, crushing his voicebox, squeezing the very life out of him. His face was purple, his eyes were popping out of their sockets. But his mouth kept moving, so I put my ear down low, right up against his mouth, as close as I could because I was now consumed with a desire stronger than I'd ever felt before, a desire to understand what he was trying to communicate to me so urgently, even at the very threshold of the end of his own existence. And when I got my ear close enough, I was able to hear the faintest trace of breath, the very last bit of breath left in his dying, thrashing corpse. And what he was saying was *"Marienbrucke."*

Then he was dead. His eyes still stared up at me, but they were the eyes of a fish sitting in a bucket of ice at the market. I don't remember picking up his knife, but I did. That was all I took. I crawled like a snake out of the trench. There were no more Germans. The ground was littered with corpses. Artillery was still being fired in the distance, lighting up the dingy sky. I stumbled back across No Man's Land to my country's side, but felt no sense of patriotism or love. France was gone. Some of my countrymen came out of their trench and retrieved me, but I didn't recognize them. They talked to me but I no longer understood their language; French now sounded foreign to me, like Greek or Portuguese. They asked me questions, but I didn't respond. All I could think was "*Marienbrucke*." Then I started repeating it;

"*Marienbrucke…Marienbruck…Marienbrucke…*" over and over and over. Whenever anyone tried to communicate with me, that's all I would say – just "*Marienbrucke*."

"They sent me to a hospital in Lyon, but I didn't get better. They couldn't make me well, so they put me out into the streets, where I became a penniless beggar, walking up and down the boulevards mumbling one word – "*Marienbrucke*" – living off the small change people would give me out of pity. Thankfully, a kindly priest took me in and I began to slowly recover, began to remember who I was, and where I'd come from. But before I could become that person again, before I could resume my pre-war life, I had to decipher the riddle of "*Marienbrucke*." I knew I couldn't be completely whole again until I found the answer. So I asked everyone I could find what it meant. I went to libraries, cathedrals, universities, and bars. Sought out poets and teachers and philosophers and students, but no one could tell me what it meant. Finally, just when I'd given up all hope, God intervened. I was sitting on a park bench one day when the most beautiful young girl I'd ever seen in my life sat down beside me. She was eating an ice cream. It was strawberry. It smelled wonderful. Then I realized, it was not the ice cream that smelled so wonderful – it was her! I stared at her in amazement for quite some time. I could not take my eyes off her. She gave me a feeling like I'd never felt before. Just looking at her filled me with all the hope and passion and light and life that the war had sucked out of me. Just as the bus approached, she finished her ice cream, turned to me, smiled, and said, "*Marienbrucke* is a place in Germany."

"I was stunned. Before I could say anything, she stood up and hurried onto the bus. Just as the bus door was closing, I squeezed through and walked down the center isle looking for her. I looked in every seat down both sides, but she wasn't there! She wasn't on that bus! That's when I knew she was an angel! Feverishly, I went to a travel agent and booked passage to Germany. I went to Munich and asked everyone I could find where Marienbrucke was. Finally, somebody told me it wasn't a place, it was a *bridge*. A bridge over the Pollat River in the town of Schwangau. I hurried to Schwangau and found the little bridge. I walked to the center of the bridge and looked at the spectacular view. It overlooked lush green fields and cows and sheep and trees and rivers and castles.

Then it hit me like a thunderbolt. This view replaced everything that had been wiped out by the war, all the beauty, animals, scenery, and trees destroyed at Verdun after we went down into the trenches. It was here, in Germany, alive and beautiful and *real*. Then I remembered the German colonel in the Kaiser helmet and handlebar mustache. The one I murdered so thoughtlessly that bitter night in the enemy trench. The one who tried so desperately, with his last dying breath, to give me this hope, to restore this dream, even as I was squeezing the life out of him with my bare hands. That German colonel *saved* me – he restored my *soul*. How did he *know*? Why did he do it? *Why*?

"And I fell to my knees, right there on that bridge, and wept like a child. And that is how I got this knife."

Gaspere stopped talking and went on with his whittling, in the dark. Nobody could speak. They waited the rest of the night in silence, but the plane never came. When the sun started coming up, Emily asked, "What do you think happened? Do you suppose it crashed somewhere on its way?"

Gaspere just shrugged, wiped his knife on his pants, and put it in his pocket. "Hard to tell."

"What are we going to do?" Constantine asked.

"I think we should go back to the house and have breakfast before the Germans come out," Gaspere said, standing up and running a calloused hand through his coarse white hair.

They trudged back to the little farmhouse in defeat. After breakfast, they all went to sleep – except Gaspere. Later in the day, a message from Rene came, via a teenage girl on a bicycle. She carried the message in a pouch of pipe tobacco, which she handed to Gaspere and then pedaled off down the road. The farmer dug down to the bottom of the pouch and pulled out a slip of paper, which he handed to Constantine. Then he lit his pipe with some of the tobacco.

Constantine quickly read the note, then crumpled it up and threw it into the fire. "The plane had to turn back because of bad weather over the channel," he informed everyone. "They'll try again when the weather clears."

"When will that be?" Rebecca asked.

"They don't know. A few days, perhaps."

"A few days? We can't wait any longer!" It was Rebecca's brother's wife, Esther. "Now I see. We'll never get out of France!" Rebecca took the distraught woman in her arms and led her into another room to comfort her.

"What should we do?" Emily asked.

"They want us to lay low here," Constantine replied. "Rene will send us another message when the plane is able to come."

They waited for two days, cooped up in the farmhouse, waiting to hear from Rene. They could only go outside at night, after dark, for a few minutes of fresh air and exercise. That's when Daniel would get Hector out for a walk, and sometimes let the children play with him – but not too rough. During the day, they stayed inside with the shutters closed, playing games, singing songs, and trying to keep their spirits up. Meanwhile, Gaspere went out and worked in his fields as usual, to avoid arousing any suspicion.

From time to time, he would burst into the house and announce, "A patrol is coming! Everyone in the basement, quickly!" They would all have to hide in the dark basement, sometimes for several hours, until Gaspere or his wife lifted the trap door and gave the all-clear. Everyone was in low spirits and feeling cabin fever. Nerves were frayed, and tempers began to flare.

Constantine did his best to reassure them. "All we can do is wait. Rene will contact us when he hears any news."

Just when morale was at its lowest, they received another message from Rene.

"What does it say?" Nikolai asked anxiously.

Constantine looked despondent. "The weather isn't clearing up as expected," he said, everyone gathered around him expectantly. "So there's a new plan. A British submarine will be dropping off a Resistance operative near Calais in three days. Rene says the submarine will take you to England."

"But that means we have to drive to Calais, to meet the submarine," Emily said.

"That's correct," Constantine concurred.

"It's a set-up," Nikolai exclaimed. "They want us to drive to the coast, where they will arrest us."

"Rene isn't setting us up," Constantine snapped. "Look, you're not thinking clearly right now, Nikolai…"

"Who can think, cooped up in this house for days on end?" Esther asked.

The Jews convened in another room to talk it over. Ten minutes later, they came out with their answer.

"We're not going to Calais," Nikolai announced. "It's too dangerous to get back in that truck and face all those Germans on the roads again."

"That's your final decision?" Constantine asked.

"We all agree. We'd rather stay here."

"Well, you can't stay here forever," Emily pointed out. "Even if Gaspere and his wife agreed, the Germans would find you sooner or later."

"Then we'll stay here long enough to figure something else out," Nikolai said.

Constantine sat down at the kitchen table and drank half a bottle of wine. Then he stood up and made an announcement. "I've made a decision. I'm going back to straighten things out with Rene. We'll come up with a new plan and I'll be back in a few days. The rest of you will stay here until you hear from me."

In the morning, Gaspere drove Constantine to the nearest train station. Everyone spent the next three days on pins and needles, waiting to hear from him. *Would things ever work out to their advantage,* thought Daniel. The Jews were quiet and worried for most of the time. Daniel and Emily spent the days cooped up in the house with them, and when the sun went down took long walks through the countryside together. Sometimes, they would stop and lay on their backs in the field where they waited for the airplane and hold hands. No talk, just holding hands and watching the clouds blow across the shining silver moon. It was a memory that Daniel would keep forever. But Emily was worried about Constantine, and couldn't hide it.

"He'll be all right, you know," Daniel assured her. "He's *Constantine*, after all."

She tried to laugh, but it was half-hearted at best.

Then, one day they received a message from him. The weather over the channel had finally cleared, so the submarine idea was cancelled and the plane would be coming again. Constantine also said that Gestapo activity in the area was so intense that he wouldn't be coming back to the farmhouse himself. It would be up to Emily and Daniel to get the Jews on the plane and bring Hector and the truck back to the circus.

That night, Gaspere led them back to the field to wait for the plane. About midnight, everyone was thrilled to hear the unmistakable whine of an aircraft engine approaching. As it got closer, the excitement mounted.

"It's here!" Rebecca shouted. "It's actually here!"

"Is this really happening, or is it a dream?" Esther asked.

The plane came down low and landed in the field. Gaspere waved his flashlight, and the plane taxied over to them. Up close, they could all see the British RAF insignias on the fuselage and wings. It sent a thrill through everyone's bodies. The pilot shut off the engine and climbed out of the fuselage.

Somehow, the plane looked disappointingly small up-close. "I expected something a little larger," Esther said.

Gaspere helped the pilot unload several cases of munitions for the Resistance, then covered the crates with hay until it could be picked up. Then the pilot glanced at the group of people for the first time, and looked surprised. "I hope you are not all planning to go?" he said in French. Expecting to hear a British accent, they were all taken aback.

"They send Free French pilots on these missions," Gaspere explained. "They wouldn't risk British pilots for this."

"They just let us use their airplanes," the pilot added.

"We are staying," Emily said to the pilot. "These six are going with you." She pointed to the Jews.

The pilot looked confused. "Six? I do not understand."

"These are the six who will be going with you," Emily repeated, a feeling of dread quickly descending upon her.

"But that's impossible," the pilot explained. "I can't take them all. This plane is too small."

Stunned, Emily finally managed to speak. "Too…small?"

"Oui, I cannot take six people in this plane. It is too small."

"Why did they send such a small plane?" Emily asked, in shock.

"The big plane isn't working right now," the pilot said simply.

There was at least a minute of silence as everyone tried to process the information.

"There must have been some kind of mistake – a miscommunication somewhere –" Emily stuttered.

"There is no mistake, mademoiselle. This is the plane we use when the big plane isn't working."

"I don't understand," was all Emily could say, her heart sinking. "You only have *two planes?*"

"The British have many planes," the pilot clarified. "But they only let us use two."

"Why…why didn't somebody tell us?" Emily asked. The pilot just shrugged his shoulders.

"We're doomed!" Esther cried out in despair. "We're never getting out of here!"

When Emily had recovered a bit, she asked "How many can you take, then?"

"Two."

"*Two?*" Rebecca asked in disbelief. "*Two?*" Then, out of sheer exhaustion, she started laughing uncontrollably. "Do you realize what we've been through?"

"No Madame, I couldn't begin to guess," the pilot said kindly.

"Then who will it be?" Nikolai demanded. "Who's going?"

"How could we choose such a thing?" Esther wailed. "It's impossible."

"Then we're all stuck here," Aaron said.

Daniel caught Emily's eye, and then looked at the children. She got it, and stepped forward. "Of course, it's the children. The children should go."

"Without their parents?" Rebecca asked.

"I won't send my darlings off with this man!" Esther pledged. "We don't even know him."

Emily spoke up again. "Look, we all know what will happen if they are captured by the Germans. Think of their future…"

"They can't be separated from their mother," Aaron, the father, said.

"They must, if you care about them," Emily argued. "It's the only thing we can do."

"She's right," Nikolai spoke up. "It must be the children. The plane is here now. You may not have this chance again."

"But they'll lose them," Esther worried. "We'll never see them again!"

"They won't lose them," Gaspere assured her. "They will be well-cared for. You will see them again, as soon as we can get you over there."

The parents thought it over. "Take them," their mother finally said. Then they got on their knees before the children and said goodbye. When she stood up, the woman said "Take them, before I change my mind," and burst into tears.

Their father helped them board the plane, and the pilot got into the cockpit and started the engine. The plane taxied away, and they watched it lift off into the late-night sky. Daniel whispered a prayer that the little plane with its precious cargo would make it safely back to England. When it was out of view, they all trudged silently back to the farmhouse and went to bed.

The next morning, Emily wrote a message to Constantine: "The big plane isn't working right now, so the pilot could only take the children. What should we do with the adults?" The message was sent along with the teenage girl, and everybody set about the arduous task of waiting for the reply.

Two days later, the reply came: "Rene says to drive them to Switzerland."

"That's his plan – *'Drive them to Switzerland?'*" Nikolai asked in disbelief.

"Is this a joke?" Rebecca laughed nervously.

"I think they're serious," Emily replied, sadly. "He also says Rene is sending an operative to straighten things out."

"An *operator*?" Esther asked.

"No, an *operative*," Emily clarified. "To see us safely to Switzerland. Rene says he's very good – we'll be in excellent hands."

"Oh, I'm sure of it!" Nikolai said sarcastically. "All of a sudden, the Resistance is going to become competent!"

The demoralized group hunkered down for another long day in the farmhouse, awaiting the operative's arrival.

Chapter 10

Alex was not what anyone expected. Arriving on foot and carrying several large bundles under his arms, the Resistance operative had pallid white skin, bleary, bloodshot eyes, and sunken, unshaven cheeks. He kept a lit cigarette in the crook of his mouth, and looked like he hadn't slept in days. Emily's heart sank when she saw him; how was this ragged skeleton going to get them to Switzerland with the countryside crawling with Germans?

The Jews were equally confused and dismayed when they got a good look at him. "Are you sure he's up to this?" Rebecca whispered to Emily. "If Rene sent him, he's up to it," Emily replied, trying to believe it herself. Once inside the farmhouse, Alex untied the bundles and laid the contents out on the kitchen table. "This is your new cover," he proudly announced. "The men will be disguised as priests, and the ladies as nuns."

"*This* is the plan?" Nikolai exclaimed in disbelief. "We're *Jewish*. No one will believe we're <u>Catholics</u>."

"Rene is aware of this?" Emily asked in alarm.

"It was his idea," Alex replied.

"This will fool no one!" Esther scoffed.

"If you've got a better idea, I'm listening," Alex said.

"Monsieur, can you get us to Switzerland, or not?" Rebecca demanded.

"Oui, Madame," Alex promised confidently. "I can get you there."

"Then we will wear the disguises, and that's all there is to it," Rebecca declared.

There was another problem a few minutes later, as everyone hurried to prepare for the upcoming journey. When Alex saw Daniel leading Hector to the truck, he stopped in his tracks and looked as if he'd seen a ghost. "What is <u>that</u>?" he demanded.

"A lion," Daniel replied. "We'll be taking him with us, back to the circus."

"We will not," Alex argued. "I will not ride in a vehicle with a dangerous beast like that."

"He's harmless," Daniel tried to explain, but the Resistance operative would have none of it.

"I'm not taking that chance," Alex vowed. "Besides, a lion doesn't work with our new cover."

He had a point there, so Daniel arranged to leave Hector on the farm during the trip to Switzerland. Then they would swing by and pick him up on the way back to the circus. The women – including Emily – dressed in the habits, and the men all looked reverential in their priest frocks and collars. "You're too young to be a priest," Alex told Daniel. "I bet you were an altar boy, weren't you?"

"*Oui*, I was."

"Well, you are once again. You will be our driver," Alex instructed him. The farmer Gaspere brought a sack stuffed with provisions and a large thermos of hot coffee out of the house and loaded them into the back of the truck.

"For your journey," he said, trying to stifle a laugh at their appearance. "I wish you luck!" The Jews thanked him for his hospitality and kissed him on the cheeks. Rebecca and Esther cried and thanked him repeatedly for his generosity and help. Then they all piled into the truck, and were off.

"Remember: you're gentiles now, so _act_ like it!" Alex called out to the Jews in the back of the truck. Daniel drove, Alex giving him directions from the passenger side. Emily sat on the bench seat between them. "We'll stay on back roads to avoid being seen," Alex said, opening the thermos and pouring his first of many cups of coffee. They drove for many hours in apprehensive silence, and were slightly relieved that there were no Germans to be seen.

When the sun went down, Daniel asked, "Are we stopping for the night?"

"No, we'll keep going," Alex replied. "Don't worry, I'll keep you awake."

Later, when Emily dozed off with her head on Daniel's shoulder, Daniel said, "You should get some sleep. I can stay awake."

"I don't sleep," Alex informed him matter-of-factly. He had been chain smoking and drinking endless cups of coffee all day. "No, really, I'm not kidding. I never sleep."

"Why not?"

"If I fall asleep, they will come and steal my dreams."

"Who?"

Alex paused and peered across at Daniel conspiratorially. "The *Belgians*," he answered slyly, then winked.

"The Belgians?"

Alex put a finger to his lips and winked again. "Sssshhh!"

The Resistance operative was quiet just a moment, then said, "And now I'm going to tell you a story that you may or may not believe. It's up to you. But it's all true, I swear it."

It all started when the glamorous film starlet Viviane Romance dropped a matchbook in the Boise de Boulogne at midnight. Alex found the matchbook. It had her address in it. He went to the address and she answered the door. "I've been waiting," was all she said, and then they engaged in a thirty-seven-and-a-half minute love affair. Although it was short-lived, it was exceptionally passionate and Alex became obsessed with the former Moulin Rouge chorus line dancer and Miss Paris 1930. Over a period of six months, he composed exactly one thousand love poems inspired by her, but didn't write any of them down.

"They all remained locked away up here –" he said, tapping his head "—all one thousand of them."

He didn't write them down because he knew his arch-nemesis, the unscrupulous Belgian poet Geert Grub, would have stolen them and published them as his own, becoming the greatest poet of all time. To deny Geert this distinction, Alex swore to never write the poems down or even speak them aloud. But Geert was unrelenting. Every day, he would follow Alex to his favorite bistro and sit at the same table in the corner partially obscured by a Madagascar fern, staring at him from across the room.

"He knew I was composing, but it was all in my mind, so he knew he would never get his hands on my work. The knowledge of this slowly drove him mad. Eventually, he took to wearing women's lingerie under his clothes and affecting an incompetent British accent. But he could never fool me and he never got his hands on my poems. The deranged Belgian grew so desperate that he hired Chinese assassins to stalk me, and I had to flee Paris with only the clothes on my back.

"To escape the Chinese assassins, I joined the merchant marine and my ship was sunk by a German U-Boat in the North Atlantic.

The U-Boat surfaced and the Germans came up on deck to shoot the survivors in the water, in order to draw sharks with the blood. Then they watched as the sharks tore the screaming men to pieces and devoured them. I used a broken oar to fight the sharks off, until I was completely exhausted. Six of us survived the attack, and floated aimlessly in a lifeboat at the mercy of the Canaries Current for five months. We tried our best to ration the little tins of water and biscuits, limiting each man to two sips of water and one-sixteenth of a biscuit per day, but soon ran out of these life-essential commodities and resorted to attempting to drink our urine.

"When that didn't work, we collected rain water and dew on a canvas tarpaulin and carefully poured it into the empty water tins to store. When it didn't rain, we caught turtles and birds and drank their blood to keep us alive. We made fishing lines with safety pins and cords stripped from the tarpaulin, and caught the small fish that gathered around the hull of our lifeboat. With these resources, we barely managed to stay alive. Fighting off fatigue and madness was also a full-time job. We kept alert by playing memory games and singing songs, but morale began to become a problem.

"At night, we studied the constellations and found Ursa Major and Ursa Minor. From the position of Polaris, the brightest star in Ursa Minor, we were able to figure out that we were drifting along the coast of Africa. Weeks and weeks passed; one seaman went mad and started drinking seawater to quench his burning thirst. He became delirious and died the next day. We slipped him over the side for the sharks to eat – one less mouth to take food and water out of our own. After a month, we realized our diet of fish, with the occasional turtle or seagull, wasn't going to be enough to sustain us for long. We became weaker and started to hallucinate from the dehydration and lack of sustenance. We couldn't look at each other. We'd become unrecognizable – no longer human beings, just emaciated skeletons with blistered skin stretched over our bones, and long hair and beards – animals, really. After two months, we'd given up all hope.

"Then we came to an island. It was a beautiful tropical island, inhabited by a civilized, friendly tribe of natives called the Umboogwa. They took us in and sheltered us, fed us and treated us just like one of their own. They were sensitive, artistic people, and physically beautiful as well, especially the women, who were all large-breasted and had thick, shiny black hair and pearl-white teeth. We spent weeks with them as we slowly recovered our strength, during which time they taught us their language and shared their culture with us.   They were very curious about our culture, fascinated with our stories as we attempted to explain the European lifestyle to them. They were fascinated, too, with our light-colored skin, and seemed to take great pleasure in admiring it and even stroking it. In fact, our skin became a sort of fetish for them, and we began to grow uncomfortable. Suddenly, the island didn't seem to be such a paradise anymore, and we secretly planned to leave as soon as we were able. That's when we realized they were just fattening us up to take our skin, and use it to create various shamanistic works of art for their sacrificial rituals. That's right, the Umboogwa were skin-worshippers! So, after one last night of celebration and feasting, we escaped to our lifeboat and resumed our trek across the sea.

"Not long after our escape, a second man succumbed. He didn't die as much as just drifted off, his eyes open, his mind just winding down into nothing like a watch that needed to be wound. We realized what we had to do, the unspoken horror, the thing no one wanted to contemplate, and we didn't toss him to the sharks. There wasn't much left of him, but he would provide us with another week or two of life, so we…

"And another month went by. No hope of rescue, no sign of land, just the endless, boundless, unconquerable ocean spanning out in all directions, a flat, three hundred and sixty degree horizon…

"*Catabolysis*, it's called – when the body starts breaking down tissues and muscle in order to keep the more vital organs such as the brain and heart functioning. The body is literally cannibalizing itself to stay alive. These are the later stages of severe starvation. At a certain point, lethargy and apathy take over – you don't really care that you are dying, and you even stop feeling pain. You become detached from your surroundings, floating in unreality,

drifting in a surreal state of non-being halfway between life and death. That is when you feel as if you can reach out and touch death itself, an apparition, a suspended vapor – the veil between this existence and the next.

"The others slipped away, one by one, over the next few weeks, until I was the last one left. *Why wouldn't I die?* The hallucinations took over. The sharks came up out of the water and they were wearing spectacles and shirts and ties, like men. They ate my comrades with knives and forks, in a civilized manner, while drinking brandy and smoking cigars and discussing politics and foreign trade. Viviane Romance, my glamorous film star, was there, playfully blowing me a kiss before walking away hand in hand with my arch-nemesis Geert Grub. I looked over the side of my boat and watched as my sea-faring comrades – all the ones who had been eaten by the sharks after we were torpedoed months ago – did an Esther Williams-style synchronized water ballet, just like in a Hollywood movie. It was my brain, blowing its last few precious calories on spectacular fantasy sequences and bizarre theater-of-the-absurd imagery. Then, one day, I too slipped under the veil and lost all consciousness.

"I am told I was found off the coast of Patagonia by an Argentine salmon fisherman. In all, the lifeboat I was in drifted a total of more than 7,000 miles. All I remember is weeks later, when I came out of my coma, clean-shaven and hair neatly cut, in the fisherman's little hut on the coast. The fisherman's wife had nursed me back to health with her hearty cooking of grilled *asado* meats, homemade *empanadas*, and goat's milk. Within a month, I was already getting my strength back enough to go out on the fisherman's boat and help him bring in his hauls of salmon. I worked with the fisherman on his boat for six months, and became a part of his family.

"Then one night in a bar in Rio Gallegos, I met an English mountain climber named Bill Tilman and his Sherpa guide, Tenzing Norgay. They had just finished a practice climb in the lower Andes and were currently plotting their next expedition to Mt. Everest. They asked me what a Frenchman was doing in Patagonia, and I told them my recent survival story. Impressed, they asked me to join the expedition. Knowing it was only a matter of time before Geert's Chinese assassins finally tracked me down, I decided to take them up on the offer and the three of us set out for Tibet the following morning.

"There were seven of us climbers, and forty-five sherpas on the expedition. We were attempting the climb over the North Ridge from Tibet. We walked in and established a base camp at the head of the East Rongbuk Glacier, on the North Col. The North Col is an icy, treacherous pass carved by ancient glaciers, and we got stopped there for several days by severe cold temperatures. Several climbers were already complaining of frostbite, and we hadn't even started up the ridge yet! It was in base camp, while waiting out the bitter cold weather, that I began to realize that the sherpas had been infiltrated by Geert's Chinese assassins! It was impossible to tell them from the real sherpas, but I thought I saw several of them sabotaging some of the ropes and climbing gear, so I alerted Tenzing and he talked to the head climber about it. Meanwhile, I made a habit of keeping my gear nearby and checking it continually for knife-cuts and other signs of sabotage.

"Finally, the weather cleared and the air warmed enough for us to start our trek up the treacherous North Ridge. We had to cross the East Rongbuk Glacier, which was covered with deep snow from the last three days of weather. It was slow going, but we made some progress and established the second camp on the slope of the ridge. The climbers with frostbite were not getting any better, so some of the sherpas broke off and took three of the British climbers back down to base camp to recover. Meanwhile, the weather turned bad again, so we couldn't push on from the second camp yet. That's when Tenzing came to me and said he'd figured out that the Chinese assassins were probably embedded with the dozen or so sherpas who came up from Nepal, and that he was not well-acquainted with them. But he promised to keep an eye on them and report back to me if he saw anything suspicious.

"While we hunkered down in the second camp, waiting for the weather to break, Tenzing discovered that the food supply had been tampered with. Most of the provisions were gone, and we were left with a few morsels of tough salted pork and a few sips of water per man per day, hardly enough to keep us going on a climb like this one. Fortunately we could eat snow to keep from becoming dehydrated, but the lack of calories would soon become a problem. Then, more bad news: the monsoon broke three weeks early, which meant heavy snow at night and slow progress during the day. Attempting to reach the summit during the monsoon was risky business, and even the veteran climbers were wary.

"The head climber, Bill Tilman, decided to split the party and assault the summit from two directions. One group would attempt the North Col pass from the west, while the other group – the one I was in – would climb the North Ridge to the summit. Some of the sherpas from Nepal – thus, the Chinese assassins – were with our team, and I was watching them very closely as we made our way up the ridge. The weather worsened as we climbed. The snow got deeper and deeper, and soon we were facing a blizzard. We had to tie ourselves together with ropes so we wouldn't get lost, Tenzing still in front leading the way. We trudged on and on. Soon, I couldn't even see the man in front of me. That's when my rope was cut, leaving me and the men behind me hopelessly separated from Tenzing's group up ahead.

"It was white-out conditions in a driving wind and we had no idea which direction we were going in. 'Climb uphill!' one of the sherpas called out to me through the blizzard. *Was it one of the assassins?* I couldn't tell! 'Keep going up!' he shouted again, so I followed his advice and kept climbing. The temperature was dropping rapidly. We couldn't see anything ahead or behind us. We were lost somewhere on the North Ridge, and conditions were getting worse the more we climbed. 'Are you sure we should keep going up?' I asked the Sherpa. 'Yes, to find the others!' he called back. We kept going until we were too exhausted to continue. My face was numb with ice, I couldn't feel my toes and fingers. We had no shelter, no source of warmth but our own bodies, so we huddled there in the snow and ice – five or six helpless, lost souls, at nature's mercy, waiting to die there on the last forlorn approach to the summit of Everest.

"It was starting to get dark. There was no way we could survive on this ridge overnight. *This is it*, I thought. *This is how I will die.* Just then, in the distance, I thought I saw a figure approaching our little group. *Probably just a hallucination*, I thought, feeling the grip of hypothermia and lack of oxygen descending over me like a shadow. Then I saw another figure, and another. They were getting closer to us. They were real! It was Tenzing, leading his party back down the ridge to find us! The sherpas with him were carrying one of the British climbers, who appeared unconscious.

"'It's impossible to go further!' Tenzing called out. 'We've got to go back down!'

I asked what happened to the unconscious climber. Tenzing said he'd been pushed down a ravine, and he had a broken leg and probably a concussion, but no one saw who did it. *The assassins!* I thought. Tenzing expertly led us all down the ridge back to our camp, cold, hungry, defeated and demoralized – but still alive. There we found out the other group met with their own calamity in the North Col.   As they were making their way through the treacherous, icy pass, something triggered an avalanche which cut them off from their camp on the Rongbuk Glacier. The blizzard had abated slightly, so we all grabbed as many picks and shovels as we could carry and hurried to dig the other team out. We spent the whole night digging frantically in sub-zero temperatures, hoping and praying that the trapped team would make it until morning. Fortunately, they were digging as best they could from their side, and met us somewhere in the middle as the sun was coming up.

They were glad to see us, but the avalanche and the bitter cold night had taken its toll.   Several of them had severe frostbite, suffering blackened noses, ears, hands and feet, and had to be carried down the mountain to safety. Two men – a British climber and a sherpa – were still buried in the avalanche – lost forever in an eternal icy grave.   The expedition was over, the summit would remain untouched for at least another year, due to sabotage and severe weather conditions. The sherpas from Nepal – the *Chinese assassins* – were nowhere to be found. The saboteurs had slipped away in the night, after triggering the deadly avalanche – an avalanche I was sure had been meant for me.

We made our way back to Lhasa to recover, and Tenzing and I parted ways a few days later. I haven't seen him since, but I thanked him for saving my life up there on that ridge that day, and we parted as life-long brothers. But before I left, I wrote down one of my best poems on a fine piece of rice paper and sealed it inside a brocade envelope with the matchbook Viviane Romance had dropped in the Bois de Boulogne that night we met. Then I gave it to Tenzing and asked him to carry it with him on his next expedition, and if he ever made it to the summit, to leave it there for me. I hope he makes it someday."

Alex's story ended quietly at dawn, when, golden sunshine streaming through the truck windshield, Emily finally stirred, yawned and stretched.

"Where are we?" she asked, trying to open her eyes.

"About forty kilometers from Switzerland," Alex answered.

"I'm hungry," Emily said. "Can't we stop for a break?"

"A very short one," Alex said, and Daniel pulled the truck over next to a field. The Jews climbed out of the back of the truck and stretched their legs. Everyone ate some bread and cheese and drank coffee and watched some cows graze nearby. Birds chirped their bright morning song from branches overhead. It was a peaceful spot, and the war seemed far away – the way France was before the occupation.

Leaning against a rock wall, Emily smiled and took Daniel by the hand. "I wish we could just stay here forever." She looked happy and relaxed. Daniel's heart swelled, and he didn't even try to hide his blush.

"Time to go, everyone," Alex ordered.

"Oh, just a little longer?" Emily pleaded.

"We've got to keep moving," Alex said. "If you ever want to get to Switzerland, that is…"

Everyone climbed back into the truck, and Daniel steered it back onto the road. Twenty minutes later, he saw something blocking the road ahead and slowed down.

"What is it?" Emily asked.

"A German checkpoint," Daniel answered.

"All right, everyone," Alex sighed. "Here we go…"

"I can back away," Daniel suggested, "and take another route."

"That would look suspicious," Alex observed. "There's nothing for it but to keep going."

Daniel approached slowly and stopped at the red and white barricade. A German sentry walked up to the cab and peered in the window. Seeing the liturgical garb Alex and Emily were wearing, he immediately pointed to a turn-off and barked "Take that road!"

"What?" Alex asked, hesitating.

"That's the road to the river!" the sentry barked impatiently. "Take that road!" The sentry touched the butt of the rifle slung over his shoulder with one hand.

"You'd better do what he says," Alex told Daniel. Daniel turned the truck and headed down the road the sentry had pointed to.

"What was all that about?" Emily asked anxiously.

"I don't know," Alex answered. "Maybe the other road is closed. But that's the way to Switzerland, so we've got to get back to it eventually."

They soon came to a small village by a river, where scores of priests, nuns, and ordinary villagers stood gathered on the banks. People lined the river on both sides, as if waiting for something to pass by on the water. Daniel pulled the truck off the road, in a spot where they could see what was going on, and waited. Not long after, a boat with a large statue of the Virgin Mary came into view on the river. The boat was flanked by barefoot priests walking along both banks of the river chanting prayers, carrying swinging thuribles of burning incense, and giving communion to spectators on the shore. Other people walked barefoot into the river and tossed written prayers on small folded pieces of parchment into the boat with the statue.

The boat was followed by other rowboats full of worshippers, chanting prayers and singing hymns. Then more people along the riverbank stepped barefoot into the water, trying desperately to get close to the statue of Mary, sprinkling infants with water from the boat's wake. Crippled people were being carried into the water – the blind, lame, missing limbs – and "dipped" for healing. Lines of women carrying infants made their way to the shore, where priests baptized them.

"The statue of Our Lady of Boulogne," Emily said in amazement. "It started in Lourdes a few years ago. It's been taken all over France to inspire a spiritual re-awakening during the occupation."

"There are actually four of them," Alex explained cynically. "All traveling at the same time in order to quicken the *re-awakening*. There's only a one-in-four chance this one's the real statue."

"It doesn't matter," Emily said, taking in the scene. "To these people, she's real."

They all got out of the truck, including the Jews, who stared at the spectacle uncomprehendingly. Not wanting to stand out, Alex instructed everyone to bow their heads and pretend to pray.

"Pretend?" Rebecca exclaimed. "I've been praying since we left Gaspere's farm!"

An old man on crutches hobbled up to Aaron. "Father, would you take me into the water and pray for my healing?" Aaron froze, looking at Alex for guidance. Alex noticed two German soldiers watching nearby and said, "You better do it." Alex and Daniel helped the old man into the water, and Aaron waded in after them.

"What do I do?" Aaron hissed in Alex's ear.

"Just sprinkle some water on him and look like you're praying." Aaron did as he was told, rather unconvincingly.

"Look at the superstitious fools!" one of the German soldiers scoffed. "What a ridiculous spectacle!"

"That's the Holy Mother," the other soldier said reverently. "Better be careful…"

"Nonsense! I don't believe in such clap-trap!" the atheist soldier thundered. Then he shouted at Aaron. "Hey, you! What good is that doing them? He's not going to be healed, and you know it! Why give them false hope?" Aaron didn't answer. "Hey, I'm talking to you, *Pere*! They're only going to be let down when all of this is over and that fake statue floats on down the river!"

"Leave him alone!" the pious soldier said. "He's a *priest*!"

"No he's not – he's an imposter!"

They all froze tensely. Aaron looked horrified.

"He's a charlatan, a con man, just like all the others!" the atheist soldier continued. He waded into the water and confronted Aaron, who was breaking out in a cold sweat and looking like he was going to faint. "I told you to stop that! You can't heal him, and you know it!"

Aaron fumbled for words. "I…I'm just praying for him…"

Nikolai intervened, taking Aaron by the arm. "Come, brother. It's time to go –"

"And look at this one! He's *blind*!" the atheist jeered. "You can't even heal yourself, how are you going to heal all of these cripples?"

The pious soldier took his partner by the arm. "Come on, leave them alone. Let's go get a beer or something." The atheist looked from Nikolai to Aaron, and back to Nikolai again.

"Ah, you're right," he finally concluded. "Let these Frenchmen take advantage of each other. What is it to us, anyway?"

"That's right, come on," his partner agreed, leading him back onto the shore.

The atheist took one last look back at Nikolai, laughing derisively. "A blind priest! What next?" Then the two soldiers were gone, and everyone breathed again.

"We've got to get out of here," Alex said darkly. "This place is giving me a bad feeling."

As nonchalantly as possible, they all piled back into the truck and Daniel guided it carefully through the streets, still thronged with religious pilgrims. Fortunately, most people were too enraptured by the glorious presence of the statue to give them much notice, and before long they'd found their way back to the main road. After two hours of uneventful driving, Emily said, "We've got to be nearing the border soon."

Alex was studying a map in his lap. "From what I can tell, we've got about fifteen kilometers to go." *Fifteen kilometers*! For the first time, Emily felt like they were actually going to make it to Switzerland. Her spirits rising, she leaned over and kissed Daniel on the cheek. Alex caught it out of the corner of his eye, and slyly smiled.

"Better be careful, kids," he said dryly. "Mixing work and pleasure can be dangerous."

"Oh, we're just very dear friends," Emily clarified.

"That's the way _you_ see it," Alex replied. "But I wouldn't be surprised if Daniel sees things differently." Emily smiled wanly, but Daniel's silence was not reassuring. "Ah, the course of true love never did run smooth," Alex continued, and then launched into a lengthy soliloquy on the difficulties and disappointments of love over the years – his brief but notably passionate encounter with the starlet Viviane Romance notwithstanding. And, as he began it, he ended the sermon with a Shakespearean flourish: "Reason and love keep little company together nowadays."

Just as he was wrapping up, Daniel saw a railroad crossing up ahead and stopped the truck. A train – a German troop train – had been derailed and was blocking the road. The cars were buckled and snarled, some even spilling out into a nearby field. Soldiers were everywhere, swarming like flies – shouting, patrolling the crime scene, scouring the nearby woods.

"Oh, no!" Alex moaned.

"Who did this?" Daniel asked.

"We did," Alex said. "The Resistance. And it looks like they did a real good job of it, too. Nice, by the book. But not so nice for _us_…" He shook his head and chuckled ruefully at the irony. Up ahead, two German soldiers with machine guns saw them and started walking toward the truck.

"What do we do?" Emily gasped.

"If you don't want to be shot, I suggest you do whatever they say."

The soldiers were tense, tired, and in no mood for niceties. "Get out!" they barked. "Get out of the truck, now!" Daniel, Emily and Alex opened the doors and got out of the cab. The soldier saw their ecumenical garb and gave them a strange look. "A priest and a nun?"

"There are more in the back," his partner called from the rear of the truck, where he was ordering the Jews to climb out. The soldiers lined them up on the side of the road and told them to put their hands behind their heads. They both gripped their machine guns tightly, watching their prisoners with cold eyes. They shouted in German to their comrades at the train. An agonizing moment later, a young officer appeared and walked up and down the line, inspecting them. The officer seemed twitchy, nervous. He looked them over distractedly, without making eye contact.

This is it, Daniel thought. *This is the end. They're going to make <u>us</u> pay for the train…*

He looked over at Emily. She was scared, but trying to look brave as the young officer paced back and forth in front of them. Finally, he stopped in front of Nikolai. "Bring him," he ordered the soldiers, then turned and walked back to the train. A soldier pulled Nikolai out of the line and led him behind the officer. When he reached the train, the officer entered one of the cars, followed by Nikolai and the soldier. Inside, the car was like an office.

"Leave us," the officer said to the soldier, who clicked his heels, saluted, and left the car. The officer slowly drew the window shades, turned on a lamp, and sat down behind his desk. "Sit down," he said to Nikolai, who felt for the chair before complying.

The officer stared at Nikolai a long time, while Nikolai stayed quiet and sweat bullets. The officer slowly pulled his luger pistol out of its holster, held it up in front of him, examined the barrel, then set it carefully down on the desk in front of him.

"Are you a *real* priest?" he finally asked.

Mortified, Nikolai gulped hard and nodded, unable to speak.

The officer looked down at his pistol, then crossed himself and said, "Father forgive me. It has been six weeks since my last confession." There was a long pause. Nikolai didn't know what to say. "Will you hear my confession?" the officer asked anxiously.

"Of course," Nikolai choked out hoarsely. "Please go ahead…my son…"

"Father, my soul is very troubled," the officer said.

"W-What is it, my son?"

The officer looked down at his hands. "Father, I've done…I've had to do things…very troubling things…"

"Tell me."

"I can't say it."

"It may help you to…talk about it."

"I am a soldier. This is wartime. I have been given certain orders…"

"My son, the good book tells us, everyone is subject to authority."

"My orders often ask me to do…very terrible things…"

"Such as?"

"Yesterday, I shot two Jews. In the head."

"How – how did it make you feel?" Nikolai heard his voice shaking. He made an effort to steady it.

"I enjoyed it."

"Why?"

"I don't know."

"Maybe you were mistaken," Nikolai suggested.

"No. I enjoyed it. Is that a sin? To enjoy it"

"The sixth commandment tells us that murder is a sin."

"But to murder, and enjoy it, I mean. Is it a *double* sin?"

"Some sins are worse than others, but all damage our relationship with God."

"Father, please be straightforward with me. My soul is in torment…"

"In the case of murder, one's enjoyment of it is irrelevant."

"What are you saying?"

"I'm saying, whether you enjoy it or not, murder is a serious sin."

"Tell me: what can I do to _redeem_ myself?" the officer asked, in anguish.

"You may be beyond redemption."

"That is not possible, with a merciful God."

"Who said anything about a merciful God?"

The officer was taken aback. "What kind of a priest *are* you?"

"I am an *honest* priest," Nikolai said. "Maybe there's no hope for you. Maybe you're beyond redemption. Maybe, if there _is_ a God, he is not merciful at all. I don't know."

"You don't *know*? Aren't you _supposed_ to know?"

"I suppose. But this collar gives me no special powers, no supernatural insight."

"But you're a man of God."

"Not really."

"Father, you shouldn't doubt your salvation."

"Why not? What assurance is there?"

"You've got to have *faith*."

"In what?"

The officer thought for a moment. "Father, I have made a confession to you. Aren't you under oath or something to, you know, make me right with God?"

"I can't do that."

"But you're the only priest I've seen for *weeks* – since I came to France. Father, I need forgiveness, I need to be made right with God – even if <u>you</u> don't believe, please, for my soul's sake…"

"All right, if it will make you feel any better," Nikolai relented. "Bless you, my son. The Lord is pleased with your repentance. Say three Hail Mary's and reflect on the goodness of God."

"Is that it?"

"What did you expect?"

"The German priests are somewhat more *strict*…"

"All right. Tell me what your German priest back home would say."

"Three Hail Mary's, two Our Fathers, one rosary, seven prayers for forgiveness, no alcohol for seven days, and reflect on the goodness of God for three days.'

"All right, do all of that then. Are we finished?"

"Are all French priests like you?"

"You'd be surprised."

Feeling "redeemed," the officer allowed Nikolai to leave. Nikolai exited the railroad car and strode on shaky legs back to the truck where the others were waiting.

"Did he interrogate you?" Alex asked.

"You could say that."

"What did he ask you?" Emily wanted to know.

"We had a…very stimulating theological discussion," Nikolai said, mopping his brow with his sleeve. "I wonder what he would do if he knew he'd just confessed to a non-practicing Jew?"

"They had nothing to do with the sabotage," they heard the officer tell the guards. "They may go on their way." The officer started to look in Nikolai's direction, then turned away suddenly and walked back to the train.

Night was falling as they once again took to the road. Alex was able to find a way around the train that didn't add too much time to their trip. When it was completely dark, he quietly instructed Daniel to pull off the road and take a narrow dirt path that wound its way down to the shore of a lake. "This is it," he announced.

He got out of the truck, went around to the back, and pulled the truck's tailgate down. The Jews climbed down and stretched their legs and backs. "We're almost there," Alex told them. "The worst part is over. A ferry will take you across the lake, and that's it." They looked around, and saw a man with a lantern a few hundred meters down the shore. He saw them and waved them over with the lantern. "That's the ferryman," Alex said. The exhausted group trudged over to the man, who greeted them with a smile. "How was your trip?" he asked.

"Interesting," Alex answered.

"Germans?"

"Oui, lots."

"Well, you made it here in one piece," the man said, pointing across the lake. "You see the light at the dock on the other side of the lake? That's Switzerland."

"Where's the ferry?" Nikolai asked.

"Ferry?" the man repeated. "No, there's no ferry. We're going across in that." He held the lantern up to illuminate a small rowboat pulled up on shore.

"In *that*?" Nikolai gasped, his eyes growing big.

"There are four of us," Rebecca said in alarm. "We can't all fit in that tiny boat."

"I will take you across two at a time," the boatman assured them.

"It doesn't look like it could make it across this lake," Aaron protested.

"I'm not getting in that boat," Esther agreed. "It's too dangerous."

"Don't you have another boat?" Nikolai asked in desperation.

"No, this is it," the boatman said.

Everyone was silent a moment. Finally, Alex spoke. "We've come too far for this to fall apart now. Look, there's Switzerland! You can see it! You're getting in that boat and crossing this lake!"

"Now, who's going first?" the boatman wanted to know.

"All right, we'll go first," Aaron volunteered. "Let's just get this over with." Aaron and Esther carefully climbed into the boat, and the boatman pushed them off and got in himself. The boat tipped from side to side precariously.

"Don't worry, I'll be back for you two in a jiffy," the boatman promised, and began to row across the lake. The rest of them watched anxiously from the shore, until the blackness of night enveloped the tiny craft.

"I hope they make it," Rebecca said, hands folded in front of her as if in prayer. They waited for two hours, with no sign of the boat's return. Finally, the light across the lake began to flash a message.

"It's Morse code," Alex said. "It says, 'Made it across safely. Boat sprung a leak. Have to find another boat.'"

Several more hours went by. Then they saw the boatman crossing back in a different boat.

"That boat looks worse than the first one!" Rebecca exclaimed. When the boatman reached shore, they could all see that the bottom of the boat was full of water.

"It's sinking!" Nikolai said in disbelief.

"Just a little water," the boatman said cheerfully, handing him a bucket. "I'll row, you two bail. We'll be fine…"

"The Resistance can't find boats without holes in them," Nikolai lamented. "We're going to lose the war!"

"Come on, I'll have you safe in Switzerland for breakfast!" the boatman promised.

Nikolai and Rebecca hugged Emily and Daniel. "Thank you for everything you have done for us, my friends," Nikolai said, his voice catching slightly.

"We will never forget you," Rebecca said, fighting back tears. They shook hands with Alex, and warily climbed into the boat. They immediately began bailing as the boatman started to row.

"Bail faster!" the boatman commanded. "We're listing! Bail faster!"

Thirty meters out, they could hear Nikolai's panic-stricken voice across the water: "There's too much water! We should turn back!"

"Nonsense!" the boatman said calmly. "We'll make it, I tell you!"

Fifteen minutes ticked by in complete silence. Emily clasped Daniel's hand so tightly, he felt the circulation in his fingers being cut off. Then, a new message from the light across the lake. "They made it!" Alex said in relief.

"Thank God!" Emily gasped, still holding tightly to Daniel's hand.

"We did it!" Daniel marveled. "They're safe!"

It was no time to celebrate – that would come later. The three of them got back in the truck and drove all night and the rest of the day back to Gaspere's farm, to pick Hector up. Gaspere and his wife were pleased to hear that the refugees had made it to safety. The typically grumpy cat took one look at Daniel and showed his disapproval at being left behind for two days by emitting a muffled, half-hearted growl. "I know you missed me, boy," Daniel said, scratching him behind the ears and loading him into the back of the truck.

Alex told them they were on their own now, that he would be making his own way back.

"What will you do now?" Emily asked.

"Check in with headquarters, make my report, then wait for my next assignment. The war is far from over yet…"

"*Bon chance*," Daniel said.

"And you two be careful," Alex replied. "There's still a lot of Germans out there!"

It would be much simpler traveling without such a large group to explain. They were simply two circus workers bringing a lion on the mend back from the hospital. Daniel cherished more one-on-one time with Emily, and even contemplated taking the long way back in order to extend the precious time with her. Then he thought better of it, as it would increase their possible exposure to German patrols, and, besides, Emily might catch on to his scheme and become cross with him.

As it was, they had plenty of time together. Emily talked of her plans after the war – of continuing in the circus business with Constantine, of perfecting their act, making it more thrilling and death-defying. Daniel felt jealous of Constantine, especially when she talked like this – but he didn't want to appear sullen, and tried not to let it show.

"What happens to the act when you have children?" he asked.

"Leave it to you to think of that!" she laughed, playfully slapping him on the arm. "Well, I suppose we'd teach them the routines and put them in the act. Why not? A real family affair."

"It sounds just *perfect*," Daniel said, unintentionally allowing a bit of bitterness into his voice. He immediately regretted it, but it was too late – he could tell she'd already caught it. Her mood changed in an instant.

"Daniel, you know I'm with Constantine," she said.

"Oui, oui – I *know*," he said, again impatiently.

She softened, reaching over and taking his hand. "Constantine and I are together, but what *we* – you and I – have is much better in a way, much sweeter…"

"This is the part where you tell me how young I am –"

"Please don't talk like that," she squeezed his hand. "I don't want it to spoil our lovely ride together. You know I love you, in my own special way –"

"That's right, like a *brother*."

She leaned over and kissed him on the cheek. "Is that kind of love so bad?"

He didn't answer. He felt like brooding a while, so she let him. They drove along in silence for about twenty minutes before he was able to overcome the pettiness. He didn't like the feeling of it, of wallowing in it – he was determined to pull himself up, to be bigger than that.

"I'm sorry," he finally said.

"You certainly are!" she teased, with her sly grin. "Now, it's all in the past. We won't discuss it anymore. What would _you_ like to talk about now? Motorcycle racing, I suppose…"

They both laughed, the dark cloud gone now, the lightness and ease of sweet friendship returning for the rest of the journey back to the little *Cirque d'Europa*.

Chapter 11

When they returned to the circus, Baron de Siklos and Monsieur Victor called an emergency meeting to deliver some shocking news. The Baron was too drunk, so the ringmaster did all the talking. During their lengthy absence, Feldcommandant Dokken, the new German commander, had become suspicious of a recent surge in Resistance activities in the area. Certain that some of the performers had something to do with it, he started ratcheting up the pressure on the little circus – requisitioning and stripping the circus trucks for spare parts, then revoking their animal permits and confiscating their animals. The circus was effectively dead.

"We cannot pay you," Monsieur Victor told everyone flatly. "The Germans have taken everything. We are closing the circus."

Sighs and gasps of dismay went up from the performers and crew alike.

"What will we do?" Madame Durand demanded, tears stinging her eyes.

"But we're family, aren't we?" Madame Olga protested. "You don't just split up a family!"

"I've been in this circus for twenty years," Monsieur Laurent, the one-armed lion tamer, lamented. "Where will we go?"

Several other performers expressed similar concerns. "We're not going to throw anybody out," the ringmaster assured them. "You may continue to live in your caravans – that is, until the Germans take them. I am sorry, my friends. I know this is your life, as it is mine. I am so sad to see it end this way…" Then Monsieur Andre took off his crumpled bowler hat and blew his nose on a tattered handkerchief. Everyone – including Lars the Helsinki Hercules – gathered around to comfort the distraught ringmaster. Even Napoleon the monkey perched gingerly on Monsieur Andre's shoulder, dabbing the tears from his eyes with a napkin.

Constantine quietly but urgently pulled Emily and Daniel aside. "We've got bigger problems," he informed them. "Rene has been arrested by the Gestapo. The cell is compromised, and the orders are to disband at once. What's worse, the Germans know everything we've been doing – the picnics, the errands – even taking Nikolai and Rebecca to Switzerland."

"How could they know?" Emily asked, her face turning white.

"They had an informer, right here in the circus," Constantine explained. "One of the clowns. The Hungarian, the one with the big ears and frizzy red hair."

"I never trusted him!" Emily said. "He was never that funny, either."

"Listen, the Gestapo are on their way here," Constantine continued breathlessly. "We've got to split up and leave, right now." He handed Daniel a slip of paper. "We'll meet at this safehouse in Dijon in two weeks. Memorize that address and then burn the paper. Get on your motorcycle and go. But don't go back to your village, that will only lead the Gestapo there. Find a place to hide out for two weeks, and then we'll meet in Dijon. Now go!"

Emily kissed Daniel on the cheek. "Be careful. We'll see you in Dijon."

Daniel ran to his tent and grabbed his bag of personal belongings, some clothes, and some money. Then he tied the bundle to the back of his motorcycle and rode away from the circus – his home for the last six months – with no idea where he was going. The only place he could think of was the little cottage in *Neufchateau*, where Anne-Marie, Monsieur Le Grun's young wife, had shown him so much kindness. Would she help him again? Daniel pointed the motorcycle in that direction and kept riding all day.

The closer he got to *Neufchateau*, however, the more a little voice in the back of his mind kept telling him it would be a mistake. Did he really want to mix Anne-Marie – and the baby – up in his troubles with the Gestapo? By the time he reached the village, he knew the answer. He decided to stay away from the warm, inviting little cottage altogether. As scared as he was, he couldn't live with himself if he endangered Anne-Marie and the baby.

So he found a meadow just outside the village and hid the motorcycle behind some trees. He would camp here until he figured out where to go. He built a small fire and sat down beside it to eat some cheese and bread he'd bought in the village. It was dark now, and a plan began to formulate in his mind as he ate his meager supper.

Constantine had said the Gestapo knew everything about the "picnics" and "errands," so riding a motorcycle though the countryside alone might arouse suspicion. His motorcycle could give him away, but he couldn't bear the thought of just abandoning it somewhere. Then it struck him: he and his bike wouldn't stand out quite as much if he were part of a race!

Rising early the next morning, he spent the day tracking down Monsieur Albert, the racing impresario, finally finding him eating his supper in a tiny bistro in the nearby village of Chateauvillain. Despite the hasty nature of the interruption, he seemed not unpleased to see Daniel.

"Well, haven't seen much of you lately," Monsieur Albert said. He had a lit cigarette in the corner of his mouth as he ate his meal. "How is the circus treating you?"

"The circus is closed," Daniel informed him. "The Germans shut it down."

"I see. I suppose it will be the racing next. A waste of petrol, I can hear them say…"

"So, there is another race?" Daniel asked eagerly.

"Oh, *oui*. In two days, starting from this village. That's why I'm here, setting things up."

"I need to enter," Daniel said urgently, then caught himself. "That is, I would *like* to enter the race. I can pay the fee."

"No need to explain," Monsieur Albert said, picking up on Daniel's anxiety. "I've seen you ride. No questions asked."

"*Merci*."

"How is the bike running, by the way?"

"*Bien*, Monsieur."

"Ah, I should have known, the way you take care of that old relic. Now, why don't you sit down and try some of their veal. You look like you haven't eaten a proper meal in days."

"I – I'm afraid I can't afford a meal *here*," Daniel said. "I've only got enough money for the racing fees."

"Don't worry about that," Monsieur Albert said, sipping some wine. "I'm running a tab here. Sit down!"

So for the next two weeks, Daniel tried to be as inconspicuous as possible. He raced when he could, and camped out with the other racers in the fields at night, trying to blend in. At the same time, he kept to himself as much as possible – the less unnecessary communication with the other racers, the less chance of somehow giving himself away. Between races, he kept the motorcycle off the roads and lived off the land – catching a fish here, trapping a hare there – counting down the days until it was time to meet Constantine and Emily in Dijon. The racing kept his mind off the Gestapo, and the hunting, fishing, and camping out under the stars kept him occupied against the nagging anxiety of his situation. Laying under the stars at night, he would think of Emily and recount their last few conversations while traveling together after Switzerland. Then he would doze off by the fire and sleep peacefully, looking forward to seeing her again soon in Dijon.

The racing was purely for sport, and for cover. He knew he had no chance of winning – the other riders were racing newer bikes with bigger engines. Still, he somehow held his own and managed to finish each grueling race out of sheer will and skill. After the third race, he still had three days left before the rendezvous with Constantine and Emily. He headed back to his secluded camping spot, planning to hide the motorcycle and lay low until it was time to go to Dijon. It was a perfect spot, off the road, behind a bank of eucalyptus trees, a kilometer away from the nearest farmhouse.

As he neared the turn-off point to his hideaway, he thought he saw the flash of a car on the road ahead. The car looked to be coming towards him, and with a start he realized it had an iron cross painted on the hood and swastika flags mounted on each fender. A German staff car – maybe Gestapo, maybe army – he couldn't really tell. Thinking quickly, he turned off the road early and hid behind some thick bushes, waiting for the car to pass. He turned the bike off and prayed they hadn't seen him. When he dared peer through the bushes, he saw the car stopped in the middle of the road, idling. *Had they seen him?* His heart stopped. He held his breath, clutching the handlebars with white knuckles. Then he waited and waited.

Finally, he heard the clunk of the car being put into gear, and it continued slowly down the road. It passed him. *They hadn't seen him!* Relieved, Daniel started breathing again. He waited ten minutes, then started the motorcycle and continued on to his hideaway for the night. He didn't build a fire that night, just in case the Germans were still in the area. He ate some bread, drank some water, then laid down on his pallet of leaves and covered himself with his jacket. It was hard for him to fall asleep, and he scolded himself for being so nervous.

They did drive on, after all. They didn't see a thing, he told himself. Just as he was drifting off, he heard it. A rustling sound in the bushes nearby, the crackle of boots on the dry forest floor. H snapped awake and sat up. Nothing but blackness all around. Was he dreaming, already? He listened for the sound again, and heard nothing. *Maybe it was an animal,* he thought. *Or just your imagination.* Spooked now, he decided to stay awake until morning. But the more he tried to stay awake, the heavier his eyes got, until, finally, he could fight it no longer and fell into a deep sleep.

He woke up suddenly with a start. The sun was shining now. He _knew_ there was someone in his camp.   Sitting up, he tried to wipe the sleep from his eyes, but blinked against the bright morning sun instead. Finally, he looked around his little camp and saw him: A German officer, sitting on a log, holding a luger pistol in his hand. The German was staring right at him, as if he'd been patiently waiting for Daniel to wake up. Then Daniel noticed he was holding something in his other hand. Squinting in the bright light, Daniel could see that it was his papers. Finally, Daniel noticed his motorcycle had been wheeled out into the open from its hiding place where he'd stashed it the night before. And with a sinking heart, he realized they had him.

The officer stared coldly at Daniel. "How long have you been working for the Resistance?" he asked, in very good French.

"I…I don't know what you're talking about."

"I know who you are, boy," the officer said coolly. "How did they recruit you? _Who_ recruited you?"

"You must have me mistaken for somebody else."

"No. I don't think so." Then the officer looked at the motorcycle. "I know this motorcycle…"

"What?"

The officer stood up and walked to the motorcycle. He examined it more carefully. "Yes, this is it…I would know this motorcycle _anywhere._"

He looked at Daniel in confusion. "How…?" Then he raised the gun again. The German stiffness and coldness was back. "You are coming with me. It would be a grave mistake to resist."

Daniel gathered up his things, and the officer said, "Bring the motorcycle." He then walked Daniel out to the road, where the staff car Daniel saw the day before was parked. The officer was alone – no driver, no guard. There was a trailer attached to the back of the car.

"Help me load the motorcycle into the trailer," the officer ordered emotionlessly. They loaded the motorcycle, and then the German motioned for Daniel to get into the passenger seat of the car. The officer got in behind the wheel and started driving, his pistol trained on Daniel the whole way.

They drove to a farmhouse nearby. They unloaded the motorcycle and hid it in the barn. Then the officer walked Daniel into the house at gunpoint. There was no one else in the house. They walked down a hallway, and the officer opened a bedroom door. "In here," he said, and Daniel walked inside. The officer closed the door and locked it from outside. Daniel waited and waited. He listened, but the officer made no sound. The rest of the house was silent. *Maybe he left me here*, Daniel thought. He went to a window, but it was locked shut. He sat down on the bed and waited, wondering what the officer was doing, what he was up to. Soon, Daniel fell asleep on the bed and slept a long time. When he woke up, many hours later, the officer was in the room with him, sitting quietly in a chair. Daniel noticed he didn't have the luger with him.

"How…how long have you been there?" Daniel asked, groggy.

"A long time," the officer answered. "I have been thinking."

"Thinking about what?"

"About what to do with you."

"What do you mean?"

"At first, I was going to turn you in. As I said, I know who you are, and what you have been up to. Yes, it's my duty as an officer of the Third Reich to turn you in…"

Daniel stiffened. "Then why don't you get on with it? What are we doing here in this farmhouse?"

"My temporary quarters. I'm being re-assigned, you see."

"Are you Colonel Fischer?"

The officer laughed. "*Nein*, he's long gone. My name is Gerhardt Schiller. I am, however, being sent not far from where he is now. But for different reasons. Not for anything I've done wrong. Sometimes a certain set of sought-after skills brings you to the same exact place as incompetence."

Daniel knew he was talking about Russia – the Eastern Front. "Why are you telling me this?"

"Daniel Renaud. As I said, I've been thinking all night. I've decided not to turn you in. Does this surprise you?"

"What do you want?"

"I'm not toying with you, Daniel. I assure you, I am in earnest. Now you're asking yourself why I would risk my career to do this. I can see it in your face. Well, rest assured, I am going to explain everything. You see, before the war I was a mechanical engineer. I was in Rome in 1927, working as a consultant for a large motorcycle company. This company was so large, that they sponsored a whole stable of racers, and built custom racing bikes for them. But there was one champion they couldn't woo. His name was Tonino Bellini, and no matter how much money they offered him, he would not race for them. Instead, he and his brothers built their own custom motorcycles, and Tonino raced them. He won race after race with his bikes, and he was the darling of Rome at that time, much to the displeasure of the big motorcycle company.

"Well, before that year's championship race, the Bellini brothers rebuilt Tonino's engine – right there, on the grounds, three days before the race! Such confidence, such nerve! They had the engine torn apart, secretly toiling away in their workshop, hour after hour, for two days. Then, being Italian, they had to take a break for a large meal. That was my chance. During their break, I picked the lock and snuck into their workshop to see their work. I knew it was wrong, but I couldn't help myself. That's when I saw it. That's when I knew it. These men weren't mere engineers, weren't simple mechanics. No, these men were _artists_. Artists whose medium was steel and rubber and iron.

"While they ate, I had thirty minutes to behold a miracle – the most beautiful piece of machinery I had ever seen. It was all laid out, there on the workbench. I couldn't believe my eyes. The pistons weren't merely rods of iron – they were *sculptures*. Balanced, symmetrical –works of art worthy of Donetello or

Michaelangelo. The cylinders were like nothing I'd ever seen before – shaped like graceful goblets, you could imagine the gods on Mt. Olympus drinking nectar from them! The cylinder heads were not merely machined, they were *sculpted*, like the bust of Venus. And the most elegant gear ratio I have ever seen…

"A mere mortal such as I should never have seen the inner workings of that beautiful engine. I knew I'd been given a glimpse into a sublime world that I wasn't worthy of, that I could never attain, and I was humbled. I snuck out of the workshop feeling like a soulless thief, a *voyeur*. Days later, when I heard Tonino rev up his motorcycle before the race, I nearly wept. All the parts, combined together, worked in divine precision, in perfect harmony – like a symphony. The idle had the quiet precision of hummingbird wings. The compression was like angels sighing. Tonino won his race, and I, I returned to Germany defeated by my glimpse of Heaven, never to return to Italy." Schiller stopped and put his head down. He took a few minutes to compose himself, then said, "The only question I have, the only mystery that remains, is, how do you come to have this remarkable machine, Daniel?"

"I…my uncle repaired a rich man's car on the road to Paris ten years ago," Daniel struggled to make it truthful but brief. "He received the motorcycle as payment and brought it back to our village. My uncle and I worked on it and got it running again…"

"Extraordinary," the officer said breathlessly. Then he became distracted, lost in thought for some time – as if wrestling with his own soul. "Do you by any chance speak German, Daniel?"

"Please tell me what this is all about," Daniel said in German. "I want to trust you, but you need to give me a reason to."

Schiller closed his eyes, almost sighing in relief. "Your German is impeccable. No one would guess you are French."

"I'm half German. My tutor was born in Stuttgart."

Schiller opened his eyes. "This is perfect…perhaps too perfect…" Daniel could tell Schiller was circling something, but not yet fully committed.

Then he very quietly explained that his own son was in the army and had been missing in action for several months. "I know I will never see him again. But you…you bear a remarkable resemblance to him…" Schiller told him the only way to save his life was for him to assume his son's identity and return to active duty in the German army.

He saw the reaction in Daniel's eyes. "Listen to me Daniel. I am not insane. The Gestapo are looking for you. They had an informant in the circus. They know everything about you, about the *Cirque d'Europa*, Constantine, the girl Emily, the intelligence you were gathering for the Resistance. They are looking for a blond fifteen year old on a motorcycle. Even if I let you go, they will capture you again, sooner or later."

"But, I have plans," Daniel informed him.

"The *rendezvous* in Dijon? The Gestapo knows all about that. Your friends will be arrested as soon as they arrive."

"I must warn them."

"It's too dangerous."

"Then, I…I will go back to my village…to my uncle…"

The officer shook his head. "*Nein*, Daniel. They will track you to your village. They will find you. Do you know what the Gestapo does to Resistance fighters? Have you heard?"

"But I was only counting train cars…"

"I know you had only one foot in the pond. The Gestapo knows it too, but it makes no difference to them. They will hang you along with the others."

"But my uncle…"

"You would be endangering him if you went back home. Think about it, Daniel. Nein, you must become my son, and return to the army. It's the one place they would never look for you…"

"It won't work…"

"I will arrange it all. You will be found wandering in the forest, a little shell-shocked, but ready to return to duty after a little rest. During that time I can get you up to speed on things."

"But they'll know I'm not your son."

"I will arrange for you to be transferred to a new unit. Non-combat. Somewhere safe. You will have new identification, papers, everything. They will never know."

"Nein…"

"It's your only chance, Daniel. We have a good army. You see how strong and well cared-for our soldiers are. Your German would more than get you by. And you would be an officer's son. I promise you, you will be safe, Daniel. Safer than facing the Gestapo…"

"Nein – this is too much…"

"It's the only way," Schiller said, reaching over and touching him gently on the knee. "Look, I can see you're just a boy, you don't deserve what the Gestapo will do to you. I can't…I can't allow that to happen. And your German is excellent. I'll coach you on the rest. I'm a good man, Daniel. I can be a good father…I can see no other way…you must be *German* now, my boy…"

Silenced by the logic of the argument, Daniel merely nodded in assent.

***

Schiller had two weeks before he had to report to his new assignment on the Eastern Front. He took Daniel and the motorcycle to his secluded farm in Saxony – Daniel riding in the car's boot, the motorcycle on the trailer, covered with a tarp. Somewhere around Frankfurt, Schiller felt comfortable enough to allow Daniel to ride in the front of the car with him. "Just remember: call me 'papa' if anyone talks to us."

The farm was a lovely, rustic place, dotted with wildflowers and tall, majestic birch trees. There was a barn and a traditional timber-framed house with cheerfully painted gables and a large, oak door. "There is nobody here now," Schiller told Daniel. "My wife lives in Berlin. She doesn't much like country life…" They stashed the tarp-covered motorcycle in the barn and went inside the house to start a fire. In the front parlor, Schiller stopped at a sideboard and picked up a framed photograph. He gazed at it fondly.

"This is Johann," he said, handing it to Daniel. Daniel examined the blond boy's face eagerly. It was like looking at his twin. "Now you see the resemblance. You are much skinnier than he was, but that's perfect. You lost weight hiding in the woods and living off the land…" Schiller added, already concocting a cover story for their scheme.

Schiller started a fire and cooked a simple but hearty supper of potatoes, sausage, and bread. "Don't eat too much," the officer warned him. "I don't want you fattened up until *after* you've been found. You'll sleep in Johann's room, the one in the back. Tomorrow morning, we'll start the lessons."

"The lessons?"

"The crash course on Johann's life," Schiller clarified, lighting a cigarette. "You've got to memorize everything about him to pull this off. And I'm going to tell you everything you need to know about army life. You're going to have to call upon your acting skills for a while, Daniel – until things become natural to you, that is."

Schiller woke Daniel at dawn, with no apologies. "We run on army time around here," the officer said matter-of-factly. The lessons began at breakfast. Schiller placed a plate with one fried egg on top of toast, two plump sausages, and a roll smeared with butter and marmalade in front of him. "Johann's favorite breakfast. Now it should become yours."

As Daniel ate, Schiller lit a cigarette and began telling him what Johann was like as a child. "He was not so different from most young boys, I suppose. He liked sports. I took him hunting and fishing, when I could. We would go swimming in the lake – that was his favorite thing. He loved dogs. He was a voracious reader. He was a good boy, loved his mother. He was our only child..." Schiller stopped suddenly, lost in thought. He looked sad for a moment, then shook it off. "Can you swim?"

"Ja," Daniel nodded.

"That's good." Schiller spent the rest of the morning and all of the afternoon showing Daniel pictures of Johann – as a young child playing in the yard, as an older boy riding his bicycle, and spending time on picnics with school friends. Daniel began to like Johann very much, and from what he could tell, Schiller genuinely loved his son and seemed to be an admirable father.

"Ah, but I should have spent more time with him – _and_ his mother," Schiller said regretfully. "I was always too busy with my work, and my family suffered for it, I'm afraid. I'm talking about before the war, before I joined the army. I had quite a career as an engineer. I was able to give them a good life, but I was unable to be a part of it myself. As a result, I really didn't know Johann as well as I should have – especially when he grew older."

Schiller grew contemplative, and lit another cigarette. He smoked it in silence, staring out the window. The farm was secluded, and the woods around it were quiet. "I want to get this farm going again, after the war. You will help me. We'll live here peacefully, growing cabbage and potatoes and asparagus. And we'll have cows. Good German beef will be in demand, and we will do very well indeed. You will find a good German wife and start a family. And when I die, I will leave the farm to you."

"What about your wife?"

"She will never leave Berlin," Schiller said dismissively.

Daniel could see it in his eyes: there was a great distance between Schiller and his wife – and not just geographically. As Schiller continued to talk, hour after hour, Daniel could see a catharsis taking place. He began to realize that the lonely officer truly missed his son and fully intended for Daniel to replace him – *permanently*. That night as he lay in Johann's bed, his cranium spinning with all the information Schiller had crammed into it, Daniel wondered what he was doing here, how he'd gotten himself into such a situation. Schiller seemed to mean him no harm, in fact was offering him protection and safety from the Gestapo for the rest of his life – *if* he was willing to turn his back on his past and become German. *Completely* German.

Daniel didn't know what to do. Escape was impossible – he was in the middle of Germany, closer to Poland and Russia than France. His only option seemed to be to go along with the officer's plan and see how things unfolded.

Over the next two weeks, each day's routine was the same, as if Daniel were cramming for a crucial exam. Schiller chain-smoked and filled him in on all of Johann's likes, dislikes, favorite foods, friends, sports, talents and skills. He tutored him on the places where Johann was raised, and a little bit about German history, music, art, culture, and geography. He gave him copious details about the unit Johann served in and the battle that decimated it. He schooled him on army life, including everything a young German private would need to know in order to serve the *Reich* properly. He gave him volumes of German poetry to read, as well as adventurous novels by Thomas Mann and Hermann Hesse – some of Johann's favorites.

Daniel soaked it up like a sponge.

"What kind of films did he like?" Daniel asked.

Schiller thought a moment, then smiled affectionately. "American westerns. He always wanted to be a cowboy."

"I like gangster movies, and musicals."

"I like musicals, too," Schiller admitted. "But Johann always thought they were effeminate." Schiller chuckled fondly, then his face grew suddenly grim.

"There's something else I need to tell you," he confessed darkly. "When Johann was a boy, I took him on a camping trip in the mountains in Austria – just he and I, father and son. We found a beautiful spot near a placid lake between two towering, tree-covered peaks, and pitched our tent. It seemed ideal to me, but Johann was unnerved by the place. 'Papa, can we not find a *different* place to camp?' he pleaded with me, but I would not listen. His intuition was telling him something, but he was just a boy and I foolishly disregarded his protests. That night, Johann was very restless and tossed and turned in his sleep. I did not hear him open the flap and leave the tent. I woke up sometime later and noticed he was gone."

Schiller hesitated a moment, his face darkening. He took a long drink of his schnapps, and continued uneasily. "I took my rifle and a flashlight and looked for him everywhere. I was beginning to panic, and feel a terrible sense of loss. What had I done? What would I tell his mother? Then, I found him, up on a ridge, the two of them silhouetted in the moonlight. It was strikingly beautiful and terrifying at the same time. Johann and a large black bear, facing each other, neither one moving. I had never been so frightened in my life. The bear could have easily crushed the boy, but was making no move to do so. Involuntarily, I called out 'Johann! Nein!' I immediately regretted it, for of course it startled the bear. She stiffened and growled, and then I saw them: two young cubs, behind her on the ridge, calling out to their mother. And I knew Johann was going to die."

Daniel was transfixed by the story. "What happened?" he squeaked out.

"I, I knew I had to kill the bear. I raised my rifle, and just as the bear lunged for Johann, I shot her. She fell to the ground, dead, but not before taking a swipe at him. Her claws made a ten centimeter-long gouge across his left shoulder. The wound healed, but the scars remained as a reminder to me, if I'd only listened to his premonition and camped somewhere else, I would not have almost lost my son."

Schiller went to a cabinet and slowly opened a drawer. He pulled out an object, visibly shuddering. He returned to Daniel and showed him the object: a large black bear paw. "Yes, I cut this paw off and kept it as a reminder, so I would never put my son in harm's way again."

Daniel stared at the gruesome memento, unable to speak.

"Of course, I failed to keep my promise," the older man admitted sadly. "When Johann enlisted in the army, Russia was on its heels. The war was going our way and I was the proud Papa. I didn't recognize the danger he was in. Ironically, I saved him from *this* bear, but I could not save him from the Russian bear."

Then Schiller looked at Daniel gravely. "There is something we must do now, Daniel. We must be very brave…"

"Nein…" Daniel said quietly, shaking his head.

"I'm afraid so," Schiller insisted just as quietly. "Johann had several physical examinations in the army. The scars would have been noted in his medical records. You must have the same scars, in case anyone bothers to check…"

Daniel just shook his head, but knew resistance was futile. Schiller was resolute. He plied Daniel with schnapps until the boy was light-headed, and a little dizzy. Then he gently removed Daniel's shirt and ran his thick fingers over the boy's left shoulder, remembering the wicked path of Johann's scars. "Yes, yes, that's it…I remember the angle *exactly*…" He gave Daniel a stick wrapped in cloth. "Here, bite down on this. It will help you bear the pain."

Then he picked up the bear paw with both hands, and placed its still sharp claws on Daniel's shoulder. "I'm so sorry, my son…" he said, plunging the claws deep into Daniel's flesh and dragging it across his shoulder. Daniel winced, but did not call out. As the fiery pain raked across his shoulder and then throughout his entire body, a calmness descended on him and he received the ordeal as something of a penance for abandoning Emily and Constantine to their fate while selfishly pursuing his own safety. Then, at peace with all that was happening, he passed out in Schiller's powerful arms.

The older man laid Daniel on a sofa and wiped the tears from his own eyes. Then he solemnly began sanitizing and dressing the wound, just as he had done a few years earlier in the mountains of Austria.

***

Every night before bedtime, Schiller would pour a glass of schnapps, light a cigar, and quiz Daniel on the day's learning. "Where did you go to school?"

Daniel hesitated.

"Faster, faster," Schiller prodded, snapping his fingers.

"*Friedrichstadt Grundschule*," Daniel answered.

"And then?"

"*Gymnasium Dresden-Plauen.*"

"What was your favorite subject?"

"Music."

"And?"

"Mathematics."

"No, no – *history*!" Schiller corrected.

"Sorry."

"Your mother's name?"

"Lise Kohler."

"Where was she born?"

"Leipzig."

"What did your father do before the war?"

"He was a chief engineer for the Mercedes-Benz company."

"Where did your family take their summer holidays?"

"The Lake District, in Austria."

"Where did you holiday in the winter?"

"The Italian Alps."

"What happened on your first time skiing?"

"I hit a tree and broke my leg."

"What happened when you tried to steal honey from the Hoffmann farm when you were eleven years old?"

"A bull chased me and gored my leg."

"What was the name of your childhood dog?"

"Buster."

"What vegetable do you hate?"

"Cabbage."

"What is your favorite dessert?"

"Strudel, with cream."

"What animal frightens you most?"

"Lions."

"Who did you take to the spring ball in 1940?"

"Sofie Muller."

"Her favorite flower?"

"Chrysanthemum."

"Who was her father?"

"Franz Muller, Vice President of the Bank of Dresden."

"What happened in the forest outside Derevnaya?"

"We were on patrol in the forest. It was late at night, very dark. We got lost. We realized there were Russians everywhere, all around us. A column of Russian T-34 tanks passed us, and engaged our main unit about four kilometers down the road. The main unit – company strength – was wiped out and we were left on our own. We tried to hide in the trees, but the Russians were *everywhere*. We knew we were surrounded, and tried to surrender. They opened fire on us, with our hands up and waving white flags. I was able to escape, and hid out in the woods until the Russians moved on."

Schiller put down his schnapps and stood up. His cigar still in his mouth, he smiled at Daniel and put both his hands on the boy's shoulders. "Very good, my boy. You are ready. You _are_ Johann now…"

Schiller walked over to a tall cabinet and opened the doors. He pulled out a Mauser rifle and handed it to Daniel. "This is like the one my son carried into battle. What do you make of it?"

Daniel hefted the rifle in his hands, trying to gauge its weight. He examined it closely, then worked the bolt action a couple of times. Schiller handed him a long bullet, and Daniel was able to chamber it. "It's ready to fire, no?"

Schiller looked pleasantly surprised. "That was marvelous. Where did you learn to do that?"

"My uncle raised me. He taught me to hunt and fish, and to fire a rifle. French rifles and German rifles aren't so different, I suppose."

"No, I suppose not," Schiller nodded. "Tell me more about your uncle."

"He is a bicycle repairman in a small village, but he taught me how to work on the motorcycle. I found out that I am able to figure out how most mechanical things work."

"That's quite an aptitude. Your uncle sounds like a good man."

Daniel thought a moment, then said seriously, "Yes, I believe he is."

***

The next morning, Schiller gave Daniel a tattered set of farm clothes, and told him to put them on. Then he put Daniel in the boot of his car and drove east for what seemed like hours and hours. Daniel fell asleep and lost track of time. Finally, he felt the car stop. He heard Schiller get out and the crunch of his boots on gravel as he walked to the back of the car. Then the boot opened, and bright sunlight flooded the compartment.

"Cover your eyes," Schiller told him, helping him climb out of the boot. "I'm sorry you had to ride back there, but you simply couldn't be seen in case we were stopped. How do you feel?"

"Queasy," Daniel replied, still retching from the exhaust fumes and the movement of the car on the bumpy roads.

"Take some fresh air," Schiller advised. "You'll feel better in a moment."

Daniel slowly let his eyes adjust to the brightness. He looked around and saw that they were in the middle of nowhere. "Where are we?"

"Russia. Remember: you buried your uniform and stole these peasant's rags in case you were stopped by an enemy patrol. You've been hiding in the woods until it was safe to come out. Wait in these woods another day, then walk west for twenty clicks. You'll find the city of Kobryn. Go straight to the garrison commandant and tell him your story. I know him – he's a good man. He'll call me immediately and I will come and pick you up. You'll speak only German from now on. If you have to speak French, throw in a few grammatical errors – Johann's French wasn't that great."

Daniel looked mortified. "You're just going to leave me out here?"

Schiller tried to be reassuring. "Now don't worry about a thing. Trust me, everything's going to work out fine."

Daniel's face still looked grim.

"Why so glum?" Schiller tried to sound cheerful. "Still not sure if you can trust me, eh? Look, why would I have gone to all this trouble? Why not just turn you in to the Gestapo straightaway, and be done with it?" Then the officer put on a big smile. "Ah, you're just a boy. Trust Papa!" He patted Daniel firmly on the shoulders, then stopped, looking worried.

"No, something is not right," he murmured, bending down and scooping up a handful of mud. He carefully smeared it on Daniel's cheeks, then wiped his hands on Daniel's shirt. "There, that's better. You've been living in the woods for weeks!"

Schiller opened the door and got behind the wheel of the car. "Don't worry – I'll be back to get you in a couple of days. Now go find a nice spot in the woods to spend the night. I'll see you soon! Remember, don't eat anything – you need to be ravenous when you get to the garrison in Kobryn."

Then he closed the door, started the engine, and drove away, waving at Daniel out the window. Daniel stood in the road and watched in disbelief as the car disappeared in the distance. *He must be insane*, Daniel thought. *This is never going to work…*

He walked off the road a safe distance and found a good spot to camp. He gathered twigs and branches, and built a lean-to for shelter. Then he lined it with leaves from the forest floor as a mattress. He felt his pockets, and found a book of matches Schiller had placed there. He gathered some kindling and built a small fire as it was getting dark. He felt hungry but vowed to follow Schiller's instructions to fast until he reached the garrison.

He sat by the fire warming his hands until it was completely dark. Then he laid down on his mattress of leaves and fell asleep wondering what had happened to Constantine and Emily, and if he would ever see them again.

Part Three
Keep Your Head Down

Chapter 12

The next morning, Daniel rose early, checked his compass, and headed west as instructed by Schiller. He had twenty clicks to cover, and he wanted to reach Kobryn before dark. He walked along a little-traveled country road, ducking into the trees and shrubbery whenever he heard a vehicle approaching. Aside from a few scattered farms dotting the countryside, he came upon no signs of civilization and, as far as he could tell, was seen by no one. After two hours, the sun was high in the sky and he began to grow thirsty.

Hearing the unmistakable sound of running water, he followed it down an embankment and across an empty field. At the edge of the field he saw a long row of tall bulrushes, and just beyond that a stream. Kneeling down carefully, he cupped the cool water in his hands and drank his fill. Just as he was turning to walk back to the road, he felt a keen sense of not being alone. He froze and scanned the bulrushes on the other side of the stream. There it was again: the sense he was being watched.

He turned to leave again, but was stopped by a rustling sound. The tall rushes parted and three rough-looking men emerged and stood in the middle of the stream. They were dressed in tattered filthy clothes, but carried a German army-issue rifle and two luger pistols.

"Are you a Russian?" one of them asked in German. He was large and powerfully built, and obviously the leader. He had a dark, unshaven face and gleaming eyes, and held a pistol in his hand.

"*Nein*. German," Daniel answered.

"Ah, a deserter, then!" the man said, smiling.

"*Nein*. I am not a deserter. My unit was wiped out, and I'm on my way to the garrison at Kobryn."

"*Kobryn*? You're nowhere near Kobryn!" the big man scoffed.

"I-I have a compass," Daniel stammered helplessly. "I need to travel west—twenty kilometers…"

"I said, you're nowhere near Kobryn," the leader repeated. "You'd better come with us…"

"*Nein*. I must get to Kobryn…"

The leader raised the pistol waist-high, pointed at him. "I said you're coming with us."

"Wait!" it was one of the others, the one with the rifle. "I don't think that's such a good idea." The leader turned and glowered at the man. "I mean, he'll just slow us down…"

"If he's captured, he'll turn us in as well," the leader said.

"I won't," Daniel promised.

"We can't take that chance," the leader decided. "You're coming with us. Deserters should stick together, after all…"

Daniel had no choice – they were armed and desperate, so he went with them. They walked north, through groves of trees and across vacant fields, careful to avoid being seen by country people or military patrols. "Where are we going?" Daniel asked.

"Not to *Kobryn*!" the big man laughed mockingly, shaking his head. "That's one of the biggest garrisons in western Russia!"

"Tell him the plan," the one with the rifle urged. The leader stopped suddenly and turned to Daniel.

"All right. He's one of us now, whether he wants to be or not. But first, introductions all around. I am Tier. That's Weber," he pointed to the one with the rifle. "And the stupid one over there is Mann. No offense, Mann. What is *your* name?"

Daniel just caught himself from saying his real name, and blurted out "Johann. Johann Schiller."

"Well, Johann, I didn't buy your story about your unit being wiped out," the leader scoffed. "Anyone with half a brain would use that as an opportunity to get out of this war permanently. Not march right into Kobryn and present himself to the commandant for further abuse. No, you're a deserter, and so are we. Let's get used to the fact and find safety."

"And where would that be?" Daniel inquired.

"We are going to jump a train to the port of Gdansk, then steal a boat and cross the Baltic Sea to Sweden."

"*Sweden*?!"

"That's right. It's a neutral country. We get to Sweden, we've got it made."

Daniel's head spun. He instantly recognized the insanity of the plan: they would surely end up at the bottom of the freezing Baltic, if they even made it *that* far. "I…I can't go to Sweden…my father will be waiting for me…"

Tier fingered the pistol in his hand ominously, scratching his nose with the muzzle. "Your father will have to see you after the war. You're coming to Sweden with us."

They continued their journey quietly, Daniel biding his time, determined to take the first opportunity to escape and make his way to Kobryn. They trudged on the rest of the day without talking, and came to a farmhouse at sundown. They stayed in the trees watching the house until dark. Satisfied there were no signs of life inside, they walked to the house and kicked the door in.

They went straight to the kitchen and started digging around for food. Weber set his rifle against a table and lit a lamp. Tier found some stale bread on the counter. "Mann, make yourself useful and look for some butter or jam," he ordered.

Just then, an old farmer came out of a back bedroom, wielding a chair leg like a club. He moved to stop Weber, but Tier grabbed the rifle and butted him hard in the head. The farmer crumpled to the floor, blood streaming from his forehead. His wife came out of the bedroom and screamed. She bent down and tried to staunch the bleeding with a dish towel.

"Lock them in the bedroom," Tier ordered. Mann and Weber dragged the moaning farmer into the back room, followed closely by the sobbing wife. Daniel glared at Tier. "What's with you?" Tier asked, puzzled.

"You could've killed him!" Daniel blurted out. "Over a few crusts of bread!"

"What are you talking about?" Tier shrugged. "They're just a couple of dumb Ruskies!"

Daniel held his tongue. Weber and Mann came back to the kitchen.

"Come on, boys," Tier said merrily. "We're not going to let a crumb go to waste. We're taking everything we can carry!" The three Germans ransacked the kitchen, filling their pockets with bread, cheese, sausages, a tin of biscuits, a bottle of vodka – even the last of the old farmer's tobacco.

As they left the farmhouse, Weber pulled Daniel aside and let Tier and Mann go on ahead. "Hey, Mann and I are just here because we don't want to be slaughtered by the Russians. Tier deserted because he killed an officer. So be careful, my friend…"

They walked on in the darkness for most of the night. *We're lost*, Daniel thought. *Hopelessly lost…*

He kept waiting for a chance to dart away into the darkness, but couldn't work up the nerve. Finally, they came to a large railway station on the edge of a town. Tier motioned for them to stop and stay hidden in the trees. There were several trains stopped in the station, each on a different set of tracks. Several of them were idling, steam hissing from their motionless engines.

"There are so many trains," Weber observed. "Which one should we take?"

"That one is headed west," Tier said, pointing to the nearest train.

"How can you tell?" Mann asked.

"I just *know*."

Mann and Weber looked at each other, but neither spoke. They followed Tier, who emerged from the tree line and walked stealthily toward the train. No one else was around. Tier examined several boxcars, then nodded his head emphatically. "This one."

He slid the boxcar door open and peered inside. Then he climbed up inside and held a hand down to help Mann up. "Now the boy," he said when Mann was inside. Weber gestured with the rifle, and Daniel climbed up into the car, followed by Weber. Everyone inside, Tier slid the door shut without a sound.

Daniel looked around the inside of the car, blinking while his eyes adjusted to the darkness. Before he could see them, he *smelled* them: sheep. The air inside the compartment was thick with their pungent odor. It didn't seem to bother the three deserters, however, who immediately got down and nestled comfortably among the sleeping animals. Nobody spoke as they waited tensely for the train to start up and pull out of the station.

Daniel found a spot to stretch out on the floor, and was just about to doze off when he heard the grinding metallic sound of the wheels turning beneath them and felt the boxcar lurch into motion. They were finally on the move, and, in their excitement, the Germans became more animated. They emptied the food from their pockets, passed around the bottle of vodka, and told stories about what they were going to do when they got to Sweden.

"I'm going to the most expensive bistro in Stockholm and order everything on the menu," Mann vowed.

"You go to Sweden, and the first thing you think about is *food*?" Weber asked incredulously. "Have you ever seen the _women_ in Sweden? They make German women look like sheepdogs!"

"That's unpatriotic at best, and possibly sacrilegious," Mann argued. "Where's your love of the Fatherland?"

"What has Germany done for _me_ lately?" Weber retorted, taking a healthy swig from the vodka bottle. He offered Daniel a stale hunk of black bread, but Daniel was too nauseated by the back and forth motion of the train and the putrid smell of the sheep to eat anything.

"What are you going to do when we get to Sweden, Tier?" Mann asked.

Tier lit a cigarette and leaned back against a sheep, both hands behind his head. He mulled the question over a moment, then said with great seriousness, "I am going to check into the first hotel I find that has a private bath. Then I am going to fill the tub with fresh milk, warmed to exactly 86 degrees, and I'm going to soak in it all night long while listening to opera on the radio."

Weber and Mann looked at each other. "Not what I would have expected," Weber commented.

"The next day, I will take a train to the city of Malmo and enroll in a trade school," Tier continued thoughtfully. "Where I will apply myself fastidiously to learn the craft of watch-making. After a thorough apprenticeship with the best watch-maker in town, I will strike out on my own and open a modest watch shop on a quiet side street. I will then woo and marry an attractive five-foot-four Lutheran woman who will bear me three blond Nordic children: one boy and two girls. They will be named Rolf, Greta, and Elise. Rolf will sweep up in the shop and eventually learn the watch-making trade from me. When I die, he will inherit the shop and pass on the enterprise to his progeny."

"My uncle was a watch-maker," Weber remarked, without missing a beat. "But I don't think he was cut out for that kind of work. He slowly went mad – something about the precision of the tiny mechanisms, the perfection of the almost microscopic works, sent him over the edge. He ended up in an insane asylum, shuffling around in his slippers, mumbling about a 'microcosm of the universe.' What makes you think you're cut out for that kind of work, Tier?"

"I like the ticking. When I was a boy, I would sit for hours listening to the ticking of my grandfather's watch. It was mesmerizing, comforting. I imagined that the ticking of my grandfather's watch emanated from the cosmos, perhaps from God himself. No one else could hear it, it was meant for me and me alone. Then an immaculate light touched my soul and I knew that the ticking was not coming from God, it was coming from *beyond* God, from somewhere amidst the foundations of Truth itself, the very pillars of the universe..."

"There's nothing bigger than God," Mann challenged.

"The *Overman*," Tier countered gravely. "The Overman buried God!"

"Oh, here we go with the Nietzsche again!" Weber rubbed his forehead, as if anticipating a headache. "So, what would Nietzsche say about beating up the Russian farmer and stealing bread from him? Isn't that immoral?"

"Morality is a construct," Tier argued. "Morality is all right for the masses – for the *sheep*. The Exceptional Man follows his own inner law. The Exceptional Man rises above the notion of good and evil."

"And what makes you so exceptional?"

"Enlightenment, my friend. Enlightenment."

"Look, I'm not opposed to the violence you perpetrated on the farmer," Weber clarified. "I am simply offended that you would use a philosopher like Nietzsche to rationalize it."

"What about desertion?" Mann added. "I suppose you would say that leaving your unit is all right because you are somehow above the law?"

"Any act is acceptable, so long as one is following one's inner law," Tier explained patiently. "This is what makes one Exceptional."

Weber, becoming increasingly agitated, could hold back no longer. "Chaos! The world would be chaos if everyone acted like you!"

"Chaos? You mean, worse chaos than this war?"

Lacking a comeback, Weber simply growled, turned away quickly, and huddled up against a sheep. "I am going to sleep now!" he huffed.

Tier merely shrugged his shoulders and began whistling opera softly – something from Wagner. The musical clacking of the metal wheels on the tracks below and the soft, swaying motion of the car quickly put Weber, then Mann, into a deep sleep. Only Tier and Daniel remained awake, but both silent. Tier glared intently at Daniel until he, too, felt his eyelids getting heavy and succumbed to the soothing motion of the railcar.

Daniel waited until he was sure Tier was asleep, then got up and stealthily made his way to the door. He slowly slid the door open, praying that the whooshing sound of the wind outside would not wake up the deserters. Then he stood watching the dark scenery pass by outside, trying to muster the courage to jump.

In an instant, he sensed someone standing behind him. It was Tier.

"Why don't you jump?" the deserter calmly asked.

"I'm afraid," Daniel admitted.

"Afraid of what – freedom?"

"The train's moving too fast."

"Make up your mind," Tier said.

Daniel was frozen. He couldn't jump. Tier reached out and Daniel braced himself to be ejected from the rail car. Instead, Tier snatched him back inside, slamming the heavy door shut.

"So. You've made your decision," Tier said coldly. "You're coming to Sweden with us." Just as he let go of Daniel, there was a tremendous explosion. The train buckled, lurched to a halt, and teetered sideways. The rail car trembled violently, emitting an ear-splitting groaning metal sound. Weber and Mann jumped to their feet amidst the bleating, panicked sheep.

The three deserters put their shoulders into pulling the heavy, warped door open, and they all spilled out onto the ground. Near the front of the train, Daniel saw partisan fighters with rifles firing at what was left of the engine, now a derailed, smoldering hulk of twisted steel. The scene quickly devolved into bedlam: train car doors flew open, and German soldiers poured out and began to engage the partisans. Soldiers, sheep, and partisans were running in all directions.

"Nice work, genius!" Weber shouted at Tier. "You put us on a train with half the German army!"

"Blend in with the sheep!" Tier shouted back, getting down on all fours. The others obeyed, trying to make a break to the tree line with the rest of the fleeing sheep. More soldiers spilled out of the train cars, overwhelming the partisans, who began retreating to the tree line as well.

"Halt!" a soldier shouted, firing several shots at the group of scampering deserters. Two more soldiers joined the first, leveling their rifles to open fire. Realizing they'd never make it to the trees, Tier and his group stood up and raised their hands. The soldiers took them up to the engine, where the Germans were assembling the tattered group of captured partisans.

"We're not partisans," Mann declared. "We're Germans!"

"Ah, deserters," a soldier said. "Just as bad."

Tier, Weber, Mann and Daniel were separated from the partisans and loaded into the back of a truck while the partisans were quickly executed only a few meters away. "This will be you in a few hours," a soldier spat on the ground and pointed at the dead partisans. Two guards climbed into the back with them, and the truck pulled away from the train.

They were silent for many miles. Then Mann looked at Tier and asked, "How would your Nietzsche get out of this one?"

Tier tried to look in control. "They are not going to shoot us," he predicted.

"They *always* shoot deserters," Weber spat.

"There's a man-power shortage," Tier said confidently. "They need every man they can get."

Weber had clearly had enough. "You have been wrong about everything since we left our unit. First, you convince us to cross the Baltic Sea to Sweden. Then you put us on the wrong train and get us captured. Why should we trust you now?"

"The Exceptional Man rises above doubt," Tier answered calmly, much like a professor addressing a philosophy class. "The Exceptional Man rises above fear."

Weber shook his head in disgust. "You're mad!" he cried, crossing his arms over his chest and turning away. They drove on in silence for three more hours. At dawn, the truck pulled into a military post with high metal fences and barbed wire and stopped in front of the commandant's quarters.

"Where are we?" Mann asked.

"Kobryn," one of the guards answered, gesturing with his rifle for them to get out of the truck. Daniel's ears perked up when he heard the garrison's name. The soldiers lined them up in front of the small building, and the commandant came out to look them over.

"They were on the train the partisans sabotaged," a guard explained.

"What do you have to say for yourselves?" the commandant demanded sternly.

"We are prepared to take up arms for the Fatherland once again!" Tier promised.

"Is that so?" the commandant asked, then turned to the guards. "Shoot them."

Weber turned to Tier. "What does the Exceptional Man have to say now?"

The commandant turned to go back inside his quarters, while the guards lined them up to be shot. Daniel called out to the commandant, "I am Schiller's son!" The officer stopped in his tracks, thought a moment, then turned back to the group. "Hold your fire," he instructed the guards, then stood directly in front of Daniel. "What was that you said?"

"I am not a deserter," Daniel said. "Gerhardt Schiller is my father."

The commandant stared at him, stone-faced, for several seconds. "Follow me," he finally said, leading Daniel into his quarters. Once inside the well-lit office, Daniel calmed down and caught his breath. He got a better look at the commandant. Colonel Franz Richter was a pale, clerkish-looking man with a surprisingly high voice and small, plump, soft hands that appeared devoid of any bones whatsoever. He wore a monocle and a red silk choker around his neck with an iron cross dangling from it. To Daniel's mind, the iron cross choker seemed oppressively tight; *perhaps that's what makes his voice so high,* the boy thought.

"What is your name?" the officer demanded in his high, squeaky voice.

"Johann," Daniel replied. "Johann Schiller."

Colonel Richter squinted at him through his monocle for a long time. "Remarkable..." he finally said. "Tell me, Johann. How do you come to be here?"

Daniel calmly gave him the prepared story, not missing a single detail: his unit was ambushed by the Russians and wiped out in near Derevnaya, after which he hid out in the woods for weeks waiting for a chance to make his way here to the German garrison.

"Remarkable," Colonel Richter repeated, after Daniel had finished. "Truly *remarkable*...and the others?"

"They are deserters," Daniel said truthfully.

Richter rang for his orderly, who entered promptly and clicked his heels. "Track down Major Gerhardt Schiller and get him on the phone as soon as possible. And bring this young man a hot breakfast at once. Oh yes – have the guards shoot the deserters," he added as an afterthought. The orderly clicked his heels again and left the office. A few moments later, two hot breakfasts and coffee were brought in and placed on the commandant's desk.

"Please, eat," Richter encouraged Daniel. "You must be famished." Daniel tucked into the aromatic plate of food as Richter poured coffee for both of them. Then he sat down, leaned back in his plush leather chair, and watched Daniel eat.

"I know your father, Johann," he finally observed, rubbing his small, sausage-like digits together as he spoke. "We were in officer's training together. He's a very good man."

"Thank you," Daniel replied, stuffing his mouth with fried eggs and bread.

"Yes, a damned good soldier," Richter continued, watching Daniel with a delightful gleam in his eye. Three rifle shots from outside the quarters made Daniel jump in his seat, but the commandant didn't so much as flinch. "We will find him and let him know that you are alive. He will be very pleased to hear the news. But there is something I must caution you about, Johann. Since you were reported missing, and presumed dead, your father has undergone something of a change..."

"A change?"

"That's right. His behavior – his demeanor – has become something of a concern to his superiors. There's an impulsiveness, an irrationality, a tendency to not accept the reality of the situation.

All natural, I suppose, under the circumstances. But all the same, you may not find him the same man you once knew…"

Daniel's eyelids began to droop. The colonel noticed. "Ah, but you have been up all night and now that you have eaten, you need to sleep. I will have a warm bunk prepared for you right away. We must have you well-rested when papa comes to claim you, am I right?"

Daniel was taken to a private bunk in the guest quarters next to the commandant's office. The furnishings were sparse, but the room was comfortable enough and Daniel slept soundly for many hours. He awoke suddenly to find Colonel Richter sitting in a chair beside the bed, wringing his plump digits anxiously.

"I have some rather unpleasant news," the commandant told him flatly. "We were able to contact your father and let him know about you. Of course, he was overjoyed and left immediately to come pick you up. Unfortunately, 20 kilometers north of here he was captured by partisans and turned over to the Red Army. He is now on his way to a Russian POW camp, I'm afraid…"

Daniel's groggy mind tried desperately to process the information. It took him several seconds to understand what the commandant was saying and realize that Gerhardt Schiller's elaborate and elegant scheme was unraveling at an astonishing rate.

"I know this is shocking news, and you may be finding it difficult to grasp its meaning right now," Richter droned on as Daniel's head spun. *The plan…the safety net…Schiller wouldn't be there to protect Daniel now…*the world seemed to suddenly be made out of sand.

"I've got more news…" Richter's voice seemed to be coming from far away now. "You are being re-assigned. I would like to keep you here, but they need men at the front. It's a combat unit. You will report in two days. They are looking forward to getting somebody with your experience fighting the Russians, I can tell you. Your father's a warrior, he'll be all right. He would be proud that you are going right back out there to defend the Fatherland, no?"

Daniel had no words. The enormity of the calamity was just beginning to sink in.

"Ah, yes. You are stunned, I know. The news was sudden. But you are a *Schiller* – you will make your papa proud. I *know* it!"

Daniel spent the next two days in a state of terror. What could he do? If he tried to leave, *he* would be shot as a deserter – just like Tier, Weber and Mann. By the time he was to depart for the front, a deadened sense of resignation had set in; this was his fate, it was irreversible. In a few weeks' time, he had gone from certain capture and torture by the Gestapo, to a sense of hope brought about by the madman Schiller and his absurd scheme, only to have it snatched away again by Schiller's untimely capture and imprisonment. It was almost too much for him to bear.

Then a truck pulled into the compound, and Richter was there to see him off. His new German army uniform felt stiff and uncomfortable. Before he boarded the truck, Richter pulled him aside solemnly and spoke to him in a hushed tone. "I know you are not Schiller's son. Johann was killed in that Russian ambush, along with the rest of his unit."

Daniel blanched. *What else can happen now?* he thought grimly.

"Don't worry, your secret is safe with me," Richter continued, placing a soft, doughy hand on the younger man's shoulder. "Gerhardt is a good man, and if he wanted to pass you off as his son, he must have a very good reason. And I think I know what it is. But that is neither here nor there now. You are off to the front. Fight the Russians like you *were* his son. Make us all proud, Johann." Then he patted the boy's shoulder and turned him toward the truck that would take him to the Eastern Front.

Stunned and reeling, Daniel walked to the truck on rubber legs. He climbed up inside and took a bench seat next to several scraggly recruits – a few older men and some boys about Daniel's age. *If this is what they're sending to the front these days, the Germans must be worse off than I thought*, he thought as he peered apprehensively around the inside of the dark truck.

The truck started up, backfired loudly, and pulled out of the camp – Richter standing at attention and saluting valiantly until it had passed through the front gates. They drove southeast for several hours, across the vast, flat steppes of the Ukraine. The terrain seemed to swallow up the tiny truck and its uneasy occupants. Daniel, who had never seen such expanses, wondered at the vastness of it. Nobody spoke, everybody feeling the same nervous apprehension the closer they got to the front.

Finally, the truck pulled into another camp with rows and rows of crude wooden barracks and a small garrison of wary soldiers. *Is this the front?* Daniel wondered, trying to get a good look at the camp from inside the back of the truck. A steely noncommissioned officer pulled the creaky tailgate of the truck down and ordered the recruits out, "*Schnell!*" The men jumped down from the truck and lined up in front of one of the unpainted pine buildings.

The noncom addressed them in a loud voice, looking them over with a war-weary indifference. "You have arrived at division headquarters. We are 18 kilometers from the front. You will enter this building in an orderly fashion, where you will be equipped with everything you need to fight the Russians. Then you will be fed a hot meal before your final trip to the front. Now inside – *schnell!*"

The recruits double-timed it into the building where each man was issued a full infantry kit: a heavy blanket and groundsheet, heavy winter coat, full ammunition pouch, field canteen and mess kit, shaving and hygiene kit, entrenching tool, gas mask, steel helmet, and an 8-pound Mauser Kar 98K bolt action rifle. A few minutes later, the men were called back outside by the noncom.

"You are now fully equipped for combat at the front," he told them. "Your Mauser rifle will become your new appendage. When you are at the front, it will never leave your hands. You will quickly come to find that it will be your best friend, and even keep you warm on those cold Ukrainian nights. You are responsible for everything you have just been given. Responsible not to lose it. Responsible not to damage it. Responsible to keep it in good working condition. Losing, misplacing, or damaging any piece of Wehrmacht property will result in a court martial. These tools you have been entrusted with by the Reich will mean the difference between life and death at the front. Take care of them as you would your own children!"

"But why do we need such a heavy coat?" one of the older men asked. "The autumn weather is very mild here."

The noncom laughed and shook his head ruefully. "You will find out soon enough!"

The men were then ordered to strap their rifles across their backs and stow the rest of their gear in the truck. "But not your mess kit. Bring that with you."

The noncom marched them to a mess wagon, where each man was served a ladle full of hot, thin broth, and a wedge of black bread.

The noncom smiled as the new recruits found a place to squat on the ground, fishing around with their spoons to find the few morsels of meat in the soup. Many of them, especially the older ones, found biting into the hard, chewy bread to be a daunting task.

"Welcome to the infantry!" the noncom beamed at them, slapping Daniel on the back. "Eat up now, lads! Back in the truck in five minutes! The Russians won't wait forever, you know!"

Bolting their food in record time, the recruits were back in the truck in four minutes flat. The noncom was pleased. "I can see that you follow orders. That will serve you well at the front!" He closed the tailgate and banged the side of the truck with a large, rock-like fist. "Good luck now, lads! See you in Moscow!" The truck ground into gear and whined its way out of the camp and across more endless steppes towards the front. Inside, Daniel took his Mauser from across his back and stood it up between his knees, which were shaking slightly.   The older man next to him was humming Beethoven. He stopped suddenly, looked at Daniel's rifle, and asked, "You know how to use that thing, son?"

"*Ja.*"

The old man, whose name was Vogel, shook his head doubtfully. "I don't know about these new rifles. I wish they'd let me bring my Mauser from the Great War. Now, <u>*that*</u> was a gun, I assure you!"

"You – you were in the Great War?" Daniel choked out.

"Last part of it. But I saw some action, let me tell you. At Amiens, fighting the French. Now that was a battle-hardened army, not like the French now. They really knew how to fight, and it was tough going."

"As tough as the Russians?"

"Don't worry, son," Vogel said dismissively. "They say the Russians aren't really that tough.   They say we'll have the Bolsheviks whipped before winter. We won't even have a chance to use these fine new coats they gave us! You'll see!"

"Who says all this?" another recruit piped up in a skeptical tone.

"Why, the *Fuhrer* – and, and Herr Goebbels and Marshall Goring. They wouldn't lie to us, would they?"

"The government, lie? Of course not!" It was dripping with sarcasm.   Somewhat offended, Vogel quieted down as the truck began to jostle violently down a very rough dirt path. He went back to solemnly humming Beethoven. The recruits bounced on the hard bench seats and slammed into one another, finding nothing inside the truck to hold onto to steady themselves. This went on for an hour, until, with great relief all around, the truck finally stopped. Now they could hear the sound of shelling, off in the distance.

"We must be getting closer to the front," someone ventured.

It was getting dark outside. Daniel peered out of the back of the truck and saw the dirtiest, most ragged soldier he'd ever seen.

"Is that one of our's?" Vogel whispered.

Daniel looked more closely. The soldier's helmet was the same shape as his own. "I think so." One of the men in the front got out of the cab and came to the back of the truck. He had a piece of paper in his hands.

"Schroeder. Coontz. Fassel. Becher."

The four men gathered up their gear and climbed out of the truck.

"This landser will take you to your new unit," he said without looking at them. Then he returned to the front of the truck. The rest of the recruits watched as the tattered soldier addressed the new recruits in their clean uniforms and gleaming new gear.

"Get your rifles in your hands and chamber a round," he ordered without emotion. "We've got a good hike to the front, but this area's hot and we may run into a Russian patrol. Now, stay quiet and follow me single file. If you get lost, your _dead_."

A chill ran up Daniel's spine. The dusty, dark-faced landser spoke with such casual indifference, as if the lives of the new men meant nothing to him. He watched the small group leave the road and disappear into the gathering darkness of the steppes. As the truck pulled away, Daniel couldn't help but wonder what would become of the four new men. _Would they learn the ropes and acclimate to their new life at the front? How long would they survive?_

The truck stopped several more times at different locations, each time leaving four or five recruits with a ragged, battle-hardened landser to guide them to their unit. At the fourth stop, Daniel listened carefully for the names being called.

"Vogel. Wilder. Kuppemann. Kindl. Schiller."

There it was – _Schiller_ – Daniel's heart leapt in his breast. Scooping up his gear, he quickly followed the others and fumbled his way out of the truck. It was surreal, dreamlike. Daniel felt somehow detached from the scene, as if he stood outside himself and merely watched events unfold.

There was the landser, covered in grime, looking much like the others. But there was something different about this one, something milder – *softer*? He looked at the recruits as if they were human beings, not merely cannon fodder as the others had. He didn't appear disdainful or indifferent – merely annoyed at having pulled this late-night duty.

The truck quickly pulled away, off to its next stop, leaving the small band alone in the vast Ukrainian night. To the south, artillery fire boomed and lit up the sky like lightning. But here it was quiet.

"Don't worry about that, you'll get used to it soon enough," the landser said in a quiet voice. "I'm Henckel. Our unit is a few clicks east. I know it's not much of a welcome, but we do it this way for a reason. If the truck pulled right up to the front to let you off like a city bus on the *Friedrichstrasse* in Berlin, none of you would make it to the trenches. Ivan watches everything we do, and that's your first lesson. Ivan sees when you eat, when you sleep – he's even watching when you go to take a shit. Never forget that."

This one talks a lot, thought Daniel. But the abundance of information and the tone of his voice was somewhat reassuring. "Now get your rifles ready, and stay with me, single file. We may run into an enemy patrol. If you want to survive, do *exactly* as I say."

Henckel struck out, moving silently over the grassy stubble of the moonlit terrain. Every few meters he stopped and listened, crouched low to the ground for several minutes, before standing again and proceeding stealthily. Then he stopped suddenly and ducked down, motioning for the others to do the same. The recruits hit the ground, face down in the prickly grass. "I thought I heard something, up ahead," he whispered to the others. "Get your rifles ready. But, whatever you do, don't shoot <u>me</u>!"

Henckel stayed still and silent for a full ten minutes. When he was satisfied there was no danger, he proceeded to slither forward. They crawled on their bellies past a burned-out village silhouetted against the moonlight. After another forty-five minutes of this, they saw a flare shoot up into the sky and explode brightly up ahead. Daniel thought it was a signal for them, that they were close to their final destination, and began to breathe a sigh of relief.

"That's Ivan, trying to light things up enough to see who they can pick off," Henckel warned. "Stay down! Ivan's flares are white, our flares burn bluer. Remember that!"

They waited ten minutes for the flare to completely die down, then proceeded with their journey. "We're almost there," Henckel told them. "The rest of the way, we slither like snakes – hug the ground, and don't put your damn heads up to look at anything!" They crawled and crawled over rough ground for about a hundred more meters. Daniel was beginning to understand why the front-line troops he'd seen so far were completely covered with soil and mud. They were all getting tired, dragging their full kits along with them, when Henckel turned and said, "We're here, lads. Safe and sound." Then he seemed to just disappear into the earth!

Daniel looked around, but couldn't find him in the dark. Then a dirt-covered arm reached up out of the earth and pulled him inside. The earth seemed to open up and swallow him whole, as it did the other startled recruits. Daniel opened his eyes and let them adjust to a dim, yellowish candle light. He was completely surrounded by glistening walls of earth. They had reached the trenches. The trench continued on in each direction, as far as Daniel could see. He sat up against one of the embankments, blinking in astonishment at the well-constructed maze of tunnels.

"Don't look so surprised," Henckel said. "This is your new home. You're going to spend so much time down here that you will begin to think you were born here." Then he addressed all the recruits, who had gathered around him in a semi-circle. "What I'm going to tell you is very important, so listen carefully if you want to get home in one piece. This trench is your safe place. As long as you follow the rules and stay down in it, it will take care of you. If you ever get the notion to stick your head out to take a look around without orders, I guarantee you there's a Russian sniper waiting to take it off for you. Are you willing to take that chance? No? Then keep your damn heads down, lads! Now, I'm going to take you to your new assignments. Yes, we've been waiting for you, and we're putting you right to work!" Then he looked right at Daniel.

"What's your name?" he demanded.

Daniel's mind was completely blank with fear and confusion.

"Come on – spit it out!"

"Johann," Daniel blurted, hoping his tongue had snared the correct name.

"No, I don't want to know your damn first name. We go by last names only here."

"Schiller."

"Well, Schiller, you come with me. I've got just the spot for a strapping young lad like you. The rest of you stay right here until I get back."

Henckel scuttled quickly away down a tunnel, Daniel following the best he could with his bulky equipment. "Come on, swim faster, little fish – I've got a lot of ground to cover tonight!" Henckel said in a hoarse bark, then winked at Daniel. They scurried like rats down a dark tunnel. Daniel began to notice some details. What he thought was candlelight was actually strings of tiny, dim lightbulbs that threw off a sickly, yellowish light – something like Christmas tree lights that come in only one color. He also noticed other soldiers – some sitting up against the earthen walls of the tunnel, writing letters or eating out of tin cans, others lying prone and trying to grab a few minutes of sleep on the damp earthen floor. They all looked dirty and unshaven, nothing like the typical model German soldier glorified in the posters, magazines and propaganda films.

Henckel turned a corner and scurried down another, narrower tunnel. Daniel, hopelessly disoriented as to which direction they were going, scrambled to keep up. His full pack and gear was feeling heavier than ever. Finally, they reached an opening at the end of the tunnel. It suddenly widened into a small enclave, large enough for two men to fit in comfortably. "Here we are," Henckel said.

Daniel blinked, rubbed sweat and dirt out of his eyes, and tried to take in his surroundings. A heavy machine gun sat on a tripod near the top of the trench, surrounded by a wall of sandbags about a meter high. Boxes of ammunition were stacked to the side, and a rough straw mattress was strewn on the floor up against the earth wall. A large landser with a week's worth of thick stubble covering most of his face was sitting against the other wall, trying to read a letter by the dim yellow light.

"I've brought your new spotter," Henckel said to the larger soldier. The larger soldier grunted without looking up. Henckel turned to Daniel.

"This ugly ape over here is Mulder. You'll be his new observer. He doesn't talk much, but he'll show you the ropes. While we're on line, this hole is your home. Make yourself comfortable. Oh, there's only room for one mattress, so you'll have to take turns sleeping. The food isn't bad though. It comes out of a tin, but it's cold and not very nourishing…"

Mulder put down the letter and glared at Daniel with large, drooping, black-rimmed eyes. "What is this? I need a new spotter, and you bring me this stunned little fish? Is he even out of nursery school yet?"

"Stop complaining," Henckel intoned. "The others weren't much better."

"Throw him back and bring me someone with some meat on his bones," Mulder growled, as if Daniel weren't even there.

"This one will do fine," Henckel argued. "You two were made for each other. I can already tell."

"He won't last two days, and you know it!" Mulder spat.

"I've got to go now," Henckel said. Daniel looked at him pleadingly: *please don't leave me here with him*…

"This is a plumb assignment," Henckel told him, turning to scurry back down the tunnel. "You'll be thanking me in a couple of days, mark my words…"

Mulder glared disapprovingly at Daniel. "What is your name?"

"Schiller."

"I'm glad you didn't tell me your first name. I never want to know it. Since you're only going to last a couple of days, the less I know about you the better."

"Why are you telling me this?"

"Oh, a sensitive one, are you? Well, on average, new recruits last two days here."

"I intend to do much better than that."

"Oh, we've got a real hero here, have we? Well, let me tell you what happened to my last spotter. He was new, like you. One night he thought he would just leave the trench and take a little stroll. It was a quiet night, like this one. On his stroll he thought he would just sneak a cigarette – no harm in that, right? Only Ivan's got perfect 20-20 vision, saw the glow at the end of the cigarette. My spotter's head was blown off by a sniper's bullet. One of those explosive rounds. One shot was all it took…"

Daniel's knees felt weak, and he was just able to fight down the urge to vomit. Mulder saw the contractions in his throat and sneered.

"Look, I, I know you don't want me here," Daniel stammered. "And I don't want to be here, either. But there's nothing either of us can do about it –"

"Yeah, yeah – the less you talk, the better it will be around here, Little Fish. So just please shut up, will you?"

"I don't see why –" Daniel began, but was interrupted by a burst of rifle fire from a few dozen meters away. The loud reports completely drowned out the rest of his sentence. Mulder snapped to attention, cocking an ear toward the top of the trench. The rifle fire continued at a steady pace for two or three minutes, while Mulder listened. Daniel's heart pounded – his first time under fire. He knew Mulder could see the animal fear in his eyes.

"Damned Bolsheviks!" Mulder shouted. Standing up, he got behind the heavy machine gun and let go a few ear-splitting bursts towards the Russian lines. Daniel had to cover his ears and crouch down in the corner of the hole. "That ought to quiet you bastards down!" Mulder shouted, ceasing the machine gun fire.

"Are—are they <u>attacking</u>?" Daniel asked in panic.

"*Nein,* they're not attacking," Mulder said scornfully. "You can pick yourself up off the ground now. Sometimes Ivan has a little too much vodka, and gets bored – especially on a quiet night like this. That's when they shoot off a few rounds, just to rattle us and let off some steam. A few bursts from my baby here usually fixes it, though…" Mulder patted the machine gun affectionately.

It seemed to work, things got very quiet on the Russian side. Daniel still looked stricken.

"Did you mess your pants?" Mulder laughed. "Look, don't worry. Everything you've heard about this place, just forget about it. It's a hundred times *worse*…"

"*Danke shoen,*" Daniel said, summoning a good dose of sarcasm. "I appreciate your kind words…"

"Get that ridiculous pack off of you before you collapse like an old mule," Mulder suggested, in a friendlier tone. "Stow your gear over there, and get some sleep," he continued, motioning to the filthy-looking mattress on the floor.

"*Nein, danke*. I'm not sleepy anymore," Daniel said, slipping the heavy pack off his back and flexing his aching shoulders.

"That wasn't a suggestion," Mulder shot back sharply. "If things are going to work out around here, you're going to have to do what I say. And right now, I'm telling you to get some sleep. Believe me, you're going to need it…"

Daniel reluctantly sat down on the mattress and tested its comfort level. He found it lacking. He gingerly laid down on one elbow, and tried closing his eyes.

"And don't take your helmet off," Mulder continued. "You'll want to sleep in your helmet around here."

"Okay, but I'm not very sleepy…"

He heard Mulder say something like "Tomorrow we'll begin your training," then closed his eyes again and quickly drifted off into a sound sleep.

Chapter 13

It seemed only minutes later that Daniel felt himself being violently shaken awake. "Come on, Little Fish – rise and shine!" he heard Mulder growling. His eyelids felt like lead, but he forced them open to see Mulder's dark, grimy face hovering over him.

"Ah, there he is – returning to paradise just in time for the fireworks show!"

Daniel sat up and tried to clear the grog from his head. With a shudder, he suddenly remembered where he was – no, it was not all a gruesome nightmare, after all.

Mulder was stuffing strips of a torn undershirt into his ears. "Get those ear plugs they gave you out of your pack and put them in your ears – *schnell!*"

"Why?"

"Stop asking questions – just DO IT!"

Daniel reached into his pack and rummaged around for the small case containing the earplugs. He found it, and began stuffing them into his ears. Looking up, he noticed the patch of sky directly above the bunker was beginning to turn pink with dawn. He saw Mulder crouching in a corner, pulling his helmet down over his head.

"What's happ—" he began, and then hell itself broke loose underneath him. He heard the terrible shriek of the incoming shells, and then the bone-rattling detonation only a few meters away from the bunker. A split second later, the ground began to heave and buckle underneath him, like the most violent earthquake. The earplugs were useless against the barrage of brain-shattering sounds. He pulled his helmet down low, tightened the straps, and tried to cover his ears with his hands.

Another hit, this one closer than the last. The earth convulsed beneath him, tossing him a full 45 centimeters off the ground. Soil, rocks, bits of concrete, and shards of lumber rained down on top of his helmet, covering the bunker floor with debris. That was followed by another even closer hit – then another. Surely, the next one would land right on top of them.

The bombardment went on and on, an impossibly long time, as the trench walls shuddered and more debris began to fill the bunker. Daniel, curled up into a ball on the mattress, clutching his helmet to his head with white knuckles, began to lose track of time. He began to lose the sound of each distinct explosion for the constant ringing in his ears. Sanity, fear, and any connection to reality was slowly being pushed out of his terror-stricken mind with each detonation and each convulsion of the earth. Each concussion physically battered him, sucking all of the air out of his lungs. He felt himself being thrown about the bunker like a rag doll, and he felt reason slipping away from him with every un-Godly impact. He was screaming as loud as he could, but could not hear his own voice.

Surely, this was the end of the world.

Then, it finally did end. Daniel lay curled up in a fetal position, still clutching his helmet with both hands, feeling nothing, with no understanding, like an inert log in a forest. He didn't know if he was alive, or dead.

Slowly, his senses began to come back to him, and he started to entertain the notion that he was, indeed, still alive. Morning sunlight now streamed in from above. He sat up slowly and looked around the shattered bunker expecting to see total carnage. It was a real mess – his pack had opened and his new equipment was strewn around everywhere – but the bunker itself was still relatively intact. Then Mulder was there, hovering over him, slapping him back to sensibility. He was shouting "Stop!" but still couldn't hear his own voice.

"You're alive! You're ALIVE!" Mulder was saying to him. He couldn't hear the words, but he could read Mulder's lips. Then Mulder was laughing madly.

"You're insane!" Daniel tried to cry, but nothing came out.

Twenty minutes later, Daniel was back. Mulder offered him a drink from his canteen, but Daniel pushed it away. "No, you must drink. Dehydration is a real problem here."

Daniel drank from the canteen, his hand still shaking, and felt a little better.

"How long did it last?" Daniel croaked out.

"Exactly one hour," Mulder replied. "They begin at dawn, and end exactly one hour later."

"Every morning?" Daniel asked in shock.

Mulder nodded. "It's their wake-up call to us. A little courtesy, extended out of the goodness of their hearts. They don't want us to over-sleep, you see…"

"How do you…"

"You get used to it. We call it '*The Concerto*.' Now, let's clean this place up…"

Daniel picked up all his gear and put it back into his pack. Mulder remounted the machine gun on its tripod and re-stacked the ammo cases. They both took out their trenching tools and shoveled all the soil and debris out of the bunker.

"Over time, it builds up the sides of the trench a little higher," Mulder pointed out, tossing the last spade-full of debris over the side. It was just all part of the daily routine at the front.

Mulder proudly looked around the straightened bunker. "There – good as new!"

They heard someone approaching through the tunnel, and both stiffened. Then Henckel poked his head in and looked around. "Ah, I see our new recruit has been initiated successfully. How did you like '*The Concerto*?'"

Daniel didn't answer. "I see. Well, if you're not sure, there's always tomorrow's performance. I brought you some breakfast." He handed Daniel a can of potted meat.

"How did the others do?" Mulder asked.

"Not as well as our friend here," Henckel replied. "One of them – Kuppemann – is still in quite a bit of shock. We took him to the infirmary. And another one – Kindl – snapped and climbed out of his hole during the fireworks. They tried to pull him back inside, but couldn't. He was running around out there, like a madman, right into a direct hit. There wasn't much left of him, I'm afraid."

Mulder shrugged, and opened a tin of pork. Daniel opened his tin and ate a few bites of the putrid meat. "Go ahead, eat it all – you've got to keep up your strength out here," Henckel urged him.

"Where <u>am</u> I?" Daniel asked.

Henckel explained that he had been attached to a rifle company of the 41st Regiment, about a hundred men spread throughout a kilometer and a half of connected trenches. Daniel was part of the

2nd platoon, which consisted of two heavy machine gun nests supported by twenty landser with rifles. "The spotter position is much sought-after. You will see a lot of action, and this fat ape here, despite appearances, happens to be one of the best machine-gunners in the Wehrmacht. Listen to him carefully." With that last bit of advice, Henckel dismissed himself, and Mulder began the day's lessons.

"This is the MG 42 *Maschinengewehr*," he began, patting the heavy machine gun proudly. "Weighs 12 kilos, fires 1,200 rounds per minute. A hundred meters in that direction lies the entire Red Army. This is the only thing standing between them and you getting your useless throat slit, so you will respect and revere this weapon with all of your heart, mind, and soul. You will treat this beautiful piece of machinery like a family member – like your own mother or sister. I will teach you how to care for her and keep her in tip-top condition, because your very life depends on it. Any questions?"

"What are my duties?"

Mulder grabbed a pair of heavy field glasses and tossed them to Daniel. "You will keep these with you at all times. Your job is to scan the enemy lines and alert me of any Red movements. But don't stand up front – always stand back here in the shadows, so they can't see the glint of the sun off your lenses." He indicated the shadow line forming a diagonal angle down the side of the bunker wall. "They see the glint off your lenses, and you're a dead man."

"Ja, I understand."

"Now, if we are attacked, you will be responsible for feeding the ammunition belt into the gun at a straight angle and with the exact right amount of slack, so we have a minimum of jamming." Mulder pulled on the ammunition belt hanging down the side of the gun, illustrating the correct angle and amount of slack. "You will also change the belts, and in the event we run out of ammo, you will run to the ammo storage trench and bring back more. If the gun gets too hot, you will assist me in changing barrels to prevent warping. Also, I will teach you how to dislodge jammed cartridges from the breech and barrel. If you learn well and follow all of my directions, we will have no trouble keeping the Bolsheviks confined to their trenches. Understand?"

"Ja. I can do these things," Daniel said confidently.

"Well, we'll see about that, won't we?" Mulder growled. "Ready?"

Daniel grabbed the ammo belt and took the slack out. Mulder squeezed off a few bursts across the steppe at the Russian trenches. The belt fed smoothly and accurately into the breech. Mulder stopped firing.

"Ja. Very good," he said, nodding. Next, he showed Daniel how to change barrels. "Open the breech like this. Take the hot barrel out. Always wear gloves so you don't get burned. Slip the cool barrel into its slot, close the breech, and pull the slack out of the ammo belt. Now you try it." Daniel switched out the barrels almost as quickly as Mulder had. The veteran gunner took a handkerchief out of his tunic and mopped his brow under his helmet. "Not bad," he admitted, surprised.

Then he thought of a sure way to trip the young soldier up. "But wait," he said gleefully. "Every ten thousand rounds or so, we need to do a thorough cleaning." He began tearing the machine gun down. He laid all the parts out on a canvas cloth on the bunker floor, and began to clean each one with a bottle of solution, an old toothbrush, and a tidy rag. Then he deftly re-assembled the gun in record time, Daniel watching carefully all the while. "It's all yours," he said confidently to the younger man.

Daniel took a deep breath, then started disassembling the gun, just as Mulder had moments before. He laid the parts out on the cloth, cleaned them with the rag, and re-assembled the gun almost as quickly as Mulder had. He placed it back on its tripod and stood aside. Astonished, the veteran gunner looked at Daniel as if he were some kind of prodigy. "Uncanny..." was all he could say. He turned away a moment to collect himself. Then he turned back around to face the boy. "How...?"

"My uncle was a bicycle repairman. He taught me how to work on bicycles, motorcycles – even cars. He taught me how to hunt and shoot rifles," Daniel explained. "If I see something done, I just know how to do it myself. That's all."

Mulder was silent a moment, then said gruffly: "Well. I see. Just take your field glasses and...and watch Ivan for a while. And don't take your bloody eyes off the bastards!"

"Jawohl," Daniel said quietly, lifting the field glasses to his eyes and looking out over the pockmarked, cratered no-man's land. He did so for four hours straight, while Mulder sat and brooded in the shade of the bunker. Finally, Mulder spoke.

"Take a break."

Daniel lowered the field glasses and sat down. Mulder handed him a canteen to drink from. "I may have been wrong about you, Little Fish," Mulder hesitantly admitted. "You've got the makings of a fine spotter. I will admit that. You've got a keen eye, and you're a fast learner."

"*Danke*," Daniel said. "What is our objective here?"

Mulder nodded vigorously. "All right. You deserve the full, absurd truth. There's a village about two clicks behind us. You passed it when Henckel brought you in last night. Nothing much, a few houses, some chickens, a few cows. Our job is to keep Ivan from taking this village. Every three weeks or so, they mount a massive attack and take it. Then we counter-attack and take it back. It just goes back and forth like that."

"How many times?"

"We've lost count."

"Why is this village so important?"

"It's not. It has no strategic value whatsoever. It's just a poor, bombed-out husk of a village."

"What's the purpose, then?"

"You tell me."

Daniel picked the field glasses up and continued his observation of the Russian trenches. "There's not much going on over there," he reported.

"Good," his comrade responded. "I'm going to the latrine. When I get back, you can take your turn." Mulder got up and left the bunker through the connecting tunnel. Alone in the eerie bunker, Daniel suddenly felt the ominous presence of the Red Army just a hundred or so meters away, and wondered what he was doing there. How did this happen? How did he end up in the middle of the Ukraine, in an army he felt no allegiance to, facing a fierce enemy so close who would treat him as they would any other German *landser*?

The hulking Mulder came crawling back from the latrine. He had a fresh pack of cigarettes, and offered one to Daniel.

"*Nein*. I don't smoke."

"You'd better start," Mulder said. "It calms the nerves."

Daniel took a cigarette, and Mulder lit it. Daniel took a puff and exhaled it quickly. Mulder laughed, and shook his head. *"Nein, nein.* Suck it into your lungs, or it doesn't do any good…" Daniel followed his instructions, and went into an extended coughing fit. Mulder laughed again. "You'll get the hang of it. Now, it's your turn to go to the latrine, but don't take too long."

"Where is it?"

"Just follow the smell."

Daniel scurried away, and was back in a few minutes. He picked up the field glasses and started scanning the Russian positions again. Nothing seemed to be happening. Then, two faint dots appeared in the sky way back behind the Russian lines. The dots gradually grew larger, and the drone of aircraft engines finally reached them.

"Airplanes," Daniel said. "Coming straight for us."

"This is it!" Mulder shouted, manning his machine gun and scanning the skies. All along the German trenches, soldiers were waking up and shouting warnings to one another. Whistles blew, and a siren went off. The planes were now a hundred meters away, coming in at almost ground level. When they reached the German lines, they turned suddenly in order to strafe the trenches laterally, for maximum effect.

The engines were deafening and frightful enough, but then the machine guns opened up and rained hell down upon the Germans in their trenches. "Come on, you Bolshevik bastards – over here for a taste of this!" Mulder shouted, opening fire as the two planes flew right over the bunker. They were so loud they rattled Daniel's teeth as he fed the belt into the gun and Mulder fired away. Daniel saw the Russian munitions striking the ground just outside their bunker.

Mulder stopped firing and waited, listening intently. The two planes turned and came back for another run, four wing-mounted machine guns blazing away and the roar of the two engines striking fear into the hearts of the German landser huddled in their trenches. Several Germans were firing their rifles at the planes as they came streaking by. Mulder pulled the trigger again, and the MG 42 sputtered to life, pouring its 8mm rounds into the sky in the path of the Russian planes. Holding onto the ammo belt with both hands, Daniel looked up and saw several rounds from the MG 42 penetrate the fuselage and tail of one of the planes as it passed overhead.

Unfortunately, there was no smoke or flame, indicating that the rounds passed through the plane without striking the fuel tank.

This time, the planes released two bombs. Daniel could just see them detach from the bottom of the fuselages, but couldn't exactly tell where they landed. When they hit, the ground shook and shrapnel and earth went flying in all directions.

The two planes finished their strafe, gained altitude, and flew back in the direction of their airfield in the east. Mulder kept firing at them until they were well out of range. Then he stopped and solemnly wiped his brow with his handkerchief. Daniel's heart was beating out of his chest.

Henckel came stumbling up the tunnel and stuck his head into the bunker. "Tunnel 7 was hit by one of the bombs," he shouted breathlessly. "We need you two to come help dig them out!" Mulder and Daniel grabbed their rifles and their entrenching tools and followed Henckel down the tunnel.

After several twists and turns through the maze-like series of tunnels, they reached Tunnel 7. There were several landser already there, frantically digging away at the collapsed earth with their spades. The platoon leader, Feldwebel (Sergeant) Toppel, was already there, directing the rescue efforts. Mulder, Henckel and Daniel quickly joined in.

"Who's buried in there?" Henckel asked.

"Kirchner, Planke, and the new guy – Vogel," someone shouted back. Several more men came scuffling up to the scene. "Go 'round and dig from the other side!" Feldwebel Toppel shouted, and they scurried away to do so. After ten minutes of intense digging, they found an arm, and then uncovered a face. "Kirchner!" someone shouted, as three men pulled the unconscious landser from his premature grave. "He's still breathing!" Two men carried him off to the infirmary, while the others kept digging, redoubling their efforts.

They unearthed a second man. "I don't know who this is," somebody said.

"That's Vogel, one of the new recruits," Henckel said, feeling his throat for any sign of life. Daniel looked down at the man, recognizing him as the older man who talked to him in the back of the truck on the way to the front. "I've got a pulse – it's faint, but he's still alive!" Henckel called out. Two men carried Vogel off to the infirmary.

"There's one more -- Planke," Mulder said, frantically digging away at the wall of dirt obstructing the rest of the tunnel. Henckel, Mulder, and Daniel dug until they were ready to drop from exhaustion. Henckel stopped. "It's no use. He wouldn't be alive this long after the collapse."

"Dammit!" Mulder shouted, sinking his trenching tool into the wall of the tunnel like a spear. Then a soldier came scampering up to them with good news. "They found Planke – dug him out from the other side!"

"Is he all right?" Henckel asked.

"Ja – he's barely conscious, but breathing."

Henckel and Mulder nearly collapsed in relief and exhaustion. Daniel followed them to the infirmary to check on the injured men. The infirmary was a narrow, poorly lit tunnel with one medic in attendance. The medic from 3rd platoon nearby had heard about the collapse and was already there to help out. The injured men lay on stretchers on the damp ground as the medics worked over them.

"How are they doing?" Henckel asked one of the medics apprehensively. Schlesser, the medic, shook his head and wiped his brow on a sleeve.

"Well, Kirchner and Planke have concussions, and Planke has a broken arm, but they should recover," Schlesser replied. "Vogel is still unconscious, but I think he'll pull through. He's in pretty good shape for his age."

Henckel and Mulder went to pay their respects to Kirchner and Planke, making jokes about staying away from collapsing tunnels and telling them to "hold on." Then the two of them, along with Daniel, and despite their exhaustion, went back to help the crew dig out the rest of Tunnel 7. As they dug, Daniel began to understand the life of a soldier at the front: eight to ten hours of sheer boredom, followed closely by two hours of sheer terror, followed by several hours of backbreaking labor. He wondered if every day at the front would be so eventful.

***

The next morning's bombardment began precisely at dawn. This time, Daniel was prepared: earplugs wedged firmly in both ears, and his helmet strapped down tightly over a pair of earmuffs for extra protection. An hour after it started, it ended, right on schedule. Opening his eyes and looking around the bunker cautiously, Daniel could see that it was slightly less disheveled than the previous morning.

"That didn't seem quite as bad as yesterday," he called to Mulder, unstrapping his helmet and removing the earmuffs.

Mulder nodded. "Ja. Partly because your nerves are getting used to it. And partly because they were concentrating most of their fire on a section to the north of us. Believe me, it wasn't so gentle there —"

He was interrupted by Henckel at the bunker door. "There was a direct hit on the communication tunnel between 3rd platoon and us! Two men are missing!"

"Who?" Mulder asked.

"Both from 3rd platoon."

"Not ours!" Mulder sighed in relief.

"But Germans, all the same."

"*Ja*, of course…I only meant —"

"Grab your trenching tools, let's go!" Henckel shouted, and left.

Daniel snatched his trenching tool and started after Henckel. Mulder stopped him.

"Don't forget your rifle. Ivan isn't taking a day off just because we have work to do!"

Slinging their Mausers across their backs, they followed Henckel through the dark maze to the communication tunnel. The damage here was much greater than the day before: the entire tunnel collapsed, filled in solid with earth for at least twenty meters. Most of 2nd platoon was here, digging, while a few sentries kept an eye on the Russians. 3rd platoon was doing the same from their side, hoping to find the missing men and meet somewhere in the middle.

As they dug, hour after hour, it became less and less likely that they would find the men alive. To compound matters, the two Russian aircraft came back to harass them every hour or so, stopping their work for up to thirty minutes at a time. Between aerial assaults, one of the victims was excavated by 2nd platoon. His skull had been caved in by a large rock that lay near him in the rubble. Work stopped while the soldier's body was solemnly wrapped in a groundsheet and returned to his own platoon.

Then the planes returned, once more, flying at nearly ground level, spraying everything in their path with deadly machine gun fire. With a groan of exasperation, everyone dropped face-down in the dirt at the bottom of the tunnel to wait it out. But one man had had enough. He stood up and fired wildly at the planes with his rifle, shouting expletives at the top of his lungs.

"Vollmer, you idiot! Get down!" Henckel shouted at him, but the soldier didn't even hear him. "He's going to get himself killed!" Henckel shouted to Mulder.

"He doesn't care anymore," Mulder replied. "And neither do I!" Mulder stood up and began firing at the planes with his own rifle. Inspired by this, a few others stood up and joined Vollmer and Mulder, as the planes buzzed directly overhead and continued to strafe the trench. Daniel looked over at Henckel for a cue.

"Don't be a fool!" Henckel shouted at him. "Just stay down until they're gone!"

At that moment, two more planes joined the fray, fully doubling the noise and chaos in the sky above them. "They're our's!" Daniel cried, spying a large Maltese cross on one of the wings.

"*Ja, Messerschmitts*!" Henckel exclaimed gleefully. "Now we'll see what those Bolshevik pilots are made of!" He and Daniel grabbed their rifles and stood up for a better view. One of the Messerschmitts peeled off and began chasing one of the Russian planes. It fired its machine guns and tore the tail section off the Russian plane. The disabled plane went into an immediate tail-spin, and went down trailing smoke. It crashed hard into the flat steppes in a spectacular fireball. The other Russian pilot decided to disengage and head home in a hurry, the two Messerschmitts in hot pursuit. They downed the second Russian plane somewhere behind Russian lines, then strafed Ivan's trenches a couple of times, for good measure.

On the way back to their airfield, they buzzed the Germans and tipped their wings, as if to say "You're welcome!" The elated Germans went wild, cheering, shouting, dancing and singing boisterously. For a brief moment, the sorrows of their grim task were forgotten, and they basked in the glory of the magnificent airshow. Daniel was too awestruck by the sheer bravado of what he'd just witnessed to do anything but gape in wonder and admiration at the unexpected show of superior air power.

But as the Messerschmitts disappeared into the western sky, the glow wore off, and the men slowly picked up their tools again and got back to work. It took the rest of the day to completely repair the communication tunnel, and there was still more bad news: the second missing man had been found, neck broken, arms and legs twisted like a pretzel.

The loss of life was a devastating blow to everyone. For Daniel, it was the first time he'd witnessed death up close. The mental image of those two twisted, mutilated corpses, his first view of the true horrors of war, would haunt him for weeks to come.

In complete exhaustion, Mulder and Daniel drug themselves back to their bunker and somehow summoned the strength to tidy it up after that morning's bombardment. Then Daniel collapsed on the mattress to get a few hours of precious sleep, while Mulder hunkered down to take the first watch.

***

The next morning's pounding by the Russians was noticeably more brutal, not to mention five minutes longer than the usual hour – payback for the downing of the two planes the day before. Surprisingly, Daniel was already feeling his nerves hardening to the daily poundings. Some men would break under the barrages, while other men took it as a personal challenge: *I can take it, Ivan...whatever you have to dish out, I can take it!* Daniel was pleased to think, at least for the moment, that he was a member of the latter group.

The rest of the morning consisted of the usual business: they cleaned up the bunker, they ate, they smoked, they went to the latrine, they took turns watching the Russians. But in the afternoon, something unusual occurred, and Daniel got his first good look at Russian soldiers.

He was looking through the field glasses when he saw them. His heart skipped a beat. Four of them emerged from the safety of their trench, carrying bundles under their arms. They looked around for a flat place to lay the bundles, and carefully lowered them to the ground. Daniel was intrigued, but puzzled – they didn't look like

233

demons, or monsters – no horns sticking out of their heads or long, sharp claws on their hands – just ordinary men in dirt-brown uniforms.

"Something's happening," Daniel alerted Mulder calmly.

Mulder was playing cards by himself. "What?"

"Four of them just came up."

"Is it a patrol?"

"I don't think so. They're setting something up, in front of their trench."

Mulder grabbed the other pair of field glasses and joined him. "Ah – they're setting up mortars."

That sounded quite serious to Daniel, but Mulder didn't seem alarmed. "Shouldn't we do something?"

"It's a trick," Mulder explained. "They want to draw our fire, make us expose our positions, so they can nail us. But we're not going to fall for it."

"Will they fire them at us?"

"They'll shoot a few rounds over our heads, try to get us to fire back," Mulder yawned. "It's not much to worry about, though."

Sure enough, as soon the mortars were set up, the Russians began a slow but steady shelling of the Germans. Most of the rounds landed away from the trenches – more of an annoyance than anything. After thirty minutes of this, Daniel asked, "How long do you think they'll keep it up?"

"Until they run out of shells, I suppose," Mulder replied, slightly annoyed.

Henckel emerged from the tunnel and stumbled into the bunker. "Nothing to worry about!" he exclaimed.

"Who's worried?" Mulder sniffed.

"Feldwebel Toppel called in an airstrike. They should be along any moment."

Then they heard the approaching drone of a Messerschmitt. It flew in low over them and headed straight for the Russians.

"What a beautiful sound!" Mulder couldn't help but gush.

"Watch this!" Henckel said, rubbing his hands together. Daniel was quickly learning: nothing raised the spirits of a German foot soldier quite like the sight of a soaring Messerschmitt.

All three watched through the field glasses as the Messerschmitt employed its machine guns to scatter the Russian troops who had been firing the mortars. They dove back into their trench as the mighty warplane swooped over them like a giant eagle. Then it banked and turned around gracefully, coming in for another pass at the mortars themselves. Its 20 millimeter machine guns chewed up the mortar tubes like they were tin cans, rendering them useless junk in seconds.

And that was that. Mission accomplished, the Messerschmitt tipped it wings and headed back to its airfield in the west. A great cheer went up from the German trenches, a roar of approval and victory that they wanted Ivan to hear over on his side.

And so it went. For days on end, the war went on like that – a tit-for-tat proposition, a deadly contest of one-upsmanship – you shoot down one of our planes, we'll obliterate your trenches with artillery, and so on and so on…

Daniel became quite familiar with this rhythm, and perhaps could be forgiven for believing the war, as deadly as it could be, was nothing more than a stalemate – much like the Great War twenty years before. The Germans, pushed back on their heels by the Red Army after the disaster at Stalingrad, never really spoke of defeat as a possibility. Surrounded by this type of optimism – along with the few small victories achieved by the Germans from time to time – it was easy to become lulled into a sense of complacency and denial that ultimate defeat could be in Germany's future.

Esprit de corps. It was something that began to bond Daniel to his comrades, whether he realized it or not.

The men gathered together and celebrated that night. They laughed and sang and toasted the Luftwaffe with schnapps. And even the most pessimistic soldier among them would not begrudge these dirty, ragged trench-dwellers a few rare moments of joy and companionship. There was enough time for skepticism – tonight, there would be rejoicing. It certainly didn't come along often enough down in the trenches in desolate, God-forsaken Ukraine.

Chapter 14

As autumn came to a close and winter approached, everyone could feel the change of weather in their bones. Those who'd been on the front for more than a year knew exactly what the coming Russian winter would bring. Newbies like Daniel had no idea what lay ahead.

One day in November, Mulder came back to the bunker from a break with a pair of boots. "Throw away those boots you're wearing, and put these on."

Daniel took the boots and looked them over. "But these are too big for me."

"Just stuff them with newspaper and wear two pairs of socks, and they'll be fine," Mulder told him. "You'll be glad to have the extra insulation when the first snow comes. You'll get frostbite in those thin, flash new boots you're wearing now." Daniel did as he was told. From that moment on, he stopped asking questions when told to do something, and just did it.

Daniel saw someone coming down their tunnel. It was Schlesser, the platoon medic. He crawled into their bunker and looked around, blinking.

"Any news about our three patients?" Mulder asked.

"I got a report from Medical Services yesterday," Schlesser reported. "They're all doing very well. They've been moved from the field hospital to a cushy convalescence center further west. They should be back with us by Christmas. Say, I need to borrow your man here to run an errand for me."

"What about Moretti?" Mulder asked. Moretti was an Italian volunteer, who usually ran errands and did odd jobs for the platoon.

"He's busy re-stocking the ammo dump. I need to borrow Schiller for about an hour."

"Take him."

Schlesser told Daniel to take the newly-repaired communication tunnel over to 3rd platoon and pick up a case of penicillin from their infirmary. Eager for a chance to get out of the bunker for a while, Daniel grabbed his rifle and started his trip. He'd finally learned his way around his own platoon's maze of tunnels, but he'd never been over to 3rd platoon, so it was kind of an adventure for him.

The communication tunnel was about a hundred meters long. When he got to the other side, there were many new faces he'd never seen before.

"Who the hell are you?" one soldier grimaced at him.

"I'm from 2nd platoon," Daniel cleared his throat. "Where's your infirmary?"

The soldier looked him up and down disapprovingly, then asked, "Why? You sick?"

"I'm supposed to pick something up."

The soldier looked away disdainfully. "Keep going straight, then make a left at the next turn."

"*Danke*."

"*Ja, ja…*"

Daniel followed the directions exactly, but couldn't find the infirmary. "That *tauschen* was just toying with me!" he said under his breath. He took another left turn, then a right, then became hopelessly lost. He finally found a tunnel that led to a wider bunker with four men sitting in it, drinking coffee. They looked up when he entered.

"Who the hell are *you*?" someone asked.

Here we go again, thought Daniel. "I'm from 2nd platoon. Where's your infirmary?"

"Why? You sick?"

"Ja, ja, I've been through all that," Daniel replied, testily. "I was told to pick something up…"

"Sit down a second," one of them said, smiling. "You look tense. Have a cup of ersatz coffee and relax." Someone handed him a cup. Daniel sat down and took a sip – nothing like real coffee, but dark and hot. "Cream and sugar?" the soldier asked, and they all laughed.

Daniel flushed bright red.

"No, really. We're okay – we're just fooling with you a little," the first soldier said. "You know, taking the piss…"

"I'm just running an errand. I need to find your infirmary."

"What's the rush? Take it easy."

Another soldier spoke up. "You new?"

"Fairly," Daniel replied hesitantly.

"It shows."

"How – how could you tell?"

"Your uniform. It's too clean." They all laughed again. Daniel noticed they were all wearing white, gauze-like bandages around their necks.

"How do you like it so far?"

"What?" Daniel asked, distracted by the bandages.

"The front. How do you like it?"

Daniel didn't know what to say.

"Speechless, I see," the first soldier – the one who did most of the talking – said. "Just remember: never turn your back on the Russians. There's only one thing you need to know: Russians are like *dogs*. No, worse than dogs."

"Worse than *swine*," the second soldier said. A third soldier spit on the ground to emphasize the point.

"We don't take prisoners," the talkative soldier said. "It would be like putting rats in a POW camp. What's the use in that?"

"And remember: Russians _never_ surrender. Even when they're coming at you with their hands in the air!" They all roared with laughter at that. Then it fell awkwardly silent.

Not knowing what else to say, Daniel indicated the bandages around their necks. "What's with the..?"

"Oh, these?" the talkative soldier said. "The fresh bandages draw the lice from our filthy uniforms."

"Really?" Daniel asked.

"Oh, yes," the talkative one continued. "You see, the lice are drawn to clean cloth. So when we put these on, the lice leave our filthy uniforms and underwear for the nice, clean gauze."

"Every two or three days, we take the bandages off and burn them," the second soldier explained. "And there you have it: almost completely lice-free. At least, for a few days, anyway..."

Daniel looked at them askance: *are they taking the piss again?*

"Here, try it," the first soldier said, handing Daniel a clean bandage. "You'll be glad you did."

Still wary, Daniel put the bandage around his neck, then remembered the errand. "Well, thanks for the coffee, but I must get to your infirmary now."

"That's right, your *important* mission," the talkative one said, and they all laughed again. It was beginning to wear on Daniel's nerves. "Come on, I'll take you."

Daniel followed the soldier to the infirmary, where the medic looked at Daniel. "What took you so long?"

"We were having coffee," the talkative soldier explained.

The medic looked at Daniel again. He was wearing a bandage around his neck, too. Then he handed Daniel a package. "Here's the penicillin. Can you find your way back all right?"

"I'll show him the way," the soldier said.

When he got back to his own platoon, Daniel dropped the package off at the infirmary and went back to the bunker. Mulder, Henckel, and Vollmer were all squeezed inside, talking and smoking cigarettes.

"What the hell is *that*?" Mulder blurted when he saw the bandage around Daniel's neck.

"I got it from 3rd platoon," Daniel explained. "They're all wearing them over there. The fresh bandage draws the lice from our uniforms."

The other three burst out laughing. Daniel flushed red again.

"No, really. That's what they told me –"

"They're pulling your leg, and you fell for it!" Vollmer exclaimed.

"Draws the lice from our uniforms – oh, that's a good one!" Mulder bellowed, slapping his knee.

"Sorry, Little Fish, but they got you good with that one!" Henckel joined in. Daniel felt like crawling into a hole somewhere. Then Mulder starting scratching himself as the laughter subsided. They all grew silent. Mulder scratched himself again. Then it became contagious and Vollmer started scratching, too.

"Do you think it really works?" Mulder asked, seriously.

"Well, *he's* not scratching!" Henckel said, pointing to Daniel.

All three looked at each other a moment. Then they got up and went to the infirmary to get bandages for themselves. By nightfall, the whole platoon was wearing bandages around their necks.

"And look: nobody's scratching anymore!" Mulder declared.

Schlesser, the medic, wasn't convinced. "Haven't you idiots heard of the *placebo effect*?"

"The *what*?" Mulder asked.

"If I give you a pill filled with sugar, but tell you it's medicine, you'll feel better just because you <u>believe</u> it's medicine."

"So, you think we're just *imagining* the lice have stopped tormenting us?" Henckel asked.

"The power of suggestion is a very strong thing," Schlesser observed.

"I don't believe you," Vollmer replied.

"I'm telling you, scientifically speaking, there's no logical reason for the lice to be drawn to the bandages," the medic argued.

"You're not a real doctor, just a *medic*!" Vollmer went on. "Why should we believe you?"

"Suit yourselves, but I'm telling you it's all in your heads."

"I don't care!" Mulder declared. "All I know is the itching has stopped! I'm wearing the bandages from now on!"

That night, it was Daniel's squad's turn for patrol. After dark, Mulder, Vollmer, Henckel, Kellerman, Himmel, and Daniel tucked their bright white bandages into their collars, blackened their faces with shoe polish, grabbed their rifles, and slithered out of their trench into no-man's land. They slowly crawled from crater to crater, stopping every few minutes to observe the Russian lines, or whenever the Russians sent up a flare. This went on for about two hours. They got close enough to the Russians to hear their voices echoing across the steppe, and stopped to listen.

"What are they doing?" Daniel asked Mulder, who was lying next to him.

"Sounds like they're just drinking and singing songs," Mulder whispered back. Daniel listened carefully, and could hear faint sounds of laughter and what sounded like a violin playing a tune. Daniel knew that while on patrol, their job was simply to make sure Ivan was staying in his trenches and behaving himself, not to engage the enemy – if at all possible.

Satisfied that the Russians weren't up to any mischief, Henckel led them away from the enemy lines to do a sweep of their own perimeter and make sure the German flanks were secure. The farther away from the Russians they got, the more their nerves relaxed and the easier they felt. Everything was quiet and as it should be on their southern flank, so they stopped to rest for a few minutes in a large crater. Daniel took his canteen out and took a swig of water.

Vollmer, who always had a new joke, broke the silence. "Hey, have you fellows heard this one? What's the difference between socialism, communism, and national socialism?"

"Please, tell us," Himmel said. He was a small, bookish-type with wire-rimmed spectacles and not much of a sense of humor. Mulder's nickname for him was "Mouse."

Vollmer launched right into the joke. "Socialism: you have two cows. The government takes one and gives it to your neighbor. Then you form a cooperative to tell him how to manage his cow. Communism: you have two cows. The government seizes both of your cows and provides you with milk. You stand in line for hours to get it, and it is expensive and sour."

"What about national socialism?" Henckel asked.

"I'm just getting to that," Vollmer said impatiently. "National socialism: you have two cows. The government seizes both cows. The next day they bring you back two goats and tell you they are cows. If you complain, the Gestapo comes in the middle of the night and you are never seen again."

"That's it? That's the joke?" Mulder asked, puzzled.

"Is that supposed to be funny?" Himmel asked.

"Take it as you like," Vollmer said, offended no one laughed.

"But I still don't understand," Mulder confessed. "In communism, they take two cows, right?"

"That's right," Vollmer agreed.

"Where did they take the cows?"

"It doesn't matter where they take the cows."

"The joke is defective. We must know where they took the cows for it to be funny."

"You're missing the whole point of the joke!" Vollmer said, exasperated.

"Will you forget about the damn communist cows?" Himmel hissed. "You two are driving me crazy! Vollmer's right: it doesn't matter where they take the cows!"

"Thank you," Vollmer said, somewhat vindicated.

"And Mulder's right: the joke isn't funny!"

"That's all I'm saying," Mulder agreed. "When a joke is missing information, it cannot be funny."

"It's not missing information!" Vollmer insisted. "It is a perfect joke. It has neither no more nor no less information than is needed."

"But it has no punchline," Kellerman chimed in.

"It may be the delivery…" Henckel added.

"Political jokes never work," Kellerman asserted.

"That's because politics and humor should be kept in separate compartments. Every comedian worth his salt knows that!" Himmel said with authority.

"It takes a special talent to tell a joke well," Henckel observed sagely.

"I bet the *Fuhrer* knows how to tell a good joke," Kellerman postulated.

"How would you ever know?" Mulder asked. "Even if it's bad, you have to laugh anyway."

Vollmer looked around in disbelief. "That's it! I'm never telling another joke! You, Himmel – you're telling all the jokes from now on!"

"But you have to have a sense of humor to tell jokes," Henckel pointed out.

"Or just make sure your joke is not *defective*," Mulder said flatly.

"SSShh! Quiet down, everybody!" Henckel hissed. He was sitting up, peering over the edge of the crater. "I think I see something…"

They all joined him at the crater's edge. "Look – over there – what is it?"

"It looks like a vehicle of some kind," Mulder said. Daniel squinted and peered into the darkness. He could just make out black tires and a dark grey body. They stayed perfectly still and watched the vehicle for a full fifteen minutes – no signs of life in or around it.

"We've got to check it out," Henckel said. "Mulder, you take Schiller and Vollmer and approach from the left. The rest of you follow me on the right." The squad slithered out of the hole and approached the vehicle with extreme caution. When they got closer, Daniel could see that it was a military staff car with a German Maltese cross insignia on the door.

"One of our's," Mulder observed. Both teams reached the car at the same time. There was nobody else around. "Somebody must've gotten stranded out here, and left it to walk for help."

"Don't touch anything," Henckel cautioned. "It could be booby-trapped." They gathered around and examined the car without touching it.

"Look at that – in the back seat – what is that?" Vollmer asked.

"It looks like a – cheese!" Himmel said.

"It _is_ a cheese!" Mulder confirmed, licking his chops. Daniel peered into the back seat and saw a large, round, yellow object, almost the size of a spare tire.

"What's it doing in the back of this car?" Kellerman asked naively.

"It could be rigged to explode," Henckel said.

"An exploding _cheese?_" Mulder asked.

"Henckel's right," Himmel said. "It could be a Russian trick."

"Or it could just be a delicious cheese!" Mulder argued. "I don't see any wires."

"Do you want to take that chance, for a few bites of cheese?" Henckel asked.

"A few _bites_?" Mulder said incredulously. "Look at the size of that thing. That would feed us for _weeks_!"

"I haven't tasted cheese in months!" Vollmer groaned.

"All right, who's for taking this cheese back with us?" Mulder asked, raising his hand. Vollmer and Kellerman raised their hands. "Come on, Little Fish – what about you? You're the tie-breaker!"

Daniel, feeling a great deal of peer pressure, slowly raised his hand. Pleased, Mulder turned to Henckel. "Well, that's it. You've been out-voted. We're taking the cheese."

"How can you be sure it's not booby-trapped?" Henckel snapped, still unsure.

"It's quite simple," Mulder explained, already having worked it out. "Schiller here will take his bayonet and very carefully feel for any wires underneath the cheese."

"Why _me?_" blurted Daniel, mortified.

"Because you're the only one with fingers slender enough to reach under the cheese without disturbing it," Mulder said convincingly. "Besides, you've got a very steady hand." He raised his own hand, which was visibly shaking. Daniel knew he was exaggerating the tremor.

"Schiller, you don't have to –" Henckel began to say.

"I'll do it," Daniel interrupted him. "On one condition: you stop calling me 'Little Fish.'"

"Done!" Mulder agreed triumphantly.

Daniel unsheathed his bayonet and studied the cheese carefully. The top of the car was down, so all he had to do was lean over the back door to reach the cheese sitting on the seat. Taking a deep breath, he reached in and slid the end of the bayonet very slowly beneath the edge of the cheese. Everyone else stood holding their breaths, like statues.

Taking shallow breaths, Daniel carefully worked the blade of the bayonet further underneath the cheese, expecting to feel it snag on a wire any second. He worked the blade around the entire circumference of the cheese – no snags, no wires.

"Well?" Mulder asked, anxiously.

"No wires," Daniel announced, re-sheathing his bayonet. Everyone began breathing again. "But you're going to have to help me lift this thing out of here."

Mulder complied with the request. They carefully lifted the circular object off the seat and out of the car. They stepped away from the vehicle, Mulder marveling at the size of the cheese. "That was one of the finest acts of bravery I've ever witnessed," Mulder told Daniel, with great admiration. "I will make it up to you – I promise."

They wrapped the cheese in a groundsheet and stuffed it into Mulder's pack. "We all agree – this is our secret, right?" Mulder said.

"Ja, ja," they all agreed.

"There's not enough to feed the whole platoon, anyway," Kellerman stated matter-of-factly.

"We took all the risk, after all," Vollmer pointed out.

"Agreed," Henckel said. "But there's still the matter of what to do with it."

"I vote we eat it!" Vollmer said.

"Of course we'll eat it," Henckel responded. "But when?"

"He's right," Kellerman interjected. "Do we eat it right away, or save it for a special occasion?"

They all thought a moment. Then Himmel suggested, "Let's save it for Christmas."

This being agreeable to all concerned, the matter was settled. "Now, we've got to sweep our northern flank before we can go home and get some sleep," Henckel said, as the squad prepared to move out. They covered a few meters at a time, stopping always to listen and observe, before moving on in the black, cratered expanse of no-man's land. To Daniel, it seemed like walking on the Moon at night – a desolate, remote netherworld, devoid of life and any other Earthly qualities.

Just as they were approaching their own position once again, Henckel stopped suddenly and motioned for everyone to hit the ground. They waited prone on the ground while Henckel watched and listened. "I heard something about ten meters ahead," he whispered to the others. "Stay here while I go check it out." They all waited silently until he came crawling back five minutes later.

"It's a Russian patrol, seven men," Henckel whispered. "Headed right for us."

"Dammit!" Mulder hissed.

"There's no time to go back. Take cover in these craters, and keep your rifles ready."

They slid down into a couple of nearby craters and waited. Daniel crouched between Mulder and Himmel. Daniel felt like his heart was trying to work its way up his throat, and gulped it back down hard. "Easy there – we're just going to let them walk right on by," Mulder whispered to him. "No use getting into a squabble tonight," he added, thinking about the magnificent cheese in his pack. What luck: this wonderful cheese just falls into their laps – a once-in-lifetime occurrence – but they may be wiped out by a Russian patrol before having a chance to eat it!

A moment later, they heard them: the tight crunch of their hard-soled boots on the short, dead grass, the creak of leather belts and straps on their uniform, the almost imperceptible rattle of someone checking his rifle. Daniel could even hear one of them breathing through his nose. They were right on top of them!

Daniel watched his comrades, still as statues, and realized how close they were to point-blank combat. At this point, *anything* could give them away – including Mulder's gurgling stomach. Thankfully, he was able to constrain that unruly organ and keep it unusually quiet. A cough, a sneeze, even so much as an innocent sniffle of the nose, and they would be fighting for their lives.

It seemed to take an eternity for the Russians to pass by. It occurred to Daniel that they probably felt the same way – that they would no doubt do anything in their power to avoid a wild gun battle on this quiet, dark night. They were out here for the same reason as the Germans: to keep tabs on the other side, make sure the enemy wasn't up to anything suspicious. Nobody in his right mind wanted to die, after all.

Finally, Henckel signaled to the others that the Russians had passed. The Germans breathed again. Henckel crept out of his crater and followed them a few meters to make sure they weren't trying to trick them by doubling back. A few minutes later, he was back: "All clear." The squad climbed out of their holes and were back in their own safe trench within ten minutes.

That ratty old trench never looked – and smelled – so good!

They sat against the glistening earthen walls, sipped from their canteens, and generally unwound from the patrol.

"How do you like that kind of cat-and-mouse game, eh, Schiller?" Mulder asked Daniel, with a sly grin. "Ha-ha, you should have seen your face in that crater! Not quite your cup of tea, I'll wager!"

"You had your eyes shut pretty tight yourself, as I recall, Mulder," Himmel remembered.

"That wasn't fear," Mulder corrected him. "I was praying, 'Oh God, don't let me die tonight without tasting this immaculate cheese.'"

"You don't believe in God," Vollmer reminded him.

"For a cheese this big, I can believe."

"It makes you wonder: how many Bolshevik patrols sat in craters trying to stay quiet, waiting for _us_ to pass by?" Himmel mused.

Mulder's smile evaporated as a chill went up his spine. He looked a little spooked. "I wish you hadn't said that, Himmel."

"Every night we come back with a full squad is a good night," Henckel concluded.

"Especially when we have something like what's in your pack, Mulder," Vollmer added.

"That reminds me – who's going to keep it until Christmas?" Kellerman asked.

"I will," Mulder answered. "I will hide it in our bunker."

"Oh, no – you'll eat it, you big oaf!" Vollman protested.

"I wouldn't," Mulder said, slightly offended. "Not one bite!"

"I don't trust you," Vollman maintained.

"Maybe we should pass it around," Henckel suggested. "You know – take turns caring for it, spread the responsibility a little bit."

Mulder shook his head adamantly. "Little Fi—I mean, *Schiller*—will keep me honest. Won't you, Schiller?"

"I'll do my best," Daniel promised.

"Ah, it's no use – we'll never get it out of his grubby hands," Kellerman said.

"I will guard it with my life," Mulder swore, putting his hand over his heart. "And on Christmas day, we will have the best Christmas feast you've ever eaten!"

***

The next morning, the trenches were buzzing with activity. It was the '*November Schrubben*,' and everyone Daniel saw seemed to have a gleam in their eye and a bounce in their step.

"What's the '*November Schrubben*?'" he asked Henckel.

"The last chance to clean up before the first freeze," Henckel replied expectantly. "That means hot water and soap – can you believe it? *Real* soap!" He said the last two words with a wonder and amazement that civilians would never understand.

After weeks of wearing the same underwear, living in a trench, and crawling on his belly on patrol, Daniel was beginning to take on the grubby patina of a long-term front-line soldier himself. Hot water and real soap was very good news, indeed!

"They're calling us by squads," Henckel explained with growing excitement. "And our squad is second! What luck, eh? The water will still be somewhat hot, and the cakes of soap will still be big enough to hold onto!" He closed his eyes and tried to imagine such luxury, here on the desolate steppes of the Ukraine.

When it was their turn, Daniel's squad proceeded to the infirmary with great expectations. They were not disappointed. True to Henckle's description, there were enough buckets of hot water for each man to have his own – of course, it had already been used by someone from the first squad.

"No matter," Mulder enthused. "It's still hot and wet!"

"They heat them over *real fires* – so that they last <u>all</u> day!" Henckel mused, smiling broadly. *Common Germans back home in their comfortable houses would never imagine such a fuss over something as simple as hot water,* thought Daniel. But after a month

247

at the front, he was more than eager to strip down and dive into his assigned bucket when the time came.

Grown men – hardened soldiers – luxuriating in the simple pleasure of washing off layers of dirt without the unpleasant sting of ice water was truly a sight to behold. And soap! Each man had his own cake to use! Such extravagance!

The *schrubben* put the whole platoon in a good mood. They laughed, joked, and got downright chatty.

"Look at Mulder!" Vollmer pointed at his comrade, stripped to the waste and washing under his arms. "There's actually a real man under all that dirt!"

"Ah – I'm beginning to feel like a human being again!" Kellerman beamed, shampooing his hair with soap.

"The only trouble is, no matter how much you scrub, you'll never *look* like one!" Henckel retorted.

"Hey, Schiller," Himmel said. "How did you get those nasty scars on your shoulder?"

Daniel put his hand over the scars. "Oh, I was attacked by a bear. I was…camping with my father in the Austrian Alps."

"How long ago?"

"I was twelve."

"Twelve?" Himmel repeated suspiciously. "Those scars look pretty fresh to me."

"What, are you a doctor now?" Mulder asked Himmel. "You've got a medical degree now?"

"All I'm saying is, there's something off about his story," Himmel said.

"Yes, I agree with Himmel," Henckel said dryly. "Don't you see? Schiller is obviously a Russian spy!"

Laughter all around.

"Don't listen to him," Vollmer said to Daniel. "You've been marked by a bear. Do you know what that means?"

"*Nein*," Daniel said.

"it's an *omen*, Schiller," Vollmer told him, with deep conviction.

"Oh, come on, Vollmer," Mulder scoffed. "You can knock it off now. Leave the boy alone…"

"I'm not joking," Vollmer insisted. "It's an *omen*. You're going to survive this war, Schiller. Don't you see? You've got the *Mark of the Bear*! The Russians can't harm you now. What's wrong with all of you? It's as clear as day!"

"That's nothing but superstitious drivel," Himmel sneered. "The '*Mark of the Bear*!' I've never heard such rubbish in all my life!"

"You're the lucky one, Schiller," Vollmer promised him, winking. "I'm a Bavarian, born and bred in the mountains. I <u>know</u> these things. Meeting that bear was the luckiest thing that ever happened to you. Mark my words!"

"Ja, danke," Daniel nodded lamely, still trying to cover the scars with his hand. *But it wasn't so lucky for the <u>real</u> Johann Schiller*, he thought sullenly.

At that moment, the air siren went off.

"Oh no, not <u>now</u>!" Mulder groaned.

Feldwebel Toppel hurried into the infirmary and blew his whistle. "In-coming aircraft!   Everyone to their stations!   *Schnell*! *SCHNELL*!"

"But we haven't finished our bath!" Henckel cried.

"It isn't fair!" Kellerman bawled, soap suds in his eyes. "We're only half done!"

Toppel had no mercy. "Everyone to your stations – NOW!"

The squad pulled on their uniforms and boots and ran to their stations, shouting oaths and complaining the whole way. The drone of the Russian engines could already be heard overhead, and huge shadow outlines of the planes darkened the trenches as they passed over them. Machine gun fire began to riddle the ground, and bombs started dropping all around the German compound.

"Ivan must've replaced those two planes the Luftwaffe shot down with a whole squadron," Mulder shouted when they were back in the bunker. He put his helmet on and manned the MG 42. Daniel had the field glasses to his eyes, carefully scanning the skies.

"I count four – no, <u>five</u> – airplanes," Daniel reported.

"Grab the belt!" Mulder shouted, ready to fire. Daniel dropped the field glasses and complied with the order. Mulder got an airplane in his sights and started to unleash a steady stream of hot lead into the blue sky just ahead of it. "It's the only way to hit them in the engines," Mulder shouted to Daniel. "Aim a few meters in front of the propellers, then they fly right into the rounds!" Daniel saw a few rounds slice into the plane's fuselage, but it kept flying with no apparent smoke or damage. "Dammit! They're flying too bloody *fast*!" Mulder growled, aiming and firing at another plane making a pass over them. The Russians flew back and forth over the German lines, strafing and bombing pretty much at their will.

The assault continued for a good thirty minutes before three Messerschmitts arrived and managed to chase the Russians off. The damage to the German compound was substantial: two trenches collapsed, the infirmary badly damaged, and the ammo dump completely destroyed. Seven men were injured, three severely enough to be evacuated to a field hospital in the safe zone.

It took two full days working around the clock to repair the damage to the trenches.

"Why did it take the Luftwaffe so long to arrive?" someone asked Feldwebel Topper.

"They're spread pretty thin these days," was all he could say. But that wasn't the only bad news. When all the repairs were done to the camp, Toppel called 2nd platoon together for a special meeting.

"The Ruskies are upping the ante," he told his assembled troops. "They're beefing up their sector with an armored regiment – twenty to thirty T-34 tanks. It looks like they're building up for a major assault."

"One infantry company against thirty Russian tanks?" Vollmer blurted out.

"What kind of help can we expect from Central Command?" Henckel demanded.

"We will be receiving support," Toppel assured him.

"What *kind* of support?" Henckel persisted.

"Substantial," Toppel promised, cryptically.

The "substantial" support was am 88-millimeter anti-tank gun with a three-man crew, which arrived two days later and ensconced itself on a knoll a hundred meters behind the German lines. After setting up, the crew came down to meet and talk to Toppel's skeptical troops.

"One 88 can take out a whole column of Russian tanks," the crew leader, Bauer, assured them with a broad smile. "We did it at the Battle of Karkhov, and we can do it here. And not only is it effective on armor, but it's an excellent anti-aircraft gun as well. Believe me, your company will be as safe as houses with us around."

Yes, Bauer and his crew were cocky, but his words were just what the unit needed to hear. Everyone in 2nd platoon came away feeling much better now that they had an 88 backing them up.

Two days later, the new gun was put to the test when a column of four T-34 tanks left the Russian lines and drove into no-man's land toward the Germans. Daniel watched through the field glasses as the 88 swiftly took out the two lead tanks, causing the last two tanks to turn around and head back. In retaliation, a Russian fighter plane, promptly dispatched to destroy the 88, quickly turned around and headed home under heavy fire from the gun.

Bauer and his crew were vigorously celebrated that evening, showered with cigarettes and bottles of *cognac* and *schnapps*. "This is the best Christmas gift we could ever imagine," Mulder joyously declared.

Chapter 15

Early December brought the first signs of snow, in the form of a serious blizzard. Daniel, Vollmer, and Himmel had been dispatched to the supply road behind lines to meet a truck and pick up a new supply of ammo, when it struck suddenly and without warning. On the way back to camp, they became disoriented as the snow fell heavier and heavier each minute. In complete white-out conditions, they soon found themselves hopelessly lost.

"I'm sure our trench is in this direction," Vollmer said, peering into the blinding whiteness.

"No, no," Himmel contradicted him. "It's *this* way."

Vollmer turned to Daniel. "Which one of us is right, Schiller?"

"I think it's this way," Daniel said, pointing in a third direction.

"Well, we can't go in all three directions!" Himmel protested.

"I'm with Schiller," Vollmer said.

"But you just said it was *that* way!" Himmel argued.

"I changed my mind," Vollmer said. "Now it's two against one. You're out-voted, Himmel."

And so they went Daniel's way – which did not take them back to the trenches.

"Admit it: we're lost," Himmel demanded. "We just keep going in circles!"

"Won't they send a search party for us?" Daniel asked.

"Not until after this bloody blizzard's over," Vollmer said. "Let's go – we've got to keep moving so we don't freeze to death."

They walked for another hour, their 8-pound Mauser rifles and the crates of ammunition becoming heavier with each step.

"I've got to rest," Himmel gasped, setting his crate on the ground and sitting on it. He was breathing heavily, ice crystals forming on his spectacles.

"Ja, but only for a moment. It's getting colder," Vollmer warned.

Daniel sat on his crate and began to wonder if this was going to be it for him – the end – frozen solid on the icy, snow-covered steppes of Ukraine. Vollmer was right: every moment they were idle, they came closer to never moving again. Daniel could already feel the icy fingers of death reaching up from the frozen ground into his extremities.

Then he saw them: several dark figures, moving toward them through the blinding whiteness. Was he imagining it? "Look!" he said to the others, pointing. Vollmer and Himmel saw them, too.

"Are they our guys?" Himmel asked hopefully.

"Can't tell," Vollmer answered.

Before Vollmer could stop him, Himmel stood and called out *"Hallo! Wir sind hier druben!"*

"Shut up, you fool!" Vollmer hissed. "They could be Russians!"

They got their answer within seconds: several shots fired in their direction.

"It's a Russian patrol – probably lost, too!" Vollmer surmised.

"What should we do about the crates?" Daniel asked.

"Forget them," Himmel replied. "Just run!"

They ran for their lives away from the rifle fire. They heard the crunch of Russian boots on the snow, pursuing them. More shots were fired – bullets whizzed by them, one just centimeters from Daniel's helmet.

"They're trying to kill us!" Himmel said, in shock.

"You're surprised by this?" Vollmer shot back. "They're *Russians*!"

They continued to run, summoning extra reserves of adrenalin and strength, not knowing where they were going – just anywhere away from the gunfire.

"They're gaining on us," Himmel shouted, stumbling in the snow. "I'm done! Let's surrender!"

"Get up, you idiot!" Vollmer reached out and pulled Himmel up. "No surrender! You know how they treat prisoners! I'd rather get shot right here!"

Vollmer and Daniel managed to keep Himmel moving forward, but the shots kept ringing out behind them.

"Look, up ahead!" Daniel shouted.

Vollmer saw it, too. "Ja, our position! It's a miracle!"

They ran the last few meters, screaming "Nicht schießen! Nicht schießen! *Wir sind Deutsche!"*

Still dodging Russian bullets, they dove headfirst into the first trench they came to.

Henckel, Kellerman, Toppel, and a few others were there.

"Where the hell have you been?" Toppel demanded.

"We got lost," Vollmer replied.

"Where's the ammo?"

"Out there. And so are the Russians!"

"I see them now!" Henckel shouted, firing over the rim of the trench. The others grabbed their rifles and joined him, sending a deadly volley out into the raging blizzard. Daniel aimed at the dark figures in the snow and fired his rifle, too. They fired back, but began to drop to the ground, one by one. Then Daniel heard Mulder's MG 42 come to life a few meters to the right, and more Russians fell. The Germans kept firing until there were no more dark figures. None of the Russians made it back home that night.

"That was pretty good thinking, leading them back here to be wiped out like that," Kellerman said.

"It wasn't planned," Vollmer admitted. "We didn't know where we were going!"

"Why don't you get lost again tomorrow night?" Henckel joked. "At that rate, in a few weeks we'll have cleared all the Bolsheviks out of this area!"

It was a great victory for the platoon and helped raise everyone's spirits – to both get their lost comrades back safely, and dispose of an entire Russian patrol in the bargain.

***

The next morning, the Russians were in a foul mood. From their point of view, their men had been ambushed and coldly slaughtered by the Germans. In retaliation, their artillery pounded the German lines for an extra fifteen minutes during the morning *Concerto.* After that, their fury spent, things were relatively quiet on the Russian side.

But not on the German side. Word was spreading like wildfire that Mulder had a special Christmas "surprise" for the whole platoon. In a tizzy, Mulder quickly set about trying to identify the leaker.

"It wasn't me," Henckel swore.

"You know it wasn't me," Daniel said.

Mulder thought a moment, then his eyes narrowed to slits. "Vollmer!"

They found Vollmer at his position in Trench 4.

"What did you do?" Mulder demanded.

"I don't know what you're talking about," Vollmer said calmly.

"If there's a scheme, I know you're behind it," Mulder fumed. "The whole platoon's talking about the Christmas 'surprise.'"

"So?"

"That was supposed to be for *us*."

Vollmer sucked in a deep breath. "All right. Look. I owed Kolb two packs of cigarettes over a card game. I told him about the cheese to pay off my debt."

"Why does everybody's portion have to get smaller to pay off *your* debt?" Himmel interjected.

Mulder buried his face in his hands for a moment. Then he fixed Vollmer with a steely stare. "You obviously don't understand the concept of the Cheese. So let me educate you. First of all, above <u>all</u> things sits the Cheese. The Cheese is magnificent and holy. The Cheese is sacred and treasured. The Cheese will sustain and nourish us. The Cheese will give us hope when we don't feel like going on. But the Cheese, as great as it is, is not *infinite*. Every time someone new is included, the Cheese gets *smaller*. Do you understand what I'm saying?"

Vollmer nodded vaguely.

"What are we going to do?" Henckel asked.

"All right," Mulder said. "To save the Cheese, we must first deny that the Cheese exists. You will go back to Kolb and tell him you were lying, that there really is no Cheese. The 'Christmas surprise' is a hoax. It was all a scheme – a ruse – to get you off the hook for the cigarettes."

"But I'll still owe him two packs of cigarettes," Vollmer protested.

"That's *your* problem, not mine!"

Henckel looked sullen.

"What's wrong with *you*?" Mulder asked.

"Now I feel guilty about hoarding the Cheese," Henckel replied. "Maybe we *should* share it with the whole platoon."

"Twenty men?" Mulder said incredulously. "Are you out of your mind? Each portion would be *miniscule*."

"But it would be fair," Kellerman pointed out.

"Who found the Cheese, eh? Do you remember?" Mulder prodded them. "It was *us*. It was providential! 'Providential' trumps 'fair.' Now, we've all got to hold together and stick to the original plan, or we all get nothing!"

***

That night, it was Daniel's turn to take *vorwartsbeobachtun gspflicht*, or "forward observation duty." The men took turns spending the entire night in a crater a few meters from the Russian lines. In the event of an attack, the observer was to fire his rifle twice and blow a whistle, to alert the Germans. Of course, nobody savored this duty, but it was a vital part of keeping tabs on what the Russians were up to.

Daniel took his rifle, his heavy winter coat, a pair of thick gloves, his canteen, and some *hartzwieback*, and crawled out to the observation position just after complete darkness. He reached the crater and settled in for a long, cold night of trying to stay alert and keeping his eyes and ears open. It was a clear night, and all the stars twinkled brightly in the sky. He was so close, he could hear Ivan talking, laughing, singing, and even smell what they were cooking for supper. Tonight, it smelled like borscht. Last week, it was beef Stroganoff.

Daniel's stomach growled. The cooking aromas were driving him mad. He was quite put out that the Ruskies were enjoying a hot, home-cooked meal while he was stuck in a freezing hole with nothing more than hard biscuits and water. But still, the wonderful aromas were better than nothing!

He made it through the night fantasizing about the wonderful meals the Russians seemed to be enjoying – taking part in them vicariously by way of nothing more than his olfactory sense and a healthy imagination. Just before dawn, after the Russians had all gone to sleep, he crawled back to his own side while it was still dark.

Everyone gathered around him when he got back.

"What was it last night?" Mulder asked eagerly.

"Borscht."

"*Borscht*," Henckel repeated dreamily.

"Describe it," Vollmer demanded.

"The meat stock was pork, I believe," Daniel reported. "I think the carrots and potatoes were sautéed in a light garlic sauce before they were added to the base. The stock simmered over a low flame for a while before the tender brisket was stirred in…"

"Stop!" Mulder pleaded. "I can't take any more!"

"This is torture!" Henckel agreed.

"Why do *they* get gourmet food every night, and all we get is cold tins of dog food?" Himmel complained bitterly.

Something strange was occurring. The men were now actually *vying* for forward observation duty – just to be able to bask in the wonderful aromas of Ivan's cooking all night. That night, it was Kellerman's turn.

"I'll gladly go in your place tonight," Vollmer volunteered.

"*Nein*," Kellerman replied. "I've been looking forward to it all week."

Everyone was waiting when Kellerman returned the next morning. He had a big smile on his face.

"Well? Don't keep us waiting – what did they have?"

"*Pirozhki*, stuffed with braised lamb, mushrooms, and onions," Kellerman said, savoring the memory.

"The bastards!" Mulder shouted, unable to control himself any longer.

"Impossible! This can't be happening!" Vollmer said in agony. "The meals are getting better and better each night!"

"It's simple," Daniel spoke up. "Every Russian unit can't be eating like this. This unit just got lucky, and got sent someone who knows what he's doing."

"That's right!" Mulder agreed. "Gourmet chefs get conscripted, too – even in Russia!"

Immediately, a whole back-story of the fictional chef began to form. Everyone collaborated, contributing ideas.

"We need a name."

"Ivan."

"No, too plain. Too obvious."

"Mikhail."

"Too Russian."

"Alexander."

"That's it! Perfect!"

"Now, where was he born?"

"St. Petersburg."

"Too cold."

"Kiev."

"Perfect!"

Day by day, to pass the time and keep from going insane, they added details to "Alexander's" story. One time, Mulder woke Daniel in the middle of the night.

"I've got it!" he said excitedly. "Alexander's father was a poor street-sweeper who finally scraped together enough money to send him to Paris to study at the *Cordon Bleu*...or, how about this: his father was an alcoholic, and his mother took in washing to save the money to send him to Paris...which one do you think?"

"I like the first one," Daniel said, closing his eyes and going back to sleep.

"Ja, I like that one better, too..."

"He should be a watchmaker's son," Vollmer said later, when Mulder ran the idea by him.

"That's not one of the choices," Mulder protested. "It's either his father was a poor street-sweeper, or an alcoholic."

"He should be a watchmaker's son," Vollmer repeated.

"Why?"

"Because I've always wondered what it would be like to be a watchmaker's son."

"This isn't about *you*, you fool," Mulder growled.

After a week of intense work, a complete life story more or less emerged: "Alexander" was a poor street-sweeper's son (or alcoholic's son, since they were unable to reach a consensus). His father (or mother) labored hard for twenty years to scrape together enough money to send him to study at the *Cordon Bleu* in Paris. While in Paris, he fell in love with a beautiful dressmaker's model named Elizabeth who had to quit modeling after a gruesome tram accident on the Rue Gay-Lussac. Alexander married the horribly disfigured girl anyway, and took her to Moscow, where they proceeded to create a family of eleven children. In the meantime, he became the head chef at the city's best restaurant, where he caught the attention of none other than Joseph Stalin. Stalin was particularly fond of his braised pheasant crepes with kipper sauce –

"Wait a minute," Vollmer interrupted. "Why doesn't Stalin tap this guy as his personal chef?"

"Idiot!" Mulder replied. "Then we wouldn't be able to enjoy his cooking *here!*"

"You're right." Then Vollmer thought of something else. "We need to be careful not to kill him."

"How do we do *that*?" Kellerman asked. "They all look the same."

"Don't worry," Mulder assured them. "Cooks are never killed in combat."

"I hope you're right," Henckel shook his head. "It would be a shame to lose Alexander…"

Eventually, "Alexander" became so real to them that they would weave him into their everyday conversations: *What would Alexander say/do about such and such…Oh, Alexander wouldn't approve of <u>that</u>…*

Above all, they continued to enjoy forward observation duty and to savor his wonderful aromas wafting across no-man's land every night.

***

The shelling began at midnight and kept up until a quarter to one in the morning. Projectiles rained down on the German lines with devastating precision, causing the earth to convulse in an apocalyptic manner for forty-five full minutes of terror. Mulder and Daniel were tossed around inside their little bunker like dice in a cup. When it finally abated, the two had been reduced to a senseless, almost comatose state. It took them several minutes to regain their ability to think and speak. Miraculously, the walls of the bunker had held, and they slowly began to realize that they were physically unharmed.

"That was a bad one," Daniel said, with deliberate understatement.

"Ivan is up to something," Mulder responded gravely. "It came hours earlier than usual. I think there's going to be an attack." They both grabbed their field glasses and started scanning the snow-covered blackness of no-man's land.

"Who's got forward position tonight?" Mulder asked.

"Henckel," Daniel replied.

"Then God help him if there's an attack."

Moments later, they heard the two rifle shots, followed by a long blast from the whistle.

Ivan was coming.

They heard the tanks first – the ground-trembling roar of the diesel engines and the terrifying squeak of those deadly steel treads. Daniel already knew that the weight of a T-34 tank could collapse a trench in seconds, burying the men inside underneath tons of earth. Men who became trapped beneath the treads of one of those monsters never survived.

"It sounds like two or three tanks coming up on each flank," Mulder guessed. "I sure hope that 88 crew is awake!"

"Why aren't they firing yet?"

"They can't fire until they can actually *see* the tanks," Mulder explained. "That's why Ivan loves to attack at night."

They both listened as the tanks continued their inexorable approach.

"Listen to me: this could get ugly," Mulder said. "If something happens to me, take the gun and keep firing. If it jams, try to clear the breech as quickly as you can and keep firing. If you run out of ammo, grab your rifle and fire like hell. Got it?" Mulder looked concerned.

"Ja," Daniel croaked, fighting off a wave of panic.

"Don't worry too much," Mulder said, turning to the machine gun. "It goes how it goes…"

The T-34s continued driving up the right and left. They were closer than ever now.

"They're trying to get behind us," Mulder surmised. Then they heard the 88 open fire from the knoll behind them. They heard the shriek of the shell as it passed right over their heads and landed right in front of one of the lead tanks, sending up a huge spray of soil and rock. Then another round screamed over their heads and scored a direct hit, knocking the tank out. That stopped the two tanks behind it, one of which broke away and moved toward the bunker while the other one fired at the 88 and missed.

At the same time, Daniel saw an entire company of Russian infantry rise out of their trenches and begin crossing no-man's land.

"Here they come!" he alerted Mulder.

Mulder held his fire. "They're still out of range."

The tank moved in front of the infantry to provide them cover. The Russians concentrated behind the T-34 and slowly followed it as it continued to approach the bunker. The tank to the right continued its volley, trying to knock out the 88, but was unsuccessful. When the Russians got into range, Mulder began firing the MG 42, but most of the Russians stayed safely behind the tank. The tank continued to crawl closer and closer, the MG 42 unable to penetrate its thick armor.

Then the machine gun jammed. "Dammit!" Mulder shouted. "You've got to get those jammed cartridges out right away!" he shouted at Daniel, who immediately went to work. Daniel opened the breech and removed the barrel, trying desperately to dislodge the jammed cartridge. While he worked, Mulder grabbed a handful of grenades and began lobbing them at the tank. One of the grenades exploded right next to the T-34, tearing off the tank's right tread. The disabled tank faltered and ground to a halt a few meters in front of the bunker.

"How's that gun coming?" Mulder shouted.

"Almost there," Daniel shouted back. "This one's really stuck…"

"Well, hurry up, would you?" Mulder lobbed another grenade at the tank, but the blast didn't penetrate the armor plating. The tank's turret began to rotate in the bunker's direction, preparing to fire right at them. Mulder threw another grenade, which disabled the turret but not the gun. Since the gun still wasn't pointing right at them, the tank driver tried to use the good tread to turn the tank in the right direction. It fired a shot which went wide, landing somewhere to the left of them. The tank driver tried to turn the whole tank again to readjust its line of fire. The driver was having great difficulty with this, but Mulder knew that sooner or later he'd get it right.

Meanwhile, the Russian troops noticed the MG had stopped firing, and were cautiously coming out from behind the T-34. Mulder threw a grenade out to keep them back a little longer. Finally, Daniel got the jammed cartridge free and replaced the machine gun's barrel.

"Ready!" he shouted at Mulder, who got behind the gun and started firing at the Russians like a madman. The Russians immediately scattered – some hit the ground, others dove back behind the tank for cover. The T-34's machine guns began firing, strafing the bunker and penetrating through the sandbags like they were made of butter.

"Try to disable the tank's machine guns with some grenades," Mulder shouted, keeping the Russians pinned down with the MG 42. Daniel grabbed a grenade and lobbed it at the tank's front-mounted machine guns. It knocked out the left side, but the one on the right kept firing.

"This damn tank's invincible!" Mulder called out. Now the Russians were getting bolder, stepping out from behind the tank and slowly making their way toward the bunker. Mulder mowed several of them down. "This barrel's getting too hot. We're going to have to change it soon!" Daniel handed him a cool barrel. Mulder changed barrels quickly and resumed firing. More Russians came out from behind the tank – their reserves seemed endless!

Then one of them ran up dangerously close with a grenade. He raised his arm to throw it into the bunker.

"*Schiller!*" Mulder shouted. Daniel grabbed his rifle, aimed, and shot the Russian in the chest before he could throw the grenade. The man fell to the ground and the grenade went off, taking out three of his comrades.

Mulder and Daniel were so absorbed in their own life and death struggle that they had no idea what was happening on the rest of the battlefield. Three T-34s had penetrated the German lines and gotten behind them, and were currently engaged in a deadly fight with the German's 88-millimeter gun on the knoll. Two T-34s were smoldering hulks of steel on no-man's land, while two others were still actively engaging the trench defenses. It wasn't looking good for the Germans; the Russians were already sending out more troops to reinforce the company they'd sent out earlier. The platoon's other machine gun nest was desperately fighting off its own attack by a T-34 and a dozen Russian infantrymen.

Feldwebel Toppel was about to order the platoon to abandon their trenches and retreat, before they were completely surrounded. Then they heard it: the beautiful, heart-racing sound of several Messerschmitt engines approaching. They were there in a flash, roaring over the German trenches, magnificently elegant machines soaring through the night sky.

"God bless the Luftwaffe!" Mulder shouted, waving madly as one of them flew overhead. "I could kiss every one of you!" The newly-arrived planes got right down to business, taking on the tanks first. The plane Mulder was waving at tipped its wings, then strafed the T-34 stranded in front of them with a deadly blast from its machine guns. Then it banked, and on the second pass took the tank completely out with its 25 millimeter canon.

The hatch opened and the crew bailed out of the burning tank. The Russian infantrymen fled, their silhouettes dark and sharp against the yellow-and-orange flames. This made them excellent targets for Mulder's MG 42, which he continued to fire nonstop. The Messerschmitt came back around and strafed the Russians with its machine guns, sending them running back to the safety of their own trenches.

Another German plane managed to destroy the T-34 threatening the other machine gun bunker, scattering the infantry it was supporting. The tanks that had gotten behind German lines were fairing no better: the 88 scored a direct hit on one of them. The other two tried to retreat, but were chased down and destroyed by the Messerschmitts before they could get back to the Russian side.

When the sun came up, Daniel looked out on the scene of carnage in a stunned silence. Burning, twisted hulks of steel dotted the cratered landscape. Columns of acrid smoke poured into the crisp early morning sky. No-man's land was littered with Russian corpses and abandoned equipment.

It was the most brutal combat he'd experienced yet. He was numb from head to toe. He had shot a man a few hours before, but he felt nothing. He knew he was still alive, but there was no joy. He knew they'd given Ivan what for, but there wasn't a celebratory thought in his mind. Just a deep, penetrating, weary *numbness*.

Mulder took one look at him, and understood. "It will pass," was all he said.

The day was spent repairing damage to the trenches and tallying the losses. Feldwebel Topple came by to relay the stats: eight Germans died in the attack, which involved the entire sector of about one hundred men. Daniel's platoon only lost 2 men: Pfeiffer and Engel. *He* didn't really know them that well, but the platoon would grieve the loss nonetheless.

Daniel's spirits began to rebound when he saw that Henckel had survived. "You made it!" he smiled.

"I wasn't going to stick around and wait for Ivan," Henckel grinned back. "After sounding the alert, I high-tailed it right back home!"

That night, the Russians didn't bother to come out and retrieve their dead. The weather turned cold and a carpet of soft new snow covered the Russian bodies in no-man's land like a thick, white, eternal blanket.

***

The next day, things quieted down as the Russians licked their wounds.

"They're not going to stay quiet for long," Topple told his platoon. "They've been bringing in heavy reinforcements and fortifying their sector – more tanks, more infantry. They're going to be making a lot more noise again – soon."

"What about us?" someone asked.

"The company commander has asked for another 88, and a tank," Toppel replied. "They should arrive in a few days."

"That's it?"

"That's all we could get," Toppel assured them. "Ivan's pushing on every sector of the front. We're already spread pretty thin, as it is…"

Two nights later, a Panther tank arrived pulling the promised 88-millimeter artillery piece behind it – effectively tripling their anti-tank defenses in one blow. The imposing combination of machinery and firepower did much to raise the moral of the men.

"Having a Panther tank sitting behind you is very inspiring," Henckel commented, and everyone agreed.

But there was more good news: the tank also brought with it a dozen *panzerfausts* – hand-held anti-tank weapons proven effective in battle against the Russian T-34 tank.

"Each bunker will be equipped with a *panzerfaust* and several anti-tank shells," Toppel assured his men, to cheers all around.

But the Russians were receiving so many reinforcements that they actually started having a manpower *surplus*. Word was coming in from everywhere on the front: the Soviets were doubling and even tripling their patrols and sending men into battle in ever greater numbers – expending their infantry in a profligate, almost reckless fashion.

"They're throwing hordes of troops at our lines up and down the front, no matter the casualties," Toppel warned his men. "Things are really going to be heating up soon."

"Where are they getting all these reinforcements?" Henckel asked in disbelief.

"From all over their empire," Himmel, the intellectual, piped up. "They've got the Bashkirs, Kalmyks, Uzbeks, Turkmens, Tajiks, Kazaks, Siberians, Chechens, Azerbaijanis, Slavs, Cossacks…"

"Ja, ja – we get the picture," Mulder stopped him.

"They will never – *ever* – run out of soldiers," Himmel added, shaking his head. "Unlike us."

It was a sobering thought, and ended the conversation cold.

The attacks continued. Every few nights, a dozen or so Russian tanks followed by waves of infantry would be thrown at the German lines in a slaughterhouse fashion. Sometimes they would know the T-34s were coming before they even heard them. When there was a head-wind, the diesel fumes would reach them even before the unmistakable squeak and clanking of the heavy steel treads. And that sound! The ominous sound that could strike fear into the heart of even the bravest German soldier. The eerie clatter of enemy tank treads had become embedded in their psyche, and would haunt them even in their dreams. It was a sound that every soldier who survived the war would remember with terror for the rest of their lives.

The new Panther tank and the two 88's greatly increased the German's ability to repel the attacks, but the fighting was still tough much of the time. The new *panzerfausts* allowed any *landser* to take out a tank on his own. But one thing more than any other contributed to their ability to turn the Russians back: air power. Everyone knew that without the arrival of the intrepid Messerschmitts and their valiant pilots each time, the battle would surely be lost.

As Christmas approached, the fighting seemed to increase in ferocity. The Russians were refusing to let up, no matter how cold the weather became. It began to wear on the Germans in frightful new ways – especially their morale.

Between attacks, however, mundane vestiges of day-to-day life would sometimes re-emerge. A minor crisis arose one day when Vollmer and Henckel came rushing into the bunker with news.

"There's talk of a major going from unit to unit looking for his stolen cheese," Henckel informed them in a hushed voice.

Mulder's face turned pale. "How do we know it's the same cheese?"

"He left it when his car broke down one night," Vollmer added. "When he went back the next day to get it, it was gone."

"If he finds out *we* took it, we'll all be shot!" Henckel fretted.

Mulder's face looked glazed with panic. "We've got to get rid of the evidence. Go get Himmel and Kellermen, and be back here in ten minutes."

The cheese was hidden behind a stack of ammo cases in the corner. Mulder took it out, unwrapped it, and found a large knife. When the squad was assembled, Mulder made them swear an oath of secrecy, and then said, "Friends, we're going to have Christmas dinner early this year." Then he solemnly began dividing up the cheese with the knife.

"I brought a bottle of cognac I've been saving," Henckel said, and passed it around as they ate. The first few bites were heavenly. They ate silently, the looks on their faces revealing something like gastronomic ecstasy.

"This is the best cheese I've ever eaten!" Mulder declared, his entire countenance beaming with hedonistic pleasure. He continued to gorge himself, admonishing the others to keep up with him.

After ten minutes of steady eating, they began to slow down somewhat.

"It doesn't taste as good as it did when we started," Kellerman said.

"I feel like I've eaten enough," Himmel agreed.

"*Nein*," Mulder said between mouthfuls. "We must eat the whole cheese!"

"But I don't want any more cheese," Himmel protested, turning green.

"You're going to eat your share, you sniveling girl," Mulder threatened. "If that major finds any cheese left, we're done for!"

Himmel tried to take another bite, but gagged loudly. Hearing Himmel, Vollmer retched involuntarily, but managed to hold it down.

"You pansies!" Mulder scolded. "Remember the firing squad!"

"But there's so much left!" Henckel complained.

"You greedy bastard!" Vollmer accused Mulder. "If you'd been willing to share with the whole platoon, we wouldn't be getting sick right now!"

"Shut up and eat!" Mulder said, but even he was beginning to feel queasy.

"I can't eat any more!" Daniel gasped, throwing in the towel. His face was a light shade of green and a sweat had broken out on his brow.

"All right. Vollmer, you eat Schiller's portion," Mulder ordered.

"Why me?" Vollmer protested.

"Because you're a Bavarian."

"That doesn't make any sense!"

"How do you expect me to make any sense when we have all this cheese to eat?" Mulder demanded.

When they had finally finished the last bits of the cheese, Daniel was lying against the bunker wall, half conscious. Himmel was passed out on the floor, and Vollmer was doubled over in pain. Mulder burped loudly.

"You're a pig," Kellerman mumbled half-heartedly.

Then Henckel's stomach gurgled loudly.

"That doesn't sound good," Mulder commented.

Henckle moaned. "My gut feels like I ate a cow!"

Vollmer's stomach gurgled louder than Henckel's. "Uh-oh." He sat up, alarmed. "I've got to go to the latrine!" He scrambled out of the bunker on all fours.

"Me too!" Kellerman exclaimed, rushing from the bunker in panic.

Himmel woke up on the floor and groaned. "My head's spinning!"

Henckel's stomach gurgled again, and he bolted for the latrine. Daniel and Mulder followed close behind.

They all had severe diarrhea for three days.

***

To pass the time in the trenches, the men played cards, wrote letters, read old, dog-eared magazines – anything to relieve the boredom. One of the latest past-times was speculating what their favorite Russian chef – "Alexander" – would do after the war.

"I think he will return to his beautiful, disfigured wife in Moscow and immediately begin working on their twelfth child," Vollmer said, with a licentious grin.

"You're an animal," Himmel said with disgust. "All you think about is *sex*."

"Oh? So what do you think he will do first when the war is over?"

Himmel thought for a moment. "I think he will open his own restaurant."

"Ja, very good," Henckel said. "With all his children helping in the kitchen and busing the tables."

"And his wife will be the charming French hostess," Daniel contributed.

"*Nein*," Kellerman contradicted him. "No one wants to eat in a restaurant with a disfigured hostess."

Everyone had to nod in agreement.

"What was her disfigurement, anyway?" Mulder asked.

"We never firmly established that, as I recall," Himmel remembered.

"Well, let's see," mused Henckel. "How about a hideous scar running down the left side of her face?"

"*Nein*. My Aunt Hilda had a scar like that," Vollmer divulged. "It always gave me the willies when she came in close for a kiss."

"How about a club-foot?" Kellerman asked hopefully.

"Idiot," Mulder scolded. "You can't get a club-foot from a tram accident. You must be *born* with it."

"How about a nice artificial leg?" Himmel volunteered.

"Not bad," admitted Mulder.

"*Ja*, she can cover it up with expensive French silk stockings," Vollmer suggested with a leer.

"There's the *sex* again," Himmel frowned.

"But I *like* the stocking part," Daniel interjected. "That way, no one will know she is disfigured except for the limp."

"Ooohh – I *like* a woman with a nice limp!" Vollmer said, with a laugh.

"Get your mind out of the gutter, will you?" Himmel grimaced, put off by the image.

"So, it's agreed then," Mulder concluded. "It's an artificial leg, which won't put the customers off the food as much."

"But what kind of food will he serve?" Kellerman asked.

"Oh, French cuisine," Himmel begged. "Let it be French!"

"What's wrong with German food?" Mulder barked.

"Why would he serve German food in Moscow?" Vollmer asked.

"We haven't established that he opens a restaurant in Moscow," Henckel asserted. "It could be Frankfurt, or Dusseldorf."

"Imbecile," Vollmer spat. "Why would a Russian open a restaurant in *Germany*?"

"*Ukrainian*, not Russian," Himmel reminded. "He was born in Kiev, remember?"

"What's the difference?"

"To a Ukrainian or a Russian, there is a great difference."

"Ukrainian, then," Vollmer conceded. "Why would a Ukrainian open a restaurant in Germany?"

"Because, we won the war!" Mulder argued.

"So, because we won the war, there are no more restaurants in Moscow? Nobody eats Russian food anymore?"

"Russian food, when well-prepared, is very tasty," Kellerman tried to point out helpfully.

"Let's stay on the topic here, shall we?" Mulder asked with some irritation. "He opens a German restaurant and serves German food to Germans in Germany. That's that."

"Then how can Joseph Stalin eat in his restaurant anymore?" Kellerman asked.

"He *can't*," Mulder pointed out as patiently as he could. "Since we won the war, Stalin will be in prison in Berlin. But if Alexander opens a German restaurant in Germany, the *Fuhrer* could be his new best customer."

"Oh, I like *that*," Vollmer called out, suddenly won over by Mulder's insurmountable logic. "You're very good at this, Mulder!"

And so it went, for long hours at a time between battles, until Christmas came and the fighting stopped for a day.

"Even Ivan won't fight on Christmas," Henckel noted.

The fighting stopped for Christmas, but so did the savory aromas from the Russian trenches. For several nights, the reports from the forward observation position had been quite dispiriting. The exquisitely tantalizing aromas had ceased to emanate from Ivan's heavy iron cookpots.

"We killed him," Henckel said dolefully. "A true artist, and <u>we</u> killed him."

"We don't know that," Daniel tried to cheer his friend up. "Perhaps he was transferred."

"*Nein*," Henckel shook his head sadly. "What unit would let a visionary like that go?"

An overwhelming sense of melancholy gripped the entire platoon, as if they'd lost one of their own. They mourned him like a brother.

Mulder was especially inconsolable. He shook his head bitterly. "This <u>bloody</u> war!" was all he could say.

Chapter 16

Two days after Christmas, the Russians mounted their heaviest assault yet. Russian artillery rained shells down on the German positions for two full hours. Then, rows of T-34 tanks began their advance across no-man's land, followed by waves of infantry. The intimidating display of force heading their way sent waves of terror through the German ranks.

"*Halt deine positionen!* Hold your positions!" Feldwbel Toppel shouted in an attempt to keep his men from bolting. The 88's behind them began firing away, taking out a few of the lead tanks – resulting in a roar of approval and cheering from the Germans. But it wasn't enough to stop the Russian armor's slow, steady advance. Each time a T-34 was destroyed, another one appeared to take its place. The 88's just couldn't keep up with the sheer numbers.

The enemy now within range, the German machine gunners began to open fire. It accomplished little, since the Russian infantry stayed safely behind their tank escorts. Now the tanks were close enough to open fire on the 88's, and did so with a devastating ferocity.

"If we lose those 88's, we're *kaput*," Mulder shouted to Daniel as they fired away on the trusty MG 42. They were now under heavy fire themselves from the T-34 machine guns. "Keep your head down, Schiller!" Mulder called out. "Remember what I told you to do if something happens to me!"

"Ja!" Daniel shouted back, feeding the ammo belt into the blazing gun's hungry breech.

Then the overwhelming fire from the tanks took out one of the 88's and its crew of three men. The Panther tank drove up and parked beside the remaining 88, and started to shell the incoming Russian tanks at a furious pace. The Russians were closer than ever now, and appeared poised to break through the German lines.

"Barrel change!" Mulder shouted. Daniel deftly changed barrels while Mulder covered him with his rifle. Daniel completed the change and Mulder resumed firing like a madman. "I don't think we'll be able to keep this up much longer!" he admitted to Daniel. The heavy metallic groan of the enemy tanks was now deafening, striking panic into the hearts of the Germans in their trenches.

Then a T-34 broke through and drove over a part of the trench to the left of their bunker. The trench collapsed, trapping two men. Another T-34 followed the first – they were beginning to encircle the German positions. The Panther tank came down from the knoll and heroically tried to stop the break through. It drove up and confronted the T-34's head-on. The tanks blasted the hell out of each other in a spectacular display of armored firepower for several minutes. When it was over, the two T-34's were twisted hulks of burning steel and the Panther moved further up to plug the hole.

That's where it met several more Russian tanks attempting to pour over the German trenches like iron cockroaches. The Panther tank fired on them valiantly, which only served to slow them down slightly. Mulder and Daniel watched this clash of iron giants breathlessly, silently praying for the Panther to prevail. Daniel looked back at the remaining 88 on the knoll behind them, just in time to see it go up in a huge pillar of fire and churning, black smoke – a direct hit. He looked back over at the tank battle raging some sixty meters to their left and saw the Panther, now surrounded by swarming T-34's, fighting for its life.

"Where's the Luftwaffe?" He shouted to Mulder, who could only look back at him hopelessly. Without air cover, they both knew they were doomed. Now, hopelessly outnumbered, the Panther was on fire, slowly dying. T-34s were breaking through, rolling over the trenches all up and down the line, followed by rivers of infantry following in their tracks.

Daniel heard the Feldwebel's whistle. *"Ruckzug! Zuruckfallen! Schnell!"* But he did not move, he couldn't move – he was completely paralyzed. He saw Mulder's face in front of his, shouting "Come on, Schiller! Let's go!" but he couldn't hear the words. All he could hear was the sound of tank shells exploding and grenades going off only a few feet away. He saw Mulder sling his rifle over his back and grab the MG-42. "Come on, Schiller! Grab the extra barrel and some ammo, and get your rifle! We're going – NOW!"

Snapping out of it, Daniel gathered the equipment and followed Mulder down the escape tunnel, leaving the cramped, dirty bunker he'd called home since he first came to the front. He could hardly believe it would be the last time he would ever see it. They scurried down the tunnel and made their way to the rear, along with dozens of other soldiers evacuating the trenches. They all climbed out of the rear trench and found themselves above ground for the first time.

Daniel looked around, in shock. Many of the trenches had caved in. Burning tanks and equipment littered the area, sending flames and acrid black smoke high into the cold, gray winter sky. Russian tanks roamed freely around the compound, firing their machine guns at anything that moved. Russian infantry were now going from trench to trench, tossing grenades down into the holes and firing their rifles at unfortunate stragglers who hadn't been able to escape.

Toppel was there, shouting at his men to fall back.

"To where?" someone shouted.

"Away from the Bolsheviks!" was his answer.

It was complete chaos. Soldiers were running around everywhere, shouting. Vollmer came running up to Toppel. "Kolb and two other men are trapped in a trench! We've got to go back for them!"

"Nein," Toppel shook his head. "It's too late!"

"We can't just leave them!" Vollmer shouted.

"I'll go back with you!" Henckle volunteered. "Show me where!" Vollmer and Henckel dove back into the smoke where the trenches used to be, totally disappearing from view.

"The rest of you men, grab whatever equipment you can and follow me!" Toppel ordered, and headed west away from the mayhem. Everywhere, Germans were fleeing, trying to fight off the Russians pursuing them. The rear-guard did what they could to slow them down, but the Russians, flush with victory, were relentless.

Most of the platoon was able to stay together: Toppel, Mulder, Daniel, Kellerman – even Himmel was there. Daniel wondered if he'd ever see Vollmer and Henckel again. They had to keep moving at an unforgiving pace to stay ahead of the Russians. Whenever they would stop for a few minutes rest in a bomb crater or in the cleft of a rocky steppe, a German soldier or two would come running up shouting, "Get up! They're coming!" In those cases, it was simply pure adrenalin that got them on their feet and propelled them forward.

They marched all day across the snowy, wind-driven steppes, with no food, little water, and even less rest. Everyone they met they would ask the same questions: "What unit are you from? Do you know where we're supposed to be going?" Nobody had any answers. Most men they met were in total shock; lonely stragglers who looked like they'd been through hell asked if they could join them. Frightened, disoriented men were seeking some form of order, some semblance of belonging.

And on and on they walked. They'd left the Russians far behind, but still they trudged on, hoping to put as much distance between Ivan and themselves as possible. Mulder stumbled on in front of Daniel, changing the heavy machine gun from shoulder to aching shoulder every few meters. No one talked much, each man saving what little energy remained to simply keep moving forward.

They walked all night, exhausted, bent-over apparitions marching endlessly over the unchanging frozen ground. They saw other groups of men moving like ghosts in roughly the same direction, but gave up trying to talk to them or glean any information from them.

By dawn, they were walking in a kind of zombie-like stupor, a dream-like, disconnected half-sleep state which seemed to conserve just enough energy to keep them moving forward. As the morning light grew, Daniel realized they were walking on some type of a trail or pathway. He began to notice other groups, streams of men moving along silently with them. About a hundred meters up ahead, more men were stopping, congregating – there seemed to be something of a sorting-out process going on.

As they got closer, they could see several officers, standing up in their open-topped staff cars, talking to groups of soldiers gathered around them. The officers were consulting lists of units and directing the men by pointing north or south. Daniel's platoon reached the knot of men and watched, uncomprehendingly, the process unfold. It began to dawn on them that they'd made it – they'd found some kind of re-assembly area with real officers they could talk to. When they reached the front themselves, an officer asked them the name of their unit.

Toppel cleared his throat and spoke up. "2nd platoon, C company." It came out in a parched croak.

"Regiment?" the officer asked.

"41st."

The officer shuffled through the papers in his hands. "Ah, yes. Your unit is re-assembling seven kilometers to the north. We have no lorries, I'm afraid you're going to have to walk it. Are all of your men accounted for?"

"All but two. They went back to try and dig some comrades out of a collapsed trench. We haven't seen them since."

"Well, be sure and report that to your commanding officer when you rejoin your unit."

"*Jawohl, Herr Leutnant.*"

"There's a mobile field kitchen over there," the officer pointed. "Get your men something to eat and drink before you head out."

They walked over to the field kitchen, a long trailer with a large window cut in the side, and joined the large crowd of men lined up next to it. Each man was given a ladle of hot soup and a large slice of warm bread. Ersatz coffee and *hartzweiback* was also being distributed, along with cigarettes. The platoon received their rations and crouched on the cold ground to enjoy their unexpected feast. The hot soup and coffee warmed them from the inside with each heavenly sip. The filthy, exhausted men began to relax and feel safe again, surrounded by so many others in their same situation. The hot meal and the presence of the officers a few meters away gave them a sense of security they hadn't felt in two days.

"I want to sleep now," Kellerman spoke up, lighting a cigarette.

"Not until we rejoin our company," Toppel ordered. "Finish up your meal. We move out in ten minutes."

They marched the last seven kilometers of their journey in better spirits, with full bellies and a concrete destination in mind. They met several other units reforming and reorganizing along the way, and by asking directions from each one, finally found their own company occupying a lonely, wind-swept patch of steppe facing east. They found and reported to the company commander, Hauptmann Klammer, who told them straight out: "The Russians are continuing their push west, right on our heels. Our orders are to dig new defensive positions here, and stop the Russian advance, at all costs. The remnants of 3rd platoon came in an hour ago." Klammer pointed to his right. "You will deploy your men and dig your trench next to them. We need to be dug in and ready to fight in twenty-four hours."

"Twenty-four hours, sir?" Toppel asked in disbelief. "My men haven't slept in two days…"

"Ivan isn't resting, and we can't afford that luxury, either."

"Jawohl, Herr Hauptmann!" Toppel saluted wearily and led his men to their new position.

"He's mad!" Mulder complained bitterly. "Dug in, in twenty-four hours – with no *sleep*?"

"You heard him," Toppel said, shrugging. "Now get your tools out and get started…"

The men wearily took out their entrenching tools and started scratching at the frozen ground. The tools merely glanced off the thick layer of ice.

"It's like solid *granite*!" Himmel exclaimed.

"This will take centuries!" Kellerman groaned.

The men set to, working feverishly for an hour. They'd only dug a few centimeters.

"Can't we just use a few grenades to break through the top layer?" Mulder asked.

"*Nein*," Toppel replied, joining in their labor with his own tool. "We'll need those when the Russians get here."

They worked and dug and chipped away a centimeter at a time. The sun went down and the temperature dropped twenty degrees. Daniel was so tired, he began to hallucinate. "Look!" he said, pointing east across the vast frozen wasteland. "They're coming! Don't you see them?"

"I don't see a thing," Himmel said.

Daniel watched, transfixed, as hordes of Cossack cavalry charged across the steppes, swords pointed forward and screaming a mad battle cry. The Cossacks were dressed in 19th Century hats and uniforms. "Don't you see them?" Daniel asked again, beginning to quake in his boots.

Mulder slapped him hard across the face. Daniel blinked away tears. The Cossacks disappeared. The men went back to work in silence.

An hour later, Daniel thought he was hallucinating again when a truck full of soldiers drove up to their position and Henckel and Vollmer jumped out of the back.

"What – you don't have that trench dug *yet*?" Vollmer shouted, with a huge grin.

"High tea went a little long, so we got a late start," Mulder deadpanned, but he was still glad to see them. The crew gathered around and slapped them on the back a few times.

"How did you make it out?" Kellerman wanted to know.

"I have no idea," Henckel replied. "We just kept running like hell until there were no more Russians!"

"What about Kolb and the others?"

They both shook their heads. "Didn't make it."

Daniel was the only one still digging.

"What's with *him*?" Vollmer asked. "Isn't he glad to see us?"

"He thinks you're a hallucination," Mulder said.

Henckel took the tool out of Daniel's hand. "Look! It's really me! Touch me!"

Daniel looked blankly at Henckel, then took his trenching tool back and resumed digging.

"I'm worried about him," Vollmer confided.

"He'll be all right after he gets some sleep," Mulder said. "Now grab your tools and give us a hand."

"I can do better than *that*," Vollmer said, stepping aside. Behind him, men were climbing down out of the truck. Their uniforms were different, not regular Wehrmacht.

"We brought the *pioneers*," Henckel said proudly. "And these fellows have the *explosives…*"

The pioneers were engineers – astute at building bridges, bunkers, trenches – anything you could imagine. They were also battle-hardened veterans, almost elite troops, experts at the art of tank destruction and demolition of almost any enemy weaponry. And they had been temporarily assigned to help C company dig in and defend its perimeter.

The platoon willingly stepped out of the shallow trough they'd managed to dig away and handed the job over to the experts. In minutes, the pioneers had blasted away the rock and frozen soil six feet deep, and left the finish work – smoothing the walls and levelling the floor – to the foot soldiers. Then they went over to offer their services to nearby 3rd platoon.

The trenches were more or less finished by dawn – not perfect, but certainly serviceable for when the Russians arrived.

"Can we get a little bit of sleep now?" Mulder asked Toppel.

"In shifts," Toppel ordered. "I want six men on watch at all times."

It was the best they were going to get. The men who got to sleep first stretched extra groundsheets over the top of the trench to block out some of the icy wind. Then they spread out groundsheets on the frozen bottom of the trench and covered themselves with their heavy coats and blankets. It wasn't exactly toasty, but not as cold as sleeping out in the open. Utterly spent, the men lost consciousness immediately and had to be violently shaken awake when it was their turn for watch.

***

That evening at dusk, a supply truck pulled up and honked its horn. The men dragged themselves out of their new subterranean accommodations and unloaded crates of ammunition and tinned rations. Mulder, who was hoping to see that mobile field kitchen drive up anytime, was especially disappointed. "More tinned mystery meat," he said, without enthusiasm.

The men set about making their new home as comfortable as possible – for a hole in the ground in the middle of winter. Vollmer and Henckel went around to other units, pilfering what they could find. They came back with empty wine bottles and some extra petrol, which was especially hard to find these days. With these items, they fashioned lamps for heat and light. Filling a wine bottle halfway with petrol, they ran a wick of twisted cotton up its neck and corked it with an empty munitions cartridge with holes bored in its side. When lit, it gave off a nice glow and helped take the edge off the constant, grinding cold.

As the days wore on, the weather continued to grow colder and colder. Daniel wondered if the temperature would ever reach a point where it could get no colder, but there didn't seem to be a bottom. The suffering increased dramatically as the Ukrainian winter settled in with a vengeance. They were men trying desperately to survive, hunkered down in underground ice boxes, in an endless, frozen, desolate wasteland, waiting for the Russians to come.

And come they did, in vast numbers. They could hear the familiar, terrifying sound of the T-34 diesel engines revving only a few hundred meters to the east. The Russians had to let them idle all night, to keep the engine blocks from freezing solid. Such extravagant use of petrol! Imagine the wasted petrol, letting thousands of tanks idle around the clock, while on the German side they were meting the rare substance out like precious ambrosia!

278

The Russian supplies – of men, equipment, tanks, food, weapons, petrol – *everything* – seemed inexhaustible!

The attacks began a few days after the Russians occupied their new positions opposite the German lines. With reinforcements arriving daily, the Russians sent out constant patrols to harass the German trenches. Extra snipers were brought in and posted around the clock – special exploding rounds would fly over the trenches anytime so much as the top of a German helmet appeared. Then the artillery arrived, and the pounding began in earnest. Not once a day, as before. Now the bombardments came two, sometimes three times a day. Would they ever run out of shells?

Finally, the tanks came, followed as always by waves of infantry. True to their reputation, the pioneers proved skillful anti-tank fighters. They crawled out of the trenches and waited for the T-34s in craters, destroying them with *panzerfausts* and magnetic bombs that stuck to the side of the tank and blew the treads off. In this manner, three pioneers managed to destroy the tanks advancing on Mulder and Daniel's position. With their tanks aflame, the infantry had to come out in the open and continue the assault on their own. Mulder and Daniel opened fire with the MG 42, and the rest of the platoon followed suit with their rifles.

Several courageous Russians rushed forward to the edge of the trench, grenades held aloft ready to throw. Mulder cut down most of them with the MG 42, but one was able to toss his grenade into the trench next to Kellerman. *"Geh raus! Handgranate im graben!"* Henckel shouted, but Kellerman wasn't able to get out in time. The grenade went off, and blew him out of the trench. Two more Russians approached with grenades. They got so close, Daniel could see their Asiatic features – a Siberian or Kazakh unit. Daniel grabbed his rifle and shot one of them, Henckel got the other one. Their grenades fell and went off harmlessly outside the trench.

"Schiller!" Mulder called, signaling him to pick up the machine gun's belt and feed him more ammo. Daniel looked out at the devastation and saw two pioneers pinned down in a crater, fighting off a dozen or so Russians. *"Runter!"* Mulder shouted at the pioneers to get down, which they did. Then he unleashed the MG on the Russians around their crater, knocking them back and clearing the way for the pioneers to crawl back to the safety of the trench. Daniel watched as one of the pioneers tried to pull his wounded

partner out of the crater, but more Russians were already converging on the crater.

"*Runter!*" Mulder called out to him again, and pushed the Russians back with more fire. Then the MG jammed. "Dammit!" Mulder yelled, opening the breech and trying to clear the jam.

"Come on, we've got to get them," Henckel shouted at Daniel. They climbed out of the trench and ran, bent low, to the crater. Daniel saw more Russians approaching, but rifle fire from the trench slowed them down. Daniel helped the pioneer pull his partner out of the crater, while Henckel fired at the Russians to keep them back. The Russians were now so thick, Henckel pulled out a grenade and lobbed it in the middle of them, sending their bodies flying in all directions.

Henckel covered them as Daniel and the pioneer pulled the wounded man to safety. Then Henckel hopped back down into the trench with them. Breathing heavily, he looked back out and saw more Russians approaching. "When will they *stop*?" he shouted in exasperation, raising his rifle and firing wildly at them. Still more Russians swarmed.

They broke through and got into one of the German trenches. "How many of them?"

Henckel asked.

"I don't know – looks like a dozen or so!" Vollmer shouted back.

"Let's go root them out!" Henckel said.

Daniel watched as Henckel, Vollmer and a few of the pioneers confronted several Russians coming along the trench toward them. The fighting was very confused and messy in the confined, dark space. It was impossible to tell exactly what was happening. He heard shouts and gun shots, and cries of pain – and then more muffled shouts, in both German and Russian.

"*Schiller – der gurtel!*" he heard Mulder shout, and it snapped him back to reality. Mulder had cleared the jam and was ready to fire. Daniel fed the belt as Mulder fired at the remaining Russians on the battlefield. Several dropped to the ground, others began slowly to retreat.

"It looks like the bastards have had enough," Mulder finally said, halting his fire. He stayed ready, however, his eyes scanning the battlefield for a renewal of the attack. A few minutes later, Henckel,

Vollmer and the others came back down the trench, covered in grime, sweat, and blood. "We got 'em," Henckel said grimly.

They retrieved Kellerman's body and wrapped it in a groundsheet. It would be impossible to bury him in this frozen ground, but at these temperatures he would keep until a proper burial could be arranged.

Daniel gazed at the white canvas-wrapped body and thought about the loss. *Poor Kellerman – good-natured, simple Kellerman...* He remembered the jokes, and the cheese, the sharing of a bottle of schnapps, and all the late-night stories about Alexander the chef and his beautiful disfigured wife, and then he turned away in disgust. *What a sad waste of life...*

Later on, some of the pioneers were huddled around a small fire in their trench, trying desperately to keep warm. Daniel and Henckel joined them to ask how the wounded pioneer was doing. One of the pioneers just shook his head gravely. They knew what that meant. The pioneers had a battery-powered radio, and were trying to tune in some news about the war.

"How is it going?" Henckel asked hopefully.

"*Nicht gut*," one of the pioneers, named Claussen, said mournfully. "The entire front has dissolved into a few isolated units trying to hold on – just a few pockets of resistance. The Russians are breaking through *everywhere...*"

Then one of the pioneers tuned something in – a faint, unclear broadcast that sounded as if it were coming from the surface of the Moon: "*Achtung!* This is Berlin! Keep fighting! Keep fighting! Victory is at hand! The Allies in the west have been pushed back to the sea! The English Channel is clogged with their bloated corpses! In the East, the Russians are being pushed back to the Urals! Keep fighting!"

"Turn that crap off!" somebody moaned bitterly. Without a word, Daniel and Henckel returned to their trench to try and get a few hours of sleep. They were awakened in the middle of the night by the sound of an airplane engine overhead. Daniel and Mulder immediately grabbed their weapons, ready to be strafed at any minute. But when the plane flew directly overhead, it wasn't bombs that it dropped. Daniel looked up warily and saw thousands of tiny bits of white paper falling to the ground, covering it like snow. Hundreds of bits of paper fluttered into the trench. Daniel grabbed one out of the air and squinted to read it. It had German writing on it.

"Soldiers of the Reich: your Fuhrer is dead. Your army has been destroyed. Your country is finished. It is time for you to surrender. You will be treated well. You will receive medical care, good food, and warm beds. You will be reunited with your families. Marshall Stalin personally promises every man will be treated fairly. Wouldn't you like to have a hot meal and a warm bed to sleep in tonight? You know it is over. Do the smart thing. Think of yourselves and your families for a change. You do not have to die. Lay down your arms! Lay down your arms!"

"Lies!" Vollmer spat. "Reunited with our families? Do they expect us to believe that drivel? They'll have us rotting in a POW camp for the rest of our lives!"

"I'd rather die fighting them!" Henckel agreed. He tore the paper from Daniel's hand and shredded it.

Mulder was busy collecting the scraps of paper from the floor. He gathered up a great stack of them and stuffed them inside his tunic.

"What are you doing?" Himmel asked.

"Don't you see?" Mulder replied calmly. "The Russians have given us a great gift, and they don't even realize it. Thanks to them, when we go to the latrine, now we will have something to wipe our asses with."

***

Daniel awoke at dawn to Mulder and Henckel counting ammunition magazines. They both looked worried. "We're running frightfully low," Henckel told Daniel. "This is all we've got left. We've got to make every cartridge count."

"The Russians have been waiting us out," Mulder explained. "Wearing us down, forcing us to use up all of our ammo. And it's working…"

Daniel had only two magazines for his rifle. The MG only had two belts of ammo left.

"What happens when we run out?" Daniel ask.

"We run like hell," Henckel answered.

The pioneers had a few *panzerfausts* and some magnetic bombs left. Sensing an attack, they were already taking up positions in craters out in front in order to surprise the tanks. Within half an hour, Daniel could hear the fearful clatter of the T34's approaching.

"Here they come," Toppel announced. "Steady now. Don't lose your heads! Make every shot count!"

When the line of tanks reached the craters, the pioneers quickly went to work on them. Two tanks were blown up, and another had its treads torn off and its cannon disabled by magnetic bombs. Their element of surprise now lost, the pioneers were at the mercy of the infantry that came pouring out from behind the tanks. The Germans in the trench laid down heavy rifle and machine gun fire to push them back, while the pioneers crawled from crater to crater searching for other tanks to destroy.

They were able to blow up another tank, but took heavy losses when a T-34 came out of nowhere and fired its cannon into a crater with three pioneers in it. They were all blown to pieces. In addition to that, the Russian infantry were swarming around them again, threatening to overwhelm them and completely wipe them out.

"We've got to get them out of there!" Henckel exclaimed, gathering together six or seven men. "Cover us!"

"I'm running really low on ammo," Mulder warned. "But I'll do my best!" Henckel and his team – which included Vollmer – climbed out of the trench and fought their way to the stranded pioneers. Vollmer, Kirchner, and Planke brought three wounded pioneers back to the trench, while the others stayed in the forward positions and helped the rest of the pioneers fight off the Russians. Daniel watched as Henckel's men and the pioneers slowly fell back to the trench, fighting every backward step of the way. Russian infantry swarmed around them like ants, firing into the retreating group.

Daniel saw two pioneers go down – both dead before they hit the ground. Then one of Henckel's men bought it. They were being massacred right before Daniel's eyes.

"We've only got a few rounds left for the MG!" Mulder declared. When it finally ran dry, Mulder and Daniel picked up their rifles and covered the retreating troops the best they could.

It was complete bedlam. Russians were running everywhere. All of them had submachine guns, and were firing in every direction like mad. Daniel saw a Russian raise his gun to shoot at Henckel, but Daniel shot him before he could pull the trigger. Six or eight

Russians then converged on Henckel, who quickly pulled out a grenade and tossed it deftly at their feet. They were blown back, their bodies sailing through the air. Then Henckel took out his last grenade and lobbed it at another group of Russians coming up on his left, wiping them out.

Then Henckel and his surviving men, along with the remainder of the pioneers, made it back to the trench – but the Russians were not letting up. "Somebody give me a magazine!" Henckel called, out of ammo. Daniel tossed him his second magazine. Henckel slapped it into his rifle and kept firing at the Russians.

There was no holding them back. Many of the Germans were out of bullets, and Russians were leaping down into the trench at several points. Petrified, Daniel looked to his right and saw a T-34 drive over the trench where Planke and Leiberman were. The trench collapsed under the weight, crushing both of them – the falling soil drowning out their screams for help. A squad of Russians leaped over the trench and followed the tank, spraying everything they saw with submachine gun fire.

To his left, some Germans were fighting off a group of Russians – in close quarters, _inside_ the trench. The Russians were now behind and all around the Germans, and it was getting difficult to tell who was who.

"I'm completely out of ammo!" Mulder said, fixing his bayonet. "It's time to go!" He grabbed Daniel and heaved him out of the trench, then grabbed the precious MG and climbed out himself. "Do you have any cartridges left?" Daniel shook his head no. "Then RUN!" They both ran, crouching low, away from the chaos of the trench. Submachine gun fire rattled everywhere. Grenades were going off, churning up the ground all around them. Daniel didn't know what direction they were running in – he was merely following Mulder.

Then they ran into Henckel and Vollmer. "I don't have any more cartridges!" Vollmer shouted, in shock.

"We're going!" Mulder shouted back. "Come with us!"

"Where are you going?"

"Away from the Russians!" Mulder screamed.

The four of them continued to head away from the trench. Daniel looked back and saw a terrifying vision of hell: the trenches laid waste, burning hulks of steel shooting flames and smoke high into the air, bodies strewn on the ground in every manner of hideous position, men running, shouting, cursing and dying in agony. Germans were limping, running, and dragging comrades in all directions away from the carnage. Russians were pursuing them and shooting them down with their submachine guns. *It's all over*, Daniel thought. *This is the end...*

They ran and ran until they couldn't see any more Russians. They saw others, running like hunted animals – men they knew, men they'd fought with. There was Vogel, the old veteran who had been injured in the cave-in before Christmas. They waved him over, and he joined them, thankful to see four friendly faces. They came upon Kirchner and Himmel, hiding in a crevice in the steppe, like frightened rabbits.

Everyone they met, they asked the same questions: "Do you have any bullets? Do you have any food?" "Do you know what happened to Feldwebel Toppel?"

But, mainly, they kept moving. "Ivan is just behind us," Mulder warned. "Ivan will forever be just behind us." They stumbled across the frozen landscape mostly in silence, not knowing where they were going, or what trials lay ahead. As long as they stayed a step or two ahead of the Russians, they knew they had a chance.

Darkness came, and with it cold and hunger. The temperature dropped twenty-five degrees in a few minutes, and the men wrapped their heavy coats tighter around their emaciated bodies. Still, they kept moving west. After an hour in the dark, they came across a small group of soldiers huddled around a pathetic fire.

"Do you know where Twelfth Battalion is?" one of the soldiers asked them.

"*Nein*," Henckel answered.

"Have you seen Karl Grasse?" another shell-shocked soldier asked. "Do you know what happened to him?"

"*Nein*," Mulder replied. "Have you any cartridges? Any food?"

"*Nein*," they answered. *Nein, nein, nein...*

They travelled on through the night, moving, always moving, to keep from freezing to death. When the pale pinkish light of dawn appeared at their backs, they finally stopped to rest.

"All right, let's see what we've got," Henckel took charge. "Come on, everyone empty his pockets – let's have it..."

They all emptied their pockets and put everything into a pile in the center. There were three tins of meat, some *hartzweiback* biscuits, about thirty grams of black bread, a bar of chocolate, and seven rounds of Mauser ammo.

"We share everything," Henckel declared. "Each man gets the same portion, and we're going to ration our food to make it last. There's a cartridge for each man. Go ahead and put it into your rifle now, in case we stumble upon any Russians or partisans."

He opened one of the tins. "We'll pass it 'round. Each man takes one bite, until the tin is empty." They retrieved their spoons from their mess kits and passed the tin from man to man. All were hungry, but no one gave in to greed – each man took a reasonable bite and passed it on. When it was empty, the last man scraped it clean with his spoon.

Henckel put the rest of the rations into his pack. They made themselves as comfortable as they could on the ground and slept like the dead for two hours. Then Henckel woke them up and they continued their march across the frozen steppes.

"Where are we going?" Himmel wanted to know.

"We are assuming they've set up an assembly point, like before," Henckel answered. "We've just got to find that assembly point, and they will tell us where to find the rest of our unit."

Just up ahead, they spied another group of soldiers walking west. "It's Toppel!" Vollmer cried. It <u>was</u> the Feldwebel, walking with Claussen and some of the surviving pioneers. They shouted out and ran ahead to catch up.

"Good to see you lads," Toppel tried to smile. "Have you any ammo? Any food?"

"Each man has one cartridge," Henckel replied. "And we've got a little food."

"So have we," Toppel said, and he added their meager goods to the storehouse in Henckel's pack.

"How far do you think it is?" Henckel asked Toppel.

"How far to what?"

"To the assembly point," Henckel clarified.

"There's no assembly point," Toppel said sadly. He told them he'd heard from an intelligence unit that the front had completely collapsed – that the German Army was in full retreat. "What's

worse, the entire division is completely surrounded. *We* are
completely surrounded. It's hopeless, lads. It's *over...*"

Henckel bristled. "We cannot surrender." Several men agreed.
"Nein." "*Nein.*"

"There are some units still fighting," Claussen piped up. "They're
trying to break through the Russians and escape."

Henckel brightened up. "Where?"

"To the northwest, and to the wast," Claussen replied.

"Then, that's where we'll go!"

They kept walking, due west, and met up with more and more
groups of men who had heard the same thing. Soon there were
streams of German soldiers trudging west, all seeking to escape the
Russians and find safety beyond their lines. Within hours, they were
on a roughly paved highway, along with thousands of men heading
west.

Up ahead, Daniel saw a commotion. An officer was standing in a
roofless staff car, talking to the passing men through a bullhorn and
pointing west. When they got up to him, they could hear what he
was saying.

"Keep going west! Some of our units were able to break through!
But you must get through the gap before it closes! You must escape
this trap so you can keep fighting for the Fatherland! You can
reunite with your units on the other side! Keep going west!"

Bolstered by this news, each man quickened his pace. There were
no illusions about stopping to sleep now – there clearly wasn't time
for that luxury. They knew they had to keep moving to escape the
Russians.

They walked for three days. Thousands of men were now moving
along the highway, almost panic-stricken, in full flight. There was
no sign of Russian tanks, but they were constantly harassed by
enemy aircraft. They went after the vehicles first, of course. Then,
after every moving vehicle had been destroyed and left as a flaming
hulk beside the road, they went after the men. The Russian pilots
seemed to have a grand time, strafing the long lines of weary
German soldiers almost at their leisure, doubling back for pass after
pass, until their machine guns ran out of bullets. Then it was back to
the airfield to be reloaded and refueled before coming back for
another run, if daylight permitted.

It became a grim exercise, the long lines of fleeing men running off the highway like a herd of cattle and flattening themselves on the hard, frozen ground while the attack occurred, waiting patiently for it to end before returning to the highway to resume their endless trek after the planes had gone. Of course, hundreds of men never did return to the highway or their long journey.

As if the airplanes weren't punishment enough, the weather turned even harsher. A stiff arctic wind blasted the faces of the men as they marched, turning them beet-red and cracking them like old shoe leather. It passed through their heavy winter coats like they were made of cheesecloth, and penetrated to the very marrow of their bones. Snow fell and piled up in endless drifts along the sides of the highway like small mountain ranges. But each man kept going, and kept others going by reminding them, *Wenn du fallst, frierst du ein – If you fall, you freeze.* When men died, their friends couldn't stop to bury them – there was no time. They were simply left on the side of the road to be covered over by the next snow.

The local population was also on the move, sometimes mixed in with the German soldiers, swelling the already great numbers clogging the inadequate highway. They travelled by all means, in carts piled high with their meager belongings, on bicycles, on farm animals, on foot – men, women and children – a testament to how much even the Ukrainian peasants feared falling into the hands of the Red Army.

Hunger drove these people – the Ukrainians, the Germans, Daniel, Mulder and Henckel. Everyone was constantly foraging and scrounging for food, but there was none to be found -- the countryside had been stripped bare. Any buildings or houses they came upon had already been stripped clean of food.

On the second day, Daniel, Himmel and Vogel spotted a dilapidated barn in a field off the highway. They formed an ad hoc foraging party and left the main group to try to scrounge even a morsel of food. Inside the barn there was only a bushel of frozen, moldy potatoes. Overjoyed, they brought back armfuls of them to their friends, who quickly stuffed them in their pockets and down their shirts to be defrosted by body heat so they could be eaten.

Daniel's feet became sore and blistered inside his boots. The boots which had done such an outstanding job keeping his feet warm in winter had suddenly become instruments of torture on this long march. Old Vogel, who had put on a brave face and hummed his beloved Beethoven heartily for most of the march, began to falter. Daniel offered to carry his rifle, and Henckel offered to take his pack, but Vogel refused any help. "Each man should be able to carry his own load!" he growled, out of breath. Determined to keep up, he stepped up his pace for a few meters, then slowed back down again.

Daniel offered a shoulder for Vogel to lean on. *"Bitte, Vater..."* The old man said nothing, but accepted the help. The extra support helped for a while, but soon Vogel was struggling again. It had become clear he was not going to be able to make it.

"Leave me here," the old man puffed.

"Nein," Daniel said. "You can make it..."

"I'll just rest here a little while, and catch up with you fellows later..."

Daniel eased him down onto the side of the road. They built up a little wall of snow around him to protect him from the lacerating wind. Vogel looked frightfully pale and weak.

"Don't worry, old man," Henckel said. "We'll see you on the other side." Henckel's comment was deliberately ambiguous.

As they marched away, Daniel looked back at their comrade and new that he was never going to get up again. As they trudged along, kilometer after kilometer, they began to notice other men who had given up, scattered along the side of the road. Some were sitting upright, frozen solid. Others were stretched out in the snow as if to take one last, eternal sleep.

Mulder was still carrying the heavy machine gun, even though it was an extra twenty-eight pounds of weight. He never let it out of his hands.

"You treat that gun like a lover," Vollmer called out to him. "When's the wedding?"

"Why don't you just leave it behind?" Himmel inquired. "It would be much easier for you."

"I was entrusted with this gun by the Wehrmacht," Mulder explained, over the sound of the howling wind. "It has saved my life many times. And I intend to return it in excellent condition at the end of my service."

Soon, they noticed columns of smoke rising up in the distance. As they got closer, they realized they would be walking right through the scene of a recent battle. Several Russian tanks and heavy field pieces lay smoldering in the snow. Frozen Russian and German corpses were scattered everywhere. To the north, the sky lit up ominously with artillery fire, and there were sounds of fighting close by to the south.

"This must be where we broke through!" Henckel surmised.

"So this is the gap, eh?" Mulder asked. "We'd better hurry through, before it closes again."

The entire stream of men had the same idea. It was less than sheer panic, but it was certainly an intentional rush, and the presence of so many dead soldiers was simply a reminder of the dangers that still lay ahead.

Daniel looked around, surveying the scene. Thousands of ragged, desperate soldiers, along with almost as many civilians, were hustling like mad to get through the battlefield. And the stream of people stretched back as far as Daniel could see. The German Army was shattered, reduced to long lines of thousands of tattered, emaciated, walking scarecrows. Some men even took on the form of living skeletons.

It was a vision of apocalypse.

Then they came to a scene Daniel could never have imagined. Thousands of men – perhaps *tens* of thousands – had stopped a few hundred meters ahead, forming an impassable wall of humanity. As they got closer, they realized the highway they were on ended at a river. The bridge had been completely destroyed, and thousands of men were massing along the riverbank like frightened crabs.

"Why don't they just walk across the ice?" Mulder asked no one in particular.

"What ice? The river is flowing water," a man from another unit answered.

The scene was utter chaos. The men along the river were being pressed forward into the freezing water by the panicked crowds behind them. There were desperate screams for them to move back, but nothing would stop the surging wall of frightened men. A few small boats and rafts arrived from the other side, but the panicked men nearly swamped them as officers tried to maintain order with drawn pistols.

"*Zurucktreten*! Step back! Step *back!*" the officers shouted, with frightened looks on their faces. Many of the lucky ones who got a place on a boat turned out to be not so fortunate when a Russian fighter plane appeared and passed back and forth over the river, strafing them. The men on the shore watched in terror as most of the boats were sunk, the men drowned in the icy churning water.

Mulder snapped. "Can't the bastards at least give us a chance?"

"Would we be so kind if we were in their shoes?" Henckel heard himself asking.

But still the crowd surged forward, willing to roll the dice and take their chances on the river rather than wait and face the Russian tanks which were surely on their way. Men were frantically tearing apart vehicles to use whatever they could find to build rafts.

"That's destruction of army property!" an officer shouted at a group of men tearing the wheels off a staff car. They shot him and continued their frenzied work.

For hours and hours, the boats went back and forth across the river, most of them sunk by the Russian planes, but slowly and surely some men were actually reaching the other side. Feeling hope, Daniel's squad kept their place in line and kept inching forward toward the river, inch by inch, foot by foot. Meanwhile, more and more soldiers and refugees were joining the throngs at the back.

"Russian tanks!" they heard someone calling from behind, and a ripple of panic visibly moved through the crowd. They felt the crowd pressing on them from behind, calling out in vain for them to stop pushing. Then they heard the clatter-clank of the approaching tanks, and the machine guns and cannons opening fire on the back of the crowd.

"Hurry! Move up!" Himmel shouted to no one and to no effect, although everyone was feeling the pressure to cross before the tanks annihilated the entire crowd. Men were launching flimsy, self-made rafts and paddling frantically into the river. Some of them floated, others did not, sinking to the bottom and taking their desperate occupants with them. Meanwhile, the tanks continued to draw nearer, chewing up the senseless wall of humanity before them.

Finally, they reached the water's edge. Toppel, Vollmer, Claussen, and Kirchner squeezed into an almost full boat, which quickly launched into the river and started its crossing. Daniel,

Henckel, Mulder and Himmel boarded a raft made of empty petrol drums and old truck tire inner tubes, and followed the boat. Despite its rough appearance, the raft was well-made and floated extremely well. The men set to paddling with wooden planks, rifles and entrenching tools – anything they could find.

They were offshore, and moving in a relatively straight line to the opposite bank! A sense of relief began to envelope Daniel as he paddled frantically. Up ahead, Toppel and Vollmer's boat was making splendid progress, when all at once, a Russian fighter swooped down out of the sky and riddled it with machine gun bullets. Daniel watched in horror as the boat took on water and began to sink. The men jumped out and tried to swim the rest of the way, but the plane came back and strafed them in the water.

None of them made it to the other shore.

Henckel pushed the horror aside. "Don't stop! Keep paddling! We're almost there!"

Miraculously, the plane turned away to terrorize another craft, leaving them free to continue their voyage unmolested. In a few minutes, they'd landed on the other side. Daniel stepped foot on the other shore, and nearly collapsed with exhaustion.

"We need two men to take the raft back over and pick up more men," someone said. "I've already been across twice, and I'm not going back!" Henckel and a man from another unit volunteered.

"You go ahead," he said to Daniel and Mulder. "I'll catch up with you!" Then he got back in the raft and went back to save a few more men.

Chapter 17

Daniel stood on the bank and gaped numbly at the chaotic scene unfolding across the river. The remaining masses still swarmed on the shore, the Russian tanks pushing them ever closer to the frigid water. Men were trying to surrender, but the tanks were disregarding their pleas and just mowing them down. Boats were still making the perilous crossing, continually harassed by aircraft. *Maybe a few more men can get across before the tanks finish them all off,* thought Daniel.

"Come on," Mulder said. "It does no good to watch. You'll be seeing it every night for the rest of your life, in color."

"But Vollmer, and Toppel and Kirchner – they're just *gone…*"

"Don't think about that now. There's plenty of time for that later."

Mulder wanted to put as much distance between them and the river as they possibly could. They started heading west, following another long line of men who'd already made the crossing. Thousands of men were now marching away from the river, at several points. Where were they going? It didn't matter, and no one thought about it. Just away from the Russians…

As they walked, Daniel couldn't help but think of their lost comrades. Toppel, the veteran sergeant and skilled leader. Vollmer – cynical, hot-headed Vollmer – the merry prankster, always eager to crack a caustic joke and bust Mulder's chops. And Kirchner, who he didn't know as well. *All gone…*

Many Russians were dying, too – but Daniel didn't *know* them. What had happened? How had his enemies, the Germans, become his friends and comrades? For months, he had lived with them, thought like them, and fought Russians alongside them. Germany's downfall, which they were experiencing ever more vividly each second, should have pleased him, not saddened him. Their Gestapo surely would have hanged him if caught, and now he was fighting savagely for the Fatherland. *You're fighting for your own survival!*

he heard an inner voice say. Nevertheless, he felt all the shame, horror, shock, and desperation at Germany's disintegration that his remaining platoon mates felt – that any true German felt, in fact.

Watching them suffer – and suffering alongside them – had made him more *like* them.

They marched a whole day before they found an abandoned barn to shelter and rest in. They slept like the dead until dawn, when they were rudely rousted by two Waffen SS soldiers with submachine guns. "*DrauBen! Schnell!*" one of them said roughly. "Outside!"

They followed the soldiers outside into the pale glow of morning. There were other soldiers there – both SS and regular Wehrmacht. An SS major stepped forward and looked them over.

"Deserters?" he asked.

"*Nein,*" Mulder said.

"Where is your unit?"

"It disintegrated when the Russians broke through," Mulder said. "Then we lost more crossing the river."

"It doesn't matter," the Major said. "You're joining us now."

"But, *Herr Haupt –*"

"We are going to fight, not run like the others," the Major interrupted him. "I have been ordered to cover the retreat. We're going back to the river to keep Ivan from crossing it – at all costs. These orders came directly from the Fuhrer. Anyone who refuses to follow the Fuhrer's orders will be shot. Now, onward to the fields of glory! Heil Hitler!"

The Major had a dark black mustache and a zealot's gleam in his eye. The skull and crossbones on his black SS cap were too intimidating for anyone to argue with. Their spirits sinking in despair, Mulder, Daniel and Himmel gathered their gear and prepared to move out.

"You will be putting that heavy machine gun to good use again," the Major said, eyeing Mulder's favorite weapon with approval. "How are your men for ammunition?"

"Each man has one bullet."

"Don't worry – we'll give you more ammo when we get back to the river."

Back to the river! Daniel's legs almost buckled. "We have to get away from this madman before he gets us all killed!" he whispered to Mulder when he had the chance. Mulder looked around at the SS men with their submachine guns, and just shook his head. "Not now. We'll find a way…"

The Zealot had them move out immediately, due east. There were about forty of them, most of them lightly armed. Daniel saw some of the SS men with heavy machine guns and *panzerfausts* – the regular Wehrmacht soldiers carried only rifles and grenades. They were all from different units – the Zealot had been gathering them up as they went along.

They picked up as many stragglers as they could find, and the healthier, uninjured ones were given the speech and pressed into service by the Zealot. Most of them took one look at the SS men and their submachine guns, and acquiesced quickly. One poor soldier had had enough, though, and refused to return to the river.

"There is nothing wrong with you," the Zealot argued. "You are able-bodied and uninjured. You are coming with us to protect the Fatherland!"

"You can shoot me, but I'm not going back and facing those Russians!" the man protested.

"As you wish." The Major pulled out his Luger and shot the soldier in the head. Then he stood over the body and said, "This man was a coward and a traitor to the Reich. Such will be the fate of all those who refuse to defend the Fatherland!"

There were no more desertions.

When they reached the river, they saw the Russians massing on the other side preparing to cross. A pontoon bridge was under construction, heavy enough for tanks to cross. It looked like several companies of infantry and a dozen tanks on the Russian side. Daniel counted some fifty or sixty men on their side. *This is suicide…*

"It will take them several more hours to finish the bridge," the Zealot estimated, scanning the bridge through field glasses. "Time enough for us to dig our defensive positions." The men set to work digging trenches as best they could in the frozen riverbank. It was tough going; the SS rolled up their sleeves and got down in the shallow slots alongside the Wehrmacht men, digging furiously before the Russians finished their bridge.

The Russian tanks fired at them in a half-hearted way as they dug. Then a couple of Russian mortars began lobbing shells over the river at them. At the Zealot's command, everybody kept digging, even with mortar shells landing all around them

"This is insane," a soldier next to Daniel grumbled as he dug. "It is hopeless. We're all going to die."

"He's lying, you know," another soldier piped up. "The orders aren't from the Fuhrer. The damn fool's just trying to be a hero, make colonel. He's going to get us all killed!"

"Well, there's nothing we can do about it, so keep digging," Mulder advised.

"I'm not fighting like this for my country," another soldier clarified. "Right now, I'm fighting for my own survival!"

"When do we eat?" another soldier asked. "We're all starving!"

An SS man nearby heard the last part. "As soon as the trench is finished – so shut up and keep digging!"

When the trenches were finished, food, water, and cigarettes were distributed. The rations were meager, but welcome: one tin of food for every two men, plus a half a liter of water and two cigarettes for each man.

"I'm hungrier now than before!" Mulder complained after devouring his half-tin of pork and turnips.

"Well, here we are," Himmel said sardonically. "Back in the trenches, waiting for the Russians to attack. Really brings back the old memories, doesn't it?"

But the Zealot wasn't going to wait for the Russians to make the first move. As soon as it was dark, he sent four of his best SS men down to the river to blow up the Russian's new bridge. The fireball was spectacular, and took the Russians completely by surprise. *Waffen SS* – these fellows didn't fool around!

"Now the Russians will *really* want to kill us!" Mulder moaned. He wasn't far off. Their brand new bridge in ruins, the Russians were swarming around on the opposite bank like angry hornets. Their tanks and mortars opened up a heavy barrage, as Mulder and Daniel settled down into their trench to wait it out. "Here it comes!" Mulder shouted. The MG 42 was set up and ready to fire, only there was no ammo yet.

Presently, some SS men came around passing out the ammo. There appeared to be no more ammo than there was food. There were two belts for the machine gun, and two magazines for each man with a rifle. "He wants us to hold back the entire Red Army with *this*?" Mulder complained, staring dolefully at the meager amount of ammunition. "Listen, Schiller: when we run out of ammo, we do what we did before."

"Run like hell," Daniel replied.

"Exactly."

Their bridge in ruins, the Russians were coming across the river in boats. Lots of them.

"At least Ivan can't get his tanks across now," Mulder said, looking a little more positive.

When the boats were halfway across the river, the Germans opened fire with everything they had. Some of the boats disintegrated under the punishing fire, sending their occupants to the bottom of the river. So many boats were sunk, that the few remaining turned back. A cheer went up from the German ranks.

"Do you think the Russians are just going to give up?" Himmel asked sourly. They looked across warily – the Russians were already preparing another wave of boats for a second crossing. This time when the boats reached the halfway mark, three Russian fighters came roaring out of the sky and began strafing and bombing the Germans viciously.

This time, more of the boats made it across. They began landing on the west bank under heavy fire, depositing Russian infantry on the shore. One by one the boats came, under air cover from the Russian planes, and landed more and more troops on the shore. The Germans were able to keep them pinned down by the shoreline – as long as the ammo held out.

Mulder had been firing conservatively, but still had less than a belt of ammo left. "It's getting close!" he said, watching as more boats landed infantry onto the shore. The SS troops were fighting like lions to drive the Russians back into the water, but they were too greatly outnumbered. Slowly, the Russians began making their way up the bank toward the Germans.

A Russian plane buzzed their trench, strafing them with machine fire and bombs. One of the bombs landed in the trench a few meters away, blowing up several men and sending Mulder and Daniel flying against the trench wall. The machine gun was knocked out, Mulder was swaying on all fours, and Daniel was barely conscious. Mulder looked over and saw Himmel, his right arm mangled by shrapnel.

Russians were now all along the edge of the trench, firing submachine guns and tossing grenades down onto the Germans. The

German line was crumbling, even the SS were running out of ammunition. And still more Russians swarmed up the embankment from the river.

Mulder grabbed Himmel and slung him across his shoulder. Then he grabbed Daniel and dragged him to his feet. "Get your rifle!" he shouted, but Daniel's ears were still ringing. Mulder grabbed Daniel's rifle and shoved it into his hands. They climbed out of the trench and started running away from the Russians, dodging machine gun fire and grenade blasts. Men were being shot and going down all around them. All the Germans in the trench were dead, and the Russians were in pursuit of the few who got out.

The Zealot, his Luger pistol in his hand, was shouting orders and firing at the Russians. Daniel saw him get hit in the leg and go down. Then Daniel lost track of him. Daniel stopped, turned, and fired a few rounds at the Russians to try to slow them down. Mulder pulled some grenades off a dead SS man and lobbed them over Daniel's head at the Russians. "Schiller, *Schnell*!"

Daniel fired at the approaching Russians until his rifle clicked empty. That was it – no more ammo. "Come here and take Himmel!" Mulder cried. Daniel did so, and Mulder unslung his rifle from his back. "Get him somewhere safe! Go!" Then he turned and started to fire at the Russians. Daniel lifted Himmel's good arm over his shoulders and helped him walk. Himmel was in and out of consciousness, unaware of what was happening. As they fled, Daniel looked back one last time and saw several Russians converging on Mulder. Out of ammo, Mulder was swinging his rifle at them. Then he got hit and went down.

"Mulder! *No!*" Daniel cried, continuing to drag Himmel along. Daniel didn't stop for nearly a kilometer. He knew he didn't have the strength to go on much longer. He found a crater and lowered Himmel into it, then got into it himself. He checked on Himmel – still alive, but breathing shallow. He stayed quiet for thirty minutes, not moving, wondering what to do next, trying to think –

Then he heard someone approaching outside the crater, making a lot of noise, dragging a wounded leg along in the snow. Was it a Russian? He waited, with no weapon except his bayonet. If it came to that, he would certainly use it, he told himself. Then the wounded man climbed down into the crater, and Daniel was relieved to see it was a tattered, blood-stained Wehrmacht uniform.

"Hallo," Daniel whispered. "Are you hurt badly?"

The soldier looked right at Daniel. It was the Zealot.

Daniel froze.

"In the leg," the Major answered. "But the bullet went through…"

In shock, Daniel couldn't help blurting out, "Herr Haupt, what happened to your uniform?"

"I buried it under the snow," the Major answered. "I took this uniform off a dead *landser*. If I were captured in an SS uniform, the Russians would shoot me on the spot."

"Are you going to surrender?" Daniel asked.

"Who knows? I want to *live*…" For a moment, the Zealot looked away in shame. "Look, there's no use in carrying on the struggle…anything can happen now."

It occurred to Daniel that this man, who had been so keen to see to it that others gave their lives for the Fatherland, was, when it came right down to it, now desperately trying to save his own skin.

"What's your name?" the Major demanded.

"Schiller, *Herr Haupt*."

"Well, Schiller, I want you to shoot me."

"*Herr Haupt*?"

"In the arm, here," he pointed to his underarm just below the bicep. "Here in the fleshy part. It will obscure my SS blood type tattoo."

"Shoot you?" Daniel repeated incomprehensibly.

"I'd do it myself, but Ivan can tell if it's self-inflicted," the Zealot said, handing Daniel his Luger. "They look for these things, you know."

Daniel reluctantly took the pistol and looked at it. The Major rolled his sleeve all the way up, exposing his SS tattoo.

"Go ahead, it's all right. I'm ordering you to!"

Daniel raised the pistol.

"A little lower – I don't want you to hit an artery."

Daniel lowered the pistol slightly and pulled the trigger.

The Major winced and swore like a sailor. "*Mein Gott*! That hurt…but it went all the way through, that's good – no bullet, and they'll never know the difference…" He took his Luger back and re-holstered it.

They stayed in the crater the rest of the night and part of the next day, sleeping and regaining their strength. Himmel was in and out of consciousness, but holding on. Around noon, they crawled out and followed the silvery pale sun west as it crossed the sky in its low winter arc. The Major fashioned a makeshift crutch out of a tree branch to help him along, and with Daniel supporting Himmel, it was slow going.

They walked alone for several hours, with no sign of the Russians. Slowly, other groups of ragged, shell-shocked, and wounded Germans began to emerge from the landscape and join them in their trek. These wandering scarecrows, in their tattered, filthy uniforms and dull, lifeless faces, staggered along asking everyone they met, "Have you any food? Have you something to eat?" They had long ago thrown away their weapons, along with any further hope of resistance. Some of them were even *looking* for Russians to surrender to.

"Has anyone seen the Russians?" these shattered men would ask.

"The Russians? They've passed us by, mate," someone would tell them. "They're already in Poland! They can't be bothered with *us*."

They walked along like this, hundreds of listless, lifeless shadows, staggering, tripping, getting back up again, always moving west in hope of finding food, someone to surrender to, or a good place to lay down and die. The farms and villages along the roads had already been ransacked for food – there was nothing left in this desolate, lifeless landscape. Everything had already been stripped away, first by the retreating Germans, then by the fleeing refugees, and finally by the advancing Russian forces. There was not a scrap of anything of value left in this starkly ravaged Land of Death.

And yet they walked on in their delirium, ghost-like husks with dark, shifting, sunken eyes and skin stretched tight over protruding cheekbones and elbows and knobby knees, until they finally surrendered all hope and sank, bovine-like, to their knees by the side of the road to die.

Daniel was delirious with hunger. Himmel's arm stank of gangrene and his head rolled around listlessly on his neck. The Major hobbled along well enough, though he complained of hunger and a slight fever. Maybe his wounds were becoming infected.

They passed by burned out villages and smoldering tanks. They passed by frozen corpses and men, by the hundreds, eating handfuls of snow in a desperate attempt to alleviate the gnawing ache in their bellies. They passed by men laughing madly, and men weeping like children, and one soldier sitting by the side of the road serenading the passing multitudes with a beautiful violin concerto.

One day, Daniel thought he heard Himmel mumbling in his ear. "Speak up," he said, a bit irritated. "What are you saying?"

"Why are you doing this?" Himmel whispered weakly. "Why don't you just leave me here?"

"*Nein.*"

"But, you never even *liked* me…" Himmel said, lapsing back into a state of semi-consciousness.

Daniel didn't like the smell of Himmel's arm. He'd been keeping it packed in snow to slow the progress of the infection, but the gangrene couldn't be completely stopped. Himmel had a fever and was delirious most of the time. *He's going to lose that arm*, Daniel thought to himself.

Later, there was something of a melee in the middle of the road ahead. A crowd of men had gathered, and were all shouting animatedly. When they got closer, they found out one man had knifed another man over a biscuit. The dead man was dragged off the road, and the victor pocketed the biscuit.

Twenty minutes later, they saw <u>that</u> man being dragged off the road with a knife wound to the chest. A different, stronger man was pocketing the same biscuit.

And so it went.

A week later, they passed a stooped-shouldered soldier kneeling in the snow by the side of the road. The man, heavily bearded and obviously shell-shocked, was repeating the same names over and over, in an almost hypnotic state: "Vollmer…Toppel…Kirchner…Kellerman… Planke…" The names stopped Daniel cold. He looked closer at the man, registering a spark of recognition.

"*Henckel?*" Daniel approached the kneeling man, who seemed to be in a trance. "Is that *you*, Henckel?"

The man ignored him, lost in his own world.

"It's me – Schiller!"

The man turned to him, listlessly. Henckel was unrecognizable – gaunt, haggard, and faded. His eyes looked dead.

"*Nein*," Henckel replied. "Shiller drowned in the river, with Vollmer and Toppel..."

"*Nein*, I didn't, Henckel! I'm alive – look at me!

"Schiller? *Nein*, Schiller drowned in the river, sunk by a Russian airplane..."

"That was the other boat – remember?"

Henckel continued his doleful litany. "Vollmer...Kirchner...Toppel...*Schiller*..."

Understanding, Daniel gently helped Henckel to his feet. "Come with us, Henckel... everything's going to be all right."

A few days later, Henckel recognized him. "Schiller!" he whispered. "Where's Mulder?"

"He was killed, back at the river."

Slowly, his old friend began to re-emerge. Daniel felt confident his battle-scarred mind would eventually heal.

Many days later, the column of marching dead was still moving west. A man ahead of them suddenly came to life and started shouting: "I know this place! I know this place! We've reached Poland! We've reached Poland!" He went from man to man, grabbing each one by the shoulders, insisting they were now in Poland. To Daniel's mind, Poland didn't look much different from the Ukraine.

Daniel's group continued to march on, hunger gnawing at them like a rapacious beast. Nobody could remember how many days or weeks they'd been walking. Daniel began to enter the feverish, dreamlike state that usually precedes the shutdown of all bodily functions. In his fever-dream, they were entering a town. They followed the stream of men, which began to swarm around the town square. There were hundreds of men there, milling about aimlessly, looking for food. There was much noise and confusion. There were trucks with men in Russian uniforms standing on the hoods. They had bullhorns and were calling out to the crowd, directing them in very broken German.

"All men in the uniform of the Third Reich, this way! Officers to the left, enlisted men to the right! Officers to the left, enlisted men to the right!"

Eventually, the throng of men began to separate and obediently follow the soldier's directions, like mindless cattle. "Officers to the left, enlisted men to the right!" The men, once they separated, were guided into different holding areas by Russian troops with submachine guns. But, somehow, they were not threatening and the herds of human cattle were not afraid. In fact, they were strangely calmed by the entire process, like sheep.

In the enlisted men's area, Russian soldiers milled about, separating the severely wounded from the un-injured. Whenever anyone protested, the guards gently told them "It's all right, the wounded will be well-cared for."

When men gathered around the guards asking *"Das essen? Das essen?"* The guards assured them, "There will be all the food you can eat!"

In Daniel's dream, his group was funneled to the right with the enlisted men. A guard came to escort Himmel away. "This man will receive the medical attention that he needs," they were told, and Himmel was gently led away. Nobody protested. The Major, who could now walk on his own, was left with the group.

Then, in Daniel's dream, they were told by more guards with bullhorns, *"Wir bringen sie zum essen!* We're taking you to the food!" They were loaded onto trucks and driven out of town. They drove for miles and miles, and judging by the position of the sun, they were heading north.

Six hours later, they arrived at a large, snow-covered field surrounded by nasty-looking rolls of razor wire. As the men climbed down from the trucks, they asked, *"Das essen?* Will there be food?"

"There will be all the food you can eat!" the guards promised.

Then the trucks drove away, leaving the men in their huge, crude, razor wire pen. Thousands of men filled the pen, and in the coming days, many thousands more were trucked in. There was no shelter, and no facilities – it was a pasture designed for cattle, and the men contained in it lived like cattle.

"Das essen! Das essen!" the men chanted, like mooing cows, but no food arrived. Instead, loudspeakers on poles blared with assurances in broken German: "Men of the Third Reich: You will be well cared for! Your wounded will receive medical treatment! Food is on the way! I repeat: food is on the way!"

In Daniel's dream, men slept out in the open, like livestock. No, livestock had barns. They smoked what cigarettes they had and relieved themselves and waited for the food to arrive. Every morning, guards would enter the enclosure and carry off the many men who had died during the night. Men surrounded the guards like zombies, begging for food.

"There will be all the food you can eat!" the guards assured them in broken German.

In Daniel's dream, every morning after the dead were carried out, guards circled the enclosure, spraying the inmates with fire hoses. The men splashed their faces, washed themselves, and opened their parched mouths to drink their fill.

In Daniel's dream, every afternoon trucks arrived and unloaded hundreds of men: Germans, Hungarians, Romanians. Every day, more men, no food. More men, no food.

In Daniel's dream, the loudspeakers blared with comforting announcements throughout the day:

"The war will soon be over!"

"You will soon be reunited with your families!"

"If you need medical attention, just call out! Our medics are waiting to help you!"

"The Soviet Union will rebuild and re-educate your nation!"

In Daniel's dream, the men called out *"Essen! Essen!"* But no food arrived. Starving men lost their minds and lacerated themselves trying to crawl through the razor wire. But most men simply huddled together in the middle of the field, like sheep.

And each afternoon, more trucks arrived and more men were herded into the enclosure with empty promises of food and medical care. Eventually, it was standing room only – no room to lie down, sit, or even squat. Men had to relieve themselves standing up. The stench became like a vapor that brought stinging tears to men's eyes. Men slept in an upright position, leaning against one another like breadsticks jammed tightly into a jar.

And then one morning in Daniel's never-ending dream, after the collection of the dead, the loudspeakers unexpectedly announced in broken German: *"Das essen ist hier! Das essen ist hier!"*

Guards walked the perimeter of the enclosure carrying baskets of stale bread, tearing off hunks and tossing them over the razor wire. "Share with your friends!" the guards called out. "There is enough for everybody!" Men climbed over each other to catch the pieces of bread, then scurried away to gnaw on them like rats. When the baskets were empty, the guards turned them upside down and shook them to show the still hungry men there was no more bread. "If you're still hungry, somebody took more than his share!"

Daniel was in a world turned upside down.

After a month in the enclosure, the SS Major still hadn't been found out by the Russians. He spoke delusionally of escape, of leading the other POW's to freedom and mounting a counter-attack against the Russians. But he had become very ill with fever and vomiting, and could barely stand on his own. Out of pity, Daniel tried to take care of him as best he could, even sharing his meager rations of bread with him.

One day, the loudspeakers announced in broken German: "We have good news! Preparations have been completed to relocate many of you to more comfortable accommodations! The relocations will begin tomorrow morning!"

The next morning, after the collection of the dead and the rock-hard bread had been tossed over the razor wire, several dozen trucks pulled up to the enclosure and guards started herding prisoners into them. The men, well-fed on their scraps of stale bread, stepped up into the trucks in rapturous anticipation of their comfortable new accommodations. Daniel, Henckel, and the Major were loaded into the same truck.

The trucks pulled out of the enclosure and drove some twenty kilometers to a train station. The men were transferred into enclosed livestock cars as the engine sat building up steam for the trip and guards paced up and down the tracks outside. Then more trucks arrived and unloaded more men, who were squeezed into the already crowded cars. This process was repeated several more times, until the men were pressed together so tightly that they could hardly breathe. And still the train sat while the engine built up and let off steam.

Finally, sometime after midnight, the train started to move, and traveled over four hundred kilometers to the west. During the journey, there was no food or water – just a single toilet break in a large field under armed guard.

Part Four
Waiting for Johann

Chapter 18

Camp Lamsdorf had served as a German POW camp for Russian prisoners until the Red Army liberated it and promptly reversed its purpose. The main compound consisted of some four dozen or so low-slung whitewashed barracks with gently-sloping roofs, surrounded by razor wire and guard towers. Each barrack was about fifty meters long and was built to house one hundred men. The Third Reich was imploding at such an accelerated rate, however, that the Russians were reeling at the sheer numbers of surrendering Germans, and it became necessary to squeeze two or three times that number into each building.

There was a six-kilometer march to the camp from the train station. "There is hot soup waiting for you at the camp!" the guards called out, to keep the prisoners moving. The Major's condition had worsened on the long train ride, and Daniel and Henckel had to hold him up between them during the march.

They entered the camp through the main gate. "Don't worry, there is plenty of hot soup waiting for you!" the guards called out.

"This man is very sick," Daniel called to one of the guards.

"If you need medical attention, just call out!" the guard replied. "Our medics will be happy to help you!"

"I'm telling you *now* – this man is very sick!" Daniel repeated.

"If you need medical attention, just call out!" the guard shouted, completely ignoring Daniel. "Our medics will be happy to help you!"

"This is a madhouse!" Daniel cried.

The men were herded into a large parade ground and directed to form lines. To get the hot soup, they had to stand through a lecture from the camp commandant. He was a surprisingly short man, but barrel-chested and powerfully built. He was in full dress uniform, his chest covered with tiny colorful medals. He mounted a platform and looked out over the haggered, malnourished group of men with a face completely devoid of emotion.

"So. This is the mighty German Army," he finally said, after many minutes. "The army of the Thousand Year Reich. The army that conquered France in six weeks. The army that attempted, unsuccessfully, to invade and subjugate the Soviet Union. Well, you see how you are now. A broken, impotent, defeated fighting force. In a few short weeks, your Thousand Year Reich will cease to exist. How do you like the way things turned out, eh?"

He gave them a moment of silence to chew on it. "Now you are under the authority of the Soviet Union. We hold your destiny in our hands. We will decide your fate. Your nation's future, and the future of its people, will be decided by Marshall Stalin."

He gave them more time to think about his words. "I am Colonel Sokolov, the commandant of this camp. For those of you who accept your defeat gracefully and resist no further, you will not find this camp such a bad place. You will be well taken care of. For some of you, it will be a better life than you will find on the outside. For those of you unable to accept this new reality, it may be quite difficult for you." And with that, the colonel stepped down from the platform and disappeared into his quarters.

The guards formed the men up and marched them to the mess hall, where each man received a ladle of hot soup. The men slurped the soup ravenously. One prisoner didn't have his mess kit. "If you lost your mess kit, you will have to find someone willing to share his soup with you!" the guard shouted, turning the man away.

After the meal, the men were assigned to their quarters. Daniel, Henckel and the Major were assigned to Barrack 12. The interior was stark: rows of bunks lined the walls, three bunks high on each side. Two wood-burning stoves provided heat, one at each end. No running water, and light was provided by two measly bulbs hanging from the ceiling. But it had a roof! Daniel and Henckel deposited the Major in a bottom bunk. His fever was worse than ever, and he was sweating and shivering uncontrollably.

"He's dying," Henckel shook his head.

"They have to provide medical care!" Daniel said. "It's part of the Geneva Convention!"

"Who are you going to complain to?" Henckel asked.

"I was a medic," a man who overheard their conversation said. "Let me take a look at him." The medic laid his hand on the Major's forehead, then opened his coat and tunic. The Major's chest was covered with a rash. "Typhus," the medic concluded grimly. "Advanced stage, I'm afraid."

"Will he die?" Daniel asked.

"Unless he gets antibiotics, it is certain," the medic replied. "But the Russians don't care. There are no antibiotics for prisoners. The best you can do is try to make him as comfortable as you can."

Daniel wet a cloth at the communal water pump outside, and laid it across the Major's forehead to try to break the fever. He offered him part of his own rations, but the Major had little appetite. He was wasting away. He slept most of the time, and when he was conscious, he blabbered on about escape and counter-attack. "There's still time to save the Fatherland!" he declared in his delusion.

Conditions in the camp were abysmal, but slightly better than the enclosure. There were no mattresses or pillows on the bunks, so men slept on the hard pinewood planks with their blanket and their heavy coat as their only covering. The barracks were heated by two wood stoves, but the ration of wood only lasted through part of the night. By morning, the inside of the barracks were bone-chillingly frosty.

Rations consisted of fifty grams of stale black bread a day. On Saturdays, a thin, watery soup was served – really nothing more than water in which turnips had been boiled. The turnips were always removed before the soup was served, and given to the guards with their meals. Many prisoners lamented the fact that the turnips were never left in the soup.

Despite what the guards said, Daniel could see no evidence of medical care whatsoever. The camp infirmary seemed to be for guards only. In this regard, the prisoners were entirely on their own.

Soon after their arrival, the prisoners were ordered back onto the parade ground for another speech by the commandant.

"Due to the devastation and destruction brought upon all peace-loving nations by the criminal actions of the Third Reich, it is necessary to rebuild Europe," Colonel Sokolov began. "As members of the Wehrmacht, it is fitting that you should all do your part in this great effort. Therefore, starting this week, every prisoner will be required to work four days a week at hard labor. This is not busy-work. You will be contributing to the rebuilding of civilization. This will be the beginning of your rehabilitation. On your work detail days, you will receive an extra ten grams of bread. The first rotation begins tomorrow at dawn.

The next morning, Barracks One through Twelve were called out onto the yard at daybreak. "You have ten minutes to collect your daily rations and be back in your lines for work detail!" a guard called out. The men scrambled to the mess hall to get their bread.

"This is the same amount we get every day," Mulder complained. "Where's our extra ten grams?"

"You will receive your extra rations this evening, when you return to camp!" a guard told them.

Before leaving, the guards walked the detail past a long storage shed, where the men picked up pick axes, sledge hammers, and shovels. Then they left the camp through the main gate and walked eight and a half kilometers to an inconceivably large hole in the ground.

"It's nice to be out of the camp, at least," Mulder said. "The work can't be that bad, after all."

They descended down into the hole on a steep, narrow path, all the way to the bottom. There they spent the day hammering and breaking down large chunks of limestone into smaller and smaller pieces. When all the large chunks were gone, the men shoveled the aggregate into large carts which were pulled to the surface by teams of mules. Then more large chunks were blasted out of the walls of the great quarry with dynamite, and the whole process repeated itself until late afternoon.

Exhausted and covered from head to toe with limestone dust, the prisoners then carried their tools back up the steep path and out of the quarry for the twelve and a half kilometer trip back to camp. But instead of receiving their extra ration of bread, they were made to line up on the yard and wait for the commandant to address them. They waited over an hour for the commandant to finish his hot supper, standing in the freezing night like shivering dogs.

"Those who fall asleep during the Commandant's address will not receive their extra ration of bread!" the guards warned them.

Finally, Colonel Sokolov emerged from his quarters and fixed them with a stony stare. Then he calmly launched into a two-hour lecture on the superiority of the Soviet system and the corrupt decadence of capitalism and fascism. Several men collapsed during the lecture, and were dragged away angrily by guards. After a long day in the quarry, Daniel's legs felt like they would buckle underneath him any moment. Several times, he had to steady himself against Henkel's shoulder to avoid the fate being meted out to those who had collapsed.

It was almost midnight when they finally received their extra ten grams of bread and collapsed like dead men on their bunks until the next morning.

On the next evening after their return from the quarry, the men were again directed to line up on the yard and wait for the commandant to address them. Forty-five minutes later, the colonel appeared and read to them selected passages from Karl Marx for nearly two hours.

The next night, it was two hours of Shostakovich blaring at ear-splitting levels from the loudspeakers.

And so it went.

On their precious days off, Daniel discovered that their main occupation consisted of trying to keep warm and nourished – a task which never seemed to be accomplished, no matter how much effort was expended on it.

Daniel spent most of his free days asking around the camp if anybody knew a Major Schiller. He met with little success until finally a prisoner recognized the name and nodded. He took Daniel to Barrack 17 and pointed out an emaciated skeleton of a man Daniel didn't recognize. Disappointed, Daniel shook his head.

"*Ja, Ja* – Major Schiller!" the prisoner insisted. Daniel approached the emaciated man and looked at him earnestly. Could this be?

"Major *Gerhard* Schiller?" he asked.

The man looked up at him hopelessly. "*Nein.* My name is *Werner* Schiller." Then he looked back at the ground lifelessly.

On his way back to his own barrack, Daniel decided the chances of finding Major Schiller here were minimal. His stomach growled, and he became preoccupied with thoughts of how he was going to keep his belly full.

"Schiller?" he heard someone say behind him. He stopped. "Schiller – is that you?" He turned around and saw another starving, filthy soldier dressed in rags, just like he was – just like *everyone* in this camp.

"It *is* you!" the soldier said, taking a step toward him. Daniel still didn't recognize him. "You – you could clear a jammed cartridge from the MG 42 faster than anybody I've ever met!"

"Mulder?" Daniel whispered. The man standing before him was a good sixty pounds lighter, and his strong, broad shoulders were now stooped like an old man's. But it was indeed Mulder!

"How – I thought they killed you at the river!"

"*Nein*. It was a flesh wound. I'm good as new!"

"Where – where are you quartered?" Daniel asked, still in shock at Mulder's appearance. Did *he* look that bad to Mulder?

"Barrack 23," Mulder replied.

"Henckel's here – and the SS Major."

Mulder looked confused. "How – I thought the Russians shoot SS officers on the spot."

"He ditched his uniform and put on a dead private's uniform."

"The bastard!" Mulder said angrily.

"He's dying, though. Typhus."

Mulder's anger subsided. "Oh. The Russians don't give medical care to prisoners here."

"I know. Come on – Henckel will be glad to see you!"

"Probably not," Mulder replied, "but let's go bother him anyway!"

On the way, they passed other skeletal prisoners milling about restlessly, lost in their own thoughts.

"The hunger – it gnaws at you day and night," Daniel said. "It's hard to think of anything else."

"They keep us like this on purpose," Mulder proposed. "If our minds are on our empty bellies all the time, we have no time to think of escape."

When they found Henckel, he was walking around and around the parade ground trying to keep warm. That's what everyone was doing. Henckel just looked at Mulder and shook his head and flashed a lopsided grin. "I am not surprised. I knew the Russians wouldn't be able to kill an ugly ape like you!"

"I'm glad to see you, too, Henckel!" Mulder smiled. "Stop walking around like that. You're using up all your calories!"

"But I've got to keep warm!"

It was like a complicated algebraic equation: how to balance the benefit of the warmth derived from physical exertion with the limited caloric intake. It was an equation many of the prisoners were unable to solve.

Daniel spent much time trying to find a guard who would be willing to help get antibiotics for the Major. Most of the guards he approached, however, quickly rebuffed him with a submachine gun barrel in his face. What was one less German to them, after all?

One day, Daniel noticed a guard he hadn't seen before. The guard watched him closely for several minutes, then began to approach him. Daniel braced himself, expecting to be kicked or yelled at to move along. But there was something different about this guard. He had a kinder face than the others.

"I see you talking other guards," he said in very broken German. "You are very…strong…" then he grimaced, knowing it wasn't the right word. "Not strong, umm…keep coming…"

"Tenacious?" Daniel asked.

"Ja, that one!" the guard smiled. "My sorry…My German is very down…"

Taking a wild shot, Daniel asked, *"Parlez-vous Francaise?"*

The guard's face lit up. *"Oui! Beaucoup mieux que l'Allemand."*

The rest of the conversation was in French.

"I went to school in Paris for three years," the guard explained. "My father was an attache there before the war."

"You speak French well."

"As I tried to say, you've been attempting to get the attention of many of the guards. Is there something you need?" the guard asked. It was a stunningly naïve question in a place like this.

"Not for me," Daniel promised. "My friend is dying of typhus. He needs antibiotics."

"I see. That could be difficult," the guard said, shaking his head.

Daniel took a chance. "What's your name?"

The guard stiffened. Daniel panicked – he'd gone too far, too fast. Then the guard softened somewhat. "My name is Yuri. What is yours?"

"Johann."

Some kind of barrier had been broken – the exchange of names, the French language. Yuri looked around nervously, but there was also a compassionate gleam in his eye. "Look, we've been talking far too long. I can't promise you anything, but I'll see what I can do. Where are you quartered?"

"Barrack 12."

Yuri smiled slightly, then nodded and walked away.

That night before lights out, two guards came in to do the headcount. One guard walked down each side, making sure every bunk was full. When the guard on Daniel's side got to his bunk, he saw that it was Yuri. Saying nothing, Yuri reached out and placed a small bundle on Daniel's bunk as he passed. Then the guards turned the lights out and left.

Daniel waited a few minutes, then opened the bundle. It was some extra bread and a few white pills, wrapped in a handkerchief. Daniel climbed down from his bunk put two of the pills in the Major's mouth, then gave him a swig of water from his canteen. Daniel checked the Major's mouth – it had worked, he'd swallowed the pills. Then he tore the extra bread in half and ate a piece, saving the rest to give the Major in the morning.

The next morning, the Major was still feverish and weak. He didn't have an appetite, but Daniel got him to take some of the extra bread with some water. He didn't seem better to Daniel, but it was still early. Daniel gave him two more of the pills and went outside.

He joined the men marching around the parade ground to keep warm. He looked for Yuri, and the two made eye contact. Yuri approached him cautiously. "How's your friend today?" he asked in French.

"Still feverish."

"Ah, it may be too late. I will bring more pills tonight though. I can only pinch a few at a time from the infirmary, or they will notice."

"*Merci*," Daniel said.

"All right, I will bring more pills tonight."

"And bread? Will you bring some more bread?" Daniel asked anxiously.

"Of course," Yuri said, and walked away quickly.

That night, Yuri brought another bundle wrapped up in a handkerchief. This time, there were more pills and bread, but also a dollop of jam wrapped in wax paper. Real jam! Daniel gave two more pills to the Major, then climbed back into his bunk and wolfed down half the bread and jam. It was heavenly!

In the morning, Daniel found Henckel and Mulder and gave them each a small piece of bread with jam smeared on top. They stood staring in wonder at the unimaginable treasure they held in the palms of their hands.

"How did you do it?" Mulder asked in disbelief.

"I can't say. Just enjoy."

"You're a miracle worker!" Henckel said, biting into his portion. They both bolted it down like hungry wolves. Daniel basked in the moment – the looks on their faces were priceless.

"If there's more, you know where to find us..." Mulder reminded him.

Daniel looked for Yuri on the parade ground. Yuri found him and came walking up very casually.

"And how is the patient this morning?" Yuri asked. He always kept a stern look on his face when they talked, in case the other guards were watching.

"A little better," Daniel said. "I think the pills are helping. But he's still not eating much."

"Ah, the fever," Yuri said. "And how did you like the jam?"

Tears came to Daniel's eyes. "It was sublime."

Yuri smiled a little. Then Daniel decided to roll the dice, and bring up something he'd been thinking about lately.

"Yuri, I know this sounds ridiculous, but I...I need to speak with the commandant."

Yuri's smile evaporated. "You're joking."

"*Non*. I have important information the commandant needs to know at once."

"That could be difficult," Yuri said, shaking his head.

"I wouldn't want to be the poor fellow who stands between the commandant and what I have to tell him," Daniel bluffed, knowing full well how much it could backfire on him. But it was worth the gamble.

"Are you in earnest?" Yuri asked gravely. "This is not some kind of trick?"

"I am serious," Daniel told him.

Yuri looked away. "I – I'm just a guard," he said nervously. "But I'll see what I can do."

For the next three nights, a different guard came to do head-count. No Yuri, no handkerchief bundles. Daniel began to panic. He'd really done it now. He'd gone too far with Yuri, pushed the boundaries of trust he'd so carefully established.

He lay in his bunk cursing his own impatience. Of course, they would be coming for him at any moment, to either shoot him or fling him helplessly into some worse kind of punishment.

On the fourth day, Yuri came up to him on the parade ground. Daniel readied himself for a tongue-lashing. Instead, Yuri smiled and said, "I hope you're ready to see the commandant."

"What?" Daniel asked in disbelief.

"You said you wanted to see the commandant. Well, I got you in. Right now."

"You mean, you're not arresting me?"

Yuri almost burst out laughing. "Of course not, come on if you still want to talk to him. He's a very busy man."

Yuri led him to the commandant's office and stayed to translate for him. "This is the prisoner – Private Schiller," Yuri addressed his commander with a salute.

Colonel Sokolov sat behind his desk and stared at Schiller. "So, what is it about?" he asked in Russian. Yuri translated for Daniel.

"Sir, a grave error has been made," Daniel croaked out, "One which I am sure the commandant would want to know about so he can correct it immediately."

"Is that so?" The commandant sat back in his chair, keeping his eyes fixed on Daniel. "How old are you?"

"Seventeen."

"Seventeen," Sokolov repeated thoughtfully. "Yes. I know they were bringing in boys of twelve and thirteen, in the end. We found their small, crumpled bodies on the battlefield. All they had left, I suppose." He spoke clinically, in a military voice, without a hint of emotion. "Go on. What is this grave error I need to know about."

Daniel's story spilled out like a geyser. He explained that he was half-French and served in the French Resistance for over a year. He told the colonel about the Gestapo and Major Schiller's scheme to have him pose as his son Johann. He explained he was only serving in the German Army as a means of hiding from the Gestapo. He ended by saying that he was sure that the commandant would want to know such news immediately and that he would not want to keep a French Resistance fighter – an ally of Russia – in his POW camp a moment longer than absolutely necessary.

The Colonel had listened patiently to Daniel's story. "Is that all?" he asked quietly.

"Oui, that's everything."

"And while you fought for the Germans, surely there were chances for you to leave. Were they watching you day and night? Did anyone physically force you to stay?"

"Non."

"Then why didn't you just leave?"

"As I told you, I was hiding from the Gestapo. The army would have been the one place they wouldn't have looked. Besides, I...I would have been shot as a deserter if I left..."

"Exactly. Shot as a deserter. That is why I cannot release you."

"I don't understand..." Daniel said in confusion. Maybe Yuri got the translation wrong...

"You see, officially, you are a private in the Wehrmacht. You stayed with your unit when, by your own admission, you could have left anytime."

"I'd seen what they did to deserters. I didn't want to be shot like the others."

"It seems to me you should have thought of that before you joined the enemy," the commandant said coldly. "So, your choices were to desert, or stay with your unit. You chose the latter. And, over time, you became one of them, didn't you, *Johann?*"

"My real name is Daniel."

"It doesn't matter."

"Does it matter to you that there is an innocent French citizen in your camp?"

The Russian looked straight into Daniel's eyes. They began to fill with tears. Daniel struggled to hold them back. "French, German – what does it matter? All that matters is that you were captured wearing <u>that</u> uniform. Look at it this way: you're one of the fortunate ones – you're still alive."

With a sinking feeling, Daniel realized it was futile – they were talking in circles.

"So, you won't release me, then?"

"How many Russians did you kill during your time with the Germans?" Sokolov asked.

Daniel knew he couldn't answer that. Sokolov said something in Russian to Yuri, and the guard ushered him out of the office.

"That went well," Yuri said when they got outside.

"I hope you don't get into any trouble over this," Daniel said.

"Don't worry, I'll be fine. A couple of extra nights of guard duty, a few hundred potatoes to peel…"

Over the next several days, Daniel began to lose hope. There was no way out. There was not enough food, no medical care. It was becoming clear that the Russians weren't planning on releasing *anybody*, let alone him. They were just going to keep them penned up until they starved to death or died of disease. He watched the Major languish in typhus, watched his friends waste away day after day, and felt himself getting weaker by the day.

One day as he was walking in those maddening circles on the parade ground, lost in thought, another prisoner said to him, "You've got to find a way to occupy your mind, or you'll go mad and die." Then the prisoner disappeared into the crowd. Daniel hallucinated it was Major Schiller, his ersatz father, and dove into the crowd looking for him.

"Major Schiller! Gerhard Schiller! *Father*!" he called and called, but there was no answer. Then he saw him nearby, his back turned. Daniel ran over to him and spun him around: "*Father*!"

But it wasn't Schiller, it was just another prisoner. Daniel hallucinated a gruesome death's head skull, with maggots crawling over it. He ran away screaming in terror. Most men didn't even notice this erratic behavior – after all, most of them were losing their minds with hunger, as well.

The next thing Daniel knew, he was waking up in his bunk, Mulder offering him water from a canteen. "What happened?" Daniel asked.

"We found you on the parade ground, squatting on the ground, rocking back and forth," Mulder told him. "You were exhausted. You slept for hours."

"It's the hunger," Henckel told him. "You'll be all right."

Daniel got up and went outside without his coat on. He looked all over the parade ground for Yuri, but couldn't find him. Would there be more bread? Would there be more medicine for the Major? Had Yuri turned against him now, too?

That night, he had a starvation-fueled dream about riding his motorcycle to a meadow where Emily was lying in the grass in the warm sunshine, her skirt pulled up to reveal part of her soft pale thigh. Then he was there, putting his dark, dirty, boney hand on her thigh and she shrank from him, and what he'd become, in fear. He woke up and began to wonder if she got away from the Gestapo. He told himself – convinced himself – that she did.

Then he remembered what the prisoner on the yard told him, and to keep his mind occupied he began to invent a whole life for her.

He fabricated everything – the village in which she now lived, the lane, the cottage, the types of windows it had, its furnishings, her new name, her job. Then he began to fabricate the people: neighbors, friends, strangers. Then she met a man – yes, his mind allowed this – and even though his psyche was disturbed, his mind couldn't stop constructing the story. Emily and her new beau went on picnics by a stream, to the cinema to see American movies, quarreled over meaningless, forgettable things, made up, made love in the grass.

Yes, he let her have a lover, to keep her happy. But he wouldn't let THEM catch up to her. Somehow he managed to keep those jackboots on the front stoop, that violent rapping on the cottage door in the middle of the night, out of the story.

He was well-pleased with the life he had invented for her, and thought about it often, adding a name here, a new detail there – children, holidays, etc. But in all of this, he allowed himself one untouchable memory, one sublime moment that belonged to them and them alone.

It was those cool nights lying on their backs in the farmer's field where they had waited for the airplane to land, holding hands and staring up at the stars together, saying nothing but pretending there was no war and they were the only two people in the world.

That was for him, and he held onto it like a rare diamond. And it was the only thing that kept him from going completely mad.

Chapter 19

A week later, the Major lost his battle with typhus. His body was wrapped in a groundsheet and carried off to be stacked in the snow with all the others. The ground was still too frozen to dig graves, so the bodies were being saved until the spring.

Daniel didn't know what to feel. The man was a patriot, a zealot, a murderer, and ultimately a coward concerned only with saving his own skin. He belonged to the SS and the Reich and Adolf Hitler – a legacy that was crumbling and would soon be gone but never forgotten. Yet he was a human being, and Daniel never regretted nursing him through his sickness and sharing his rations with him.

That day, the guards called everyone out onto the yard for a special address by Colonel Sokolov. The men lined up in their squads and the colonel slowly ascended the steps of the platform. He stared at them a full sixty seconds before speaking.

"Your Fuhrer, Adolf Hitler, is dead," he told them in a cold voice. "He shot himself in the head in Berlin, and his body was burned by his assistants. His remains are now in the possession of the victorious Red Army. Germany surrendered this morning. The war is over. Your glorious Third Reich is now a part of history." Colonel Sokolov never tired of twisting the knife when he had his victims down.

"When are you going to release us?" someone shouted.

"That is up to Marshall Stalin. When I hear from Moscow, I will let you know. In the meantime, please continue to enjoy your stay at Camp Lamsdorf." The Colonel descended the steps and walked back to his quarters.

The stunned prisoners continued to stand in their lines a while, letting the information sink in. Then they slowly began to disperse and go about their business of surviving another day.

Later, Yuri approached Daniel on the yard.

"I am sorry about your friend," he said. "I've been waiting for a chance to talk to you. I've been thinking about what you told the commandant. I believe your story. I know you're not a German."

"*Merci*," Daniel said.

"Listen, we've got to get you out of here. If we don't, you'll die here. They'll never release you properly, because they'll never admit they put a Frenchman in a POW camp. In Soviet Union, we don't admit mistakes. But I know another way. I have been working on a plan."

"What is it?" Daniel asked.

"You must escape," Yuri whispered. "I'll help you. On Wednesday nights, a friend of mine has watch duty in guard tower six. Occasionally, I keep him company, and we share a bottle of vodka. It would not be out of the ordinary for me to visit him this Wednesday night. I'll be sure and distract him – get him good and drunk – while you make your escape."

"How?"

"I will give you wire cutters. You will cut your way through the fence under the tower, while I distract my friend above."

Just then, another guard came walking by, close.

"You dirty German pigs disgust me!" Yuri shouted at Daniel in anger. "Your uniforms are filthy and you stink like a sewer!"

The other guard stopped and looked at Daniel, then at Yuri. "Is everything all right here?" he asked.

"This filthy pig wasn't watching where he was going, and almost bumped into me," Yuri said. "I think I'll just stay here and chew on his ass for a while!"

The other guard laughed. "Anything to relieve the boredom!" and went on his way.

"You're too lazy to wash, you sit on your fat asses all day, and then all you do is beg for more food!" Yuri went on, until the other guard was out of ear-shot. "Sorry about that."

"That's all right. So, I escape alone?"

"No. You need others, to help each other make it out of Poland. Find some men you know – men you trust – not more than four, and let them know about the plan. But be careful – choose only men you trust. There are informants among the prisoners. If one of them rats you out, you will be shot for planning to escape. And I will deny everything."

"But suppose we make it through the fence. Won't they come after us?"

"That's what everyone thinks." Yuri swept his hand toward the rest of the camp. "All these Germans, sitting here waiting to die, won't risk an escape because they think they'll be hunted down."

"Won't they?"

"No. Believe me, Daniel: the war is over. Germany has surrendered. If you make it out of here, they won't even bother coming after you. Why would they? The war is *over*."

"But won't your friend get in trouble?"

"Don't worry about him. His uncle is a colonel. Nothing will happen to him."

Daniel looked at Yuri a long time.

"I know what you're thinking. You can trust me, Daniel. You've got nothing else. There are no plans for a proper release of prisoners. If you don't get out now, you'll *die* here – or worse, be shipped to a camp in Siberia."

It was Friday. Daniel had five days to decide and find five accomplices. Of course, Henckel and Mulder would be the first he would tell. He found them on the yard, and they huddled together stamping their feet to keep them warm.

"When is it to be?" Mulder asked.

"Wednesday night, after lights out," Daniel replied.

"Five days? It's not enough time!" Henckel said.

"How do you know we can trust this guard?" Mulder demanded.

"He left the wire cutters under a loose floorboard under my bunk while we were on work detail. They are there now – I checked a few minutes ago."

"What if it's a set-up," Henckel said. "What if he just wants to help his friend capture us and foil an escape? To boost his own career, get a promotion."

Daniel shook his head. "I don't think so. There's something *different* about Yuri."

"He's a *Russian!*" Mulder hissed.

"He brought medicine for the Major, and extra bread for us. You tasted the bread and jam yourselves. Why would he do that?"

"To win your trust, so he could set you up with this phony escape ploy," Henckel surmised.

"I trust him," Daniel insisted. "Besides, we're all going to die in here, anyway!"

"So we can die now, or die later," Mulder said. "At least this way, we can choose when we die!"

"All right, supposing we do this," Henckel said. "How will we know when it is safe?"

"Yuri will signal us with a flashlight, from the tower. One flash means go, two flashes means stay put. But we need two more men. Who can we trust?"

"Petersen, the medic from our barracks," Henckel said. "He's a good man."

"I know someone, too," Mulder said. "Wissel, from my barracks. He's strong, and he's talked about getting out of here before."

"Good," Daniel said. "Go get them. We'll meet back here in thirty minutes."

Half an hour later, they were back with Petersen and Wissel. Daniel explained the plot to them. Wissel was for it, but Petersen wasn't so sure.

"How can we trust the guard?" Petersen asked. "He's a Russian!"

Daniel explained how Yuri had helped the Major and brought them extra bread. "And he has promised to bring us extra bread for the escape. I trust him."

"It's a trap," Petersen said. "I'm not coming."

"Then you will rot here forever," Wissel told him. "It's your choice. I'm going with them."

"We need to know now, Petersen," Henckel told him.

"Then it's no. I just don't feel right about it." Petersen walked away.

"Do you think he'll rat on us?" Mulder asked.

"No, he's a decent fellow," Henckel replied. "He's just afraid…"

"We need one more man," Daniel said.

"Why?" Wissel asked. "The four of us can do it ourselves."

"Let's keep our eyes open and ask around, all the same."

Energized by the thought of escape, Daniel went over and over the plan in his mind. A new-found sense of hope began to take hold, replacing the fear and helplessness that had engulfed him for so long.

After lights out that night, Daniel checked under the loose floorboard. The wire-cutters were still there, safe and sound. He'd taken the bottom bunk after the Major died so he could keep watch on the secret compartment under the floor.

Henckel shook him awake in the middle of the night in a panic. "What about the space between the two fences – you know, where the guards patrol?"

"It's taken care of," Daniel assured him. "Yuri will wait to give us the signal until the guards have passed. They won't even see us."

"But what about the other towers?" Henckel asked. "Won't they see us?"

"*Nein*," Daniel whispered. "We won't be in their line of sight."

"All right, but how do we *know* they won't come after us?"

"Henckel, we've been over all of this before," Daniel said. "Now, stop worrying and go back to sleep, will you?"

The next morning, a new batch of prisoners arrived. More and more had been arriving every week, causing a shortage of bunks. It was getting to the point where the new arrivals would have to start sleeping on the floors of the barracks.

Ten men out of this batch were assigned to Daniel's barrack. The prisoners seemed to look worse off than Daniel, Mulder and Henckel had when they arrived, if that was possible. They arrived hoping for food, medical care, and sleep – roughly in that order. After being in camp for thirty minutes and seeing the condition of the long-timers, however, all their hopes were dashed.

"We walked for twenty days to surrender to the Americans, but they just turned us over to the Russians," one of them told Daniel, with tears streaming down his cheeks. These new men had to find out of the way spots to roll out their groundsheets and threadbare blankets on the floor.

They were surprised to see Himmel among the new prisoners – minus an arm. Himmel had been assigned to their barrack with the others. "When they separated me from you, I was taken to a 'hospital' and stacked alongside hundreds of other severely wounded," Himmel told them. They were left there for days with no care – left to die or recover on their own, the Russians didn't really seem to care which. Then a Polish doctor working for the Russians took pity on Himmel, realizing he could save his life by amputating his gangrenous arm. The Russian doctors laughed at the Pole's compassion for a German, but let him do the operation anyway just to humor him.

"While I was recuperating in a different convalescent hospital I had a very interesting meeting," Himmel told them, looking straight at Daniel. "There was a German prisoner there – a *major* – who had lost his mind." Daniel's heart skipped a beat at the word *major*.

"The orderlies told me that at first the Russians thought he was faking it," Henckel continued. "But over time they became convinced he was truly mad. His name was Major *Schiller*." They all looked at each other: an odd coincidence. "In certain moments of near lucidity, the major told me he had a son named Johann. He described him to me. That's when I knew it was <u>our</u> Schiller he was describing! In his madness, the major insisted he was going to escape and make his way back to his farm, where he is convinced his son will meet him. So, why didn't you tell us your father was an officer?"

They all stared at Daniel, who said nothing.

"This is really nothing," Henckel finally said. "He probably didn't want to make a big deal out of it. He just didn't want any special treatment."

"The fact that he fought alongside us in the trenches and never mentioned it – never used it to get out of crappy details – says a lot about him," Mulder agreed.

"And there is something else," Himmel went on suspiciously. "The major said he was from Saxony, and had the accent to back it up. But *you* don't sound like a Saxon. You don't round your vowels like they do. So, where are you *really* from, Schiller?"

"My father was an engineer when I was very young," Daniel said. "He worked in Italy for two years. During that time, my mother and I lived with relatives in Stuttgart."

"Oh, Stuttgart," Himmel opened his eyes wide. "I taught music in Stuttgart before the war. At the Conservatory. What part of the city did you live in?"

"Bad-Cannstatt."

"Oh yes, I know it well!" Himmel said. "Charming town. Lovely festival, held in the Fall, as I recall."

"*Ja.*"

"And you must have been acquainted with the Wilhelma Zoo, and the natural mineral spas..." Himmel went on tossing out local references like a Michellin Guidebook. Luckily, Daniel was able to keep up only because his tutor had described the wonders of the city in such vivid detail during their lessons so long ago.

"But the accent – Stuttgart is closer, but it still isn't quite right, is it?" Himmel asked, staring hard at Daniel. "No, there's kind of a western flavor to it – I'll get it yet, you know!"

"You've been doing this ever since you met Schiller," Mulder said. "Don't you think it's time to knock it off?"

Soon it was lights out, and, lying in his bunk, Daniel's thoughts were, for once, not on hunger or escape. Gerhard Schiller was *alive* – that was good news to Daniel. And now Daniel knew that Schiller expected to meet him back at the family farm, provided they could both escape successfully. And, maybe someday, if his mind healed enough, Schiller might be able to help Daniel track down Emily and Constantine. Daniel drifted off to sleep that night with more hope than he'd had in months.

***

Since Himmel was unable to work in the quarry, he was promptly put to work in the camp kitchen. After his first day, he came back to the barracks before lights out very excited. "Come here," he said to Mulder, Henckel and Daniel. They all gathered around Daniel's bunk, where Himmel showed them his pockets were full of bread crumbs.

"Is that..?" Henckel asked hesitantly.

"When we cut the bread, there is always crumbs," Himmel told them. "I just scoop the crumbs into my pocket when no one is looking!" He gave each of them a handful of crumbs, careful not to let anyone else see. "There's only enough for us – unless I can find a coat with bigger pockets!"

The men quickly vacuumed up the meager calories from the palms of their hands and licked them clean.

"You've finally found a way to make yourself useful!" Mulder said, slapping Himmel on the back.

"We expect you to volunteer for kitchen duty every day!" Henckel said, not joking.

After lights out, they told Himmel of their escape plan. He said he was in. He wouldn't be much use with only one arm, but they just didn't have the heart to leave him behind.

Two days before the escape, tragedy struck. They were working in the quarry when a harness on a mule team snapped and a cart full of limestone chips was cut loose on the ramp going up to the surface path. There was no way to stop the ton of runaway rock, and a man was pinned against another cart and crushed to death. A crowd quickly gathered to pull the cart away, but it was too late. Mulder, Henckel, and Daniel pushed their way to the front to see who it was, and, in horror, realized it was Wissel.

Wissel, their escape partner. Now there was only Daniel, Henckel, Mulder, Himmel – and possibly Petersen, if they could ever talk him into it.

Wissel's body was wrapped in a groundsheet and carried back to camp by four men that night – Daniel, Henckel, Mulder, and another prisoner named Dangler. He was stacked in the snow with the other winter deaths, and would be buried with the spring thaw.

The next day, one day before the escape, Daniel was called into the commandant's office. Daniel walked in on rubber legs, with a mouth like cotton. *Did he know?*

Yuri was there to translate, but he did not look at Daniel.

"I have good news!" Sokolov said. "I referred your case to my superiors in Moscow. Despite your lack of papers, we believe you are a French national. The Soviet Union does not wish to incarcerate allies. Therefore, you will be released immediately. You are free to go..."

Daniel was too stunned to say a word.

"There is just one condition," Sokolov went on. "That you sign this document. Then you are free." He picked a piece of paper up off his desk and held it out to Daniel.

"What does it say?"

"It merely states that your incarceration here was a simple mix-up – that it was no fault of the Red Army – due entirely to the fog of war, and that the situation was corrected as soon as it was brought to our attention."

"That's acceptable, I suppose..."

"Also, that you agree to read this script while being filmed by a Red Army film crew." Sokolov tossed him a script. Daniel could see that it was written in French:

"M treatment while under the care of the Soviet Union was according to the Geneva Convention. I and my fellow prisoners

*were well-fed, well-sheltered, and received excellent medical
attention. Our required work was meaningful and humane. Our
living quarters were comfortable and warm, and we had plenty of
time to pursue optional educational opportunities as well as leisure
activities."*

"'*Meaningful and humane work?*'" Daniel asked. "A man was
crushed to death yesterday in the quarry. His name was Wissel. He
has a family in Frankfurt."

"Accidents happen in many work places."

"But these are all lies," Daniel said. "What will you do with the
film?"

"What do you care?" Sokolov asked impatiently. Then he calmed
himself and tried unsuccessfully to smile. "It will be used to show
the world that things are not so bad here. To assure our allies that
the Soviet Union is committed to the Geneva Convention and human
rights as it goes about the noble task of rebuilding Europe."

"You want to use me for propaganda."

"Call it whatever you like," Sokolov said. "You will be back in
France in two days. Isn't that what you want?"

Daniel thought of Mulder and Henckel and the others, counting on
him for the escape. Perhaps they could still escape, on their own.
But he knew he could never bring himself to say those lies into a
camera and then leave his friends behind in this place.

"No," Daniel said quietly.

"But, a month ago you came to *me* – and now you turn your nose
up at our offer? This has all been arranged – the film crew is on its
way – what am I to tell Moscow?"

"Tell them what you like. I'm not doing this."

The colonel poured a glass of vodka and took a long drink. He sat
the glass down on his desk, appearing to be calmer. "All right. You
are not thinking clearly. You have twenty-four hours to make a
decision. After that, the offer is withdrawn and you will rot here for
the rest of your miserable life – I will personally see to it!"

Yuri escorted him out of the commandant's quarters and across
the yard toward his barrack. "Is the escape still on?" Yuri asked.

"Oui. We're all ready to go – except for poor Wissel."

"Wednesday then – as planned," Yuri nodded, turning abruptly
away.

***

At two o'clock in the morning, guards busted into Daniel's barrack shouting for everyone to get up and get dressed. "Outside, now! *Schnell!*"

Outside, they were ordered to run around the yard in a wide circle. "*Lauf!* Run! *Schnell!*" the guards shouted. Barking dogs were brought out on leashes, adding to the noise and disorder. Then several guards with firehoses came out and began spraying the prisoners as they ran by. Soon, they were all soaked with cold water, but the guards kept them running.

"If you stop running, you will freeze to death!" the guards called out. The dogs barked. The men ran, the men were soaked, and the men ran again. It went on like this for an hour. Daniel looked at the commandant's quarters as he ran. The lights were on, and he could see Colonel Sokolov's silhouette in one of the windows, watching them.

No, I will not sign your paper, he thought, *even if you make me run all night...*

The next morning, the guards called the entire camp to line up on the yard before breakfast. Thousands of haggard prisoners stood at attention, waiting for the commandant to finish his hot breakfast and address them. Finally, he ascended his platform and glared at the assembled men.

"We have uncovered an escape plan," he told them matter-of-factly. Daniel's heart stopped. *Breathe*, he told himself. He looked at Henckel, who looked stricken. They both looked at Mulder, who had turned as white as milk. *Just keep breathing*, Daniel told himself.

"The beginnings of a tunnel was found underneath a barrack in the Romanian section," Sokolov went on. "Thankfully, they didn't get very far, because the ground is still too frozen."

Daniel felt his heart start beating again – the initial jolt of adrenalin began to subside.

"The prisoners responsible have been identified and will spend six months in solitary confinement. The guards will be doubled. The entire camp will be on half rations, until further notice." Then he left the platform and the prisoners were dismissed for morning rations.

"Is he crazy?" Mulder exploded. "We can't even survive on full rations, let alone half!"

"Quiet down, you oaf," Henckel hissed. "We're getting out of here, remember?"

"Did you hear him? The guards will be *doubled*," Mulder argued.

"I'll talk to Yuri," Daniel said. "I'll see if we can still do this or not."

Daniel stayed on the yard, waiting to spot Yuri. Finally, he saw him and caught his eye. They met behind one of the barracks, where there was less traffic.

"Can we still do this?" Daniel asked urgently.

"Sure. It's still possible," Yuri assured him. "Even with doubled guards, it will still take them fifteen minutes to walk the perimeter of the camp. Just watch for my signal. Everything will be all right."

Despite Yuri's assurances, Daniel carried around a heavy sense of fear all the rest of the day, like a rock in his belly.

That night after lights out, Daniel checked the secret compartment under his bunk. Yuri had left wire cutters, a compass, and extra bundles of bread for them. He waited a half an hour, then slid out of his bunk and whispered to Henckel: "Let's go." Most of the prisoners were already snoring loudly. They crept to Mulder's bunk. He was wide awake. "It's time."

They collected Himmel and crept outside, careful not to wake anyone. They were already wearing their heavy coats and blankets – they slept in them every night for warmth. Each man carried a bundle of bread. There were never any guards inside the compound at night – they would all be patrolling the camp perimeter, between the two fences.

They walked quietly through the snow along the side of their long barrack, all the way to the back. "There's the guard tower Yuri's in," Daniel pointed it out. Then they waited in the dark, rubbing their hands and arms to keep warm. Daniel heard someone creeping up from behind, and froze. It was Petersen.

"I want to go with you, after all!" he whispered.

"That's fine," Daniel said. "We have plenty of bread."

They saw two guards walk by between the fences. A few moments later, they saw one flashlight signal from the tower –one for "go." Daniel gripped the wire cutters tightly. The fear was gone.

He ran thirty meters to the first fence. He cut a one meter vertical slit in the fence and spread the wire enough for a man to pass. Then he crawled through and ran to the outside fence, where he cut the same type of slit. The others were already passing through the first fence, as Daniel crawled through the outside fence and waited. Daniel looked in both directions and was relieved to see no guards. Mulder was the last man through both fences. After going through, he carefully pulled the slit back together and re-tied the wire, to make it look seamless. Then he dusted the ground between the fences with his coat, to wipe away their footprints.

When they were all through the fences, they ran away quickly to the west. A light snow was falling, already obscuring their tracks. By morning, when the guards would notice them missing, they would be miles away and there would be no way of tracking them.

They were free! They ran west all night long and didn't get tired – they were free men at last!

"Yuri's plan worked brilliantly!" Daniel exclaimed.

"He's the only Russian I would kiss right now, if I could!" Mulder said.

"But I wouldn't want to be his friend tomorrow!" Henckel said.

"Don't worry about *him* – his uncle's a colonel!" Daniel replied, and they all laughed.

Chapter 20

They ran across fields and through the woods, over frozen streams and up snowy hills. At dawn, they finally stopped and ate some of the bread Yuri had given them. It tasted good, and they wanted to keep eating – but they knew it had to last as long as possible.

"It's about three hundred kilometers to Germany," Henckel observed.

"This bread's not going to last that long!" Mulder said.

"We'll have to come up with alternate sources of food," Daniel replied. "But we've got some time to figure it out."

They slept for an hour on the cold ground, while the dim winter sun rose a little higher in the sky. Then they awoke and continued their trek. They kept off the main roads, kept to themselves to avoid detection. There was the problem of the uniforms – as tattered as they were, they were still recognizable as Wehrmacht and therefore would definitely give them away.

That problem was solved later that day when they came across a small village, and watched it carefully from the woods for any signs of life. There were none, so they very carefully made their way into the hamlet and saw why it was so quiet. The whole village had been massacred. Men, women, and children lay in the streets, in house and shop doorways, and even hung from trees by their necks. It was a sight that made Daniel's skin crawl.

"The Russians!" Mulder spat. They all knew the Russians had been going from village to village, accusing Poles of collaborating with the Germans. It didn't have to be true to bring harsh reprisals by the Russians – truth had nothing to do with it. It was Red Army *policy*.

As gruesome as it was, they knew they had to pick through the dead and find some suitable clothing to conceal their identities as soldiers. A coat here, a shirt there, a hat here, a pair of breeches there – soon they were all dressed in their new role as Polish peasants.

"We're exchanging our Ukrainian lice for Polish lice," Mulder cracked.

Then they burned their old uniforms. Before they left, they went through the houses searching for food, but everything had been picked over by the Russians. They found a few potatoes, which they stuffed into their pockets, a box of wooden matches, and a sharp carving knife. Then they left the eerie village with chills running up their spines.

After a few days, they had put many, many kilometers between them and Camp Lamsdorf. But they were also almost completely out of bread. Their constant fear of being tracked down by the prison guards had been replaced by an urgent need to find more food – and quickly. They stopped in a heavily wooded area to rest, while Daniel set about devising a way to get sustenance. Daniel had the men gather all the sticks and twigs they could find, and he showed them how to make a number of falling traps to try to catch small forest animals. They used what remaining bread they had and a few bits of potato as bait to lure the animals into the traps. The first two days proved unsuccessful, but on the third day one of the traps snared a wild rabbit. It was winter-lean, but it would be enough to keep them alive for a few more days.

They dressed the rabbit and built a fire to cook it over, and that night they had a wonderful meal to share. After eating, they sat in the glow of the fire and talked about what they were going to do when they finally made it home.

Mulder was from Bremen. "The first thing I'm going to do is drink a barrel of good German beer," he said dreamily, with a gleam in his eye. "Then I'm going to get a job at the Mercedes factory and buy a fine house in town. After that, I will find a wide-hipped Northern woman with a wild laugh, who will bear me three strapping sons."

"No girls?" Petersen asked.

"No girls," Mulder affirmed. "They are only trouble."

Henckel was from Heidelberg. "First, I will soak in a hot tub for a week. I'm even going to *sleep* in it. Then I will work in my father's glove-making shop and marry a girl named Elsa. She has buck-teeth, but she has long blonde hair and her *strudel* is out of this world!"

Petersen was from Schwandorf, a small town in Bavaria. "My brothers and I have plans to go in together and open a sweet shop. Then we will decide who will get to marry Margaret, because we were all wooing her before the war but she never could make up her mind!"

Daniel said he would go to his father's farm where they will raise cows for milk and to sell for beef. "Then I'll get my old motorcycle running again and look for a race to enter."

"No special girl to marry?" Henckel asked.

"She is very far away," Daniel said sadly. "I don't know if I will be able to find her."

Himmel was from Nienberg. "I don't know what I will do," he said. "Who's going to hire a one-armed music teacher?"

Over the next few days, they stayed in the forest, trying to trap more animals. It was peaceful there, and the war seemed far away. Also, spring was coming, and the weather was warming up a bit. Animals were beginning to emerge from their winter dens. They trapped another hare, and a hedgehog, which was tough and gristly and had a wild, unpleasant flavor.

Noticing that the streams and ponds were beginning to thaw, Daniel had an idea for catching fish. They worked for two days weaving twigs and sticks from the forest floor into a kind of enclosed basket with a door on one side. Then they broke through the ice of a pond and submerged the basket with a heavy rock.

"I'm hoping the fish will swim into the basket, but not be able to find their way out again," Daniel explained. Several hours later, they brought the basket up and garnered six fish! That night, they feasted on fish slow-roasted over a hot fire.

The basket trick worked so well that soon they had fished out the pond. They moved the basket to a stream and caught more fish than ever.

"This is all very fine, but we can't stay here forever," Henckel said.

"That's right – we need to be moving on if we are going to make it back to Germany," Mulder agreed.

"Tomorrow we'll catch as much fish as we can," Daniel said. "Then we'll smoke them to take with us."

The next day, they caught a dozen fish and built a make-shift smoker out of branches and leaves. Then they lit a fire inside it and began smoking the fish. "The smoke will preserve the fish, so it will last longer," Daniel explained.

But the heavenly smell of smoking fish drew a hungry black bear, who came sniffing around the smoker and refused to go away. Everyone grabbed branches and tried to shoo the bear away, but he wouldn't leave.

"If we all charge him at once, he'll get scared and run away," Mulder suggested, disastrously. The bear stood his ground, lunging at Mulder and missing him by centimeters with his sharp claws.

"We're only making him angrier!" Henckel pointed out.

"You fellows back away," Daniel said. "Let me try." The men backed away, but held onto their branches just in case. Daniel approached the bear with both hands held in front of him, palms out. The bear growled fiercely. Daniel took another step toward him. The bear stopped growling. With each step Daniel took, the bear seemed to become calmer. Daniel very slowly reached into the smoker and pulled out two fish. He showed them to the bear, who drooled and licked his chops. Daniel tossed the fish several meters away, into the bushes. The bear looked at Daniel, then at the smoker, then back at Daniel. He stepped closer to Daniel.

Daniel's heart pounded, but he showed no signs of fear. He felt like bolting, but kept his feet stuck where they were. The others were frozen, holding their breath in sheer terror.

The bear was right in front of Daniel, but did nothing threatening. Then it stretched its neck way out and sniffed Daniel. Daniel didn't move. The bear turned around and went to retrieve the thrown fish. It found them in the bushes, and went on its way.

"Somebody please tell me what we just saw!" Petersen gasped.

"You see, Vollmer was right!" Mulder cried in relief. "He has the Mark of the Bear! We're going to be all right!"

They wrapped up all the smoked fish and broke camp that afternoon, leaving their comfortable, temporary forest home behind. They walked due west for the rest of the day and all that night, carefully staying away from main roads to avoid Russian patrols and communist partisans. The expanse of woodland and grassland of western Poland seemed endless, but they knew that each step brought them closer to Germany and to home.

When all the smoked fish had been eaten, they were hungry again. They were in a hurry to get home, but that haste cost them dearly in calories, and soon their stomachs were empty and growling once more.

After two days without a bite, they came across an abandoned farmhouse. Desperate for food, they went inside and began scouring it for any morsel. The kitchen was picked clean, and they began ransacking other rooms. Himmel went down into the basement and called back a moment later, "Hey, I found a sack of turnips!"

Then there was a terrible explosion, and flames and smoke poured up from the basement doorway. "Himmel – *no!*" Henckel shouted, too late. They rushed down into the basement, but there was nothing they could do. There wasn't even enough of Himmel left to collect and bury. Everyone knew: it was either the work of the Russians, or their paramilitary counterparts, the communist partisans.

"The bastards!" Mulder shouted. "Booby-trapping rotten turnips! For what? The war's over!"

"As irritating as Himmel could be, I'll miss him," Henckel said, bowing his head.

Driven by hunger, the four of them pressed on. The next morning the sun rose like a pale flare, casting an orange-pink glow on the rope-like wispy clouds strung across the sky. They had spoken very little all night, instead saving their waning energy for the critical pursuit of finding food. It was only the beginning of spring, and the countryside had been stripped bare by the merciless winter and hordes of refugees.

Then, mirage-like, they saw a farmhouse nestled in a grove of tall spruce trees. They waited, hidden in the woods, for an excruciating two hours, watching for any signs of movement. When they were sure no one was about, they crept in for a closer look. There, next to the barn, was a pen with a single scrawny goat in it. There was no debate; their stabbing hunger compelled them to abandon any scruples and seek only survival.

Noiselessly, they made their way to the pen and opened the creaky gate as slowly as possible. Daniel kept watch on the house, while the others slipped a rope around the goat's

neck and led him out of the pen. Petersen kept the goat's mouth clasped shut with both hands as they absconded with the bearded beast.

"There's not much meat on him," Mulder observed, disappointed.

"It'll do for a good meal tonight," Henckel replied.

They led the goat a few hundred meters from the farmhouse, into a thick wood for cover. They could wait no longer. Petersen and Mulder prepared a fire while Daniel and Henckel killed and dressed the goat. The gnawing pain in Daniel's gut overrode any sense of pity for the animal, which was now the only thing standing between them and utter starvation.

Roasting the meat was absolute torture. "Let it cook!" Henckel warned the famished men several times. "You'll be sorry if you don't!" When the meat was ready, Henckel cut off big chunks of it with the carving knife and handed everyone a hearty portion. The men ate ravenously and quietly, except for the occasional grunt or sigh of pleasure.

The men leisurely ate their fill. When they were finished, the carcass was stripped clean of meat. "We'll take the bones with us to gnaw on for a few days," Henckel said, leaning back on an elbow and enjoying the warm glow of the fire.

"How far do you think we've come?" Mulder asked.

"I would say about a hundred and fifty kilometers," Henckel estimated.

"We're only halfway to Germany, then," Mulder pointed out.

"Each step brings us that much closer to home," Henckel observed.

"But home may not be like what we remember," Petersen said. "You heard the talk, before we left the camp. The Allies destroyed the cities with bombs. The Russians are taking their revenge, violating women and murdering innocent people."

"That was all rumor," Mulder scoffed. "Men's imaginations running away with them. How do _they_ know?"

Petersen shrugged. "Like you, I hope it's not that bad. But I have a feeling life is going to be much different than it was before the war."

"The Russians won't be here forever," Mulder predicted. "They will want to go home, see their own wives and families."

"Yes, but more will come," Henckel said.

"Well, I am from Bremen," Mulder declared. "So I will live in the Allied zone, under the British or the Americans. It won't be so bad."

"If you can get there," Petersen cautioned.

"Oh, I will get there, my friend. If it takes me the rest of my life."

Their bellies full, the satisfied men drifted off into a deep slumber, one by one. Exhausted by several days without sleep, they'd neglected to designate a watch rotation before passing out. As the night wore on, the fire burned out, and the forest grew quiet.

Just before dawn, Daniel awoke suddenly to the sound of footsteps in the leaves on the forest floor. Whoever was approaching was not trying to be quiet about it. Sitting up and rubbing their eyes, the men were astonished to see six men dressed in peasant's clothes and armed with Russian rifles standing over them. They wore caps and red armbands, and were as dirty and unshaven as the Germans were.

"How are you sleeping, comrades?" one of them asked sarcastically in Polish. He had a lit cigarette in his mouth and beady, penetrating eyes. The others stared down at them with stony faces.

"I see you had a fine meal last night," the leader with the cigarette said, switching to broken German. "I hope it was very tasty. You are German, yes?"

The men said nothing.

"Deserters? Runaway POW's?" the partisan leader tried again. "Oh well, it doesn't matter. You have stolen a goat – the People's goat. It didn't belong to you, but out of your corrupt greed, you took it for yourselves. That is exactly the kind of selfish thinking we have come to change, comrades."

"We were starving," Daniel offered weakly.

"Yes, many people are starving," the leader said. "But they do not steal from their neighbor. Many people must suffer to bring change. It is necessary and expected, is it not?"

The Germans stayed silent. The leader withdrew a few feet and consulted with two of his men while the others kept watch on the Germans. From the looks on their faces, Daniel could tell that danger was imminent. The leader and his consultees seemed to be discussing what was to be done with them. Catching snatches of the conversation, it seemed to Daniel that one of them was lobbying for taking them alive and turning them over to the Russians, but the leader seemed somewhat unimpressed with that option.

The sun was just beginning to rise in the east, creating a pale yellow glow over the tops of the trees. Daniel, Henckel and Mulder exchanged furtive glances. It was written on all of their faces: they were going to be shot, or turned over to the Russians, which was equally unacceptable. None of them wanted to go back and rot away in a POW camp. Henckel cocked his head slightly toward the trees – a silent signal to run for it while they had the chance. Petersen saw it, too. Mulder nodded *Let's go!*

Before the leader and the two others could rejoin them, the Germans sprang to their feet and took off like rabbits for the trees. Darting off in different directions, Daniel toward the darkness between the trees about thirty meters away. He heard the partisans shouting and firing their rifles behind him, but kept running fast. He heard bullets whizzing past his head, and ducked down low to avoid them. He tripped over a log, fell flat on his face in the dirt, but immediately got up and kept running, expecting to feel a bullet penetrate his back at any moment.

Glancing to his left, he heard a shot fired and saw Petersen stumble and go down. Still he kept running and running. He heard more shots. To his right, about twenty meters away, he saw Henckel get hit and go down. He didn't get back up. *Henckel!*

Daniel looked all around, but couldn't see Mulder anywhere. Had he made it to the trees? Then, Daniel was in the trees, enveloped by their darkness, as he heard the partisans running after him and firing wildly. Scrappy Daniel: no heavy rifle or pack to carry, able to outrun the men by dodging between, over and around trees, branches, and fallen logs in the thick wood. Eventually, he couldn't hear them anymore, and slowed his pace. Had they given up on him?

He stopped briefly to take inventory of his possessions. He had the compass in his pocket, and the carving knife tucked into his belt. He had a dozen or so matches wrapped tightly in wax paper to keep them dry. But he had no food. He decided he would – he *must* – continue west, make it to Germany.

He walked for three days in a hunger-crazed stupor, across fallow fields stripped bare of any crops and through dense wooded areas that were largely uninhabited. He counted footsteps and tried to forget the sight of Henckel and Petersen being gunned down in the night while running away from the partisans. He sipped water from streams and slept fitfully at night, trying desperately to remember Remy and the boys and the childish games they played in *Nulle*, and the graceful contours of Emily's face.

Emily. Where was she now? Had she survived the cataclysm, as he had? Sometimes, he didn't have the energy to remember her face. She was slowly fading from his consciousness. His spirit was fading, and hunger was consuming him. It was all he could do to keep putting one foot in front of the other, kilometer after kilometer, as he crawled slowly toward no promise of safety.

On the fourth day, the world was swirling around him. He was hallucinating again; the T-34's were coming, followed by the Russian infantry. They were right on his heels, driving him, keeping him moving, pressing him on. He came to a road that had telephone poles along it – a major road. It was swarming with peasants, refugees – a massive stream of humanity flowing west. He thought he was still hallucinating. Without thinking, he dove into it and was carried along with the flood.

Blend in, he told himself. *Become one with them.* It was dreamlike. Some had carts laden down with their belongings, others carried suitcases or children strapped to their backs. Some were on bicycles with flat tires, elderly souls rode in wagons pulled by their children or grandchildren. The sides of the road were littered with dead bodies, a few abandoned cars, and even an old piano that several men were cannibalizing for firewood.

He walked and walked in this sea of humanity, the desperate, the half-living. A man was screaming somewhere up ahead for no apparent reason, other than he had just lost his mind. Most were silent, wordlessly trudging on, willing to face death itself to escape the horrors of Russian occupation. Where were they going? It didn't matter – somewhere safe, somewhere *away* from the Russians. Daniel's strength was flagging. He didn't know how he would be able to keep on. He fed off the energy of the mob and, somehow, they all kept moving inexorably forward.

He didn't know how many days he'd been with the refugees when he found her. She was kneeling along the side of the road, over the bodies of an older man and woman. She was a waif-like figure wrapped in a tattered grey coat, her light brown hair tucked into a dirty silk scarf. Lost in a state of insensibility, the girl was about Daniel's age and very pregnant. Daniel stopped in his tracks and watched her, scores of refugees surging around him like minnows. He watched her for minutes; she didn't stir. How long had she been kneeling there?

No one else seemed to notice her, or even care. Daniel approached her and touched her shoulder. "Come on," he said gently. "You'll die here." She was unresponsive, rigid – almost catatonic. He took her arm and began to lift her up. She turned her head and looked up at him with large, brown, uncomprehending eyes. There was a hollowness in them that haunted Daniel. "This is no good. You must keep moving."

She looked back down at the old couple. "*Matka. Ojciec.*" It was Polish for "mother" and "father."

"They are gone now," Daniel said gently. "You must come with me."

The girl allowed herself to be pulled to her feet. Shaking with weakness, she collapsed against him and hung on his arm like a rag doll. *She's been kneeling here quite a long time*, he thought. Gradually, the stiffness in her legs began to diminish and she was able to walk with assistance. It was slow going at first, but soon they were moving along with the flow of people again, Daniel holding her upright and keeping her steady. They had walked in silence for several hours when Daniel realized she was growing weaker with each step. She was emaciated. He knew he had to get her some food, or the baby would starve to death inside her. He began asking everyone around them, everyone he could find: "*Essen? Essen?* For the girl and the baby – *essen?*" The refugees were like zombies, unresponsive, uncaring, half-starved themselves.

Finally, an older woman whose husband was pulling an over-loaded cart like a beast of burden took pity on them. Reaching into the back of the cart, she pulled out a cloth sack and produced a small piece of bread. She passed it to Daniel discreetly, so no one else would see.

"This is no place for a girl who's having a baby!" she scolded him in Polish, then turned away to rejoin her husband. Fighting the urge to devour the bread himself, he led the girl off the road and sat her down in the grass. He handed her the piece of bread and made motions for her to eat it. She shook her head.

"For the baby," Daniel urged her. She seemed to understand. Mechanically, she raised the bread to her mouth and nibbled at it in tiny bites.

"My name is Daniel," he told her. It felt strange saying his real name.

"Karina," she said, swallowing dry bread. She seemed to be getting her appetite back now.

"Where are you from?" he asked. She shook her head. She didn't understand much German.

"Well, I don't know Polish, so this will be quite interesting," he said, smiling. The faint glimmer of a smile fluttered across her delicate lips, then she looked away shyly. When she had finished the bread, he helped her up and they continued their journey. He watched her and wondered how far along she was. Eight months? Nine months? It was hard to tell. He knew her condition would slow him down, but he also knew he could never leave her behind.

After walking awhile, Karina began to revive. *"Soldat?"* she asked meekly, in German. It took Daniel aback.

"No. Well, I *was*…but I'm not now." She looked puzzled. He didn't know how to explain. It occurred to him that her baby's father was probably a German soldier, and that he was now either dead or in a Russian POW camp. Looking at Karina, he could tell she'd been through it – traumatized by war, abandoned, both parents dead – he could only imagine the extent of suffering she had endured. And now carrying a new life inside her, a life that would be joining her in this upside-down world in a few short weeks.

He spent the next several days keeping her moving forward and trying to find a nice family who might take her with them. All of his queries were met with shaking heads and the same answers: "We can't possibly take on another mouth to feed." Some of them felt guilty enough to toss him a crust of bread or a dried fish or a potato, but no one would accept responsibility for her.

"She looks like she's about to pop any day now," one old woman told him. "We just can't cope with that right now…"

The morsels of food were welcome, but not nearly enough to sustain a young woman carrying a child. Daniel, for his part, made sure every bite went to Karina, while he continued to go without.

"You must eat, too," she said in Polish.

"I will be all right," he lied. Hunger was consuming him.

From time to time, he watched her as she rummaged through a small cloth bag she wore strapped across her shoulder underneath her coat. In it she carried a well-used silver-plated hair brush, a faded length of purple ribbon, a small music box, and a dog-eared photo of her family – her, her parents, and a young man who must have been a brother. Daniel assumed the young man was killed in the war.

These items, along with her coat, scarf, a worn dress, and some old shoes, were her only earthly possessions.

They trudged on and on, feet blistered and burning, past fields strewn with demolished military vehicles and bombed out villages. Once, they passed some Russian soldiers on the side of the road, trying to get a motorcycle with a sidecar started. They looked strong and well-fed, and their uniforms were new and clean. Daniel stopped and watched as one of them repeatedly tried to kick start the motor.

"It's not getting any petrol," he blurted out, before he could stop himself. The soldiers stopped and stared at him. Daniel tried to look unafraid.

"The tank is full," one of them said in broken German.

"I…I could take a look at it for you," Daniel offered.

"Do you know motorcycles?"

Daniel nodded. The soldier got off the bike and waved his hand in invitation. Daniel went to work, checking the fuel line and carburetor.

"The fuel line is clogged." The Russians watched in wonder as Daniel deftly disconnected the line and cleared the blockage. The soldier got on and it started right up. Pleased, he patted Daniel on the back.

"How can we help you?"

"*Brot…brot…*"

The Russian pulled a sack out of the sidecar and handed it to Daniel. He reached inside and pulled out a sandwich, staring at it in disbelief: thick slices of bread, ham and cheese stacked between them. He began weeping uncontrollably. The soldier nodded at the sack, and Daniel looked inside again – a half dozen wheat cakes, each one a sumptuous meal in itself. It was beginning to dawn on Daniel that their lives had just been saved – and by enemy soldiers, at that.

"*Da svidaniya!*" the Russians called out, taking off on their motorcycle and honking the horn. Daniel and Karina stepped off the road and sat down in the grass to enjoy their meal. The sandwich was more than enough for both of them; they would save the wheat cakes for the coming days.

Not having to worry about food for several days was a profound relief. Such a luxury had a tremendous effect on their spirits – Daniel hadn't felt so good in months, it seemed. They laughed and cried and ate until they were satisfied, and then they laid back in the grass and slept peacefully in the sun – Daniel's hand clenched tightly around the sack containing the life-giving wheat cakes. Karina slept with her head tucked against his shoulder and a smile on her lips. They weren't going to die after all – at least not yet.

Chapter 21

The next day, the sky turned dark with gathering clouds and it began to rain. The throng of desperate souls kept trudging on, Daniel and Karina with them. Thankfully, the road was paved, but the rain turned each side of it into a churning sea of mud. Daniel took his heavy coat off and draped it over Karina's head and shoulders. In this way they marched on, day after day, through the torrential rain, soaked to the skin but determined to keep moving west.

On the fourth day of rain, Karina's labor pains began. Her contractions were about fifteen minutes apart, and it became difficult for her to walk. Then her water broke and the contractions became more frequent.

"*Nadchodzi!*" she gasped, clutching her abdomen in pain. "It's coming…"

Daniel held her upright, trying not to panic. He tried to get the attention of the refugees around him, but they just shook their heads and walked right by them. Then a man and woman pulling a cart with several children in it stopped next to them.

"The baby's coming – *NOW!*" Daniel shouted in German.

"Put her in the cart!" the woman ordered, shooing her own brood out of the way. The man helped Daniel get her into the cart, where she laid back on a pile of blankets. The woman propped some rolled up clothes under her head for a pillow while Daniel tried to shield her from the rain with his heavy coat.

"*Dankeshon,*" Daniel said in relief. "Will she…will she be all right?"

"She will be fine," the woman assured him. Her name was Lena, and her husband was Oskar. They were from Leszno, where Lena had worked in a hospital until the Russians came. The children gathered around the cart and watched with large round eyes as their mother went to work on Karina. She worked with a confidence and calmness that reassured Daniel and greatly comforted Karina.

"This baby's coming fast," Lena observed, feeling Karina's taught abdomen. "It'll be over soon."

And so it was. In twenty minutes, Lena held a shrieking six-pound baby boy in her hands. With great efficiency, she cleaned the infant off with a damp cloth and wrapped him in a soft blanket – all in a day's work. Then she laid him on Karina's breast and mopped the new mother's brow with a handkerchief. The baby began to quiet down.

"She's so young, but her baby is healthy and she's got to be a mother now!" Lena observed stoically, satisfied with how things turned out. "You will stay with us until she can walk on her own. Do you have food?"

"A little," Daniel answered.

"Well, you'd better feed her something. She's got to keep her strength up."

Daniel reached into the sack and pulled out one of the last wheat cakes. He broke it in half and gave the piece to Karina. The other treasured piece he carefully put back in the sack. Karina ate slowly, smiling down peacefully at her newborn son.

She named the boy Jakob, after her father. They stayed with the family for three days, while Karina regained her strength and Lena coached her on the basics of motherhood. "This is no way for a young couple to start a family," Lena said, shaking her head and watching the long line of refugees ahead. "But everyone's lives have been turned upside down by this war. We just have to learn to make do."

On the morning of the fourth day, Karina and her baby stepped down from the cart and the older couple's children piled back in. The rain had finally stopped, and it was a fine early summer day.

"I don't know how we can thank you," Daniel said to Oskar and Lena.

"Just take good care of her," Lena said. Then they wished the young couple luck and went on their way. The food was almost completely gone, but Daniel and Karina marched on, taking turns carrying little Jakob, somewhat less miserable than they were before.

Hearing a commotion in the procession up ahead, they quickened their pace to find out what was happening. *"Deutschland! Deutschland!"* they heard someone shouting. *"Wir sind in Deutschland!"* A minute later, they were passing a road marker announcing the border between Poland and Germany. Refugees with the strength left to do so cheered and threw their caps in the air.

"Nonsense!" shouted an old man waving his cane. "We've still got a ways to go to get away from these stinking Russians!" But for most, making it to Germany was a real morale booster. They soon came to a town where every other building seemed to be destroyed. Whole streets were decimated, deserted, homes bombed out and raked by machine gun fire. They walked past a school that was on fire, a gutted police station, a smoldering orphanage. Dogs chased rats and squirrels through the rubble where dirty children played in the filth.

In the center of the town there was a large church, and refugees crowded around it shouting for food. A priest stood at the door waving his arms in the air. *Kein essen!*" he shouted at the mob. "We ran out of food days ago! Come back in a day or two, we will have more then!"

"We'll be dead by then!" someone shouted back. "Open up! Let us in!"

The priest tried to close the church door, but the crowd surged forward and forced their way inside, brushing him aside like a leaf. The mob, half mad with hunger, began ransacking the church.

Others threw bricks through shop windows and then poured inside in hopes of finding a piece of bread or a morsel of cheese. But not a crumb could be found.

"Let's go to Dresden!" a man shouted. "There will be food there!" A large group of refugees followed him out of town because he seemed to know what he was talking about. Daniel and Karina went along with them – things in Dresden couldn't be worse than here.

On the road to Dresden, there were Russian tanks with their crews sitting on top of the turrets smoking cigarettes. They sneered and laughed at the refugees in their tattered clothes and gaunt, dirty faces. "Go back to Poland, you filthy dogs!" they jeered, but did nothing to stop the flow of people.

When they got to Dresden, there was no way to prepare for the horror they encountered there. The entire city had been levelled. There was not a single building left standing.

"Did the Russians do this?" someone asked in shock.

"No, the Americans and the British," another man said, pointing to the sky. "Fire-bombing by the Allies."

They shuffled through the ruins of the shattered city in silence, unable to summon words. They saw no one, except a man in a threadbare police uniform sitting on a pile of bricks, holding his head in his hands. He looked up at them with red-rimmed eyes as they approached.

"You're wasting your time," he told them. "There's nothing here. There's no food in the cities. Only rioting and starvation. You would do better going to the country." Then he stopped talking and lowered his head back into his hands.

Listlessly, the refugees began breaking up into smaller groups and dispersing into the countryside. Daniel, Karina, and little Jakob struck out on their own. "I know a place," Daniel told her. "If I can find it!" They left Dresden and headed south through the countryside. The hunger was back, stabbing at their insides like daggers, and Daniel knew he had to find food quickly for Karina and the baby.

He found a straight tree branch and split the end, forcing a stone into the split to create a two-pronged fork. Then he went hunting for snakes. Three hours later, he had caught a fat, two-meter long Aesculapian serpent and skinned it with the knife. Then he started a fire and cooked the snake meat slowly over it skewered on a branch. Fat ran off the yellowish-white meat and sizzled on the fire in a tantalizing manner. He had eaten snake meat before, but Karina was skeptical.

"Go on, you must eat it," Daniel urged. "It's all right, I promise!"

Grimacing, she took a hesitant bite, the small taste quickly jump-starting her appetite. When she had devoured that piece, she eagerly asked for more.

"If I can catch one of these every day or so, we should be all right," Daniel told her, knowing she only understood a small percentage of what he said.

It took Daniel six days to find the farm. His memory was foggy, but he knew it was about thirty kilometers southeast of Dresden. When they arrived, he recognized it immediately: there was the old timber-framed farmhouse with the gaily-painted gables, the old barn, the colorful wildflowers, and the tall birch trees. It was all just as he'd remembered it.

There was Schiller, looking ten years older and bent over, standing at the gate watching the road. He looked startlingly thin. His tattered officer's uniform hung on his bony frame like a tent, and there was a distance of ten thousand years in his weathered grey eyes. He didn't recognize Daniel. "Have you seen my son, Johann?" the old man asked, staring right through Daniel like a madman.

"I *am* Johann," Daniel said.

"No, you're not Johann. I am waiting for *Johann*."

"Papa – it's me!"

The old man shook his head sadly. "No. I am waiting for Johann."

Daniel realized that the Russians, believing he'd truly lost his mind, must have released him and somehow he made his way back here. He tried to lead him into the house, but Schiller wouldn't go, wouldn't leave his post at the gate, watching and waiting to see his son Johann walk down the road, like a faithful dog waiting for its master.

Daniel brought Karina and the baby into the house. She was elated to see real furniture and beds – real, soft *beds!* And a roof over their heads! He set about making a crib for the baby out of a dresser drawer, while she cleaned up in the washroom. Then he went outside and discovered three or four chickens in the yard – there would be eggs! Real, fresh *eggs!*

In a matter of days, they had settled into an easy routine. During the days, Daniel would take Schiller's old rifle into the woods and hunt rabbits and deer. He also dragged the old motorcycle out of the barn and began to work on getting it running again. Karina took care of little Jakob and cooked the meals, and showed a great aptitude for getting the household in order in no time. Every night, she nursed Jakob and put him to bed to the sounds of her little music box. The infant would fall asleep to the dulcet strains of *"Moonlight Sonata"* – one of the tunes old Vogel would hum back in the trenches.

Schiller stood at the gate all day and well into the night, until he was coaxed inside with the promise of a hot meal and a tumbler of *schnapps*. As the weeks passed and the summer waned, Schiller's mental state and physical health continued to deteriorate. He stopped eating and seemed to lose interest in living. No longer able to stand at the gate, he kept up his watch for Johann from inside the house. Daniel and Karina cared for him the best they could, but knew it was only a matter of time.

Daniel got the motorcycle running, but petrol being an issue he had to use it sparingly. He hunted and fished in nearby streams with Schiller's old rod and reel, and, gradually, he and Karina began to put a little bit of meat back on their emaciated bones. Karina even devised a way to bake a type of ersatz bread with flour made from wild almonds. Then, in early autumn, Schiller finally died. Daniel buried him in a lovely spot beneath a birch tree behind the house, with a picture of his beloved son Johann on his chest.

And life went on for Daniel, Karina, and the baby. They had shelter and food, and they were happy. They learned to communicate in a somewhat strange mixture of German and Polish. There were increasingly tender moments between them, and the way she looked at him with her large, sad, soft green eyes left little doubt about her feelings toward him. The suffering and deprivation of their exodus had somewhat obscured her comeliness, but here on the farm, with water and soap and other such amenities, her true beauty began to emerge.

On one of his hunting forays, Daniel discovered a lovely lake in a secluded valley. It was well-stocked with fat, strapping fish, and he quickly caught all he could carry home. The next day, he brought Karina and Jakob back for a picnic. They spread a blanket on the shore and ate a satisfying lunch of cold rabbit stew and smoked salmon, washed down with a bottle of white wine from Schiller's cellar. Then Karina gave the baby his lunch and put him down for a nap.

It was a lovely fall day, and it soon grew warm enough to wade into the water. Feeling playful, Karina couldn't help but splash Daniel several times.

"Oh, that's how it's going to be, is it?" he laughed, splashing her back. She stood her ground, dousing him several more times before he picked her up and carried her out to a deeper place.

"*Nie rob tego!*" she screamed. "Don't do it!"

He counted to three – *eins, zwei, drei* -- and dropped her in. She went under, and popped up seconds later completely soaked. She pushed him hard, and he fell backward and went under as well. Then he stood up, picked her up again, and carried her back to the shore. He gallantly laid her on the blanket to dry in the sun, and sat down beside her. The baby slept through it all.

He looked down at her, lying in the sun with her wet, light brown hair cascading over her soft white shoulders. He bent down over her and kissed her very softly but very deliberately for a good long time. She closed her eyes and forgot about all the suffering and starvation and pain of war and thought about this moment and this moment only. From now on, the war would be a distant memory and this happy time of living on Schiller's farm would be the new reality. This would be *their* lake, and young Jakob would grow up with a wonderful father who would teach him to fish and hunt, and who would bring him swimming here in the summers. Right now, at this moment, she was as happy as she'd ever been in her life.

On the way home, they found a stray cow grazing in a field. There was no one else around, so Daniel calmly and carefully approached the bovine and slipped a rope around its neck. They led the cow out of the field and onto a dirt road back to the farm. After a kilometer, they came across an old farmer wearing a frayed, weather-beaten cap on his white-haired head. He carried a gnarled tree limb as a walking stick, and was smoking a misshapen, hand-rolled cigarette.

"Ah, you have found my cow," he said in German. "I thought the Russians took her. But she must have escaped on her own."

Daniel held the lead line out to him. "If she is yours, please take her."

The farmer looked up at the sky and rolled the cigarette around in his mouth a while. "Let me ask you something. Where do you live?"

"We're staying at the old Schiller place."

"Schiller, eh?" the old farmer spat tobacco onto the ground. "Thought he died in the war."

"*Nein*," Daniel answered. "He died just last week, on his farm."

"Well, that's certainly news," the farmer said, lost in thought. He didn't seem to be in a hurry to reclaim his cow. "Tell me: have the Russians been by much lately?"

"*Nein*," Daniel replied. "Not at all."

"Well, they've been by my place quite a bit. And each time they visit, they take away more of my animals with them. Would you mind keeping this cow at Schiller's place for a while, so they can't steal *her*, too?"

"Of course not. We'd be happy to help out."

"You'll have to milk her every day," the farmer said. "But you get to keep the milk."

"It's a deal," Daniel said, shaking the farmer's hand.

The farmer said his name was Heinz Fassel, and every few days he brought another animal to Schiller's farm to shelter it from the Russians. After a few weeks, the place looked and sounded like a thriving farm. Daniel soon found himself busy caring for a veritable menagerie – pigs, goats, geese, sheep – even an old plough horse named Otto von Bismarck. When the pig turned out to be a pregnant sow, Daniel found himself in charge of a whole pen full of piglets.

"They were born here, so they're yours," farmer Fassel said of the piglets – as well as any other animals born on the premises.

Then one day the Russians stopped coming to Fassel's farm. Soon after, he visited Daniel and Karina, but not to take any of the animals home with him.

"I'm not as young as I used to be," he told them, chewing on a crooked hand-rolled cigarette. "Both of my sons were killed in the war, so it's only me and my wife running the place now. Soon, we won't be able to manage all these beasts anymore. I think they should just stay here, with you young folks…"

As over-worked as he felt, Daniel agreed to keep the animals, and things began to settle into a predictable, if sometimes hectic, routine. Thoughts of France, and even Emily, began to grow dim in Daniel's mind. In the spring, he would plant potatoes and cabbages, beets and carrots. He would make this place a working farm, maybe someday even raise cattle for beef, just as old Schiller suggested so long ago. He would marry Karina and raise Jakob as his own son, because, as he was just beginning to realize, he'd fallen deeply in love with the girl.

For now, winter was fast approaching, and they would be warm and fed. The great suffering they had both endured – he on the front in the Ukraine and she in Poland – would eventually fade into the distant past as they made a new life together.

Late one night, long after Karina and the baby had gone to sleep, Daniel sat in the kitchen thinking by candlelight. He played Karina's music box and thought of Remy and the boys and lazy summer days growing up in the French countryside. He thought of the musty smell of rubber and oil in the old bicycle repair shop. He thought of his picnics with Emily and the shabby little circus, and of saving Nikolai and his family from the Gestapo. He thought of Mulder and Henckel and the stolen cheese and freezing to death in the bloody, lice-infested trenches at the front. He thought of old Vogel humming Beethoven and Vollmer's boat getting hit on that icy river and his friend Yuri's acts of kindness when they escaped from the POW camp. He thought of meeting Karina, alone and pregnant, on that tragic road in Poland, and wondered how such a sublime thing could happen amidst all the chaos and suffering of war.

He thought and thought, until the wee hours of the morning, trying to remember everything, trying to sort it all out, to make sense of it all. Then, just before dawn, he took a pen and several pieces of writing paper from Schiller's old oak desk. He sat down at the kitchen table and, in the quiet of the morning, began writing a letter to his uncle back in the tiny village of *Nulle*.

About the Author

Marc Sercomb lives in the foothills of Los Angeles with his wife Robin, two cats, two motorcycles, and a chestnut Tennessee-Walker horse named Whiskey. A life-long Southern Californian, he attended California State University, Northridge, where he studied Journalism and English Literature. He has been a teacher for twenty-three years.

An avid reader of both fiction and nonfiction, World War II and European history have always been of particular interest to him. Marc likes to spend his spare time watching movies with his wife and cats, hanging out with good friends, and riding his motorcycles in the beautiful mountains of the Angeles National Forest.

He wanted to write a book about the miraculous resilience of the human spirit and the unexpected kindness of strangers and enemies during dark and dangerous times. Of *Picasso's Motorcycle* he says, "This story kind of haunted me for a while. That's how I knew I had to write it."

www.ingramcontent.com/pod-product-compliance
Lightning Source LLC
Chambersburg PA
CBHW050857130726
47900CB00013B/161